ASHES

Books in the World of Raphtova

The Reawakening Trilogy
Spark

Ashes

Ablaze

Tales of the Inn
The Curse of the Stoneskin (coming soon)

Operation Brooch (coming soon)

The Wanderer (coming soon)

Leane Winger

ASHES

Book Two of the Reawakening Trilogy

This is a work of fiction. The characters, places, and events recorded in this work are the product of the author's imagination or are used fictitiously. Any resemblance to actual persons, living or dead, is purely coincidental.

1. Edition, 2023
Copyright © 2023 by Leane and Jesse Winger
All rights reserved.

ISBN 978-1-7777664-7-4

Published by Leane Winger, Mackenzie BC, Canada
leane.n.winger@gmail.com
leanewinger.com

Cover design by Aiden Walker

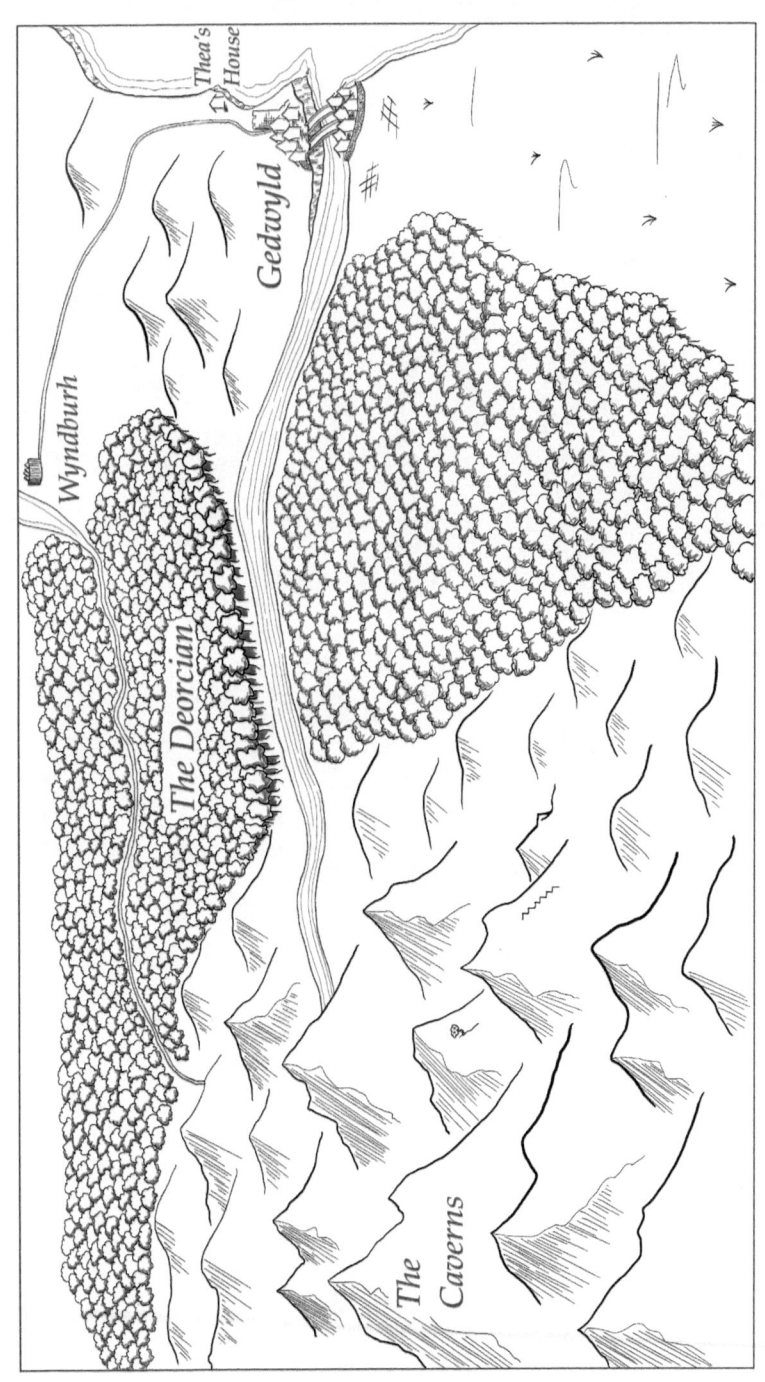

The old building stood empty. Ancient vines clung to its high stone walls and wrapped around its arched gates. The wind hissed through the barren courtyard and whistled across the smokeless chimneys. Inside, every room was bare. Nothing adorned its walls or filled its cavernous emptiness.

Once it had been full of people. The hearth fire had blazed brightly and the air was filled with laughter and the smells of good food. The stables overflowed with the horses of passing travellers, and the ocean docks bustled with shipments from far across the sea.

Some time later, a great lord bought the building, eccentric and mysterious. The walls were draped with expensive tapestries, and those who came to visit wore velvet and silk. Ships brought strange curiosities and expensive materials, most of which were never seen again.

Storm clouds rolled across the world of Raphtova. The building felt them deep within its stones. Visitors came in the night, cloaked in black. Whispers floated through the air, speaking of danger, betrayal, war. The words of power inscribed above the door provided safety—for now—but that was not enough.

The people left. They did not say where they were going, but the fire on the hearth burned out, and darkness fell across its light-filled rooms. The courtyard was overrun with weeds, and the gardens grew wild. Occasionally a small group of travellers would take shelter within its walls, but they always left within a day or two, glancing nervously over their shoulder as they left.

Alone, the building waited, as Raphtova continued its orbit of the great planet Micai, and Micai continued its path around Allumen, circle after circle. No news came to say whether the war was over, but the tide on the sea continued to flow and the seasons came and went. From its place high on the bluffs above the sea, the building watched the world go by, and waited.

Today, however, things were different. Today a wagon arrived, filled with chairs and tables and crates. The one who seemed to be in charge of the wagon was an Elf. Her amber diamond skin still showed hints of roughness, a sign that she had only recently reached adulthood. She looked up at the building with an eager gaze, amethyst eyes glimmering in the light.

Another Elf was with her, who appeared to be about her age. His skin was red granite and he watched the first Elf with a warm, thoughtful gaze.

A third traveller dropped down from the cart in a clatter of chain mail and assorted weaponry. His head and chin were covered in a wild mass of hair, and he appeared for all intents and purposes to be a middle-aged man, except that he was unnaturally short. Calling gruffly to the other inhabitants of the wagon, he began to unload its cargo.

Everyone chipped in with the work, stacking baskets and crates just inside the arched gateway. Laughter and snatches of song drifted through the air for the first time in many, many circles.

When the cart had been unloaded, the driver said goodbye and turned it back down the old, rutted lane, leaving the two Elves and the short man behind. After the cart had rumbled out of sight, they stepped through the gate and crossed the courtyard, looking up at the ancient building with interest and anticipation.

There was something different about these people. They looked as if they meant to stay.

The Elf they called Thea opened the door.

Chapter One

"You're right." Roland stared around the empty room, running his hands through his thick, mosslike hair. "It does look like it was made by Elves."

"Like the fireplace there." Thea gestured. "It's just like the one in Uncle Mykyta's office."

She stared around the large room, taking it all in. Dark wooden beams spanned the ceiling. The floor underfoot was smooth and polished. It was just as empty as when she had last seen it, nearly two cycles ago.

"So it really is abandoned." Roland ran a hand along a dusty windowsill.

Thea nodded. "The Lord of Gedwyld said no one has lived here for as long as any human can remember."

"Because it's haunted?" Roland gave her a sidelong glance.

"That's what he said, but I didn't notice anything like that when I was here before."

She could almost see Elora standing at the window, bow in hand, watching for the monsters that had chased them all the way from the Deorcian. Arl had stood by the door, ready to fight anything that might follow them inside.

Thea's eyes took in the writing above the door. Elvish writing, calling on the power of the Deity to keep evil away and protect all those within its walls. Because of that magic, the monsters couldn't get close.

She glanced at Roland. He was staring at the walls with a distant expression, unaware of anything else around him.

"Roland," Thea protested, "not right now." Grabbing his shoulder, she gave him a gentle shake.

Roland startled, his emerald eyes turning to focus on Thea's face.

She laughed. "There will be time for vidlas later, if you really want to."

Roland shrugged. "I just wanted to check the walls, but they seem solid enough."

Thea frowned. "Why wouldn't they be solid?"

"Because the building is so old. If Elves lived here it must have been before the Great War, and you saw the buildings in Enzhelika. That city was abandoned and it crumbled into ruins. This house is as solid as if it was just made."

Thea's gaze returned to the carvings above the door. *Safety. Protection.* Did the door's magic also protect the building itself somehow?

Roland looked up at the doorframe. "I wouldn't have noticed those carvings if you hadn't told me they were there. They're almost impossible to see."

Thea nodded. "I only saw them because of my spirit sight. It's like the words are glowing."

Roland grinned. "Well I can tell you the walls are made of solid rock and the mortar isn't crumbling." He winked. "At least my deep sight is good for something."

"Your sight is good for lots of things," Thea protested, though of course she liked her own elf-sight better. She never would have started serving the Deity or left Lyudmyla if it hadn't been for her spirit sight.

Roland glanced around the room. "Where's Ulfgar?"

Thea's heart sank. "Ulfgar!" Leaving the great room, she passed through the empty kitchen and into the pantry with its bare shelves. The trap door leading to the wine cellar was open. Thea crouched above it. "Ulfgar! We're going to start bringing everything in now!"

Ulfgar's gruff voice grumbled up from the depths beneath her feet. After what seemed like a long time, his heavy footsteps echoed on the stairs and his head emerged, squinting in the light.

"What?" he grumbled.

Thea tried to ignore the heavy smell of wine on Ulfgar's breath. "We're going to bring everything in now. Want to give us a hand?"

"Want to?" Ulfgar frowned. "I only came for the drink."

"I know." Thea gave a wry grin. "It won't take long if we all work together."

Ulfgar nodded sullenly and heaved himself up the remaining steps.

Thea's gaze lingered on the shadowy wine cellar beneath her feet—the only room in the old building that wasn't empty. Ulfgar knew it well, and the events of the past few cycles had only seemed to strengthen his desire to drink himself into oblivion.

Leaving the cellar door open, Thea followed Ulfgar and Roland out to the pile of furniture and boxes in the courtyard.

"Give me a hand with this table, Ulf," Roland called, heaving one side off the ground. Thea picked up a chair and led the way back into the ancient building.

The table and chairs were set by the fireplace. They

seemed small in the vast emptiness of the bare room.

Roland stepped back and cocked his head. "You might need some more furniture." He glanced at Thea with a grin.

"It will come soon enough." In her mind, Thea could see the room filled with tables and chairs, ready for anyone who might want to come and stay, but the influx of Littles into Gedwyld had made it a challenge to find any furniture at all.

The boxes and crates held a mismatched assortment of supplies needed for setting up a home. There was basic kitchen equipment and some tools, a few blankets, and enough food for the first few days.

Thea carried the box of blankets upstairs. Setting down her burden, she walked past the bedrooms to the farthest room of all. It was a private suite, having a small sitting room connected to a bedroom, with large windows that looked out over the sea.

The other bedrooms were empty, but this one had a bed frame in it.

Footsteps thumped up the stairs. Thea returned to the hallway to find Ulfgar and Roland carrying one of the mattresses.

"You want this room, Ulf?" Roland nodded towards one of the doors.

Ulfgar shrugged and heaved the mattress over his shoulder.

Thea went back downstairs and brought the box of food into the pantry. It didn't take long to set everything out on the bare shelves.

"Thea!" Roland's voice drifted through the silence of the house.

Returning upstairs, Thea passed Ulfgar's room. He

sat on his mattress, rummaging through the enormous backpack he carried wherever he went.

Roland was waiting in the sitting room with the large windows. He smiled when he saw her. "Your room is ready. Come have a look."

Thea stepped into the bedroom. The bed frame now had a mattress on it, and the bed had been made, with the blankets folded neatly back. Beside the bed was a small table, on which lay a few pieces of paper and a fountain pen.

Thea looked at Roland in surprise. "Where did that come from?"

"I made it." A proud smile creased Roland's face. "When we learned we wouldn't be able to get your furniture right away, Kais helped me find some wood and tools. I thought you'd like to have a little writing table you can use till your bigger one comes."

Thea crouched beside the table. It was well made and meticulously polished, its edge carved with a narrow pattern of vines and flowers. Roland hadn't made anything like that since he started sailing on the Eagle. She smiled. "It's beautiful. Thank you so much."

Rising, she looked around the room. Her room. From the windows, she could see the gardens and outbuildings, overgrown with weeds and ivy. Beyond the gardens, a door in the surrounding wall led out to the bluffs overlooking the sea. Allumen's light glittered on the deep blue water far below.

Ulfgar's heavy footsteps thumped through the door. "Sure is empty in here," he muttered.

"The wagon from Gedwyld will come soon enough," Roland countered. "We'll have this place ready to go in no time." He glanced at Thea. "Then you can come back

8

to Lyudmyla with me."

Thea's heart sank. "I said I'll think about it. Do you want to see the gardens?"

Roland grinned. "Sure."

Ulfgar grunted.

Thea led the way down the stairs and out into the courtyard. On one side of the gate, a low building had clearly once been a stable. Beyond it, a moss-covered structure seemed to be built right into the wall. Ducking through the low door, Thea found she couldn't see much in the shadowy darkness.

"Storage, maybe?" Roland speculated, looking around the small room. "There's a fireplace, though, which seems odd."

"That's a forge." Ulfgar emerged from behind Thea's elbow, eyeing the structure with grudging interest. "It's old. Haven't seen one like this in ages."

Thea glanced down at the stocky man. "You know much about forges?"

Ulfgar's shoulders hunched up into a shrug. "I was a blacksmith once," he muttered. "Long time ago."

Thea wondered how long ago it could have been. According to her understanding of human appearances, he shouldn't be much older than his forties. Maybe circles seemed longer to people who weren't made to live forever.

Ducking out through the door, they returned to the bramble-filled gardens.

"I'm going in," Ulfgar muttered.

"Okay," Thea gave him a smile. "Just let us know if there's anything you'd like for your room."

"It's not my room," Ulfgar snapped. "I'm not going to be around long enough for that."

He stomped off towards the house, leaving Thea and Roland in silence. The dry grasses rustled in the sea breeze.

"You said there was a dock?" Roland asked.

"I think there used to be." Thea turned back to Roland with a smile. "Let's go look."

Skirting the rest of the gardens, they passed through the door in the wall and found themselves on the bluff overlooking the sea. Below them, an old path wound in tight switchbacks all the way down to the shore.

"You sure get a nice view from here," Roland mused, staring out at the glittering waves. He never spoke about it, but Thea knew he missed the sea. Sailing had been his life, until he lost his place on the Eagle.

Roland glanced at Thea, eyes twinkling. "Race you to the bottom."

Thea grinned. "Ready when you are."

"Go!"

Thea raced after Roland, tumbling from boulder to boulder along the narrow, winding path. Her tough, stonelike skin protected her from most bumps and bruises, as it did for all the Elves. Legs scrambling, she made it around the first switchback, and ran on.

Roland was still ahead. As Thea rounded the next switchback she glanced at the water far below. It looked deep enough. With a great leap, she flung herself off the cliff.

Hurtling past jagged rocks and boulders, she plunged head first into the churning sea. The shock took her breath away. Propelling herself back to the surface, Thea took a great gasp of air. The water was cold. Kicking her feet, she swam back towards shore.

Roland tumbled down the last of the path and waited

with his hands on his hips, breathing heavily.

"I still won," he called as Thea pulled herself up on the rocky shore.

"No, I won," Thea retorted. "I made it to the bottom first."

"The bottom of the *path*."

"Well, you should have said." Thea tried to glare at him, but she couldn't help laughing. For a moment she'd felt like she was back home in Lyudmyla. Not that she wanted to be there, of course.

Roland grabbed her hand and helped her up.

Doing her best to ignore the cool breeze that chilled her through her wet clothing, Thea looked around the rocky shoreline. Some old wooden pilings were all that remained of what must have once been a dock. "I guess the protection magic didn't reach this far."

Roland nodded. "It looks like a good place for a dock, though. We'll have to rebuild it, then the Raven will have somewhere to tie up."

"You think the Raven will come?" Thea glanced at Roland. "Svetka's your friend, not mine."

"She'll come," Roland grinned, "if your uncle tells her to. No one says no to the Chancellor."

"I wouldn't put it past her."

Roland shook his head. "Svetka's no fool. She knows how authority works."

"And she hates it."

Roland laughed. "I never said she didn't. Still, your uncle is a good boss. I enjoy working for him. Mostly. At least I can still sail sometimes, even if it's just to deliver letters."

They made their way back up the long, winding path.

"It's a long way to carry cargo," Roland mused as

they reached the top of the bluff. "I wonder if the people who lived here had an easier way up."

"I don't know." Thea looked around the rocky bluff. There didn't seem to be any other way down to the old dock site. "We don't know anything about the people who made this place. Just that they were Elves."

"Well, I've never met an Elf who would carry a boatload of crates up a steep path if there were any other options available." He scanned the cliffs with a keen eye. "They would've had some kind of system. It's just a question of whether it survived."

"If it didn't, I'm sure we can figure something out," Thea grinned.

"First things first." Roland looked up past the wall to the old stone building beyond. "We need to get your house ready to be lived in."

That night, Thea lay in her new bed, warm and comfortable. Half asleep, she looked around the shadowy room with a contented smile, imagining what it would look like once it was fully furnished and decorated. It was bare and empty now, but soon it would really feel like home. Slowly her eyes drifted shut.

Something jolted Thea into wakefulness. She stared into the darkness, heart pounding, as a wailing cry filled the air around her.

What was that sound? Thea froze, unable to move as the pitch of the cry rose higher and higher until it felt as if her ears were going to explode. The sound was all around her, pulsing through her body and her mind. She couldn't think. She couldn't breathe.

It stopped. Silence rang in Thea's ears as she took a

trembling breath. In the blue-green light of night, the room around her was empty and still.

Pounding feet thundered through the silence and Roland burst, breathless, into her room.

"What was that?" He demanded, his eyes wide with alarm.

"I—I don't know," Thea stammered. "I never heard anything like that before."

Ulfgar appeared behind Roland, a half-asleep scowl just visible beneath his tousled hair. "That hurt my head," he muttered, rubbing his forehead.

Thea glanced at Ulfgar's bloodshot eyes. His evening spent in the wine cellar probably didn't help.

"Whatever it was, it didn't sound natural." Roland's eyes scanned the room carefully. "Could you tell where it was coming from?"

"No. It seemed to be coming from everywhere."

Roland nodded slowly. "Let's see what we can find."

The night air was cold. Thea grabbed her oilskin cloak from where she'd hung it on a bedpost and followed Roland.

They examined the bedrooms and the upstairs meeting room, but nothing seemed strange or out of place. Cautiously, they walked down the stairs into the great room below. Grumbling, Ulfgar plodded along behind them.

The great room was dark and empty, except for the table and chairs tucked close to the fireplace on the far side of the room.

They walked through the shadowy kitchen, the pantry, and down into the deep darkness of the wine cellar, but there was nothing to be seen that hadn't been there before.

"Well?" Ulfgar muttered, after they returned to the great room.

Thea frowned. "I don't understand. *Something* must have made that noise."

"Should we look outside?" Roland asked, his gaze moving to the large windows, through which the blue-green light of Micai glimmered faintly.

"But it was so loud. I thought—"

The wailing cry began again. It was low, almost beyond hearing, then rose quickly higher and higher. It filled the air around her. It filled her mind until it was impossible to think about anything else.

Crouching on the ground, Thea covered her ears.

When the shrill wail faded into silence, she looked up again. Roland seemed shaken. His hand rested on the long knife he always carried at his belt.

Ulfgar's eyes darted around the room. "Ghosts and spooks," he muttered. "They said this place is haunted."

"It can't be haunted," Thea protested. "Nothing evil can enter here."

"Just because it's haunting doesn't mean it's evil," Ulfgar muttered. "How do you know how that magic door works?"

"I guess I don't really," Thea admitted, looking up at the door. The inscription on the doorframe seemed brighter in the gloom of night. "I just know the musharocs couldn't follow us in here."

Roland moved back to Thea's side. "Can you see anything? With your spirit sight, I mean."

Thea shook her head. She'd been looking, but she couldn't see any sign of any spiritual presences.

"So we look outside?"

Thea nodded.

Thea and Roland searched the courtyard and all of the outbuildings, but there was nothing to be seen. Ulfgar followed them, glancing from side to side with a suspicious gaze.

Finally they stopped by the gate and stared out across the overgrown fields and patches of woodland that surrounded the old walls. Overhead, the planet Micai filled the sky. Its gentle blue-green light glimmered on each leaf and stone. Thea listened to the usual sounds of night—the chirp of frogs, the rustle of small creatures scurrying through the grass, the owls calling in the distance.

"Whatever it is, I don't think it's out there," Thea reflected aloud as they turned back towards the shadowy stone building.

Roland nodded. "It's just strange that we couldn't see anything."

Thea shivered and pulled her cloak tighter.

They returned to the great room in silence.

"I'm going back to bed," Ulfgar muttered. Stumping across the room, he disappeared up the stairs. Soon the sound of his snore drifted through the silent building.

Roland watched Thea with a worried gaze. "Is there anything else we can try?"

Thea sighed. "I guess we should sleep, if we can."

Roland nodded and together they walked back upstairs.

Alone in her room, Thea stared out the window for a while, watching the light of Micai shimmer across the sea.

The haunting wail began again, rising up all around her as if the walls or the air itself was crying out. It pierced through her, almost painful in its urgency.

When it faded away, a soft knock filled the silence.

"Come in," Thea called.

Slowly, the door opened and Roland stepped into the room. "You heard it again?"

Thea nodded.

"Should we ... do something about it?"

Thea's gaze returned to the window. Outside, the world was peaceful and quiet. "I don't know what we can do."

"I would just hate for something to—" His voice faltered, and his gaze fell to the floor.

"We're safe here," Thea insisted. "I'm sure we are." In her mind, she could still see the musharocs soaring through the air, screeching in fury, unable to reach their prey. "You should sleep, if you can." She offered Roland an encouraging smile.

Concern etched Roland's forehead, but he gave a reluctant nod. "Good night, Thea."

Thea watched Roland go, then walked slowly back to bed. Hanging her cloak over a bed post, she lay down and pulled up the blankets.

She was almost asleep when the cry rang out again. She lay, motionless, as the wail echoed on and on, rising higher and higher until her head pounded. Finally it died away, and she fell asleep.

What seemed like moments later, the wailing cry jolted her from her sleep again. Thea groaned and covered her head, but it was impossible to fall back asleep until silence descended.

The cry rang out again.

And again.

Thea tossed and turned as the cry dragged her into wakefulness over and over until at last the first golden glimmers of daylight pierced through the darkness of night. Staggering to the window, she watched Allumen emerge from its nightly eclipse, its brilliant light shimmering through the golden rings of Micai.

Thea rubbed her aching head. Time to check in. Kneeling by the window, she waited.

Allulien's warm presence flooded the room. Thea looked up and saw her General, larger than life and translucent as swirling water. The brightness shining from within them filled the room with golden light.

"Welcome home, Thea," Allulien smiled. "You have waited a long time to return here."

Joy filled Thea's heart. "Thank you. I'm so glad to be back."

Allulien's eyes sparkled with light. "Are you ready for your orders?"

"Yes, Allulien."

"Take the time to get to know your new home. Make it you own, repair what has been broken, and bring life back to this forgotten place."

Thea smiled. "Thank you, Allulien. I will."

The warm glow of Allulien's blessing washed over her as her General's presence began to fade.

"Wait!" Thea called. "What was that crying sound last night?"

Allulien's piercing gaze was stern, yet twinkled with joy. "What did you learn about it?"

Thea hesitated. "It sounded urgent, almost as if it was trying to say something." Her eyes widened. "Could I use my magic to understand it?"

Allulien smiled. "Why don't you try that tonight?"

Allulien disappeared, but with her spirit sight Thea could still feel the imprint of their presence, left behind like a footprint.

After making her bed, Thea wandered down to the kitchen where she found a roaring fire in the oven and Ulfgar busily cooking a pan full of eggs. He grunted a greeting as she entered, but otherwise seemed uninterested in speaking to her.

Hearing footsteps on the stairs, Thea returned to the great room.

"Good morning." Roland smiled when he saw her, but his eyes looked tired. "Did you get much sleep?"

"Not really," Thea admitted.

Roland nodded. "Did Allulien say anything about it?"

Thea shook her head. "Just a reminder that I could have used my comprehension magic to try to understand it."

"By the fourth or fifth time that cry happened, I was sure tempted to try banishing it." Roland gave a wry smile.

"I'm glad you didn't. I'd like to know what it is first."

"I know. That's why I didn't." Roland yawned. "I'll need an extra long sleep during staph today. That was a rough night."

Thea nodded and stifled her own yawn.

A crashing sound echoed from the kitchen, followed by muffled curses.

"Can I help?" Roland called.

"Go away," Ulfgar grumbled. "I'm fine."

"Did Micai say anything?" Thea asked Roland when the din from the kitchen had settled down.

"Told me to stay alert, get sleep when I can, and be ready for anything." He gave a wry grin. "You know how Micai is."

Thea smiled. She did know. "I guess we'll just keep

our eyes open."

After breakfast, Thea set about cleaning the old building from top to bottom. Just because it was in excellent repair didn't mean the passing of time hadn't left any toll. Dust and cobwebs filled every corner.

Roland and Ulfgar helped, but even so they had only finished cleaning the upper floor by the time workday was over.

After a quick bite to eat, Thea threw herself into bed, exhausted.

When she woke, staph was over and half of restday as well. The house was quiet and empty. A quick check in Roland's room showed that his hunting knives were missing, so she knew where he had gone.

Ulfgar's snore drifted up from below.

After rousing Ulfgar out of his drunken stupor in the wine cellar, she gave him the task of cutting back the brambles in the courtyard. Thea found a shovel in the old gardener's shed and started tackling some of the tougher weeds.

A couple of measures later, Roland returned with two rabbits, already skinned and prepared for cooking.

Thea looked at the result of their efforts in the garden. It was barely a dent in the work that had to be done. Putting away the shovel, she followed Roland into the house.

They ate a simple stew and watched the light of Allumen flicker behind the rings of the planet Micai on its way to its nightly eclipse.

Thea's heart beat loud in her ears. Would the strange wailing cries happen again? What could she learn about them? She went through the motions of getting ready for bed, then lay in the darkness and waited.

She didn't have to wait long. The wailing cry rose around her like a wave of sound. Using the magic given to her by Allulien, Thea listened to the cry again.

It was a call. A call for something missing and far away. Now that she listened to it again, the sound did not seem menacing or frightening. It throbbed through her body like a lonely cry. Something was gone. Something was lost.

Thea pulled the blankets tighter and waited. Finally the cry died away and she heard the knock she had been expecting.

With a creak, the door opened. "Thea?"

"Yes, Roland?"

"I'm planning to sit up and watch tonight. Just so you know."

"Do you want me to sit up with you?"

"It's okay. There's no point in all of us losing sleep."

Thea nodded. "Anything I can help you with?"

Roland frowned. "It's just ... are you sure you didn't hear anything like this when you were here before?"

"No. Nothing like this." There had been the screeches of the musharocs outside, but that was entirely different.

"And you were here overnight?"

"Two nights."

"Okay." Roland didn't seem satisfied, but he didn't push the question anymore. "Good night, Thea. Sleep well."

Thea didn't sleep well, but she dozed between the haunting cries.

Chapter Two

Thea stood at her window, looking out over the gardens. They looked much better now. The weeds and brambles were gone. The pathways were swept and the few surviving ornamental shrubs had been carefully pruned. Inside, everything had been scrubbed until it shone, and the few things that were broken had been repaired. Roland had spent the last couple of days measuring logs for rebuilding the dock, and Ulfgar had lent a hand in the work when he wasn't busy drinking.

They still had no idea what was causing the strange wailing cries.

The cries had continued night after night. Thea and the others tried staying up all night to watch. They tried ignoring it and going back to sleep. They searched the house and grounds again and again, but there was nothing to be found. Whatever caused the chilling sound, it seemed unaffected by anything they did. It wasn't causing them any harm, besides affecting their sleep, but Thea had a sinking feeling that she would have to figure out what was causing it before anyone would be willing to come and live there with her.

"Thea!" Roland's voice echoed up from downstairs. "Thea, the Littles are here!"

With a gasp of delight, Thea ran downstairs and out into the courtyard.

A large wagon pulled by two oxen rumbled in

through the gate. The wagon was piled high with boxes and crates, and seated precariously on top were several Littles—humanlike in appearance, but considerably smaller. They waved greetings as she approached.

"Thea!" A voice that Thea knew well rose loud above the hubbub.

A tall, Elf-like figure leaped off the back of the cart. Her skin gleamed green in the light and her strange white and green hair blew wildly in the wind.

"Sylica!" Thea grinned as her exuberant friend bounded across the courtyard to embrace her.

"I heard there was a wagon coming, so I just had to come and see you!" Sylica beamed, waving enthusiastically at Roland and Ulfgar who had also emerged from the door. "Look at this place, it's so pretty now! I knew you would get everything looking so good. Do you want a candy? I brought lots!"

"How are you doing?" Thea asked, accepting the handful of candy being thrust her direction.

"I'm doing really well!" Sylica beamed. "I've been having so much fun in Gedwyld!"

"I'm glad." Thea smiled. "I was hoping you'd come visit sometime."

"There was something I was supposed to tell you." Sylica's face clouded with a frown for a moment, then burst out in a grin again. "I remember! Elora and Kais say hi. They wanted to come, but then they didn't."

"How are they doing?" Roland asked.

"They're doing really well." Sylica nodded sagely. "They finally got all their wedding presents put away, I think. You know they kept on getting more and more presents? Their house was right full to the top! They had to give a lot of them away, but Elora made me promise not to tell anybody. She sent this for you!" Sylica reached into her bag and handed Thea a large wooden spoon with a beautifully carved handle. "She liked it but they were given eight of them or something like that. She thought you could use it."

Thea accepted the spoon with a smile. "You'll have to thank her for me."

The other Littles who had come with the cart gave their greetings. Thea welcomed them all by name. "Come in!" she urged them. "Come get something to eat, then I'd love to hear what you think of the house."

The Littles followed Thea inside, while Roland and Sylica took care of the oxen.

"Would you like something to drink?" Thea offered, pulling empty boxes and crates around the hearth as impromptu seats. She gathered a mismatch of assorted cups from the kitchen as the Littles made themselves comfortable.

Gili hopped up to help pass out the cups.

"How are the Littles in Gedwyld doing?" Thea asked as she pulled up her own chair.

"We all have our own homes now," Alya replied, stretching her feet out towards the fire. "It was nice of the Middles to share their homes for a while, but it's much nicer having our own."

"I'm so glad. Everyone is finding work alright?"

Alya nodded. "Us pipers have lots to do, of course. Others are working on the farms or up at the castle."

"And Sami's working at the house of healing, of course," Talia added.

"Are Faris and the others recovering well?"

Alya nodded. "Sami says Faris should be able to go home soon, and he's taken the longest to get better.

Dana has her own place down by the wall, and most of the others have family to take care of them."

"You have a home now too," Talia grinned, turning to Thea. "It looks very nice."

"Lots of space." Tam's eyes twinkled.

Alya set down her cup and eyed the room with a judicious gaze. "What do you need for it? Water pipes? Heat pipes?"

"The house doesn't have any sort of pipes," Thea replied. "Whatever you want to do with it would be wonderful."

The Littles shook their heads.

"I don't know how the Middles were happy living like this," Alya frowned. "No running water, no sewer, no heat unless the room has a fire. You'd never see Littles living like that."

Tam gave a good-natured shrug. "If you don't know what you miss, how can you miss it?"

Alya made a face. "You'd think they could have figured it out."

Thea smiled. "You said the pipers have been busy?"

Alya nodded. "All the Middles want pipes in their homes now, and they pay us very well."

Thea gave an apologetic smile. "I'm afraid I don't have much to pay you with."

Alya waved her hand. "That is different. You saved us from the dark things and brought us to our new home. For you, this is a gift."

Thea smiled. "Thank you. That is very kind."

Clattering and thumping echoed from the courtyard.

Roland opened the door. "Anyone want to help unload the wagon?"

Everyone jumped up to lend a hand, and soon the

wagon's contents had been piled in a corner of the great room. Not much of the furniture Thea ordered was ready yet, but there were a couple of bedframes and mattresses, as well as more kitchen supplies. A pile in another corner held the tools and materials the Littles had brought for their work.

Ulfgar disappeared into the kitchen, and soon the table was loaded with bread, potatoes, and sausages.

As everyone ate, Sylica shared all about the recent dance the Lord of Gedwyld had hosted at the castle, as well as several other community events that seemed to blend together into an endless, enthusiastic tale.

After supper, Thea showed the Littles to an unoccupied bedroom upstairs, while Sylica opted to sleep by the fireplace.

Finally Thea climbed into her own bed and fell asleep.

She woke as Allumen's first rays emerged from their eclipse, feeling more rested than she had in days. Kneeling by the window to check in, she waited to hear if Allulien had any orders for the day.

A murmur of voices floated up from downstairs. She hadn't heard from Allulien since she first moved in, but that didn't really surprise her. Allulien wanted her to settle into her new home, and that's what she would do until new orders came.

Thea skipped down the stairs and waved a greeting to Sylica and the Littles who were already eating their breakfast.

"Thea?" Roland followed her down the stairs. "Could we talk for a moment?"

"Sure. What is it?"

"How did you sleep last night?"

"I slept fine. Why?"

There was something strange in Roland's expression. "You didn't wake up at all?"

"No. Did you?"

"No."

Thea's eyes widened. "Nothing woke us all night!"

Roland glanced around the room with a frown. "What changed?" His eyes fell on the table where Sylica and the Littles talked cheerfully over their breakfast. "They came."

Thea stared. It seemed preposterous, but what else could explain it? "Maybe the cry will happen again tonight?" she suggested, but somehow she knew that it wouldn't. How on Raphtova could her guests be connected with the strange cries that had been haunting them every night?

"You didn't hear it when you were here before." Roland stared at the table with an intent expression. "Sylica was with you then, wasn't she?"

"And Elora, so it could be something to do with the Littles."

"Should we ask them about it?"

"Not yet." The last thing Thea wanted to do was frighten their guests away.

Roland gave her a doubtful glance. "Alright."

Thea and Roland joined the table.

"Hi Thea! Hi Roland!" Sylica greeted them as they approached. "I woke up and I was hungry so I made some porridge in the kitchen. I hope you don't mind that I used up all the oats because I was really hungry and Alya, Tam, Talia, and Gili came down too and I thought they must be hungry but I think I made too much because now they aren't hungry anymore but there's still lots in the kitchen. Are you hungry? You must be because it's breakfast time but you haven't been downstairs yet. Did you sleep well? I slept great! Sleeping by the fire is so nice and cozy. I sleep by the fire when I stay over at Elora and Kais' house because Sami has the extra room and Zaki sleeps in the attic. I thought sleeping in the attic would be fun too but Zaki didn't want to share it with me."

Roland leaned close to Thea's ear. "Has she taken a breath yet?"

Thea laughed. "Excuse us, Sylica. We'll get some of the porridge you made and be right back!"

"Of course," Sylica beamed. "I hope you like it. Sami was teaching me all about how to make porridge. First you take the oats and then you—"

Thea extricated herself from the cooking lesson and headed for the kitchen. Sure enough, Sylica had cooked up an entire bag of oats into her pot of porridge. Thankfully there was another bag, Thea knew, tucked away somewhere in the pantry.

Ulfgar emerged from the wine cellar, bleary-eyed and yawning.

"Good morning, Ulfgar," Thea smiled. "Want some porridge? There's lots."

Ulfgar stared at the pot in consternation. "How much did you make?"

Thea laughed. "That was Sylica. I didn't think to hide the kitchen supplies."

Sylica's continuing chatter drifted through the air as Ulfgar dished up a bowl.

"I'll be downstairs," he muttered, and stumped back towards the wine cellar.

Thea returned to the table and pushed Roland off towards the kitchen to get his breakfast. The Littles had already finished eating.

"We want to start our work now," Alya said, staring up at Thea with her large blue eyes. "Do you have any instructions?"

"You're the experts," Thea smiled. "Whatever you want to do will be fine with me."

Alya nodded in appreciation and gestured for the rest of the Littles to follow her upstairs.

Thea finished her breakfast as quickly as she could, beneath the endless flow of Sylica's chatter, then went to find the Littles.

They were in Roland's room, examining the chimney that stretched up along the wall from the great fireplace downstairs.

Alya looked up from her work as Thea entered. "This room will be warm, but we need to get the heat to the other bedrooms. We can build a pipe from here through the floor. It shouldn't take too much work."

"That would be wonderful, thank you."

The Littles conferred together in their own language. Tam pulled a thick pencil from behind his ear and started making marks on the floor.

Alya turned back to Thea. "The toilet room will be downstairs. We could make it upstairs, but that is harder."

"Downstairs is just fine," Thea assured her.

Alya nodded. "Come see where we want to make it."

Thea followed the Littles down the stairs and into the small lean-to. When Thea had arrived, it was full of cobwebs and scraps of wood. Now it was neatly swept and cleaned. The firewood that Ulfgar collected was stacked neatly on one side.

Alya tapped the wall. "This room is made of wood, which is easier to work with than stone. With the whole space we can fit two toilets and a bath room."

Thea considered this. "What if we don't use the whole space? It would be nice to still have room to store firewood."

"Some people like to have a moving tub," Gili offered. "You could have it upstairs and move it from room to room, wherever you want it."

"They are more work to fill up," Alya countered, "and there won't be any pipes upstairs."

Tam scratched his head. "There might be space under the stairs."

Alya nodded. "Let's see." She turned to Thea. "We will start taking things apart and see what we find."

"That sounds good to me," Thea agreed. "Let me know if you need anything."

The Littles grabbed their tools and got to work. Thea joined Sylica and Roland, sitting by the fire.

"Hi Thea!" Sylica paused in her tale to greet her friend. "I was telling Roland about this time when I was up at the castle and I really wanted to see the view from the tower, so I was trying to climb up it, but I guess I'm not so good at climbing because I only got partway up and then I got stuck, so I was hanging there and down below was the cliff and the sea, and I was thinking it wouldn't feel very good to fall down all the way onto the rocks so I was trying not to fall, and then a guard saw me and there was all this shouting and yelling, except the shouting and yelling wasn't helping me get anywhere—"

Pulling up a chair, Thea settled down and let Sylica's

chatter wash over her like the warmth of the fire. It was nice to have more people around. The house was much too large for just her, Roland, and Ulfgar, and soon she might not even have them. Roland would have to go back to his work in Lyudmyla, and no one knew how long Ulfgar would stay around. It was one thing to live in this old empty building with its wailing cries when there were friends with her. She didn't like the thought of living there alone.

"Thea?" Alya's strikingly blue eyes stared up at her.

Startled by the Little's sudden appearance, Thea gestured for Sylica to be quiet. "Yes, Alya?"

"I think you should see this."

Thea glanced at Roland, then followed Alya into the lean-to. A few of the floorboards had been pulled up, and the rest of the Littles were staring down into the shadowy hole. Alya gestured towards it.

Kneeling down, Thea peered into the gloom. Beneath the floor, stairs led down into darkness.

"Roland?" Thea called, but Roland was right behind her. He crouched over the hole.

"What's going on?" Sylica asked, squeezing into the crowded lean-to. "Is there something down there? Can I see?"

"Can you get Ulfgar, please?" Thea asked, watching Roland closely as he saw what lay beneath the floor.

"Ulf-gaaaaarrrrr!" Sylica called, skipping out of sight.

Roland glanced at Thea. "This might explain things."

"Explain what?" Alya asked, catching Roland's expression.

"We've been hearing … sounds." Thea explained. "At night. We couldn't find where they were coming from."

"You didn't know these stairs were here?"

Thea shook her head. "Were they boarded up, do you think?"

"Not boarded up. Hidden." Alya looked around the room with a keen eye, saying something in the language of the Littles. The rest of the Littles jumped up and started searching around the lean-to.

"We're looking for something?" Sylica bounced back into the room. "I like looking for things! It's like a treasure hunt!"

"What's going on?" Ulfgar emerged from behind Sylica, filling the room with the smell of wine.

"Look here!" Gili cried, gesturing to a small crack in the floor.

Alya slid her thin fingers along the crack. "There's a hook. Is there anything it could attach to?"

"That iron ring in the rafters?" Tam offered.

"Right." Alya grinned. "Who's got a rope?"

Roland ducked out of the room and returned moments later with a length of rope. He threw it on the ground in a loose coil, ready for use.

"Put the end through that ring in the ceiling," Alya ordered, and nodded with approval as he did so. "Now slide the end through that crack on the floor. See how it goes under the catch? Now tie it."

With a flick of his wrist, Roland tied a knot and pulled the rope tight. He grabbed the end of the rope that hung loose. "We need to tie this off somewhere."

Alya nodded. "I'm guessing ... there!" She pointed to a pair of inconspicuous nails sticking out from the walls of the lean-to. Thea had noticed them when she was cleaning, but hadn't thought anything of them.

"Right." Roland grabbed the rope and pulled.

With a grinding creak, a portion of the floor began to

rise, revealing the stairs that stretched down into darkness.

Ulfgar stared.

"A secret passage?" Sylica squealed. "That's so exciting!"

Roland fastened the rope around the nails and returned to the top of the stairs.

"What's down there?" Sylica demanded. "Is there treasure?"

"We don't know," Roland replied in an even voice. "We haven't been down there yet."

Sylica gasped in excitement. "Can I come?"

Thea glanced at Roland. "I think—"

"I'll go down." Roland interjected. "I'm the one with protection magic."

Thea had to admit that was true.

"I won't go far," Roland assured her.

Thea nodded. "Do you need anything?"

Roland drew his knife. "A light would be nice."

"I'll get one." Talia slipped out the door. The rest of the Littles crowded around the top of the stairs with Sylica, peering down into the darkness.

Talia returned and gave Roland one of the small lanterns that the Littles used, filled with gently glowing fungi.

Holding the lantern in one hand and his long knife in the other, Roland stepped down the stairs and disappeared into the gloom.

Ulfgar pushed past Thea and thumped down the stairs after him.

"Ulfgar!" Thea hissed. His belt clattered with axes, knives and other weapons. How he always had his weapons on his person, Thea didn't understand, but she had to admit that he was always prepared.

"Can we follow them?" Sylica whispered in a voice that filled the room.

Ulfgar was out of sight now, but Thea could still hear him, thumping and clanking in the darkness below.

"Pleeeeaaaassseee?" Sylica begged.

Thea glanced at the Littles. "I guess so," she conceded. "Do you have any more lanterns with you?"

Alya nodded and returned with two more lanterns. Thea took one of them.

The Littles looked up at her with big eyes.

"You don't have to come if you don't want to," Thea assured them. "We won't be gone long."

Sylica hopped from foot to foot in breathless anticipation.

Nodding to Alya, Thea gripped the lantern tightly and stepped onto the stairs. Moving down, step after step, she was soon beneath the floorboards, leaving the light of day behind.

The small lantern gleamed with its strange green light, only just illuminating the old stone walls and dust-filled cobwebs.

Behind her, Sylica squealed in hushed excitement.

At the foot of the stairs, a long corridor stretched into darkness. Scuffling noises and hushed whispers echoed from beyond her sight, though with her spirit sight she could see Roland's spirit, bright in the gloom, and the spark of life deep inside Ulfgar's calloused spirit. Thea hurried towards them, aware of Sylica's spirit shining like a beacon behind her.

The stone walls that she passed reminded her of the walls of the building up above, but darker and dirtier. The stones beneath her feet were worn with age.

Finally the light of her lantern illuminated a door. Through it she could see the light of Roland's lantern.

"Roland?"

In the dim green light, Roland glanced up and saw her. "Come in," he gestured. "It seems fine."

Thea stepped through the door and looked around. It was a large room, about half the size of the great room upstairs, and filled with a host of strange-looking contraptions. Tables were covered with bottles and vials, shelves were piled with tools and packages, crates and barrels lined every wall. A strange smell lingered in the air.

"I'd suggest not touching anything," Roland added. His eyes widened slightly as he saw Sylica following close behind Thea. "*Please* don't touch anything." He glanced around the strange room in alarm.

"What is this thing, anyways?" Ulfgar muttered, staring at a large tub connected to a rat's nest of wires, tubes, and pipes.

"Oh! Oh! I know!" Sylica skittered over to his side. "That's a thingy! I saw one of those before!" Her eyes caught Roland's glare and she froze, her hand extended halfway towards poking it.

Ulfgar grunted. "And I don't suppose you know what this is, then?" He gestured to a glass ball suspended over what appeared to be a small pile of charcoal.

"Sure. That traps the magic in the—oh!" Sylica stared around the room, her eyes shining. "It's like Uncle Bob's workshop! See? There's the magic holder thingy and the seeing small things machine and the spinner arounder and everything! This person was an Uncle Bob!"

"A what?" Ulfgar frowned.

Thea looked around the room with a new fascination.

She'd heard about Sylica's Uncle Bob. "This person made magical things?"

"Of course they did!" Sylica beamed. "Why else would they have a magic holder thingy?"

"Magical things?" Roland looked at Thea in surprise.

Thea nodded. "Ever met Sylica's candy bag?"

"Yes, but—"

"It never runs out."

Roland blinked. "Really?"

"Want to see?" Sylica squealed.

"No, it's okay. I believe you." He turned to Thea. "If the person who lived here made magical things, that would explain the door."

"That's right," Thea agreed.

Roland looked around the room with interest. "Do you suppose some of these things are magical?"

"Of course they are!" Sylica grinned. "You can't have a magic holder thingy that isn't magical. And *that's* magical," she pointed to a small hammer hanging above one of the desks. "And *that's* magical. And *that's* magical!"

"Really?" Roland glanced at Thea. The stack of papers Sylica had just indicated certainly looked like normal papers.

"She can see magic," Thea explained, watching Sylica bounce around the room. "I don't know how, but every time I cast magic around her she can see it, as if the magic is a visible thing. Maybe it's a kind of elf-sight?"

"Magic sight?" Roland frowned. "I've never heard of something like that befo—don't touch that!"

Sylica put down the glass bottle with a guilty expression. "Why?" she protested. "I used to touch everything in Uncle Bob's workshop. Nothing bad ever happened!"

"This person was not your Uncle Bob," Roland retorted. "We don't know what they were like, or what they left behind."

With a creaking clatter, the cupboard doors on the far side of the room swung open.

"Ulfgar!" Roland groaned.

Oblivious, Ulfgar stalked towards them, carrying a large forging hammer. "Can smell smithy tools anywhere," he muttered. Holding the hammer up to the light, he turned it this way and that. "Best one I've ever seen."

"It's shiny, isn't it?" Sylica grinned.

Thea gave her a sharp glance. Did that mean it was magical? She tried to get a look at the hammer, but there didn't seem to be anything unusual about it.

Ulfgar swung the hammer onto his shoulder and looked around the room. A spark of eagerness glinted in his eyes.

Thea held her lantern over the papers on the desk. They didn't have any writing on them, just scribbles and sketches of things she didn't understand.

Her eyes moved to the shadowy corners of the room. Was this where the noise had come from? It was possible—there were so many strange machines and tools—but what exactly had made the sound, and why? She had heard the cry calling out for something, but why would a tool call for someone? And why was it silent last night?

Ulfgar and Sylica continued to explore the room, poking and prodding things with unwary interest.

Where was Roland? There—staring at the wall with the half-vacant gaze that Thea knew well.

"Roland?" She spoke in a low voice and waited.

At last Roland shifted and turned to look at Thea. His eyes shone in the lantern light. "There's another room!"

"What?" Thea stared around the room, but she couldn't see any other doorways.

"Over here." Roland led Thea back into the shadowy corridor.

"Hey! Where are you going?" Sylica called after them.

Roland felt along the wall across from the door. "I saw it," he said, as if to himself. "There's something over here."

Thea ran her hand along the smooth, close-fitting stones. "But there isn't any door."

"Where was it?" Roland muttered to himself. "It starts here ..." he walked along the wall. "And it goes to here. A smaller room than the other one ..."

"Need help?" Ulfgar asked from behind Thea.

"We're looking for a hidden door or something." Thea looked the wall up and down. "There's a room behind it."

"Oh! Me! Me!" Sylica squealed, pushing past. Dropping the lantern she had been carrying, she began pushing the stones, one after the other, as if one of them was sure to be the key.

"I can hit it," Ulfgar offered, swinging the hammer experimentally.

Thea cautioned him to wait.

A few moments later there was a *clonk* and an excited squeal from Sylica. A portion of the wall swung inwards, leaving a dark opening before them.

Sylica leapt towards it, but Roland held out an arm

and stopped her. Lifting his lantern, Roland examined the doorframe and the floor beyond. Cautiously he stepped inside. Thea heard his sharp intake of breath.

"What is it?" she whispered.

For once, Sylica was completely silent.

Roland glanced back and gestured them forward. As Thea stepped through the door, the light from her lantern reflected on a wall filled with swords, knives, shields, and armour.

Sylica gasped. "It's treasure!"

"An armoury," Roland replied, his eyes fixed on the glimmering sight before them.

"Can we touch them?" Sylica whispered.

"I don't see why not," Thea said cautiously. "Just be careful."

Everyone scattered around the tiny room to examine its treasures.

"Look at the shiny dresses!" Sylica squealed.

"Those are armour, Sylica," Thea explained, but they *were* shiny. Each small plate of metal twinkled like a green star in the lantern light.

Ulfgar lifted a large, two-headed axe off its hook on the wall, examined it, and gave it a couple experimental swings. "Hm," he muttered. "That's really well balanced. Never seen that done properly before."

Roland looked at the embossing on one of the shields. "Do you recognize this symbol, Thea?"

Thea frowned. "It looks Elvish to me, like the symbol for one of the houses, but I don't recognize it."

Roland nodded.

"What are all these things doing here?" Sylica asked, knocking on a gleaming helmet.

"Being hidden, I imagine," Roland replied. "The real

question is: why were they left behind?"

Thea's gaze roamed across the gleaming weapons. "And what should we do with them?"

"What do *you* want to do with them, Thea?" Roland gave her a keen look. "This is all yours now, you know."

Thea swallowed uncomfortably. The house was hers. The Lord of Gedwyld had told her no one owned it, and as far as he was concerned she was welcome to it. But surely these weapons and armour belonged to somebody.

"I wonder if we should leave them here," she said slowly. "I need a little while to think about this. They look like they're really valuable."

"They're really well-made, if that's what you mean," Ulfgar muttered under his breath.

From the corner of her eye, Thea caught his expression as he set the axe back in its place on the wall.

"Ulfgar ..."

He looked up with a frown. "What?"

"I think you should have that axe."

A startled look passed through his eyes. "What?"

"I'd like you to have it."

He frowned. "Why?"

"Because you're my friend."

An expression Thea couldn't explain wound its way across Ulfgar's face. Then he scowled and turned away. "I don't make friends."

Thea lifted the axe down and held it out. "Take it, Ulfgar. If not as a friend, at least as a thanks for all your help."

Ulfgar looked at her with a wary expression. Slowly he reached out and took the axe. "Thanks," he muttered, but his eyes glittered as he stared at the weapon in his hands.

Thea turned her attention back to the others. "I'd like you to have something too, Sylica." Her eyes roamed around the room and settled on the armour Sylica had admired. She lifted it off its stand and held it up. It was surprisingly light.

Sylica gasped. "I get to have the shiny dress?"

"Armour," Thea corrected. "Do you think it will fit?"

Sylica was already gone, dancing around the room with the armour jingling in her arms.

Thea smiled and turned to Roland. "What would you like to have?"

He glanced at the ground. "I don't need anything."

"No, really. What would you like?"

Roland looked at her for a moment with an expression she couldn't define. It looked like he wanted to say something, then his gaze turned to the row of glittering weapons. "I usually fight with a knife," he offered.

Thea looked through the knives and chose one with a carving of a bird on the handle. "It looks a bit like a raven, doesn't it?" She smiled.

"Thank you." Roland accepted the knife as Thea handed it to him. "What are you going to take?"

Thea shook her head. "I'm not going to take anything."

"You made the rest of us take something. Why shouldn't you?"

Thea shrugged. "I have Raybow. I couldn't ask for anything else."

"What do you use for close range?"

Thea made a face. "I try to avoid fighting at close range."

Roland's smile was grim. "Sometimes you don't have a choice."

"I guess." Thea sighed. "What would you suggest?"

"A falcion is an all around useful tool," Roland suggested, pointing out a sword with a slightly curved blade. "Spears are good too. I'd suggest a staff, but I don't see one here."

Thea looked through the weapons and eventually chose the falcion that Roland had pointed out. She also took four small knives, beautifully shaped, with gemstones in their handles.

Leaving the secret door open, they returned along the corridor and back up the stairs into the lean-to. The Littles stared in surprise as Thea and the others emerged, carrying their new weapons and armour. Their eyes opened even wider when Thea gave each of them one of the small knives.

"Excuse me, what is this for?" Gili asked.

"It's a gift. For you to use."

"But it's so fancy," Gili protested.

"It's just a tool," Thea smiled. "It doesn't really matter what it looks like."

"Oh ... thank you," Gili replied, but her big eyes didn't leave the glittering knife resting in her outstretched hands.

Chapter Three

Thea returned to the great room, leaving Sylica and the Littles talking in an excited huddle. Setting her falcion on the table, she sat by the fire, staring into its flickering depths. Footsteps approached.

"Well that answers some of our questions."

Thea glanced at Roland. "We still don't know what was making that noise. Or why."

"We know where to look now. Once Sylica and the Littles leave we'll have a chance to figure it out."

"Figure what out?" Sylica bounded towards them. Her armour jingled like windchimes, scattering prismed light across the room. "What are we looking for?"

Thea gave Roland a sidelong glance. "There was a strange wailing noise, but we couldn't figure out where it was coming from. It sounded like it was calling for something. Did your Uncle Bob ever make anything like that?"

Sylica frowned slightly. "I don't think so." Her countenance brightened again. "But he did make a bell that rang whenever I was coming to see him!"

"So he could have made something like that?"

"Uncle Bob could make anything! Like the Big Book says: The only thing prettier than magic is even more magic!"

Thea considered her for a moment. "Did you know the person who lived here?"

"Nope."

Thea sighed. "We heard the cry every single night, except last night. The only thing that changed was that you and the Littles came."

"I guess it wanted some Littles nearby," Sylica grinned. "I like having Littles nearby too."

"But ... why?" Thea protested. "And how do we make it stop?"

"Just keep some Littles around. Sounds easy to me!"

"We don't even know if it is the Littles. What if it's something to do with you?"

Sylica looked perplexed. "But I *am* a Little!"

"Uh—" Roland began.

Thea sighed. Despite Sylica's stonelike green skin and height, she was still adamant that she was a Little.

Roland shifted in his chair. "Want me to start unpacking these boxes?"

Sylica jumped up. "I like unpacking! I am really good at taking things out of boxes. Want to see?"

"Just a moment," Thea laughed, intervening before Sylica managed to pry the box open. "Let's take it into the kitchen first. Roland, these other ones go out to the gardener's hut."

"I'll get Ulf to help me." Roland glanced around the room. "Where is he anyways?"

Thea stood up. "I'll find him."

She went down to the wine cellar, but to her surprise Ulfgar wasn't there. She checked his room upstairs, but he wasn't there either. Where had he gone? She hadn't seen him go outside.

Roland passed by carrying a large crate. He stopped when he saw her face. "What is it?"

"Do you know where Ulfgar is? I haven't seen him."

Roland frowned. "Did he come back up from the workshop with us?"

Thea's eyes widened. "Maybe he didn't."

Returning to the lean-to, Thea took one of the lanterns from the chattering Littles and went back down the stairs.

As soon as she stepped into the workshop she saw him, sitting on the floor with his chin resting in his hands. His new axe lay on the floor beside him.

Thea hurried over. "Ulfgar, is something wrong?"

Ulfgar frowned up at her, as if surprised by her presence.

Roland stepped into the workshop, followed by Sylica.

"You brought the whole parade?" Ulfgar muttered, getting to his feet.

"Sorry." Thea smiled apologetically. "I hadn't realized you stayed down here. Is there something we can do to help?"

Ulfgar eyed the room darkly and gripped the shaft of his axe. "Doesn't make sense," he muttered. "Workshop down here. Forge up there. It's too far away."

"What do you mean?" Thea frowned. "You just go up the stairs and across the garden. It's not that far."

"No blacksmith keeps his forge that far from his workshop. There must have been an easier way to get there."

"Oohh!" Sylica clapped her hands. "A secret tunnel?"

Thea glanced at Roland. If there was, could his elf-sight find it?

"I'll try," Roland nodded.

Sylica was already scrambling along the wall, dodging boxes, crates, and various strange machines.

Thea glanced at Ulfgar. "If there *was* a tunnel, where do you think it would be?"

Ulfgar frowned for a moment. Marching up to an empty piece of wall, he swung his axe into it with all his strength. The wall shattered and collapsed, leaving a gaping hole that stretched out into darkness.

"Ulfgar!" Thea gasped.

"A secret tunnel!" Sylica squealed.

Ulfgar stepped through the hole and was lost in the shadows.

Thea hurried after him into the darkness. Reaching out, she felt smooth stone walls on either side of her. Ulfgar was right. There was a tunnel.

Cautiously, Thea shuffled forward. Green light glowed behind her. Roland was following with the lantern.

The floor of the passageway was polished and smooth, sloping gently upwards.

If the tunnel ended near the forge ... Thea quickened her pace. "Ulfgar!" she called, "Maybe I should—"

With a rumbling crash, light streamed down the tunnel to meet her.

Moments later, Thea stepped over a heap of rubble into the small stone hut that held the forge.

"That's more like it," Ulfgar muttered, brushing cobwebs off his shoulders.

Thea shook her head. "Don't you think we might have liked to keep the door?"

Ulfgar shrugged. "It was stuffy down there."

Roland and Sylica emerged from the tunnel.

"Wow." Sylica looked around the shadowy room. "What's that?"

"It's a forge," Ulfgar explained. "For blacksmithing."

"Did this Uncle Bob make things in here?"

Ulfgar nodded. "Here and the workshop below."

Sylica opened a drawer that Thea hadn't noticed before. It was filled with tools. "They sure left a lot behind." She shook her head. "Uncle Bob never left things behind."

"I wonder what happened?" Roland mused. "If they were an Elf they wouldn't have died."

"Maybe they left when the Great War started." Thea stared out the door towards the old stone building. "All the Elves left then and went back to their island."

"*Our* island." Roland's words were low, at the edge of hearing. Thea pretended she hadn't heard.

Stepping out into the garden, the cool breeze made Thea shiver.

"You should get wind chimes for your garden," Sylica suggested, skipping after her. "Wind chimes are so pretty and they turn the wind into music! I like music a lot. Did you know I started learning how to play the flute? But then I stopped because I kept dropping it. I like dancing a lot more anyways."

There was a stir of movement by the house. The Littles approached through the garden, carrying their new knives.

"Thea," Alya looked up with her piercing eyes, "my friends and I have decided that we will make a second toilet room for you. A private one for your room upstairs."

Thea looked at them in surprise. "That is very kind of you, but you said it would be hard to make a toilet room upstairs."

The Littles looked at each other.

"You have given us a lot," Alya explained. "We want

to do something for you."

"You are already doing something for me," Thea protested. "That is all I need."

Alya held up a hand. "The tools you gave us will make it much easier. Look." Lightning quick, she swung her knife at a stone on the ground. The stone sliced cleanly in two.

Thea stared. "What ... how ..."

Alya picked up the rock, and with her knife scooped out a bowl-shaped hole, as easily as if the rock had been soft wood. "This will make our work much easier."

Thea stammered. "I—I'm glad. Roland, did you see that?"

Roland had seen. He was staring at the knife. "How did it do that?"

"Maybe it's magic." Alya shrugged. "We heard you talking about magic."

Roland pulled out his new knife and looked at it closely. Thea could almost feel him weighing whether to try it or not. With a quick slicing motion, he brought it down on another rock. The rock fell apart in two equal halves.

Everyone stared.

"How can it be that sharp?" Roland whispered, staring at the knife in his hand. Gingerly he felt the edge that had struck the rock. "It should be dull. Or broken. But it's completely undamaged."

"Sharp and strong, eh?" Ulfgar muttered, lifting his large axe.

"Ulfgar don't—"

Ulfgar swung his axe with all his strength, striking a large rock by his side. With an explosion of sound, the rock splintered apart, sending fragments flying every direction.

Thea threw herself to the ground.

"Ulfgar!" Roland yelled.

As everyone cautiously got back to their feet, Ulfgar stared at his axe with a gleam in his eye. "No troll is going to bother me now."

"Really?" Thea looked at their weapons with renewed interest. "Are these for fighting trolls, do you think?"

"Of course," Sylica grinned. "Those are trollsbane weapons, didn't you know?"

Thea stared at her. "No. I didn't. How did *you* know?"

"The magic is right on them. See? The shiny pattern right there."

Thea looked at the hilt of her sword where Sylica had pointed. There was nothing there. But Sylica could see magic in a way no one else could.

"Are all of the weapons we took trollsbane weapons?"

"Yup." Sylica grinned. "There were only trollsbane weapons in there. I guess whoever made them had a lot of problems with trolls."

"We do not expect to be fighting trolls," Alya gave an amused smile, "but these will help us in our kind of work."

Thea turned back to Sylica. "If the weapons are magical, what about your armour?" She gestured to the glittering mail that Sylica still hadn't taken off. "Is it magical too?"

"Oh, it's one-size-fits-everybody armour. Uncle Bob did that on my clothes all the time because I kept growing so much."

Thea looked at the mail shirt with interest. It fit Sylica remarkably well. "It's armour that can fit anybody?"

"Watch this!" Sylica pulled the mail shirt off and dropped it over Gili's startled head. With a clatter, the armour shrunk to fit the Little's lithe form.

Thea stared at it in astonishment. The armour looked as if it had been tailor fit for Gili's body. "How does it do that?"

Sylica shrugged. "I don't know. You'd have to ask Uncle Bob."

"But—" Thea protested.

Sylica took the mail shirt off Gili and pulled it back over her own head. It fit her perfectly. "It's so shiny," she beamed, then did a little dance, scattering rainbows around the courtyard.

The next day was grey and dreary. Thea finished her check in and came downstairs to find that the Littles had already started their work for the day. They didn't need anything from her, so she went into the kitchen to get some leftover porridge for breakfast.

As she was eating, Roland joined her.

"I was thinking about the workshop downstairs. There was a hidden door to the armoury and a hidden door to the forge. What if there are other doors we haven't found yet?"

"You want to look?"

Roland nodded. "It will take a while, because I don't want to miss anything. You'll be okay unpacking by yourself for a while?"

"I don't mind," Thea gave a reassuring smile. "Besides, I'm sure Ulfgar and Sylica will help me if I need anything."

Thea spent the next while reorganizing the pantry.

There were boxes of things that had been sent out from Gedwyld, and it would be nice to know where everything was when she needed it. When that was finished she swept the kitchen and did the dishes. She was just finishing when Sylica joined her.

"How are things going upstairs?" Thea asked.

"Really good!" Sylica beamed. "I thought maybe I should bring up snacks because it's nice to have snacks when you're working. The Big Book says that, you know."

Thea suppressed a smile. "Bring up whatever you think they'll like."

As Sylica bustled around the kitchen, Thea went out to the great room and cleared the table. Opening the box of medical supplies from Sami, she started laying them out on the table.

"Can I help you?" Sylica asked, returning from her snack delivery.

"Of course."

As Sylica carried on a one-sided conversation about the different kinds of bandages, a movement from across the room caught Thea's attention. She glanced up and saw Roland hovering around the doorway that led to the lean-to. There was excitement in his eyes.

Thea turned to Sylica. "Excuse me for a moment."

She joined Roland in the lean-to. "What did you find?"

"There's something. I think there's another room, or a tunnel. I wanted to get you before I tried to open it."

Thea could feel Roland's excitement. "Should I get Raybow this time? Just in case?"

Roland glanced towards the stairs. "It wouldn't hurt."

Silently, Thea and Roland slipped upstairs. The Littles were busy cutting and measuring things in Thea's bedroom. Thea grabbed her cloak and pinned it in place with the small flower brooch. Slipping Raybow's baldric over her shoulder, she clipped the bow in place, hanging down her back.

Stepping out of her room, she saw Roland hang a coil of rope over his shoulder. All three of his knives were on his belt. He gave Thea a sheepish smile. "It doesn't hurt to be prepared."

Thea felt her excitement rising. It was probably just another tunnel leading to one of the outbuildings, but what if there was something more?

They hurried back down the stairs and stopped short as Sylica bounded to greet them.

"Where are you going? Can I come?"

"We were just going to look downstairs some more," Thea explained, glancing at Roland.

"With a rope?" Ulfgar stalked towards them, his hands on his hips. "And your bow?"

"We think there might be another room."

Sylica squealed in delight.

"Right." Ulfgar sighed and cracked his knuckles. "I'm coming too."

"Me too!" Sylica grinned.

"Alright." Thea couldn't help smiling. "We'll just leave the Littles to their work."

"Hey!" Sylica protested. "I'm a Little and I'm coming!"

"Okay, we'll leave the *small* people to their work. How's that?"

"Excuse me!" Ulfgar grumbled. He glared up at Thea from under his bushy eyebrows.

"We will leave the *house repair professionals* to their work." Thea laughed and shooed everyone towards the lean-to.

The Littles had left two lanterns by the top of the stairs. Thea took one and Sylica snatched up the other.

Thea led the way down into the shadows. "Where did you see it, Roland?" she asked over her shoulder.

"Walk to the end of the corridor," Roland replied. "I saw something behind the stones in two places." His eyes scanned the walls, as if to get his bearings again. "There," he pointed to the wall near the end of the corridor, "and there." Roland pointed directly beneath his feet.

Thea stared. "There's something below us?"

Roland nodded.

Sylica's mouth was a big O. "How do we get down there?" she asked in an excited whisper.

"Possibly through there," Ulfgar muttered, eyeing the patch of wall Roland had indicated. "Right about there, was it?"

Roland nodded, then dodged out of the way as Ulfgar swung his axe at the wall. It shattered with a resounding *crash*. Rock dust filled the air. Thea coughed and covered her face with her sleeve.

"We could have just figured out how to open it," Roland muttered as the dust began to settle. He took the lantern from Thea and held it through the opening. "It's a tunnel."

"Can I go first?" Sylica squealed.

"I think I'll go first," Roland replied steadily. "But thanks anyway."

He stepped over the rubble and Thea followed close behind him.

"Do you see anything yet?" Sylica asked from behind Thea's shoulder.

"Not yet."

The corridor was perfectly flat and ran on for a little while before turning sharply.

"There's stairs here," Roland whispered. "Watch your step."

Thea followed Roland down, step after step. The corridor turned again, and Thea stepped out into a room, smaller than the workshop but larger than the armoury. Barrels and crates were stacked in every corner. Metal brackets hung on the walls. She shivered in the cool, damp air.

"Ooohhh," Sylica breathed. "It's kind of spooky down here."

"It was probably some kind of storage room," Roland mused. "Interesting—the door isn't hidden this time."

There was a door, made of wood and reinforced with iron bars. As Roland went to investigate it, Thea looked at the crate beside her. It was nailed shut.

"Should I see what's inside?" she asked the group at large.

"Ooo yes!" Sylica squealed. "Maybe it's more treasure!"

Thea pulled out her knife and eyed the crate critically. "It just looks like a normal crate. Like we use for shipping things at home."

Roland glanced towards her.

"I mean in Lyudmyla," Thea added quickly. With the edge of her knife she pulled out the nails and carefully lifted the lid. The crate was filled with bolts of cloth.

"It's fabric." Thea gestured for Sylica to bring a lantern closer.

"Fabric?" Sylica protested. "That's not very exciting."

"It doesn't have to be. Look at this. It's good quality material, and it hasn't gone musty or anything."

"Maybe there's something more interesting in this one." Sylica gestured to a larger crate.

Thea wandered over to look. The crate had a label on the side. "Sailcloth," Thea read aloud.

"How do you know that?" Sylica protested.

"Because it says so." Thea pointed at the label.

"No it doesn't."

"It's Elvish, Sylica."

"Oh."

Roland was examining some kind of small mechanism attached to the door. Thea went to join him. "Any luck?"

"It's locked. I'm guessing it needs a key of some sort."

Thea frowned. "Do you think we can get it open without the key?"

"Wait—" Roland cried as Ulfgar's axe swung through the air. The door splintered in two.

"Ulfgar, you ... you *doorsbane*!" Roland sputtered. "What if we want to be able to close it again?"

"I'll make you a new one," Ulfgar grumbled. "You wanted it open."

In the shadows beyond the door, something moved.

Chapter Four

With an explosion of splintered wood, something erupted from the shattered door. It ricocheted directly towards Sylica.

"Look out!" Thea cried.

The black missile slammed into Sylica's chest and she fell backwards with a cry.

Thea grabbed Raybow.

A seething black mass writhed on top of Sylica, pinning her down. It had legs, a body, a head. Thea's mind slowly pieced its form together. It was a ... dragon?

The creature flopped off of Sylica and started nudging her side with its muzzle.

Thea lowered Raybow and stared. It was a small dragon, about the size of a large dog. It had beady black eyes in its narrow, lizard-like face, and its black leathery wings were tucked up against its sides. It gleamed strangely in the lantern light.

Sylica sat up and gasped in delight. "It's a baby dragon!"

"Careful!" Roland gestured everyone back. "We don't know what it's going to do."

Sylica scooped the dragon up in her arms and let out an ear-piercing squeal of delight. The dragon wriggled faster than ever, knocking Sylica back to the ground. With its front feet on Sylica's chest, it started licking her face.

"Um—" Roland said and looked at Thea.

"It doesn't seem to be dangerous," Thea hazarded. "But what is a dragon doing here?"

Roland's hand still rested on one of his knives. He eyed the dragon suspiciously.

Sylica struggled to sit up again. "Baby dragon!" she squealed, throwing her arms around its writhing form.

"Sylica," Thea cautioned, "we don't know what it's doing here."

Sylica scratched the dragon on the back of its head. "Who's a good baby dragon? You are!"

The dragon wriggled so hard it fell over with a *clunk*.

Thea and Roland exchanged a look of surprise.

Ulfgar stalked forward and tapped the dragon with the butt of his axe.

Clunk. Clunk. Clunk.

Ulfgar looked at it in bewilderment. "It's a tin can," he muttered. "A tin can, but it's acting like it's real."

"I'm going to call you Daisy." Sylica beamed at the small dragon that was now sitting and looking up at her expectantly. "We are going to be best friends!"

"Sylica," Thea pulled her aside. "I don't think it's a real dragon."

"Of course it's a dragon," Sylica chided. "This is Daisy and we're best friends."

Roland ran a hand through his curly hair. "Can I have a closer look at ... Daisy?"

"Of course you can," Sylica smiled. "Daisy, stay!"

Roland knelt beside the strange little dragon. "Look." He gestured Thea closer. "You can see the rivets along the sides. There's a hinge here at the jaw."

"A tin can," Ulfgar muttered.

"A metal dragon?" Thea frowned.

The dragon bounced up and rubbed itself against Sylica's legs.

Thea turned to Sylica. "Is there any magic on this dragon?"

"Of course," Sylica beamed. "It has *alive* magic on it."

Thea looked down at the wriggling mass of metal and rivets. "The magic is making it alive?"

"It seems so," Roland frowned. "In some way or other."

The dragon rolled onto its back and Sylica started scratching its tummy. Something gleamed in the lantern light.

Thea leaned closer. "What's that?"

Everyone gathered around. There was a panel on the dragon's stomach, held in place with some kind of latch. The dragon lay very still, as if waiting for something.

Gently, Thea reached out and pushed the latch. With a soft *click* the panel swung open.

Inside, gold and gemstones glittered.

Sylica gasped. "It's a *treasure* dragon!"

Ulfgar stared. "That's a lot of gold."

The whole inside of the dragon was a hollow cavity, filled with coins, gems, and jewelry.

Gingerly, Thea lifted up a necklace strung with diamonds. It glittered green in the lantern light.

"Wow!" Sylica thrust both of her hands into the mass of treasure. Coins and gemstones tumbled across the floor with a clatter.

"Careful," Roland cautioned. "Let's keep everything inside until we go back upstairs."

Thea nodded and returned the necklace. Ulfgar scooped the gems and coins off the floor. When everything was inside, Thea closed the panel with a *click*. The dragon rolled over and jumped to its feet.

"Now what?" Ulfgar scratched his beard.

"Take it upstairs and have a closer look, I guess." Thea glanced at Roland. "Do you think this is what made those cries at night?"

"Could have been," Roland frowned. "But why? And why did it stop when Sylica and the Littles came?"

Thea watched the strange metal dragon rub itself against Sylica's legs. "It seems to like Sylica a lot." It was strange. Why did the dragon act like that? It was almost as if the rest of them didn't exist at all.

"Let's bring it upstairs where the light's better." Roland's hand left the knife at his side. "Will it follow you, Sylica?"

"Come, Daisy!" Sylica called, skipping towards the stairs. The dragon trotted obediently after her.

"Hold on," Roland called. Taking one of the lanterns, he leaned through the broken door. "Another storage room. Alright, let's go upstairs."

Sylica and Daisy led the way up the stairs, past the workshop, and into the lean-to. Sounds of thumping, sawing, and lively chatter drifted down from Thea's room. The Littles were still hard at work.

Back in the great room, Sylica flopped down in front of the fireplace. The dragon lay on the hearth beside her, curling up like a cat.

"Anyone want a drink?" Ulfgar muttered.

"You know, I wouldn't mind one." Thea rubbed her head. A magical workshop, a hidden armoury, and now treasure hidden in a strange, metal dragon. What was she going to do with it all?

A great deal of thumping and grumbling came from

the direction of the cellar, then Ulfgar came into view, carrying an entire barrel on his back. With a grunt, he lifted it onto the counter that separated the great room and the kitchen.

"Don't have to walk so far now," he muttered to himself. Disappearing back into the kitchen, he reappeared with four mugs, which he filled and brought to the table.

"Thanks, Ulfgar." Thea sipped from her mug reflectively.

Roland eyed the dragon. "How do we get the panel open?"

Thea touched the hard metal of the dragon, now warmed by the fire. How had Sylica gotten it to roll on its back? Feeling a little foolish, she gave it a tummy scratch.

The dragon rolled onto its back and lay still.

Gently, Thea pressed the latch and the panel swung open. She steadied herself with a long breath. "Okay. Let's see what we have here."

Thea picked up a handful and spread it out on the hearth. The firelight glittered on the tumbling gold.

"Ooh. Shiny!" Sylcia sat up, eyes shining.

"You can help," Thea smiled. "Just be careful."

Together, they emptied the dragon of its treasure. Everyone gathered around, poking and prodding, turning over coins in their hands, holding up multifaceted gemstones to the light.

"A locket." Roland lifted a piece of jewelry from the pile. "I wonder if there's anything in it." He fiddled with it for a while, then handed it to Thea. "Can you get it open?"

Thea turned the locket over in her hands. It clearly

had tiny hinges along one side, but there was no sign of how to open it. "I'm scared to try," she confessed. "I don't want to break it."

Roland took the locket back. "I'll try my sight on it later. Maybe I can see what's inside. It could tell us about where all this came from."

Thea looked at the treasure, now scattered around the hearth. "Are there any other clues?"

Ulfgar piled all the coins together. Some of them were clearly Elven. Others had Elvish text, but didn't look like any coins Thea had seen before. Others bore strange text from entirely different languages.

The gemstones didn't hold many clues, though they were beautiful and clearly very valuable. The jewelry seemed to encompass many different styles, though they had in common that they were all, as Sylica declared, "very shiny".

As everyone sorted through the glittering treasures, Thea tried using her comprehension magic. Would that help her understand where they came from?

Roland glanced up sharply as Thea's magic swept over the treasure.

Thea shook her head. "It's from all over. Some is Elvish, but I don't know enough about other cultures to identify the rest of it. Whoever collected this treasure travelled a lot more than I have."

Roland nodded. "What are we going to do with it?"

Thea sighed. "I don't know. Let's sort it all out and count how much there is. We can use the money to furnish the house and do more repairs, but I'm not sure about the gems or the jewelry. We'll keep them in the armoury for now."

"What about Daisy?" Sylica demanded.

Thea looked at the strange little dragon. It lay on its back with its panel open, perfectly still. What would happen to the dragon if the treasure wasn't inside it? Gingerly, Thea closed the panel. The dragon hopped to its feet and shook itself.

"I don't know what to do with it," Thea confessed. "I'm guessing it's the dragon that was making so much noise every night, so I don't like the idea of shutting it up again."

"You would *never* shut Daisy up like that!" Sylica cried, aghast.

"No, of course not," Thea assured her.

Clonk. The dragon's mouth opened. A long red tongue shot out, struck one of the coins, and pulled it into the dragon's mouth with a *snap*.

Thea stared. "Did you see that?"

Everyone watched as the dragon ate the coins, one after another.

"Hey!" Ulfgar frowned, snatching up one of the coins before the dragon could get it. "We weren't finished with those yet!"

"I guess that's a good place to keep it all safe," Thea mused, watching as the dragon moved on to the gems and the jewelry, smacking each piece with its sticky tongue.

Thea lifted a thin gold chain out of its reach. Surely it would break, being smacked like that. She would put it back in through the panel once the strange little dragon had finished collecting the rest.

Small twinkles of colour glittered along the chain. Thea held it up to the light. Tiny gems, almost smaller than sight, were threaded along the delicate chain.

"You could keep it, you know," Roland smiled. "It's

very pretty."

Sylica dangled a gem-studded belt in front of the dragon's face. It gobbled it up, then looked around for more.

"You're a hungry little dragon, aren't you?" Sylica cooed, scratching it under the chin. The dragon sniffed around for a while, then lay down beside Sylica with its head resting on her knees.

A clattering on the stairs announced the Littles' approach.

"A longer day today," Alya said, crossing the room, "but we wanted to fill up the holes before we—" her eyes widened. "What's that?"

The dragon bounded towards the Littles.

"That's Daisy!" Sylica grinned. "We found her downstairs."

The Littles eyed the strange metal dragon cautiously as it circled around them, sniffing as if it was looking for something.

Finally it returned to Sylica's side, curled up, and lay down. Sylica yawned.

Thea turned back to the Littles. "Would you like something to eat before staph?"

"We already ate," Alya replied. "Would you like to come see our work?"

Thea and Roland followed the Littles upstairs. A portion of her bedroom had been divided off, and an array of pipes had been inserted through the walls and floor.

"We don't have all the pieces we need," Alya explained, "but when we've done what we can we will go back to Gedwyld for the rest."

"Thank you," Thea smiled. "It's looking wonderful."

Beaming with pleasure, the Littles trooped out of the room.

Roland lingered after the others had gone. "You're going to rest now?"

Thea nodded. "I think I'll sleep for a bit."

"Okay. Have a good sleep, Thea." Roland gave her a smile and closed the door behind him.

Thea dragged herself into the world of wakefulness to find that staph was already over. Outside, rain pattered against the window.

Sitting up, Thea stared out the window for a while. Grey mist streamed past in ragged threads. On the sea, breakers rolled.

There was a gentle knock at the door. "Thea?"

"Come in," Thea called. She smiled as Roland peered around the door. "Yes?"

"Do you mind if I come in? It's just ... it's been so busy we haven't had much time to just be together and talk. I miss that."

"Of course you can come in." Thea slid over to make room for Roland to sit beside her on the bed. "It has been busy, hasn't it?"

Roland nodded.

They sat in silence for a while before Roland ventured, "How are you feeling about your house? Do you like it?"

"I do." Thea's gaze took in her simple, empty room, now littered with Littles' tools. "It hasn't exactly been what I expected, but when the rest of the furniture comes I think it will feel more like home."

"You want to stay here?"

"Of course." She gave him a knowing look. "This is

where the Deity wants me to be."

"Just because the Deity wants you to live here doesn't mean you can't come back to Lyudmyla with me, for a little while."

"I know." Thea sighed. "But I don't want to come back. I want to be here, to make this a place where people can come, meet friends, and learn about the Deity. I can't do that if I'm gone."

Roland nodded glumly and stared out the window towards the sea. After a while, he spoke. "I know what I want, but it seems the more I chase it, the farther away it is."

Thea shifted so she could look in Roland's eyes. "Roland, you serve the Deity. If the Deity wants you to do something, there will be a way."

"But it seems so impossible."

"Get to know the Deity more. Spend time with Micai. I don't know how many times I felt like something was impossible and Micai helped me through it." She gave a fond smile. "Say hi to them for me."

"I will." Roland's keen glance sent a shiver down her spine. Then he smiled sheepishly. "Should we go see what everyone else is doing for restday?"

Downstairs, the Littles were sitting around the fire, listening to Sylica tell a story about her Uncle Bob. Daisy lay curled up by Sylica's side. Outside, the wind whistled through the courtyard.

Sylica paused her tale as Thea and Roland approached, giving them a cheerful wave.

"The rain has stopped for now." Roland glanced out the window. "Maybe I'll take the chance to do some hunting."

"Could I come with you?" Alya asked, rising from her

seat.

"Of course," Roland smiled.

"I'll come too!" Gili grinned.

Thea pulled a chair up to the hearth. At her side, Talia was whittling a piece of stone.

Talia caught her surprised glance. "Why not?" she smiled. "These knives can do more than cut pipes." She held up what looked like the crude form of a bird. "I'm not very good at it yet."

"I think it's wonderful, Talia," Thea replied, admiring her work.

Tam had been systematically cutting a piece of rock smaller and smaller to see how small he could make it.

"I'm glad you're enjoying the knives," Thea smiled.

"I'll sweep up," Tam offered, trotting over to the corner where the broom leaned against the wall.

After the hunters left, Talia and Tam retired to their room, leaving Thea and Sylica alone by the fire.

Sylica lay on the hearth, humming a little song. Her emerald-like skin glimmered in the firelight.

Thea watched her for a while. "Are you happy living in Gedwyld, Sylica?"

"Hm?" Sylica looked up and grinned. "Of course I am! I have so many friends there, and there are so many fun things to do! I can visit Sami at the healing house, or go with the pipers while they work, or visit all the people on market day. Sometimes I visit the guards at the castle or I go out to the farms and talk with the workers in the fields. It's great!"

Something seemed forced in Sylica's smile. "But what?" Thea hazarded.

Sylica put her chin in her hands. "Sometimes I feel like people aren't really my friends." She frowned.

"Everyone is my friend, of course," she added quickly, "but they always seem to be happy when I go away." Her face creased in a look of thoughtfulness that Thea hadn't often seen. "I don't think that's how friends should be."

"I'm sorry," Thea stammered, unsure of what to say. It was true that many people found Sylica's exuberance more than a little trying, but Sylica had always seemed obliviously cheerful through it all.

"But that's okay—" Sylica's buoyant nature returned like the snap of an elastic, "—because Daisy is my best friend now! Aren't you, Daisy?"

She scratched Daisy under the chin, and to Thea's astonishment the dragon began to purr.

"Have you seen Ulfgar since staph?" Thea asked.

"Nope. Who's a good baby dragon?" Sylica cooed, holding Daisy close.

Thea glanced around the room. "I'll go find him. Maybe he wants to join us for a while."

Leaving Sylica and Daisy by the fire, Thea walked over to the stairs that led down to the wine cellar. She could hear a small shuffling movement in the shadows below her feet.

Carefully, Thea walked down the stairs into the pungent air of the wine cellar. As her eyes adjusted to the darkness, she saw Ulfgar sitting hunched in the corner, his new axe leaning on the wall beside him. The coin Ulfgar had taken from the dragon lay on the floor. He was glaring at it.

"Would you like to come upstairs, Ulfgar?" Thea asked.

"Hmm?" Ulfgar grunted, looking up at her. His eyes were bloodshot.

"We're sitting by the fire and talking. Would you like to join us?"

"No."

Thea decided to try again. "Come on, Ulfgar. We'd like for you to join us."

Ulfgar gave her a suspicious glance. "Why?"

"Because you're our friend."

"You are not my friends." Ulfgar glared. "I don't make friends."

"But—" Thea stammered.

"Every time I care about someone they are wrenched away from me." Ulfgar's eyes burned. "Every bloody time. I refuse to care and I won't. I won't lose it all again."

Thea's heart ached. She knew so little about Ulfgar's story or how he had lost so much. "Is that something to do with Finni? I heard Micai call you that once."

"Finni is dead." Ulfgar's eyes could have bored holes through her skull. "I am not that man anymore. Now I am going to drink, and you are going to leave. me. alone."

Slowly, Thea walked back up the stairs, leaving Ulfgar in the shadows below. She wanted to help him, but what could she do?

By the fire, Sylica was lost in her own little dream world, happily singing a song while Daisy slept beside her.

Thea sat alone with her chin resting in her hands.

After a while, Roland, Alya, and Gili returned from their hunt.

"We got a deer!" Roland called through the door. "Anyone want to help gut it?"

"I will!" Sylica jumped up.

Daisy trotted after her.

"No, Daisy." Sylica turned to the little dragon. "You stay here by the fire. I'll be back soon."

Sitting back on its haunches, Daisy cocked its head and whined.

"Good girl, Daisy," Sylica beamed and skipped out the door.

Thea watched with interest as the strange dragon started to pace the room. Back and forth it paced, its black metal gleaming in the light.

Thea glanced around, but there was no one else there to see the little dragon's strange behaviour.

"It's okay, Daisy," Thea said, but it paid no attention. It seemed to be growing more and more distressed.

Should she go get Sylica? Thea glanced out the window, but she couldn't see where Sylica had gone.

The dragon sat in front of the door and gave a long wailing cry. It echoed through the air, sending chills through Thea's body.

She knew that cry.

Footsteps clattered down the stairs, and Tam and Talia burst into the room.

"What was that sound?" Tam stammered, his eyes wide with fright.

Thea gestured to the dragon, sitting attentively in front of the door, waiting.

The door burst open and Sylica scampered into the room.

The dragon jumped up. With its two front legs on Sylica's chest, it licked her face excitedly.

"Hi Daisy!" Sylica beamed. "Did you miss me?"

"Apparently it did," Thea muttered. Through the open door she caught sight of Roland. They exchanged a glance.

"Sylica," Thea looked from her friend to the wiggling, puppy-like dragon. "Are you *sure* you never saw this dragon before?"

"Nope, never." Sylica grinned. "Why?"

"Because it only cries when you're not here."

"Aww, she missed me!"

"Before she even met you?"

Sylica didn't seem to care. She danced off towards the fireplace, with the dragon scampering along behind.

"Mystery solved?" Roland muttered to Thea under his breath.

"I guess so," Thea replied, "but it left another three behind!"

Roland nodded thoughtfully.

The Littles offered to prepare the evening meal, and soon delicious smells wafted out from the kitchen.

When the food was ready, Thea approached the stairs to the wine cellar.

"Are you coming for supper, Ulfgar?"

No response came.

Thea returned to the others. The Littles had cooked up quite the feast, with thick stew, flatbread, a salad of fresh foraged greens, and even a pie made from stewed berries. They sat around the hearth on crates and boxes and chatted cheerily while they ate.

Thea listened, but found that she didn't have much to say. Roland came and sat beside her.

"At least we don't have to worry about that sound anymore," he said in a low voice.

Thea nodded. Watching Sylica and Daisy, she was quite sure Daisy wasn't going to be left behind when Sylica left. They'd just have to decide what to do about the treasure first.

"Daisy," Sylica's voice rose above the chatter. "Why won't you eat?"

"What's wrong?" Thea glanced at Sylica, who was waving a piece of bread in front of the dragon's snout.

"Daisy won't eat anything!"

"It's not a real dragon, Sylica. Maybe it doesn't need to eat."

"Daisy is a real dragon," Sylica protested. "Maybe she just doesn't like bread." She seemed to consider this for a moment, then pulled out the bag that always hung at her side. "Want a candy, Daisy?"

"Sylica!"

The dragon's long tongue shot out and snatched the candy into its mouth.

Sylica squealed with delight, feeding Daisy candy after candy.

"Should we stop her?" Roland whispered in Thea's ear.

Thea felt like they should, but couldn't think of a good reason to. After all, it wasn't like the dragon could get sick. Could it?

After the evening meal, Roland went to bed, and soon the Littles followed. Thea sat by the fire for a while longer, staring at its flickering flames and listening to the wind-driven rain pattering against the windows.

From the hearth by her feet, a snore rose through the air. Sylica lay with her arms wrapped around Daisy.

"Good night, Sylica," Thea whispered, and walked softly to the stairs. At the door to her room, she paused. Something was missing.

Of course. Every night since he had come, Roland had always been there to say good night, but he'd gone to bed early. She glanced at the door to his room. It was closed. He must have been very tired.

As Thea got ready for bed, she felt something in her pocket. It was the delicate necklace she had taken from the dragon's treasure. She laid it on the small table Roland had made her. Maybe she would keep it after all. Roland thought she should.

Thea lay in bed and listened to the sound of the rain until she fell asleep.

Chapter Five

Thea stretched her wings and dove through the sky, the wind rushing by as she swept towards the sea far below. Allumen's glow warmed her scales and tingled through her coursing blood. Down, down she swept towards her prey—a fish so large that humans in their tiny boats could only dream of. She dove towards the glittering sea, snatching the fish in her powerful claws. Beating her wings, she rose again into the sky. Now for somewhere to rest and enjoy her meal.

As Thea soared above the sea, the distant mountains rushed closer, rising to pierce the sky. Yes. Here she could rest. She landed upon the highest crag and saw Raphtova stretched out below her like a tiny map. The fish was good. It sated her hunger. For now.

Taking to the air once more, she swept through the mountains, searching. Yes, there it was. Her cave. She landed in the remote mountain valley, peaceful and still. The cave mouth opened wide before her and she swept inside, her tail cutting a swath in the pebbly ground behind her.

Home. The gold was calling to her. She entered the treasure room and crawled on top of the great heap of gold and jewels, padding about to make a comfortable bed in the midst of it.

Surrounded by her hoard, Thea rested and watched the light twinkle around her. With a claw she fingered a delicate necklace. It looked familiar.

Thea woke to find Allumen's light streaming through the window. In her hand she was holding the necklace from the dragon treasure. She stared at it, memories from her dream streaming through her mind. It had been so real. It was hard not to feel that, if she tried, she could leap from her bed and fly.

She shook herself and stepped gingerly out of bed. Absentmindedly, she slipped the necklace into her pocket. It would be amazing to be able to fly, to feel the rush of the wind racing past her like in her dream.

Thea knelt by the window to check in. The view from the top of the mountain had been incredible. She'd thought she'd enjoyed good views before, but that was like being on top of the world.

Right. Checking in.

Thea tried to focus, but soon found her mind wandering again. Maybe she should get up for a while and try again later, when the vivid images from her dream had faded a little.

Roland's door was ajar. Thea peered inside, but he wasn't there.

Finally she found him in the gardens. He held a knife in each hand, swinging them in smooth, glistening arcs.

Thea watched in silence until Roland looked up and waved for her to join him.

"What are you doing?" Thea asked.

"Training," Roland smiled. "I used to train every morning back home. It was about time I started again. I like to do it as a part of my check in with Micai." He swung his knives from position to position.

"Any word from Micai today?"

"No. I'm having a hard time focusing," Roland admitted.

"Same." Thea made a wry face. "I keep thinking about the dream I had last night. I was a dragon. It was very real."

Roland gave her a sharp glance. "You had a dream about dragons too? I dreamed I was a dragon hunting monsters."

"I dreamed that I was flying." Thea smiled at the memory and fingered the necklace in her pocket.

Behind her, the door to the kitchen opened. Ulfgar stumped down the stairs and glared up at them with bloodshot eyes. "Let me guess. You both had a dream that you were a dragon last night, didn't you?"

Thea stared at Ulfgar. "What?"

"We did," Roland said. "But—"

Ulfgar held up his coin. "Dragon treasure."

Thea frowned. "I don't understand. Daisy looks like a dragon, but that doesn't mean it's actually dragon treasure. It could have come from anywhere."

"I'm not talking about that tin can. I'm talking about real dragons. This treasure came from real dragons."

"How do you know?"

"Trust me. This isn't my first run in with dragon treasure. The dreams tell you if nothing else does."

"What do you mean?"

Ulfgar gave her a frustrated glare. "Look. Dragons are magic. They use the treasure to keep their magic going, right? They sleep on it and that's what keeps them alive. The problem is that once a dragon has taken a coin, or anything else, it has the dragon's touch. It wants dragons. If it's claimed by someone else, it tries to turn them into a dragon."

Thea stared at the coin in Ulfgar's fist. "The treasure is trying to turn us into dragons?"

Roland's eyes were wide. "Can it actually do that?"

"Never heard." Ulfgar frowned. "It usually drives people raving mad first."

"Can we make it stop?"

"Never heard of someone who could."

"Then what do we do with it?"

"There's only one thing you can do. Take it back to the dragons."

Thea stared at Ulfgar. They couldn't really take the treasure to the dragons, could they?

"Where are these dragons?" Roland asked.

Ulfgar shrugged. "Up in the mountains. Somewhere."

Thea's mouth felt dry. "You really think we have to take the treasure to the dragons?"

Ulfgar nodded glumly. "At least the treasure can carry itself."

Thea looked at Roland in alarm. *Daisy*. What would Sylica say when she learned they had to take Daisy back to the mountains?

Roland frowned. "Is the metal dragon also trying to turn us into dragons?"

"Don't imagine so." Ulfgar scratched his wild beard. "Dragon treasure is usually gold and silver and jewels, not tin cans."

"And we didn't notice anything as long as the treasure was locked away. If we keep it inside the dragon will we have some protection?"

Ulfgar glared at Roland. "I'm not the expert on this, okay? I'm just telling you what I know."

How did Ulfgar know so much about dragon treasure, anyways? Thea looked at him with interest, then realized she was fiddling with something in her pocket. Slowly she pulled out the delicate golden chain. Dragon treasure.

"Probably slept with it by your bed, didn't you?" Ulfgar gave her a knowing look. "How about you?" He turned to Roland. "Probably have that locket with you now."

"No, it's upstairs."

"Check your pockets."

Roland reached into his pocket, frowned, and pulled out the locket on its chain. "I swear I left it in my room."

Ulfgar shook his head. "You grabbed it when you weren't paying attention. Dragon treasure is like that." He shivered. "I'm going to feed mine back to that tin can. You should too."

Ulfgar stumped back towards the house. Thea and Roland followed.

They found Sylica sitting in front of the fire with Daisy by her side. The Littles had begun their work for the day.

"Hi Thea! Hi Roland! Hi Ulfgar!" Sylica smiled. "Isn't it such a nice day out? I was thinking about coming outside too but the fire was nice and warm so I stayed here."

"Did you have a dream about dragons last night?" Thea asked as they joined her by the fire.

"Nope. No dreams at all. Did you have any dreams, Daisy?"

Daisy looked up at Sylica expectantly and cocked its head.

"Sylica," Roland looked her straight in the eye, "are you *sure* you didn't have any dreams about dragons? Nothing about being a dragon at all?"

"It would be so fun to be a dragon," Sylica's eyes sparkled. "Then I could *fly* and I would love to fly! And I could have lots of treasure and everyone would be my friend!"

"Did you dream about that?"

"No."

Roland tried again. "When we were looking through the treasure, did you keep anything out?"

"No. Why would I?" Sylica frowned. "I let Daisy eat it all back up. I think she was hungry."

Thea looked from Roland to Ulfgar. Sylica hadn't kept a piece of the treasure, and she hadn't dreamed about dragons.

"I've got something else for Daisy." Thea pulled the necklace out of her pocket.

Daisy perked up and started sniffing the air.

Thea held the delicate chain tightly. It took all of her strength to hold it out towards the strange little dragon.

Daisy sniffed it experimentally, then with a smack of its tongue snatched it out of Thea's hand. The necklace was gone.

A strange feeling rushed over Thea, like a piece of herself was missing. She shook herself and the feeling passed. "Your turn," she nodded to Roland and Ulfgar.

A strange look crossed Roland's face as he held out the locket. "I never got a chance to look inside," he murmured, but his voice seemed very far away.

"You can do that later," Thea urged him. "We're just storing it."

Roland nodded and let go of the locket. The little dragon gobbled it up.

Ulfgar flipped his coin in the air. As it fell he reached to grab it, but Daisy's tongue shot out and snatched it out of the air.

A brief look of anger crossed his face, then he snorted. "That's done then." He shoved his hands in his pockets and stalked across the room.

"Oh! I want to feed Daisy something too!" Sylica looked around. Off the table she grabbed a golden belt, studded with gemstones.

Thea stared. "What was that doing there?"

"I don't know." Sylica waved the belt in front of Daisy, who obediently ingested it.

Thea glanced at Roland. She was sure the belt hadn't been lying on the table a moment ago, and Sylica had said she hadn't kept anything out.

Sylica looked from Thea to Ulfgar to Roland. "You are all acting very strange."

"It's the dragon treasure," Roland explained, sitting down beside Sylica. "We need to bring it back to the dragons."

Sylica's face lit up. "Can I come? I'd love to see a dragon!"

Roland glanced up at Thea.

"We haven't quite figured out what we're doing yet," Thea explained. "It's all pretty new."

"I can take it." Roland spoke in a low voice. "It's time for me to get back to my work in Lyudmyla. I can travel through the mountains on my way."

Thea's heart sank. She wasn't ready to say goodbye to Roland yet.

"I think—" she stammered, "—since we found it in my house, I should probably come. Just as far as the mountains."

Roland gave her a thoughtful glance. "You could carry on with me to Lyudmyla, you know."

"Right now we should focus on getting to the mountains," Thea replied, trying to ignore the suggestion.

"Hooray!" Sylica cried, jumping to her feet. "We're going on an adventure to the mountains to see the dragons!" She skipped around the room, sending Daisy scampering in circles after her.

Thea suppressed a smile. It *would* be fun to travel again. "I wonder if Elora would come with us?" she asked aloud.

"We should ask her!" Sylica jumped up and down. "I bet she would *love* to come!"

Thea glanced across the room at Ulfgar's brooding figure.

Ulfgar saw her glance. "We're leaving tomorrow," he muttered and stalked out of the room.

So Ulfgar was coming too. Their whole travelling party would be together again ... except Arl. Nothing could make up for Arl's absence, but it would be wonderful to have everyone else together again.

"We should get packing, then," Roland grinned. "Tomorrow morning we'll head down to Gedwyld and ask Elora if she wants to come."

Thea ran up to her room and set Raybow and her cloak on her bed. Rooting through the storage crate in the corner, she pulled out the small handbag she had used for her trip from Lyudmyla. She would bring it, but it wouldn't fit everything she wanted to bring this time. Maybe she could buy something larger in Gedwyld.

She fingered the knife that Svetka had given her during her escape on the Raven. She always kept it on her belt. What else would she need?

Wind hissed past the window. Thea stared out at the

grey horizon. Her last journey had been during the Great Heat, but now it was the Second Slowing. It would be much colder, with the Great Sleep approaching. They would need to bring blankets, and warmer clothes.

Thea spent the rest of workday preparing food and packing supplies from the pantry. It was a strange sort of packing, since none of them had proper packs, except Ulfgar. Thea put everything they wanted to bring into baskets. They'd have to carry the baskets as far as Gedwyld, then they could buy proper backpacks.

Thea eyed the pile of supplies with a critical eye. She'd travelled with a Dryad who owned nothing and carried nothing, and she'd learned to make do without much of what she had thought was necessary. This time, however, it would be nice to travel with a proper waterskin, a compass, and some of the other things she'd had to make do without on her last journey.

Thea, Roland, Ulfgar, and Sylica met again in the great room.

"I told the Littles we're leaving tomorrow," Roland said. "They're happy to carry on with their work here, and they'll close things up when they leave."

"That's good," Thea smiled. "I've collected the supplies we have, but there are a few things I'll need to buy in Gedwyld."

Roland fingered the knife at his side thoughtfully. "I imagine it won't always be safe in the mountains. You'll bring your falcion, won't you Thea?"

Thea nodded. "You'll have to teach me how to use it, though." She gave a wry smile.

"What do you have for weapons?" Roland turned to Sylica.

"Oh! I'll show you!" Sylica skipped out of the room and returned with what looked suspiciously like the leg of a table with metal spikes attached to the end. In her other arm she carried what may have once been a tower shield, but it had been battered beyond any recognizable shape.

Ulfgar stared at them in horror.

"I brought them with me," Sylica beamed, "because Elora says you always have to be prepared."

Ulfgar stalked over to Sylica and took the makeshift mace and shield out of her hands.

"Hey! Where are you taking them?" Sylica protested.

"I'll be right back," Ulfgar muttered and stalked out of the room.

Sylica frowned after him for a moment, then turned to the little dragon at her side. "Who's excited to go on an adventure? You are!" She patted Daisy on the head.

Thea and Roland exchanged a glance. What would happen to Daisy when they got to the mountains?

Remembrance swept over Thea like a wave. She hadn't gone back to finish her check in. Excusing herself, she hurried up the stairs to her room. It was filled with tools and bits of pipe.

The door to Roland's room was open. Thea slipped inside and knelt by his small window. Carefully she stilled her mind and her spirit.

Allulien. Thea spoke silently within her heart. *We have to bring the treasure to the dragons. Is that right? Or is there something else I should do?*

She waited. Across the hallway she could hear the chatter of the Littles as they worked. The wind hissed through the eaves. Allulien did not speak.

What should she do? She needed to return the

treasure to the dragons so that no one would be harmed. That was within the Deity's will, to protect others from harm. Allulien could have spoken if it was important that she stayed behind. They didn't, so she was free to go.

Thea glanced thoughtfully around Roland's room. He didn't have much—a mattress on the floor and a blanket. The rope that Khariton had given Thea was coiled in the corner. Two of Roland's knives lay neatly beside it, along with his belt pouch.

He had been travelling light, sent to help her when she needed help the most, but he had not come to stay long. He had his work in Lyudmyla. Thea wondered how soon her uncle might be convinced to give him another leave of absence.

After staph, Thea went down to the armoury. She would need money if she wanted to buy things in Gedwyld, but the coins from the dragon treasure should not be used.

In silence, she stared at the glittering wall of weapons, armour, and shields. What should she sell? After contemplating for a while, she chose a sword. Bringing it upstairs, she set it with the rest of the things on her bed, then went to find the others.

Roland sat on the front step, sharpening his knives. In the courtyard, the Littles had set up an impromptu shooting range and were throwing their knives. Sylica scampered back and forth, fetching the knives from the target. A loud clanging sound echoed across the courtyard.

"Where's Ulfgar?" Thea asked.

Roland shrugged. "He took an armload of something into the hut where the forge is and he hasn't come out since. It sounds like he's making something."

Thea watched the Littles at their sport for a while. It seemed strange that she was leaving so soon, when she'd barely had a chance to get settled in. Still, the dragon treasure was technically hers, which meant it was her responsibility. The house would still be there when she got back.

Soon it was time for the evening meal, but Ulfgar didn't come in.

"I'll bring some food out for him," Roland offered.

After he returned, Thea shot him a curious glance.

"He's making something," Roland confirmed. "I stayed to watch for a bit, but he didn't want to talk." His gaze strayed in the direction of the forge. "You can tell he's good at it."

After the meal, Sylica and the Littles pulled their chairs around the fire.

Roland stretched. "I think I'll go to bed. It will be an early day tomorrow."

"I'll go to bed too." Thea got up and followed Roland. At the door to her room she stopped and looked back. "Good night, Roland."

Roland smiled. "Good night, Thea. Sleep well."

Thea slipped into her room and shut the door. Outside, the last light of day faded into the darkness of an overcast night. In the garden below her, red light flickered from the open door of the forge hut. The ring of a hammer echoed through the night.

Chapter Six

Thea woke as the first light of day gleamed across the sea. Kneeling by the window, she waited to hear what Allulien would say.

There was no word, but she felt peace deep within her spirit. She was doing the right thing, and her friends would be there with her.

Grabbing her cloak, she pinned the brooch in place and slipped Raybow's baldric over her shoulder. The falcion hung at her side.

She went downstairs to get breakfast.

"Hi Thea!" Sylica called from the kitchen. "We ran out of porridge, so Daisy and I made more!"

Thea stared at the massive potful bubbling on the stove. "Sylica!"

"It's okay," Sylica protested, gesturing to the counter. "There's lots more oats!"

Thea stared at the massive bag of oats that filled half the counter. She had never seen it before. Where had it come from? Sylica certainly hadn't brought it with her from Gedwyld.

Before Thea could question her, Sylica skipped away.

Filling her bowl, Thea ate quickly, then carried the baskets out from the pantry and set them by the table. She glanced up as Roland came down the stairs. His face bore a thoughtful expression.

He smiled a brief greeting, then went into the kitchen.

Thea's gaze followed him. The unexplainable bag of oats still sat on the counter.

The front door swung open and Ulfgar stomped inside. His face was smudged with soot, and he carried a large bundle wrapped in cloth. Laying it on the hearth, he gestured for Sylica to join him.

Opening the bundle, Ulfgar lifted up a new mace. It was made of metal, with a long smooth handle. At the striking end, the metal arched out into six points, sharp and deadly.

Sylica stared, taking the mace gently in her hands. "It's so shiny," she breathed, eyes glittering. Then she frowned. "What did you do with the old one?"

"I burned it." Ulfgar turned back to the bundle and lifted up a new shield. It was as tall as he was, perfectly curved, with the bottom corners cut into sharp spikes. Its smooth, strong metal gleamed in the light.

"I said I'd make you new ones," Ulfgar muttered. "I didn't think I'd still be here to do it, but ..." He scowled and shoved the shield into Sylica's arms. Turning away, he stumped off towards the stairs.

"Thank you!" Sylica called after him.

"I'm going to get my bag," Ulfgar grumbled and disappeared up the stairs.

Sylica squealed with joy and danced around the room, waving the mace and shield, her glimmering armour jingling. Daisy scampered after her.

"Careful of the floor!" Thea cried as one of the spikes on the shield gouged a deep scrape in the polished wood.

"Oops." Sylica froze. "Sorry, Thea."

Thea sighed. "It's alright." She caught a glimpse of Roland watching from over the kitchen counter. His eyes twinkled.

The Littles trooped downstairs to say goodbye, followed by Ulfgar carrying his massive pack. Stomping past them, Ulfgar lifted the keg off the counter and attempted to balance it on top of his oversized pack.

Thea watched him in dismay. "Ulfgar, what are you doing?"

"Bringing the drink," Ulfgar muttered. With a grunt, he managed to strap a belt around the girth of the barrel. "That should hold."

Staggering beneath the weight of his load, Ulfgar eased himself sideways through the door.

Roland followed. His knives and pouch were on his belt, along with the lantern Alya had said he could keep. He'd attached his bedroll to the rope, which was slung over his shoulder.

Thea handed one of the baskets to Sylica and carried the other. They stepped out the door, with Daisy scampering at their heels.

Alya waved and closed the door behind them.

Thea's new home was only about a measure's walk north of Gedwyld, and soon they could see its great stone walls in the distance. The towers of its castle rose high on the cliffside, overlooking the sea.

There were no guards at the gate. Passing through, they walked along the winding, cobbled streets, turning many heads as they passed. Thea and Roland exchanged a glance. Hopefully the strange little dragon wouldn't cause trouble.

"Oh look, Daisy!" Sylica squealed. "We can go see all

our friends!"

"Not this time," Thea cautioned. "We can't stay for long."

"There's Dib the baker!" Sylica waved excitedly. "He's one of my best friends too! Hi Dib!"

"Don't—"

It was too late. Sylica dashed up the street, her shield and mace bumping wildly over her shoulder. Daisy galloped along behind her. Overhead, a pair of crox wheeled and dove, cawing loudly.

"Sylica!" Thea yelled.

"I'll go get her," Ulfgar grumbled. "Meet you at Elora's."

Soon Thea and Roland turned onto the lane where Elora and Kais lived in the lower part of town. As they approached, Thea caught sight of Elora, who appeared to be hammering new shutters into place. Her mass of dark curly hair was tied back from her face, and a couple of spare nails were clenched between her teeth. She wore a serviceable-looking brown tunic and green trousers. It was still strange to Thea to see her without her black scouting clothes or a quiver of arrows at her belt. As it was now, she looked remarkably like her grandmother, only younger.

"Elora!" Thea hurried down the street towards her.

Elora looked up, her face breaking into an enormous smile. "Thea!"

Thea crouched down and embraced her friend.

"It's good to see you," Elora beamed. "Come inside!"

Elora's thin face had rounded out somewhat since Thea had last seen her. She picked up her tools and led the way into the house.

Thea ducked through the low doorway. Elora and

Kais had done a lot to their house since she had last seen it. Pictures hung on the walls, and the rustic, handmade table held a vase of late-blooming wildflowers. There were no more piles of things in the corners waiting for a place to belong.

"Kais!" Elora called up the stairs. "Thea and Roland are here!" She put the kettle on the fire and pulled up some chairs. "We were hoping to see you soon. What brings you to Gedwyld?"

There was a creak from the stairs and Kais bustled into the kitchen. He was a bit taller than Elora, with sandy-brown hair and a gentle face. He looked from Thea to Roland with a pleased expression, as if taking them in.

"It's good to see you, Kais." Thea crouched down and embraced him warmly. "I love what you've done with your home."

"It does finally feel like home." Kais looked around the room with a fond smile. "How is your new place coming along?"

"It's coming along." Thea caught Roland's eye. "We had some unexpected difficulties."

Elora gave her a keen glance. "Really? Like what?"

"It turns out there really was something to the reports of it being haunted. Every night we could hear a strange cry, but we couldn't find where it was coming from."

Elora frowned. "We never heard that when we were there."

"I know, but we found out what it was."

Elora leaned forward, an eager glint in her eye.

"It was dragon treasure."

"Dragon treasure?" Elora leaned closer.

Kais looked at Thea in surprise. "What do you mean?"

"Treasure from a dragon's hoard. I don't know how it got there, but it's dangerous to keep it. We have to get it back to the dragons as soon as we can."

A look of longing crossed Elora's face. Kais squeezed her hand.

"That's where you're going now?" he asked.

"Yes. We were wondering if you'd like to come with us, Elora."

Elora and Kais exchanged a long glance.

Elora sighed and turned to Thea. "I wish I could. But you see, Kais and I are expecting a baby."

Thea looked at Elora in wonder. "You're pregnant? Congratulations, Elora and Kais, that's wonderful!"

"Thank you." Elora gave her a wry smile. "I just wish it wasn't stopping me from coming with you."

"But we completely understand," Thea assured her, "and that's such exciting news."

"Congratulations," Roland added. "I wish your family all the best."

"Thank you," Kais smiled. "I'm sorry that Elora can't go, but if there's anything we can do to help you on your way, you only need to ask."

"We're just going to buy a couple of things in the market," Thea explained, "and then we're ready to go. It wouldn't have been a lot of warning, if you were going to come." She smiled apologetically.

"Does that mean you have the treasure with you now?" Elora eyed her curiously. "Can I see it?"

"Yes and no." Thea made a wry face. "It's with Sylica at the moment."

Elora's eyes widened. "And she's here in Gedwyld?"

"Ulfgar's keeping an eye on her," Thea explained with sudden misgiving. "They should be here soon ..."

A sudden commotion erupted in the street outside the house and the door burst open. Sylica tumbled inside, followed by Daisy clomping along on its four metal legs.

Ulfgar jumped in after them, stuck his head out the door and yelled, "That's all, folks! Go on, now!" He slammed the door shut and leaned his back against it, breathing heavily. The barrel on top of his pack teetered at a precarious angle.

Elora grabbed a knife off the mantle. "What is that?" she demanded, staring at the dragon.

"Hi Elora!" Sylica called cheerfully. "This is Daisy. She's my best friend, and we were having so much fun! Did you know a guard's buckle can come off if it's pulled strong enough? Daisy thought they were yummy."

Ulfgar glared. "We did not need to know that."

Daisy started sniffing around the room. Elora looked at it suspiciously. "That is not a real dragon."

"No it's not," Thea agreed, hushing Sylica's protests. "It's a dragon treasure carrier, of some sort. We don't know how it works the way it does, but the treasure is inside it. That's what we're taking to the dragons."

Relaxing slightly, Elora set the knife back on the mantle and shook her head. "The Great Big Big knows how much I wish I could go with you." She sighed.

"Elora is finding that city life isn't much to her liking." Kais gave her a compassionate smile. "But this is where we have work, for now."

Thea thought for a moment. "Elora, could you do something for me? Alya and the others are at my house while they finish their work, but after that the house will be empty. Could you check on it every now and then for me while I'm gone?"

Elora's eyes brightened a little. "We could do that. For a while anyways, until the baby comes."

"Thank you." Thea smiled. "I'd really appreciate that."

"Daisy!" Sylica's warning voice rose from across the room.

The little dragon froze, its tongue stretched out towards a silver candlestick sitting by the fire.

"No, Daisy," Sylica chided. "Leave it."

Slowly the dragon retracted its tongue and slunk away.

"Good girl, Daisy," Sylica beamed. "Who wants a candy?"

Daisy perked up immediately and caught the candy out of the air.

The stairs creaked. Peeking around the corner, a slender Little with pale skin stared at Thea from behind a shock of dark hair.

"Hello, Zaki." Thea smiled.

Zaki caught her eye, then disappeared back around the corner.

Elora glanced towards the stairs. "He came down? I wondered if he might."

"How is he liking Gedwyld so far?"

Elora shrugged. "I honestly don't know. He almost never leaves his room except to eat, and even then we have to pester him."

"He'll be alright." Kais laid a reassuring hand on Elora's arm. "It was hard for him that Arl died, especially after losing his parents." His gentle eyes turned to Thea.

Thea nodded. "I'm glad you're both here for him."

"Is Sami home?" Roland asked.

"No," Elora replied. "She works most days, but I'll tell her you were here. She'll be sorry she missed you."

Someone hammered at the door.

"Open up!" a voice called. "Castle guard here. Open up!"

"Oh." Sylica gave a guilty smile. "That might have something to do with us."

"You think?" Ulfgar muttered.

Thea stared at Elora, aghast. "I don't have time to deal with this."

"Go out the back door." Elora gestured her away. "I'll explain things to the guard."

"Will the guard listen?"

Elora grabbed the knife off the mantle and slipped it through her belt. She gave Thea a sly smile. "I think the guard will listen."

"Sylica! Roland! Let's go!" Thea called. "Ulfgar!"

Kais showed them out the back door with a smile while Elora went to speak to the guard.

"Okay, Ulfgar," Thea said as soon as they were on the street. "You take Sylica to the western gate. I'll buy the supplies we need and meet you there."

"Hey," Sylica protested. "Wasn't Elora supposed to come with us?"

"I'm afraid she can't, because she's going to have a baby."

Sylica squealed in delight. "A baby? I have to go see her!"

Thea grabbed Sylica's arm as she turned to dash back the way they had come. "Not right now. She's busy. You'll have to see her later."

"Oh. Okay." Sylica's frown disappeared in an instant. "We should get her a present!"

"We don't have time for that right now."

"I know!" Sylica brightened even more. "We can give her some treasure! She'd like that!"

"No." Thea replied firmly. "That treasure is going to the mountains and nowhere else."

"But I was thinking—" Sylica began, scurrying off down the street.

"I'll come with you," Roland muttered to Ulfgar, and they hurried after Sylica.

After they had gone, Thea made her way up to the merchants' district. Her business didn't take long. After examining the sword, the merchant she brought it to offered a trade for whatever she needed from the shop, as well as twenty silver pieces. As she left, she caught a glimpse of the merchant staring in awe at the sword laid out on the counter in front of him. Thea had a sneaking suspicion it was more valuable than anything else he had in his shop.

She met the others by the western gate. From Roland's expression she could tell that escorting Sylica that far had been an adventure of its own.

Dislodging a pack of crox from a nearby alleyway, they rearranged their supplies. Roland declined carrying a pack, choosing instead to wrap his extra gear inside the blanket he carried slung over his shoulder. Sylica chose a large basket pack, which she filled with food, bandages, and other supplies. Thea chose the leather, waterproof pack, and took everything they didn't want getting wet.

Ulfgar didn't touch his pack. Thea eyed it with its barrel balancing precariously on top. "Are you sure—"

Ulfgar growled, and Thea decided to leave well enough alone.

Thea held up the baskets they'd brought from home. "Now what do we do with these?"

"I'll run them up to Elora's," Roland offered. "They could probably use them."

Thea reached into her bag. "Here. Take these to Elora as well." She handed fifteen of the silver coins to Roland. "Maybe they'll do some work on the house while we're gone."

Roland nodded and started up the street at a jog.

Thea and the others left the city and started the long trek past Gedwyld's surrounding farms.

As they were passing the final field, Roland caught up with them.

"So," he grinned, "what's the plan?"

"Well," Thea glanced around their small group. Everyone was watching her. "We need to go to the mountains, and this river comes from the mountains. That's all I really know." She watched the river sweep past them towards Gedwyld and the sea. It was wide and deep here, flowing with irresistible strength.

"So we're just going to follow the river and hope we find the right place?" Ulfgar gave her an incredulous side-eye.

"That's all that I know to do," Thea admitted. "Dragons *are* very big. Once we get close enough we should be able to find them."

"A lot can happen between now and then," Roland added, watching the forest with an eager expression. "Maybe we'll meet people on the way who can point us in the right direction."

Thea gave him a grateful smile. "Alright. Let's go!"

They followed the river until staph, then found a good spot for a campsite. Away from the cool winds off the sea, the hottest time of the day was still quite warm. Thea leaned back against a tree. Her legs ached.

"We'll trade off watches while we sleep," Roland said, making himself a mattress of fallen leaves.

"But it's safe here," Sylica protested. "Nothing bad happened all the way before."

"The Generals took care of that, remember?" Roland spread his blanket over the pile of leaves and tucked in the sides. "It won't be as dangerous as the Deorcian, but that doesn't mean it's safe."

"Oh. Okay."

Ulfgar shifted a large rock so the top was flat and set his keg on top.

"You can use this bed if you like, Thea," Roland offered. "I'll take the first watch."

As soon as Thea lay down, she was asleep.

She woke to find that staph was almost over. Ulfgar snored between two large tree roots and Sylica lay curled up beside Daisy. Roland knelt beside Thea.

"Sorry to wake you," Roland gave a wry smile, "but I can't keep my eyes open."

Thea scrambled to her feet. "You could have woken me before now."

Roland shrugged. "You were all so tired."

"You're tired too." Thea urged him towards the bed. "I'll watch now."

Thea sat in the warm light of Allumen and waited. Light rippled across the river as it flowed past. Birds scratched among the dirt and stones. A squirrel scampered up a nearby tree.

With nothing to do, Thea sat and thought, watching

Allumen's light cast dancing shadows through the trees overhead.

When she was a child, her tutor had taught her about Allumen—that it was named after Allulien, the greatest of the Generals. Her tutor had always been very insistent on that, that Allulien was the greatest of the Generals. She'd never met another Elf who would admit that. As far as most Elves were concerned, Enkeli was the greatest, because Enkeli was the General of the Elves. Not that they actually served under Enkeli at all. It was all show and dead ritual, nothing more.

Through a gap in the trees, Thea caught a glimpse of the great planet, beginning its journey across the sky to eclipse Allumen and bring night. Fond memories of Micai rose in her mind, sitting by a fire together, sharing their mug of beer. Everything seemed so much simpler when Micai talked about it, when Micai spoke about showing mercy.

One by one, Thea's companions roused to wakefulness.

"Who said this was a good idea?" Ulfgar muttered, stretching as if he had a crick in his back.

"Hello, Daisy, did you have a good sleep?" Sylica cooed, scratching the dragon on the back of its head.

"You know it's not really alive," Ulfgar grumbled.

"Yes she is," Sylica retorted. "Daisy is just as alive as you are."

"That's not saying much," Ulfgar muttered.

"*More* alive then." Sylica crossed her arms and stuck her chin in the air. Daisy licked it enthusiastically.

Ulfgar stumped over to his barrel.

"Hey, Ulf!" Roland called across the campsite. "Want to see if you can find us something to eat?"

Ulfgar frowned. "Suppose I can."

"Oh! Me too!" Sylica jumped up, tumbling Daisy off her lap.

Ulfgar looked at her in alarm.

"I know," Roland interjected. "I have a hook and line in my pouch. Do you want to try fishing, Sylica?"

Sylica thought that was a great idea, and Ulfgar, relieved, went the opposite direction.

After Roland got Sylica set up by the river, he returned to Thea. "Want me to help you train with that falcion? If you're carrying a weapon, you should know how to use it properly."

"Thanks," Thea grinned.

Roland showed her the different positions, attacks, and defences, then drilled her until she was out of breath.

"That's good," Roland smiled. "We can take a break if you want."

Thea nodded and sank to the ground. Roland sat beside her.

"We do a lot of training back home. That's mostly Khariton's doing, but Micai thought it was a good idea. If I'm going to protect someone, I need to have the strength to do it." He smiled. "It feels good to be training again."

Down on the riverbank, Sylica sat on an old, rotting log, swinging her feet.

"She's got her line right in the shallows," Roland commented. "She's not going to catch anything there."

"I'll go tell her." Thea stretched her aching muscles and wandered down towards the river.

Sylica stared out at the shimmering water, her armour twinkling in the light. Daisy sat beside her. It made a beautiful, though rather odd, picture. Thea found herself hesitating. Did it really matter if Sylica's line was in the weeds?

Sylica sighed and put her chin in her hands. "Daisy, I know you're not a real dragon."

Daisy cocked its head and whined.

"I know. Just like I'm not a real Little."

Thea stared in shocked surprise. Did Sylica really just ...

"I don't fit in. I'm different."

Daisy watched Sylica intently, as if taking in every word she said.

"Maybe I'm just too excited all the time." Sylica seemed to consider this, then sighed. "But if I'm not a Little, what am I?"

Daisy lay its head on her lap.

Sylica wiped her eyes with the back of her hand. "Oh Daisy." She hugged the strange little dragon. "You understand, don't you?"

Thea wasn't sure what to do. She wanted to comfort her friend, but she couldn't confess that she'd heard what she just heard. Sylica had never, even for a moment, expressed any doubt that she was not a genuine—though rather overgrown—Little. How had this change come about? And what did that mean for Sylica?

Sylica started humming a little tune.

Thea took a cautious step closer. "Sylica?"

Sylica looked around and gave her a big smile. "Hi Thea! Isn't the river so pretty? Daisy and I are having so much fun fishing! I wonder if we'll catch a shark!"

"I—I don't think there's sharks in this river," Thea stammered, unsure of what to do with the sudden direction of the conversation.

"That's okay," Sylica continued without missing a beat, "then we'll probably catch a giant octopus or maybe a sea monster! That would be fun! I wonder if sea monsters taste good? Or maybe Daisy and I will make friends with the sea monster, won't we, Daisy? And then it can take us on adventures under the sea."

A large ripple coursed across the river. In its wake, the water began to bubble and churn. Thea stared in alarm. What was in the river?

Oblivious, Sylica chattered on. "Actually, not a sea monster. Maybe a dolphin. Or a whale! Then I could teach it to do tricks. Oh! I could teach you to do tricks, Daisy! Roll over, Daisy! Roll over!"

Daisy rolled over, and landed in the river with a splash.

"Daisy!" Sylica laughed, clumsily pulling the dragon back onto shore.

The river flowed smoothly along its banks once again.

Giving it a cautious glance, Thea walked back up the bank to where Roland was waiting.

Sitting with her chin in her hands, Thea watched Sylica attempt to teach Daisy to speak.

The river had started churning when Sylica was talking about sharks and sea monsters, then stopped as soon as she was distracted by something else. Was it just coincidence? There had been too many coincidences over the past few days.

Thea glanced at Roland. "You know how Sylica does strange, magical things sometimes, but it doesn't feel like magic?"

"You mean the time she made the path through the

middle of the fire?"

Thea nodded. "It never happened much, and it was always when we were in danger. Now I'm seeing strange things I can't explain almost every day, and Sylica doesn't even seem to notice."

"You think it's Sylica making those things happen?"

"It's always connected to her somehow. She told me that sometimes she wants things to happen and they just happen, but it hasn't been like this."

"You're worried about her?"

Thea stared down at the riverbank. Sylica was throwing rocks into the rippling water. "I think it got worse after we found Daisy."

Roland glanced out through trees. "All the more reason to get to the mountains, then."

Thea nodded. If the dragon treasure was gone, maybe Sylica's strange magic would go back to normal.

Chapter Seven

As they set out the following morning, Thea did her best to keep an eye on Sylica, but she didn't notice anything unusual. Sylica skipped along the riverside path with her usual enthusiasm, directing her continual stream of chatter towards Daisy when no one else seemed to be listening.

Gradually the rough dirt path dwindled into an animal track, then disappeared among the trees. A lone crox peered at them curiously from a branch overhead.

Ulfgar led the way through the forest, with Sylica scampering at his heels. Thea found herself walking beside Roland. Allumen's light filtered through the trees, casting a mosaic of shadows over the forest floor.

"What do you miss about Lyudmyla?"

Thea froze. "What?"

Roland shrugged. "You've been gone a long time now. I was wondering if there's anything you miss about it."

Thea's mind raced. "I ... I don't really think about it much, to be honest." She shot Roland a sharp glance, but he seemed to be genuinely curious. "I miss hill-tumbling, I guess. People look at you funny when you do that out here."

"What, you miss me beating you all the time?" Roland's eyes twinkled.

"Hey!" Thea protested. "You know I won at least half

the time!"

"Not when your uncle was playing."

Thea made a face. "Uncle Mykyta has to win at everything. You know that."

"You used to go up to his office a lot."

"When I was in trouble, you mean?"

"Other times too. I've heard stories."

"From who?"

"Mykyta. He talks about you a lot, you know."

Something uncomfortable twisted in Thea's gut. "That doesn't mean I should go back."

"I wasn't saying that."

An uncomfortable silence grew to fill the space between them.

"I ... I guess I miss the days when we'd both be free and we could go down to the harbour and watch the ships, or climb right to the top of Larsya to see the view." Thea shrugged. "Things like that."

Roland nodded. "I miss that too."

The silence settled in to stay.

No one talked much as they made their way west along the river—with the exception of Sylica, of course. Roland seemed lost in thought and Ulfgar stomped along in a dour mood. Even the river was silent, rushing smoothly along its current-swept banks.

With a scream, Sylica disappeared.

Everyone stared at the dark hole in the forest floor where Sylica had stood a moment before.

Thea hurried closer. The hole was narrow, but very deep. "Sylica!" she called. "Sylica, are you okay?"

Roland threw his bedroll on the ground and untied his rope.

"I'm okay," Sylica's voice echoed up from the depths

beyond their sight. "It's very wet down here."

Daisy ran around the rim of the hole, whining like a lost puppy.

"I'm throwing a rope," Roland called down the hole.

"Yay! A rope! I like—ow! That hit me on the head!"

Roland leaned over the hole. "Can you climb, or should we pull you up?"

"Oh, I can climb. I like climbing a lot! One time I climbed all the way up a—"

Roland glanced at Ulfgar. "We'll pull her up."

Sylica finally emerged from the hole, clinging to the rope like a bedraggled rat. Her clothes and pack were soaked, and her skin was streaked with mud.

"*Never* do that again, do you understand?" Ulfgar glared at Sylica. "You have to watch where you're going or you'll get yourself killed!" A look of consternation flashed through his eyes. He shook himself and turned away. "Not that I care," he muttered.

Roland stood at the edge of the hole, staring down into its murky depths. "Who would leave a hole like this? Someone could get hurt!"

"What happened?" Thea asked Sylica, helping her find a seat and remove her pack. "Didn't you see the hole there?"

Sylica held Daisy's wriggling form as the little dragon licked her face. "It's a well, actually," she explained, a grin splitting her face. "You know how there's all these stories about how someone fell down a well? I was just wondering what it would be like to fall down a well, and now I know!"

Thea stared at her.

Sylica frowned. "It turns out it's just like falling. And getting wet. The stories make it sound a lot more interesting than that."

"Sylica!" Thea glared. "Did you make a well appear just so you could fall down it?"

Sylica blinked. "How would I do that?"

"I don't know. Sometimes you make things happen because you want them to. I don't know how you do it."

"Maybe it was already there."

"And you just happened to fall down a well right as you were wondering what it would be like?"

"That was pretty handy, wasn't it?" Sylica grinned. "Now I know what it's like!"

"But how—" Roland stammered, "why—"

"Didn't you ever wonder what it was like to fall down a well?"

"No!"

"I bet Daisy wonders about it sometimes. Don't you, Daisy?"

Thea gave a helpless shrug.

"Can't leave this here," Ulfgar muttered, kicking a stone into the hole. "Someone might fall in."

Thea turned to Sylica. "Can you make it go away?"

"What?" Sylica frowned.

"The well. You made it. Make it go away."

"How do I do that?"

"I don't know. You're the one who did it!"

"But I didn't try to do it!" Sylica protested. "It just happened!"

Thea and Roland exchanged a concerned glance.

"No point standing around," Ulfgar grumbled. "Let's find a big rock or something."

That night, Thea sat and stared into the flickering flames of their campfire.

It wasn't Deity magic. That was the strangest part of Sylica's strange, unexplainable magic. When a servant of the Deity cast a spell, other servants of the Deity could feel it happening. They could tell where it was coming from, and sometimes even have a sense of its purpose and what it was going to do. Sylica's magic wasn't like that. Thea couldn't feel it happening, it just happened. A well had appeared, as if it had always been there. But it hadn't. Thea was certain of that.

The logs in the fire settled, sending up a shower of sparks. Sylica lay sprawled out along one side of the campfire, with Daisy curled up nearby. The firelight glimmered on her smooth, stonelike skin.

Ulfgar lay with his head on his hands. His empty mug lay on its side, its last dregs staining the moss a deep red.

Beyond Ulfgar, a deeper shade moved among the shadows.

Thea froze, her spirit sight tingling. Something was out there, staining the darkness an even deeper black.

Silently, she reached for Raybow.

With a moan, Sylica rolled over in her sleep.

Something in the shadows moved.

Without taking her eyes off the surrounding trees, Thea laid a hand on Roland's arm.

Roland's eyes opened. He saw her, then reached slowly for his knife.

Thea gestured him closer. "There's something out there."

"Where?"

Thea pointed.

With a slight nod, Roland crept closer to the fire, grasped the end of a burning brand, and held it aloft.

The sudden light flared across the crouching forms of two wolf-like creatures. They snarled and their shadows seemed to grow larger, stretching out in every direction as if to swallow the light entirely.

"Careful—" Roland called, gesturing Thea back.

A wolf leapt, and fell with Raybow's arrow piercing its throat.

"What the—!" Ulfgar bellowed, suddenly buried beneath the wolf's heavy corpse.

The second wolf turned to run, and collapsed as Roland's knife severed its spine.

Kicking and grunting, Ulfgar extricated himself from beneath the wolf.

"Shadow wolves?" Roland frowned. "What are they doing this close to Gedwyld?"

"Beats me," Ulfgar grumbled. "I thought they lived in the Deorcian."

Roland stared out through the trees, but everything seemed silent and still. "I figured we'd run into trouble eventually, but I didn't think it would be this soon."

Ulfgar grunted and eyed the dead wolves. "Didn't seem like too much trouble."

"It could've been if Thea didn't spot them in time. We'll have to be more careful."

After dragging the dead shadow wolves out of their camp, Ulfgar lay down again and closed his eyes, but this time his great axe lay close at hand.

Roland cleaned his knife on a patch of moss. "I'll cast shield over our campsite. That should give us some protection if there's any other shadow wolves in the area."

Thea felt the warmth of magic wash over her. She returned her second arrow to her quiver.

Sylica rolled over and snuggled closer to Daisy.

"You go ahead and sleep, Thea," Roland nodded. "I'll keep watch for now."

They travelled more cautiously after that. During the day, Thea used her magic to bless their travel, and Roland cast shield over their camp at night. Ulfgar always kept an axe close at hand.

Sylica didn't seem concerned, even as they drew closer to the Deorcian. She happily talked with Daisy, danced along the riverbank, and asked endless questions. Her strange magic surges continued with alarming regularity, but it didn't seem that there was any way of stopping them.

Across the river, the trees became larger and darker. Light didn't penetrate through their thick, moss-covered branches.

Thea had only ever seen one forest like that. She glanced at Roland. "It will be safer on this side of the river?"

Roland watched the far riverbank with a distrustful gaze. "We can hope so."

Workday was almost past when they saw the first burnt trees. Soon all the trees on the northern bank were scorched and black, piercing the sky like charred spikes.

Thea stopped and stared across the river, her mind filling with the roaring of the flames, the bellowing of the monsters, the scream of the night mare, and the horrible moment it killed Arl.

Tears stung her eyes. It was easy enough not to think about it, with the excitement of exploring her new home. Here it all came back like a wave.

Roland squeezed her hand. "Let's keep going."

Everyone was silent as they passed the place where the Littles had spent the night after their ordeal. Ulfgar trudged along with his head sunk down between his shoulders. Even Sylica seemed pensive and withdrawn.

The intense light of staph gleamed down through the branches overhead, but they walked on. Weariness dragged at Thea's limbs, but she didn't want to be the one to suggest stopping. It was better to leave that place far behind.

A noise drifted through the trees. Thea froze and strained her ears to listen. A rumble of stone. A cry that sounded like pain.

The others heard it too.

Thea scanned the trees. Where was it coming from? Away from the river, deeper in the forest.

Thea hurried through the undergrowth. Pushing her way through a thicket, she stepped into the clearing beyond.

Trolls. A whole group of them. Their attention was on something beyond them—a lone figure crouched with their back to a tree.

One of the trolls swung its fist. The figure dodged the punch and struck up with their weapon, which appeared to be some kind of long staff, with a spike and an axe head on the end.

Another troll roared and swung its arm.

A brown blur streaked down from the trees and landed on the troll's head. The troll staggered back and waved its arms around its head, as if trying to get something off its face.

In the gloom beneath the trees, the lone figure's spirit shone with light.

With a roar, Ulfgar leapt from the shadows. His axe swung through the air, struck a troll, and split it in two.

The other trolls wheeled, stared, and turned to run.

"Charge!" Sylica yelled. Swinging her mace, she sent a troll ricocheting off a tree.

Roland's knife flashed in the light and another troll crumpled to the ground.

An arrow from Raybow struck the final troll in the shoulder, and the lone figure's halberd knocked it to the ground.

The figure turned to glare at her rescuers. She had fur-covered legs and hooves that looked remarkably like a goat's. Her upper body was tanned and bare, and two sharp little horns poked out from her neatly braided hair.

Thea looked at her in wonder. "You're a Faun."

"I had that," the Faun retorted, gesturing at the fallen trolls.

"I see," Thea replied. "I hope we did not interrupt you."

"I've been keeping an eye on you for a while now." The Faun flicked her braid back over her shoulder. "I was just clearing these trolls out of the way for you."

The Faun was taller than the average Little, but still shorter than Thea. Her eyes sparkled with light.

"Thank you for your thoughtfulness." Thea tried to understand the expression on the Faun's face, but it eluded her. "My name is Thea," she added. "We are just passing through."

"I am called Zanele. And—" Zanele's eyes darted around the trees for a moment. "You can come out, Cheeky."

A flying squirrel swooped down from the trees and

landed on Zanele's shoulder.

"This is Cheeky, my companion. Cheeky, this is Thea. And some people."

"This is Roland, Sylica, and Ulfgar." Thea quickly made her introductions.

"And that?" Zanele eyed the metal dragon at Sylica's side.

"That is Daisy."

Zanele seemed to take this in stride. "Pleased to meet you. If you are travelling further west today, you should come with me. There are other trolls south of the river today."

"We can deal with a few bloody trolls," Ulfgar muttered.

"And my leader told me to bring you to him," Zanele continued, "so if you refuse I will have to fight you."

"We have no interest in fighting," Thea said quickly, putting a warning hand on Ulfgar's shoulder. "Who is your leader?"

"You will see." Zanele gave a cocky smile. "Follow me, and if you see any large rocks be careful. It might be a troll."

Thea followed Zanele through the trees, with the others following close behind.

"Can you tell us where we are going?" she ventured, when Zanele did not offer further information.

"It is not far. I could say, 'behind the fir trees just this side of Forgotten Swamp', but I don't think that would tell you much."

Roland quickened his pace to fall in step beside Thea.

"You saw light?" he asked under his breath.

Thea nodded. "A servant of the Deity."

"Good." Roland's hand left the hilt of his knife. "We will see where she takes us."

They walked through staph and part of restday before Zanele turned to look back at them. "Wait here."

In a flash, she disappeared into the trees.

Ulfgar glared at the forest surrounding them. "If she leads any monsters here, I'm going to put my—"

"She won't." Thea gave him a reassuring smile. "Trust me."

Roland nodded, but his hand rested on the hilt of his knife.

Thea shifted uncomfortably. Zanele would come back soon. Wouldn't she?

Light shone through the forest. Two spirits were approaching. Thea stared. They were brighter than any spirit she had ever seen, even brighter than Davis's.

"Thea!"

Roland's low voice brought her back to the present moment with a gasp.

In front of her stood a Faun, holding out his hand in greeting. He was like Zanele in appearance, except that the skin of his upper body was umber and his horns were larger and curved like a ram's. There were silver streaks in his dark, curly hair.

At his side was a giant eagle. It stood taller than the Faun and hopped along after him, looking around the forest with its piercingly black eyes. On the other side of the Faun walked a pure white stag.

"Thabani, at your service." The Faun flashed a brilliant smile as he shook Thea's hand. He gestured to the eagle at his side. "This is Kaji, my companion, and this is Ember."

The stag stepped forward, and as it did so it shifted

and changed into the form of a human, naked, with pure white skin and hair. "Hello," Ember smiled, "welcome to all of you in the name of the Deity."

Thea stared at the Dryad in wonder.

Roland's eyes widened. "Thabani, of the Ithemba?"

"That's my name," Thabani turned to Roland with a wink.

"I'm Roland, from the Messengers."

"Roland!" Thabani's face lit up and he clasped Roland's hand. "So I get to meet you at last!"

"It's a pleasure to meet you, Thabani." Roland smiled. "I've heard so much about you."

Thea looked from Roland to Thabani in surprise. "You know each other?"

"Thabani is the head of the Faunish Resistance," Roland explained, turning to Thea. "Micai has told me about him."

"Likewise," Thabani grinned. "We were very excited to hear about the Messengers. That's just what we need to keep all the branches of the Resistance connected."

"How have things been here?"

"Oh, the usual. We've been on high alert for a while now, since we heard that the Spark might be passing through. It takes all hands to keep our forest safe for travel, never mind what goes on north of the river. Still in good spirits, though. What brings you through here? A message from Mykyta?"

"Not this time," Roland grinned. "I'm on my way back to Mykyta now, but first I'm taking Thea to the mountains."

Thabani glanced at Thea with a grin. "Ah yes, the charming young lady."

Thea's face grew hot. "Sorry for staring at you earlier.

Your spirit—and Ember's—are the brightest I've ever seen. I didn't know anyone could have a spirit like that."

Thabani stared at Thea with widening eyes, as if really seeing her for the first time. "You're the Spark." His voice was low and hoarse. "You've come." He turned to face the trees behind him. "Zanele!" he yelled, "Why didn't you say it was the Spark? We should've had all hands out there!"

"Pardon me?" Thea ventured. Her mouth felt dry. "The what?"

"The Spark." Thabani looked at her. "The one lighting the Deity's flame in Raphtova. The whole Resistance knows about the Spark. We just didn't know who it was."

Thea looked from Thabani to Ember to Roland. Suddenly she felt very small. "I'm Thea."

"Lady Thea," Thabani bowed and took her hand. "Welcome to the Resistance."

Ulfgar cleared his throat.

"This is Ulfgar," Thea hurried to introduce her friends, "and this is Sylica. And that's Daisy."

Thabani nodded graciously. "You are all very welcome. Come and meet the Resistance."

He led the way, with his majestic companions following on either side. Thea and the others followed—down a tree-covered slope, past tangles of undergrowth where they had to walk in single file.

Pushing through a screen of branches, they found themselves in the midst of a camp. Small huts were nestled beneath the trees. A large bower covered a bare patch of ground where several Fauns were busy preparing the evening meal. Two large fires blazed in a clearing, and hammocks hung from tree to tree, swinging gently in the breeze.

"Welcome to Pinehome," Thabani grinned, waving greetings to several of the Fauns who waved back. Delicious smells filled the air. Young fauns skipped across the clearing and blinked at the newcomers with large, curious eyes. Sitting by the fire, a mother Faun nursed her baby. Across the fire, two Fauns were busy fletching arrows. On the far side of the clearing, a wolf with golden eyes lay in the shadow of a tree.

Everywhere Thea looked, she saw spirits that were filled with the light of the Deity.

An osprey dove overhead, carrying a large fish in its talons. As it descended, it tossed the fish in the air, shifted into a Faun, and landed on its hooves, catching the fish in its hand moments later.

Laughter and cheers rang around the clearing.

"Come sit by the fire," Ember urged Thea and her friends. "You must be tired."

Sylica had long gone, running to join the children at their games. Thabani moved among his people, talking and laughing.

Thea picked up the bag Sylica had left behind. Her shield and mace lay in a heap beside it.

Ember smiled. "I have a place where you can set your bags. There is no need for you to be encumbered."

Ember led Thea, Roland, and Ulfgar to a sheltered spot by a corner of one of the huts. Thea left her pack and her weapons leaning against the wall. She was among the people of the Deity. She wouldn't be needing them.

"Come!" a Faun called. "Come eat!"

Everyone gathered around the bower where the food had been prepared. Thea listened to the chatter all around her. Most of it she couldn't understand, being in the language of the Fauns, but a bowl was thrust into her hands and filled with fish, roasted roots, and small bread-like cakes.

Thabani lifted his hand for silence and started to sing. The rest of the Fauns and Dryads joined in.

Thea touched her own ears with magic, so she could understand the words.

Praise the Deity, praise.
Praise for this food, praise.
Praise for this day, praise.
Praise the Deity, praise!

The food was delicious. Thea's bowl was filled again and again, and she found herself laughing and chatting with the Fauns around her as if she had known them all her life.

There were almost as many animals in the camp as there were Fauns. A cat wound its way between her legs. Two young crox tumbled over each other in their eagerness to collect fallen scraps. A short, stocky Faun had a snake draped around his neck. A ruddy-haired Faun had a falcon on her wrist.

Thea caught a glimpse of Zanele with Cheeky on her shoulder. Thea waved a greeting, but Zanele turned and disappeared into the crowd.

A Faun sitting by the fire held up a flute and started to play. Several of the Fauns gathered around him and started a dance.

"I like dancing too!" Sylica cried, racing to join them. Soon she was spinning and twirling in their midst, a whole head taller than the tallest of the Fauns. Daisy capered about as if it, too, enjoyed dancing.

Someone got out a drum. Someone else started playing a small harp that they set on their lap.

The music was infectious. It wound its way around the clearing, a lively, joyful tune. One by one, people set down their chores and joined the dance.

Children jumped and twirled. Mothers danced with their babies on their hips. Young couples spun each other around, while others joined hands in a large circle, weaving in and out. Even Ulfgar tapped his foot along to the music.

Roland grabbed Thea's hand. "Want to dance?" he asked, his eyes twinkling in the light.

Thea nodded and they were swept into the dance. Circle after circle, they spun around one fire, then the other. She danced with Roland until the tide of the dance swept them apart. She danced with Thabani. She danced with Sylica. She danced with Ember.

From across the fire, Thea watched in disbelief as Sylica grabbed Ulfgar and dragged him into the dance. He was laughing. He was actually laughing!

Intoxicated with the joy of the dance, Thea grabbed Roland's hand and spun him around. The music was inside of her, pulsing through her body. Night fell, and the dance carried on. Thea whirled from partner to partner until finally she collapsed, exhausted, at the side of the clearing.

Beyond, the dance continued. Thea watched the swirling kaleidoscope of dancers spin by her, every eye shining in the firelight. In the bower close by, two Fauns were making love.

Thea felt the music wash over her, calling her back to the dance.

Across the fire, she met Roland's gaze. There was something in his expression that she hadn't seen before. It was filled with desire and passion and a deep, unspeakable joy. It reached out to her, and Thea's heart leapt to respond.

Something woke inside of her, tingling through her blood. It was warm and irresistible, like the music. Her heart beat faster.

Ulfgar collapsed to the ground beside Thea, laughing until he couldn't breathe.

"Oh, I'm going to feel that tomorrow," he wheezed, taking in great gulps of air. He wiped tears of laughter from his eyes. "I haven't danced like that since ... since ..." His face clouded and his shoulders sagged. "Damn," he muttered, staggering to his feet. "Where's that barrel?"

"Ulfgar!" Thea called.

Slowly, Ulfgar turned and looked back at her.

"You don't need that."

Thea watched as pain filled his eyes.

"Yes." Ulfgar muttered. "Yes, I think I do."

Turning, he stumbled away.

The music had lost its magic for Thea. She sat and watched the dance with her chin in her hands and a deep sadness in her heart.

Thabani came and stood beside her, the giant eagle at his side. He watched the whirling dancers as they turned round and round, the firelight reflecting in his eyes. Perhaps it was the pain in her own heart, but Thea thought she saw pain in his eyes too.

Thabani noticed her gaze. He smiled, but the smile seemed sad. "We dance with all our heart because we also fight with all our heart." For a moment, his youthful face seemed old. "You see them so, and tomorrow they will give their lives if it is asked of them. We keep this forest safe from the hand of the Fallen General. With a life like this, tomorrow is never a guarantee."

Thea looked at Thabani with sudden understanding. "It was you who kept the southern way safe for the Littles to pass."

"That was us." Thabani smiled and stroked Kaji's feathers. "Micai's orders: Secure the southern banks. The Spark is leading the Littles out of the Deorcian."

"Micai is your General?"

"Sure is," Thabani winked.

"Micai told me the Resistance was in place. I didn't realize that was why it was safe across the river."

"We keep our heads down. That's the best way not to lose them." He tapped his curly head with a grin. "As long as the Fallen General doesn't know about us, we stand a chance of fighting another day."

"Is that really all you do? Fight the darkness?"

"That is what the Deity has called us to do, and we'll do it until the day we die. Won't we, Kaji?"

The eagle nudged Thabani with her giant beak. He gave her a scratch. A faraway look was in his eyes.

"I've been doing this since I was twelve, when our last leader was found dead, torn apart by musharocs. We all know we'll die doing this. It's just a question of when."

"How old are you now?"

"Twenty-five. That's getting up there for a Faun," he winked, "but I'm not slowing down. I'll go out flying." He caressed Kaji's head. "Now off you go," he said to the giant bird. "Find yourself something to eat."

Kaji shook herself and spread out her massive wingspan. As she took to the sky, the rush from her wings made the flames of the fires leap and dance.

Cheers rang out around the clearing and the musicians sped up their tune.

Thea looked at Thabani. The silver in his hair glistened in the firelight.

"Why didn't Micai tell you my name?"

Thabani shrugged. "You're the Spark. That was all I needed to know."

He walked away, leaving Thea alone in the shadows.

Thea watched the Fauns weave their patterns around the dancing flames. They were so young. Every one of them would barely be considered more than an infant in the circles of the Elves, yet here they were, ready to die in the service of the Deity.

And Thabani was getting old? He was only twenty-five! No wonder they danced with such abandon. The nights they had for dancing were so few.

Across the clearing, she watched the snow-white Dryad playing with the children. As a Faun, Ember leapt into the air and did a flip, changing into a monkey, a fish, and then a turtle, before turning back into a Faun just in time to land on the ground.

The children laughed and clapped their hands.

Ember was so different than Arl. Thea remembered Arl's stern expression and unimpressed glare. And yet—there was something alike. Ember's glance took in the clearing in a way that showed that they were watching. If anything was going to happen to someone, it would have to go through Ember first.

Ember saw her gaze and smiled.

With a leap, Ember shifted into bird form and

flapped up onto a large branch. Flipping backwards, they shifted back into a Faun, dangling from the branch by one arm.

The children jumped up and down, reaching up with their arms as Ember pantomimed being in terror of falling. Letting go, they tumbled towards the shrieking children, shifting into a large spotted toad just in time to land in a child's outstretched hand. The children laughed and cheered.

Hopping out of the beaming child's hand, Ember shifted back into Faun form, ruffled their hair, and strode off into the dance.

A few moments later, Ember joined Thea. Shifting into the form of a pure white Elf, they sat beside her with their legs stretched out towards the fire.

"They are fun, aren't they?" Ember beamed, watching the children jump and dance.

Thea watched the Dryad with a thoughtful gaze. "You live so much longer than them. Don't you?"

Ember nodded. "A Dryad's seed lives four hundred circles before it returns to the ground. I have walked two hundred of those circles already."

"Then you must have seen so many generations of Fauns!"

"I have." They watched the dancing Fauns with glittering eyes. "I knew their grandmothers and grandfathers, and *their* grandmothers and grandfathers."

"Why are you here?"

"The Fauns are my people. I live with them, and I protect them with my life."

"But you're a Dryad."

"I am a protector. I cannot deny my nature. Or my

General." Ember smiled.

"Who is your General?"

"Micai, the Protector, as it is for many of my kind."

Understanding grew in Thea's mind. "Micai is the General of the Dryads?"

Ember nodded. "We take to service under Micai more readily, though Dryads can be found in the service of any of the Generals."

"Who is the General of the Fauns?"

"Allulien."

Joy filled Thea's heart. Of course Allulien was the General of the Fauns. They were so full of joy and life, so loyal to the Deity and faithful in the Resistance. She smiled. "Allulien must love them very much."

A smile gleamed in Ember's eyes. "I believe Allulien does, and I do too. They live with so much joy and passion. Raphtova is a better place because there are Fauns in it."

Thea watched the Fauns whirl past, lost in the abandon of joy-filled dance. An ache throbbed, deep in her chest. "Their lives are so short. Isn't it sad, knowing they will all die?"

"It is sad." Ember watched Thea with a thoughtful gaze. "You are just learning about that sadness, aren't you?"

Thea nodded.

Ember stared across the dancers to where Thabani stood beside Roland, deep in conversation. "Thabani is my seed brother. I will fly with him until death."

"But when he dies what will you do?"

"Stay right where I am. There will always be more people to love."

Thea watched the Dryad in silence. Beneath the

sadness and the joy, she could feel a deep, lasting peace.

"Could you speak with Ulfgar sometime?" Thea asked, her voice barely above a whisper. "I think he needs to hear about that."

Ember nodded. "I will do that, if the Deity gives us time."

With a rush of wind, Kaji appeared, silhouetted against the night sky. She soared to the ground, landing beside Ember.

Ember shifted into a pure white eagle, just as large as Kaji. They spoke together in low clucks, then took to the sky, Ember following close on Kaji's tail.

Thea caught Thabani's expression from across the flickering fire.

Gingerly, she skirted the clearing, avoiding the revellers who seemed unconcerned by the departure of the eagles. Thabani gripped the handle of the dirk at his side, staring at the place in the sky where the eagles had disappeared.

"What's going on?" Thea whispered, stepping beside Roland.

"Kaji saw something," Roland whispered. "Ember has gone to see what it is."

They didn't wait long. Soon Ember returned, alone, and swooped down to Thabani's side, shifting into Faun shape as their hooves touched the ground.

Ember and Thabani spoke together in low, urgent voices. Thea waited, hardly daring to breathe.

Thabani turned to the dancers and spoke two words.

Silence fell across the clearing. Without a word, the Fauns began to put out the fires and disband their camp.

Thabani gestured for Thea and Roland to join him.

"The enemy is on the move." He looked at Roland. "Did Micai tell you anything about this?"

Roland shook his head.

Thabani gave him a keen glance. "With the Littles gone from the Deorcian, it's gone from bad to worse. There's nothing to hold back the spread of the monsters. We don't know where they come from, but there are more every day. Now Kaji has seen a company travelling north through our forest. If they're joining the monsters in the Deorcian, that's bad. If they're here to find us, that's even worse."

Thabani paced, his hands behind his back. "There's been no sign that he knows about us. No enemy has escaped to bring him news. We could hide and let them pass by, but they're passing this way. If there's any chance they know we're here ..." He glanced at Ember. "Ambush. Aspen Valley."

Ember nodded and disappeared among the bustling Fauns.

"We'll set up an ambush." Thabani turned to Thea and Roland. "That's our best chance of stopping them. Will you join us?"

"Of course!" Thea cried.

"Yes," Roland replied at the same moment. He shot Thea a grin.

"Thank you." Thabani regarded them seriously. "May the Deity watch over us this night."

Thabani strode across the clearing.

Hurrying after him, Thea stared around in disbelief. The huts were gone. The charred remains of the fires were swept away. If she hadn't seen it with her own eyes, she never would have known there had been a camp in that clearing.

"Come on!" Roland gestured Thea towards the place where their bags lay in a conspicuous heap. Ulfgar was there, his head resting on his pack.

"What's going on?" he grunted, opening one eye.

"Enemy troops, heading this way." Roland swung his bedroll over his shoulder and ran to join Thabani and the rest of the Fauns.

Thea grabbed Raybow and her bag.

Ulfgar closed his eyes again. "Am I supposed to come or something?"

"You can if you want to." Thea turned to go, then stopped to glance back. "We like it when you're with us."

Fauns ran back and forth across the clearing. In the midst of the chaos, Thabani called out orders.

He waved as Thea approached, gesturing to a Faun at his side. "This is Ayanda. She will stay with you for the fight."

Thea nodded. "What's the plan?"

"Plan?" Thabani's eyes twinkled. "If we made a plan, the enemy would figure it out. As it is, they have no idea what to expect."

Thabani spoke something to Ayanda, then turned to the rest of the Fauns. Silence fell, and Thea felt the ringing of comprehension magic in her ears.

"The enemy is coming." Thabani spoke in a low, clear voice. Thea realized she was understanding the Fauns' language. "Ember reports thirty trolls and ten humans at least, but there may have been more in the shadows. Three of them look like casters."

At Thea's side, Ayanda's eyes widened.

"But we are the Resistance!" Thabani's voice rang louder. "The Fallen One will not have his way in our forest. We fight for the safety of all the peoples of Raphtova and we will not let this danger pass by us to reach them. Be ready for anything, and watch for my signal." Thabani lifted his hands. "The protection of the Deity be on the Resistance this night!"

The Fauns clustered together, hugging, kissing, patting backs and butting heads. Then, like a mist, they dispersed into the night.

Thea looked at Ayanda at her side. Like all the Fauns she had goat-like legs and a bare, human-like upper body. Her horns curved back from her head like two long blades, and a curved sword hung at her belt. She carried a young Faun on her hip.

As Thea stared, the little Faun blinked up at her with large, innocent eyes.

"This is Inyoni." Ayanda smiled. "She is five cycles old tomorrow."

Inyoni made a kissing sound, then giggled.

Thea looked at Ayanda in surprise. "Are you taking her with you?"

"Of course." Ayanda tousled Inyoni's curly hair, revealing her tiny horns. "Why would we send our children away? We live by the Deity's protection, in camp or in battle."

Around them, the clearing was almost empty. Thea watched Sylica busily collecting her pack and weapons, with Daisy at her side. Ulfgar wasn't there.

"Sylica!" Thea called, and waved for her to join them. She glanced at Ayanda. "Where do we go?"

"Follow me."

Thea followed Ayanda as she slipped through the undergrowth. "You can do magic?"

"Yes. I follow the way of Allulien."

Joy rose in Thea's heart. "Allulien is my General too!"

"Good." Ayanda shot her a brilliant smile. "This will be fun. You and I will face the casters."

"The casters?"

Ayanda's expression became grim. "You think only the servants of the Deity can do magic?" She crouched behind a tree and peered into the shadows beyond. "The Fallen General had the same ability as any other General to give magic to those under his command, before he fell. Now he uses that power for evil, to give magic to those who serve him."

"But that magic came from the Deity! How can it be used to do evil?"

"The Deity gave it, and magic given cannot be taken away. Even our magic could be used to do harm if we chose to, but Allulien would have a thing or two to say about that the next time we checked in." She held a finger to her lips. "Now come."

Thea followed her guide through the shadows, with Sylica and Daisy trotting along behind. Soon they climbed what appeared to be a bit of a bluff, rising through a clearing in the trees.

"Aspen Valley is down there," Ayanda whispered. "We think they're coming that way."

Sylica and Daisy joined them, clanking and glimmering in the planet-lit night.

"I do not know your names," Ayanda said, turning to greet them.

"I'm Sylica."

"And your companion?"

"This is Daisy."

Ayanda nodded. "I am Ayanda. This is Inyoni and my

companion Biti." She gestured to a small black bat, hanging off one of her horns. "Fauns like to have a companion, to be with us in life and in battle."

Sylica beamed. "I like having a companion too!"

Ayanda nodded. "Good. Now we wait."

"Wait for what?" Thea whispered.

"For the signal."

"What's the signal?"

Ayanda shrugged. "Your guess is as good as mine. We'll know it when we see it."

An eagle's cry rang out through the night. Overhead, Kaji soared into view with Thabani clinging to her back, his dirk unsheathed in his hand. As Kaji wheeled, Thabani leaped, plummeting towards the ground.

A white blur shot past. Catching Thabani in their talons, Ember barrel-rolled as a volley of arrows whistled through the air and the forest below them erupted with shouts and cries.

Ayanda grinned. "I think that's the signal."

Chapter Eight

Thabani and Ember disappeared beyond Thea's sight. All around the valley, the shouts and cheers of the Fauns rang out.

Ayanda gestured Thea forward. "Come on! Let's go find some casters."

Thea's eyes widened in alarm. "Find them?"

"What? You think they're just going to come to us?"

Thea heard a squeak, almost beyond the edge of hearing, and a small black shadow zipped past.

Ayanda smiled. "Biti will help us."

As silently as she could, Thea followed Ayanda through the deep darkness beneath the trees. Shouts and the clashing of steel echoed towards them. Glimpses of light and shadow flickered across Thea's spirit sight.

Something crashed through the trees. Ayanda grabbed Thea's arm and pulled her down into the undergrowth.

A large troll lumbered past, its rough, stonelike skin glinting in the light of Micai.

With a shout, two Fauns erupted from the trees. Their spears struck the troll with the scrape of metal on stone.

The troll roared and heaved a massive boulder through the air. It struck a tree, which splintered and collapsed.

Biti darted past.

"There's a caster!" Ayanda hissed, pointing beyond the troll.

Thea stared. There—a figure lurked in the shadows, nearly invisible in black robes and hood. It was the right size and shape to be human, but where its spirit should have been was nothing but a dark void.

Horror crept down Thea's spine. It was different than the darkness she had seen in the Elves or many of the people she had met. This darkness wasn't an absence of light, it was a darkness given in the service of evil.

The figure gestured and a surge of magic burst through the forest. Vines whipped out of the undergrowth, tangling around the body of a nearby Faun, pulling him to the ground.

The troll struck the entangled Faun with a sickening thud. The Faun cried out in pain.

More trolls burst through the trees as the first troll staggered back, a green snake wrapped tightly around its neck.

"What do we do?" Thea hissed, then realized that Ayanda was gone.

Combat raged all around the shadows where Thea hid. A troll stumbled back, almost colliding with her. It turned with a snarl.

"Who wants to meet my shiny new mace!" Sylica's voice rang over the chaos. She appeared in a blur of green, swinging her mace above her head. Her shield gleamed in the light of Micai.

The troll hesitated. Sylica's mace struck its face with a resounding crack.

Thea ducked behind a tree. Heart pounding, she

scanned the shadows, trying to find the caster.

There.

From the branches above the caster's head, a Faun leapt with knife raised.

Vines erupted from the trees, wrapping tight around the Faun, pinning her to the tree.

The caster raised their hand.

Thea threw magic at the caster. The two spells collided and disappeared.

With a hiss, the caster turned and saw Thea. Their face looked like an ordinary human face, but the hatred in their eyes made Thea's blood run cold. The caster lifted their hand and magic surged.

The ground at Thea's feet boiled and began to rise.

"Look out!" someone yelled.

From the ground, a large, dirt-covered creature emerged, crawling its way into the light. It had no face or features, but somehow it looked at Thea and snarled.

Thea scrambled back as the apparition swung a clawed, arm-like appendage towards her.

Ayanda appeared, striking at the monster with her curved blade. Inyoni clung to her back, giggling.

Where the blade struck, a swath of dirt fell to the ground. The monster shifted, and its missing flesh regrew.

"Damn," Ayanda muttered, dodging back as the monster lashed out at her.

Thea stared at its seething form. It didn't have any spirit inside it at all.

"Stay back!" Ayanda called, gesturing Thea out of the monster's reach.

With a thundering roar, another monster emerged from the dirt behind them.

Thea wheeled to face it.

"Biti!" Ayanda yelled. "Where's the other caster?"

The bat darted away, but the first monster's arm swung again, striking the little bat from the sky.

"Biti!" Ayanda leaped. Her hands closed around the little bat as she tumbled to the ground.

From her mother's shoulder, Inyoni stuck out her tongue at the seething monster.

With a chorus of cries, more Fauns burst into the clearing. Leaping towards the first monster, their javelins sunk in deep and the monster roared.

"Come on Daisy!" Sylica burst into view. Swinging her mace with gusto, she threw herself at the other.

The first monster shifted and roared with the rumble of falling dirt, evading every thrusting attack of the Fauns. With a strike quicker than lightning, it hit one of the Fauns in the chest and sent her flying backwards.

Thea gripped her falcion, but before she could strike, a clawed arm struck her shoulder, knocking her to the ground.

With a hiss, the monster seemed to grow larger. Grabbing a Faun with a root-like tentacle, it dragged him, screaming, towards its gaping mouth.

With a surge of magic, Ayanda waved her arm at the monster. It crumbled into dirt.

Staggering to her feet, Thea gasped for breath.

Where the other monster had been, Sylica continued to pound a heap of innocuous dirt.

Thea watched her for a moment. "Sylica. I think it's dead."

"And don't do that again," Sylica muttered, shaking her finger at the dirt.

In the shadows, Thea caught sight of one of the

casters. Their hood had been torn back, revealing a young, bearded face. The caster raised his hand.

"Counterspell!" Ayanda hissed. "I'll take care of the other one!"

Heart pounding, Thea threw her magic at the caster. The swell of magic stopped.

The caster locked eyes with Thea and started his magic again.

Thea countered it.

The caster smiled, ever so slightly, then started his spell again.

Again Thea countered it.

With an explosion of pain, something struck Thea's side and she fell, hitting the ground with a heavy thud. Spots swirled in front of her eyes. Gasping, she struggled to get up as a troll's fist swung at her face.

The troll roared, then crumpled and fell to the ground. Behind its prostrate form, Ulfgar grinned at Thea, his great axe coming to rest on his shoulder.

He grabbed Thea's hand. "Up you come." Pulling her to her feet, he gave her an appraising look. "You alright? Good."

"Stop that!" Sylica yelled.

Thea turned and saw the caster. She felt the swell of magic.

Flame engulfed the caster, leaving nothing but a bit of charred ash.

Daisy closed her mouth and sat down, a look of complete bafflement on her metallic face.

Everyone stared.

"Good girl, Daisy!" Sylica beamed, patting the dragon on the head.

Ayanda sheathed her sword. "That is a very

interesting companion you have."

"Oh yes," Sylica nodded enthusiastically. "Daisy is the best companion in the world!"

Inyoni rested her head on her mother's shoulder.

Thea turned to Ayanda. "How did you make the monster disappear like that?"

"Counterspell." Ayanda stroked Biti's crooked wing with a forefinger. "It undid the magic holding it together." She shook her head. "It took a lot of magic, but I couldn't let it hurt Msizi like that."

Thea stared out across the valley. The trees didn't grow as thickly that way. Through the shadows she watched the dark, creeping things—trolls, and other shapes that were harder to see.

A glimmer of light caught her eye. Roland leapt out of a tree, rolled, and stabbed a shadowy figure in the gut.

A troll erupted from the shadows, swinging its fist. Roland dodged the blow and the troll charged after him.

Taking three quick steps, Roland reached the closest tree, ran partway up its trunk, and launched himself backwards. Flipping, he landed on top of the troll. With a surge of magic, his knife gleamed and he plunged it into the troll's stony back.

Thea watched as Roland leapt to the ground, his red granite skin gleaming in the light of Micai.

Something moved in the shadows beyond him. Roland jumped back as a boulder hurtled through the air. Magic surged. The rock struck the empty air in front of Roland and shattered.

Flourishing his knives, Roland leapt towards the hidden troll.

Ayanda gave a low purr in Thea's ear.

Thea looked at her in surprise, but Ayanda just winked. "I'll take a piece of that if you don't."

Thea stammered. "I—I don't—"

A mischievous gleam twinkled in Ayanda's eyes. "We all see it, sweetheart."

Thea felt her face get hot. She glanced around to find that the battle had moved on. Sylica was already halfway across the clearing, thundering towards a pack of trolls. Mace and shield waving, she bellowed, "Charge!"

"Excuse me," Ulfgar muttered and ran after her.

Thea glanced across the valley. She couldn't see Roland anymore.

"Come on." Ayanda slipped into the shadows and Thea followed.

"Watch for magic, or anything that seems unnatural," Ayanda hissed. "If the third caster is still alive, we need to find them."

They dodged from shadow to shadow, while Inyoni babbled cheerfully at her mother's side.

"What kind of magic can the casters do?" Thea asked, peering through the gloom.

"They enhance things, mostly. Like the vines and dirt monsters those casters were controlling. They take things and twist them to do what they want. Otherwise, they're a lot like us Allulien casters. They can use comprehension and charm." Ayanda gave Thea a sidelong glance. "Charm is the most dangerous of all. It affects the mind."

They crept through a thicket. Thea was aware of every stick cracking beneath her feet compared to her silent companion, but Ayanda didn't seem to care.

"Charm can influence decisions or confuse

someone's thinking," Ayanda continued, "but with a lot of magic behind it, it can completely change what someone is going to do, or make them do something they don't want to." Pausing, she shook her head. "Fauns can't be charmed. That's part of how we were made. I've seen it done on some of the Dryads, though." A look of pain passed through her eyes.

Crouching behind a tree, they watched a company of trolls tramping through the brush.

"Give it a try. Charm them," Ayanda whispered. "Confuse what they are doing."

Thea sent out her magic. She watched as the trolls looked around, as if suddenly at a loss as to why they were there and what was going on. One of the trolls punched another on the shoulder, and soon they were brawling and tumbling along the ground. Muffled grunts and shouts ricocheted through the trees.

Two Fauns ran by. Magic surged and the knives of the Fauns gleamed as they threw themselves at the trolls.

"I blessed their weapons," Ayanda whispered with a smile.

Thea and Ayanda crept on.

"Try to save some of your magic, if you can," Ayanda whispered. "We still don't know if there's another caster out there."

"How do you know how much magic you have left?"

"You can feel it inside you. That warm glow left by Allulien's presence, that is the feeling of the magic. After a while you get used to judging how much you have."

Ulfgar charged past, brandishing his axe.

Thea and Ayanda reached the far side of the valley

without seeing any sign of the third caster. Overhead, the blue-green expanse of Micai filled the sky, casting dappled shadows through the scattered trees.

Thea frowned. "Maybe the last caster is dead?"

A commotion of shouts and cries erupted from a distant cluster of trees.

Ayanda's mouth stretched into a thin line. "I doubt it."

"You both doing alright?" Roland appeared out of the shadows beside them.

"Yes." Thea shot him a glance. "Seen any casters lately?"

Roland shook his head. "No, I—"

Ulfgar stumbled into view, locked in combat with a human-shaped figure. Ulfgar gripped his axe as the human tried to wrestle him to the ground. With a growl, Ulfgar twisted away and gave a stunning blow with the butt of his axe.

A pack of trolls emerged from the distant trees.

"Hey Ulf!" Roland called, "Want a lift?"

Running towards the stocky man, Roland grabbed him around the shoulders, and with a spin, flung him at the oncoming trolls.

Ulfgar plummeted through the air, crashing through the ranks of the trolls with a triumphant yell.

Beside Roland, the human stared at Ulfgar in bewildered shock, until Roland punched them in the face.

Ulfgar's roar echoed across the valley.

"Got to go!" Roland gave Thea a grin and took off towards the melee.

Thea stared after him. "Should we help?"

Ayanda watched the fight with an amused

expression. "I think they can take care of it."

An eagle swooped overhead, silhouetted in Micai's light.

From the shadows, a bowstring twanged.

The eagle screeched in pain. Wheeling, it dove towards the shadow, talons outstretched. Striking its prey, the eagle lifted the shrieking human into the air and dropped them.

The eagle's feathers gleamed white as it banked once again and dove towards Thea. As Ember reached the ground, they shifted into human form, screaming in pain as their flesh shifted around the arrow lodged deep in their shoulder.

"Ember!" Thea gasped.

Ember staggered. "Come quickly. The caster."

"Where?" Ayanda demanded.

"Follow."

Ember ran, with Ayanda and Thea following close behind. Blood covered Ember's shoulder and dripped down their side.

"Can't we help you?" Thea pleaded, but Ember ran on, until Thea's heart pounded with the effort of keeping up.

At the edge of a clearing, Ember staggered, clinging to a tree for support. "Out of magic," they gasped. "Couldn't counterspell anymore."

"Ember—"

Ayanda laid a hand on Thea's shoulder. "Look!"

In the middle of the clearing, a human figure stood alone, robed in black.

Not alone—a Faun crouched in front of them, tensed to strike.

From the shadows, the wolf with golden eyes leaped

at the caster. Without a glance, the caster waved a hand and the wolf tumbled back, crashing through the underbrush.

The Faun leapt, but the caster pointed a finger and the Faun was blasted backwards, tumbling head over heels to land in a heap.

A shadow swooped across the face of Micai. Diving like an arrow, Kaji plummeted towards the caster. Magic surged, but Kaji veered away.

That moment, Thabani leapt off Kaji's back. With his own flash of magic, he brought his dirk down on the caster's head. The black robes fell to the ground.

Rising like a spectre behind Thabani's back, the caster struck out with a long, thin dagger. It glanced off Thabani's skin with a shower of sparks.

Thabani turned to face the caster with a surge of magic, but the caster raised their hand and the magic disappeared.

With their other hand, the caster punched him in the stomach.

Thabani staggered back, crouched in a defensive stance. They stared at each other for a long moment, the air crackling with the contempt in their eyes.

Thabani sprang forward, magic flaring.

As the caster moved to counterspell, Thabani struck with his dirk.

Steel rang out as the caster parried with their dagger.

Thabani twisted his blade and the dagger tumbled to the ground.

A blast of magic knocked Thabani off balance. The caster kicked him in the chest, and he fell to his back with a thud.

Ayanda lunged forward and magic surged, but the

caster counterspelled, without even a glance her direction.

Kaji dove, but the caster pointed a finger and a sudden blast of air sent the giant eagle tumbling back into the trees.

The caster set their foot on Thabani's chest and raised a hand. Magic swelled. Thabani stared into the caster's face with fearless eyes.

Thea threw all the rest of her magic at the caster. The two spells collided, shimmered, and disappeared.

The caster hissed. Scanning the shadows, their eyes locked onto Thea's. With a gesture they sent Thabani tumbling through the air.

Ember leaped, and with a scream of pain shot through the air on eagle's wings, catching Thabani moments before he hit the ground.

The caster's eyes hadn't left Thea's. They were probing her. Watching.

The caster smiled.

Thea felt her limbs go leaden. *You don't want to fight.* Something spoke with her own thoughts. *You want to sit down and go to sleep.* Her legs started to collapse.

She tried to fight it, but the weight dragged her down. It was crushing her. Filling her mind with thoughts she didn't want to have.

"Hey!" Sylica's voice rang out beyond her shrinking world. "Hey! Stop that!"

Sylica stormed between Thea and the caster, grabbed something unseen, and pulled.

With a wrench, the presence left Thea's mind. She staggered, gasping for breath, and realized that Roland's arms were around her.

The caster stared at Sylica in shocked disbelief.

Quivering with rage, Sylica yanked the unseen thing in her hand. The caster staggered forward.

Throwing the unseen thing aside, Sylica marched up to the caster with her hands on her hips. "That's not nice!"

The caster's eyes flared with hatred. With a gesture, magic burst towards Sylica, but she knocked it aside as if it was a tangible thing that had been thrown.

Roland stared. "We should help her!" His concern-filled eyes turned to Thea. "You're okay?"

Thea nodded.

Drawing his dagger, Roland ran towards the caster.

A dark figure erupted from the shadows, tackling Roland to the ground.

The caster flung another spell. Again, Sylica knocked it aside.

Roland rolled on top of his attacker as another shadowy figure burst out of the trees.

From the far side of the clearing, a group of trolls charged.

Fauns leapt out from the shadows, intercepting their rush towards the center of the clearing. Shouts and cries filled the air.

Behind Sylica, the ground began to boil and rise. Sylica grabbed something out of the air and yanked. The caster staggered to the ground, rolled, and struggled to one knee, gesturing at Sylica's legs.

Sylica kicked. Something unseen ricocheted back and struck the caster in the face.

Combat raged all around them. Thea slashed a troll with her falcion. Ayanda round-house kicked a human in the side of the head.

In the center of the clearing, the caster staggered upright and spat blood. Summoning a massive surge of magic, the caster thrust it at Sylica. Gripping her shield, Sylica blocked it. The caster sustained the spell, driving the magic at her with incredible force. Sylica staggered back and braced herself, her shield lifted above her head.

Thea ran towards her, then ducked as a sword swung over her head. A troll collapsed to the ground, blocking her way. She scrambled back. A cloaked figure leapt out and Roland tackled it to the ground.

In the center of the clearing, Sylica was forced back a step, then another step.

Ayanda grabbed Thea's arm. "Do something!"

Thea looked at her helplessly. "I'm trying! I can't get there!"

"Then shoot them! You have a bow!"

Snatching Raybow from her back, Thea sighted along the arrow. The combat surged past. She aimed, and let the arrow fly. It blazed with white light, passing through the melee, and struck the caster in the chest.

Sylica staggered as the caster sank to the ground.

All around the clearing, the trolls wavered, looking uneasily towards the lifeless heap that had once been the caster. They seemed smaller than they had before.

Sylica glared. "And no candy for you!"

One of the trolls took a step back, turned, and ran away through the trees.

All around the clearing, trolls scattered. The Fauns charged after them.

"Don't let them get away!" Ayanda's voice rang above the noise. "Keep the forest safe!"

Thea took a long, unsteady breath. Roland appeared

beside her. "Where's Thabani?"

Thea stared at the chaos spreading out in every direction. A flash of white showed through the gloom under the trees. "Ember will know."

As Roland hurried to find Ember, Thea's gaze returned to the middle of the clearing. Sylica stood alone in the midst of the scattering trolls and triumphant Fauns.

Thea hurried to join her.

Sylica stared at the lifeless form by her feet. Her hands were shaking.

"Sylica, are you ..." The words died in Thea's throat. Sylica's face was ashen, frozen in an expression of horror. Thea wrapped her arms around her friend and held her close.

Slowly, Sylica's body stopped trembling and she lifted her eyes to Thea's face. "Nobody uses magic to hurt my friends."

Thea tried to smile. "Thank you for saving me. I ... I have no idea how you did that."

"I just grabbed the magic." Sylica's voice seemed quiet and far away. "It wasn't nice magic." She stared out through the gloom. "Where's Daisy?"

Daisy leaped out of the shadows. Planting her muddy paws on Sylica's chest, she started licking Sylica's face.

Sylica sat in the dirt and held Daisy's wiggling, blood-smeared form.

Thea knelt beside her. "Are you going to be okay?"

Life began to sparkle in Sylica's eyes again. She looked up at Thea. "Want a candy?"

Thea grinned. "I'll take you up on that later." Standing, she glanced around the clearing. The last remains of combat had moved beyond her sight. The

Fauns that remained nursed bloody limbs and spoke to each other in low voices.

Thabani stepped out from the trees. He limped, with his arm draped over Kaji's back for support. Beside him, Ember eyed the clearing with glittering eagle eyes. One wing dragged on the ground, bloodied and limp.

"I see the caster fell." Thabani gave Thea a cheerful wave. "That was a close one for a while, wasn't it? Let me guess—the last of them turned tail and ran."

Thea nodded. "I think some of the Fauns are trying to stop them."

Thabani grinned. "The chase is on." He nodded to Kaji, and she took to the sky.

Ember watched her go with longing in their eyes.

"Not this time, my friend." Thabani stroked Ember's back. "You need that arrow removed before you fly anywhere."

Zanele emerged from among the Fauns. Seeing Thabani and Ember, she strode to meet them.

Dropping her satchel on the ground, she examined the arrow protruding from Ember's shoulder. "A deep muscle shot," she muttered. "Was it poisoned?"

She glanced at Ember's glittering eyes and frowned.

A Faun approached with a basin of water. Zanele barked out an order and another Faun hurried to join them.

Zanele spoke with Ember in a low voice, then opened her satchel. Getting out a large piece of gauze, she held the shaft of the arrow in her other hand and gave Ember a nod.

Ember's form began to shift, and Zanele pulled out the arrow, quickly covering the wound with the gauze. The snow-white Faun collapsed, unconscious, into the arms of the waiting Fauns. Gently, they laid Ember on the ground.

Thea watched in horrified fascination as Zanele opened a small sealed pouch and drew out a needle attached to some kind of thin, strong thread. With small, even stitches, she sewed together the wound and tied off the thread. Laying her hand over the wound, she closed her eyes.

Thea felt the surge of magic.

A wound appeared on Zanele's shoulder, just like Ember's had been. Her face contorted with pain.

As Thea stared, the wound on Zanele's shoulder started to fade. The skin drew together and the blood disappeared. Zanele shuddered and opened her eyes. Her shoulder was left without a mark.

Zanele lifted her hand off Ember's shoulder. The stitches were still there, but the wound was almost completely gone. The red, inflamed swelling had disappeared.

Thea looked at Zanele in wonder. That was Raphea magic—the magic of the Healer.

Zanele glanced up at the Fauns who stood close by. "Ember should not fly for three days, to ensure this heals properly." Taking a bottle of salve from her bag, she spread a generous layer across Ember's shoulder and wrapped it in a bandage.

Standing, Zanele wiped her hands on a towel. "Thabani? Let's have a look at you."

"I am well," Thabani assured her. "See to the others first."

She gave him a keen glance. "I saw that limp. Come here."

Settling Thabani on a smooth patch of ground,

Zanele examined his leg. It lay bent at an unnatural angle. She made a small sound with her tongue. Cheeky's head poked out of her bag, disappeared, then reappeared with a small vial clutched in her mouth. The little flying squirrel scampered over to Zanele and dropped it in her outstretched hand.

Zanele opened the vial and handed it to Thabani. "Drink this."

Thabani obediently drank.

Ayanda laid a hand on Thea's shoulder. "Come. There is clean water and bandages. Care for your own wounds, then you can help those who need it."

Thea followed Ayanda to a place where several buckets had been set, along with a pile of clean towels.

"We bring all that we need when we go to fight," Ayanda explained, pointing out a heap of bandages. "We do all that we can at the site of the battle, because the scent of blood is already here. When we are finished we will find a safe place to rest."

Inyoni splashed and played in one of the buckets, laughing in delight as her little hooves churned up the water.

Thea wetted a towel and found a place to sit that was out of the way. Gingerly, she wiped the blood and dirt off her skin, wincing as she tried to avoid the scrapes, welts, and bruises.

The imprint of the caster's magic lingered in her mind. It left a raw, vulnerable feeling.

Roland joined her. "I think we got them all. Kaji and one of the Dryads are doing a last sweep of the area." He eased himself to the ground. His clothes were torn and smeared with blood and grime.

Thea offered him the towel.

"Thanks." Roland gave a tired smile and started wiping his face. He winced.

"Here." Thea took the towel. Finding the cleanest corner, she wiped the blood off his face. A large patch of skin on his cheek was raw and red. Gently, she cleaned the dirt off as well as she could.

"Sorry," she whispered as Roland flinched again.

"It's okay." Gripping her other hand, Roland held still while Thea finished. Finally she set the towel down.

"Thank you." Roland smiled and caressed her cheek.

There was that look in his eyes again. Thea's heart started beating faster. She wanted to say something, to tell him how important he was to her, or to ask—somehow—that he could keep looking at her like he was right now.

She couldn't find any words to say.

Around the clearing, the Fauns chattered cheerily as they cleaned their gear and dressed their wounds. Zanele moved from person to person, chittering to Cheeky as she worked. The little squirrel darted in and out of Zanele's satchel, fetching gauze, bandages, and small vials of liquid.

Thabani hobbled across the clearing with his leg in a brace, patting backs and giving hugs.

"I'd like to speak to Thabani." Roland smiled at Thea. "Want to come?"

Thea nodded.

Thabani was talking with Ulfgar, who bore a large bandage wrapped around his head, but otherwise appeared unscathed.

Thabani waved for Thea and Roland to join them. "I was just telling Ulfgar he's got quite the battle plan—tackle them head on, sometimes quite literally!"

He laughed and slapped Ulfgar on the back. "I'd gladly have him by my side in any fight."

Ulfgar clutched his helmet and beamed through his tangled beard.

"And Roland, Thea, the Deity knows how much we needed you today." Thabani gave a deep sigh. "That's the end of that, though. Hopefully we'll get a rest before the Resistance is needed again."

His eyes wandered around the busy clearing. For a moment, his face looked tired. "Three lives lost today, and a few more that will have to lay low for a while. We've had worse, but that never makes it easier."

Kaji soared into view, carrying a lifeless bundle. Gently, she set it on the ground and took off again into the sky.

Thea watched the Fauns in silence. She had never seen so many hearts so completely given to the Deity. There was sorrow in their eyes, but also joy, and a determination that took her breath away.

By the buckets of water, Sylica industriously washed the blood and grime off Daisy's scales.

How had she been able to counter the caster's magic like that? Thea had never heard of anything like it. Clearly the caster had been very powerful, but Sylica had stood firm when no one else could. It was impressive, and completely baffling.

If asked to do it again, though, she would probably say she had no idea what to do.

In the shadow of the trees on one side of the clearing, several Fauns were digging with small spades. Other Fauns carried the bodies of the humans and laid them beside the growing hole.

As Thea watched, two Fauns set down a body. It was

a woman with dirty blonde hair. Beneath the blood and grime, Thea could just see the freckles on her face. Beside her lay a middle-aged man with a shock of dark hair and pale skin.

Thabani limped to Thea's side. "They're just ordinary people. I know. It's hard to see it for the first time."

Thea stared at the lifeless figures as they were lowered one by one into the open grave. Tears stung her eyes. "Couldn't they have followed the Deity, if they'd just had the chance?"

"Who knows what chances they've had or why they chose the Fallen One. Fear, maybe, or whispered lies that twist the mind. Maybe they craved the power that was promised to them." He sighed. "It didn't save them, in the end."

"But what about mercy?"

Thabani set a gentle hand on Thea's shoulder. "Sometimes mercy looks like judgment."

With a hobbling gait, he turned and walked towards the middle of the clearing, where a large pile of branches and logs was being assembled.

Thea followed. Sylica skipped around the clearing, playing with the little Fauns. Roland helped heave more branches up onto the pile. Ayanda stood watch over the Fauns who had died as they were washed, then lifted one by one onto the pyre.

As everyone gathered around, Thabani raised his hand for silence. He spoke in the language of the Fauns, his hand resting on Kaji at his side. Thea had no magic left to understand what he was saying, but she knew that he was speaking his last words over the Fauns who had given their lives.

The fire was lit, and as it spurted and started to grow,

the Fauns began to sing. It was a beautiful, haunting song. Tears glimmered in every eye as the flames rose higher and higher.

Ember stepped beside Thea. "Like the Fauns," the Dryad whispered. "They burn so bright, and then they're gone." Their eyes flickered in the light of the flames.

One by one, the Fauns returned to their tasks. Some finished burying the humans. Others put the dirty towels in the buckets and carried them away.

Thabani turned to Roland and sighed. "We can't linger long."

Roland glanced at the fire that still glowed hot.

"Swift Wing will stay behind and make sure the fire does not spread to the trees." Thabani gave a friendly wave to one of the Dryads. "The rest of us will go find a camp for the night."

Thea looked around the clearing. The Fauns had left no sign of their presence or the battle that had so recently raged, except for the blazing pyre and the scattered, stone-like remains of the trolls.

Ulfgar trundled up to join them. His large pack was on his back again, its barrel strapped tightly in place. Thea realized, in surprise, that Ulfgar hadn't taken his pack with him into the fight. She'd never seen him leave his pack behind before.

He caught her glance. "The barrel survived!" he called with a triumphant smile. Light gleamed inside him in a way that Thea hadn't seen since he fought to get the Littles out of the Deorcian.

Joking and laughing, Ulfgar strode among the Fauns, swapping stories and beaming beneath his tangled mess of a beard.

At Thabani's word, the procession of Fauns set out into the forest. Thea followed Thabani and Ember through the trees, with Roland close behind her. Their pace was slow because of Thabani's limp, but when the Dryad offered to carry him, he refused. "I'm not the only one with a hobble today," he grinned. "We'll take it slow. You can go on ahead and find a good place for us, if you like."

As Allumen's light began to brighten the overcast sky, they arrived in another clearing. All around Thea, the Fauns bustled about. Fires were lit, huts erected, and screening walls thickened. In hardly any time at all, the new camp looked remarkably like the one that had been taken down.

"Get what sleep you can," Thabani urged Thea and her friends. "There are plenty of others who can take watch. Sleep in a hut if you want, or by the fire. Our home is yours."

Some of the Fauns were already settling down to sleep. Others started cooking food, while others grabbed their weapons and climbed into the trees or slunk into the underbrush.

Roland lay down by the fire. Ulfgar got himself comfortable with his head resting on his pack, and Sylica cuddled up beside Daisy. Thea set down Raybow and her bag. She didn't know how serious Ayanda had been, but she decided to stay pretty close to Roland, just in case.

Chapter Nine

Thea woke to someone shaking her.

"Lady Thea." Thabani's voice was urgent and low. "Sorry to wake you, but I need to speak with you right away."

Thea blinked and stared blearily around the clearing. Nothing had changed in the time since she had fallen asleep. From the light in the sky, it looked like not much time had passed either.

Beside her, Roland startled into wakefulness. "What's going on?" he asked, reaching for his knife.

"Come." Thabani gestured for them to follow.

Gingerly, Thea and Roland tiptoed past Ulfgar's recumbent form and the place where Sylica lay curled up beside Daisy.

At the edge of the clearing, Thabani turned to them with a grim light in his eyes. "Word from Micai. You need to leave. Now."

Thea's eyes widened. "What's wrong?"

"The Enemy knows the Spark is here. I don't know how, but he knows. You must leave as soon as possible, before he tries to find you."

Roland's gaze turned to Thea, his forehead creased in concern.

Thea frowned. "What about the Resistance? Will the Enemy send more troops here?"

"The Resistance will carry on. We always do."

Thabani's face was grave, but his eyes twinkled with light. "We will do whatever we can to help you on your way."

Thea hurried back to her sleeping companions. "Sylica. Ulfgar. Wake up. We have to go."

Groaning, Ulfgar sat up. "My head ..." he rubbed the offending extremity. "Didn't drink enough yesterday." Pushing himself up from his hands and knees, he stumbled over to his keg.

Sylica stared sleepily at the sky. "Is it today or tomorrow?"

"It's today." Thea picked up Raybow and her bag, slinging them over her shoulder. "I'm afraid we didn't get to sleep much, but Micai says we need to go, before the enemy finds us."

Sylica frowned. "I thought they all died."

"All the ones we were fighting, yes. There are others."

"Oh."

As Sylica stood up, Daisy pranced around her feet, begging for attention.

"All that work and we don't even get a break," Ulfgar grumbled. "Should just bloody lie down and give up." He put his hands over his ears. "And make your tin can stop yapping. It's hurting my head."

Sylica sat on her bag and pouted.

Thea sighed. Ulfgar's spirit was cold and hard, as if all the life Thea had seen in it before had only been a dream.

Gesturing for the others to follow, she made her way back to the place where Thabani and Roland were talking.

Thabani looked up as she approached. "Lady Thea, I am sorry that our time with you has been so short.

Where will you go now? What is your quest?"

Thea glanced at her companions. "We have something with us that belongs to the dragons. We are taking it back to them."

Thabani's eyes widened. "To the mountains? Maybe it's good you can't stay long. We've already seen snow on the higher slopes."

Thea smiled apologetically. "I know it's not a good time with the Great Sleep so soon, but we don't have a choice."

Thabani made a wry face. "It's never a good time for travelling in the mountains. Prepare yourselves to leave. I'll see how I can help you." Turning, he strode away.

Sylica blinked at Thea. "We're really leaving?"

"I'm afraid so."

Sylica scampered off, bidding a tearful farewell to every Faun she could find.

Ulfgar took the opportunity to ingest as much alcohol as possible.

Roland leaned close to Thea and spoke in a low voice. "I was talking with Thabani. He's afraid the enemy we fought might have had a way of communicating with the Fallen General, and that's why he knows you are here. We need to avoid contact with the enemy, if at all possible, for the next while. Hopefully we can get away without being noticed."

"But why would the enemy be looking for me in particular? I'm just an Elf."

Roland shrugged. "This whole Spark thing is new to me too, but the Fauns seem to think you're important." He grinned. "I think you're important too."

Ulfgar grumbled and pulled his helmet down over his eyes. "A puffed up head. That's all she'll get at this rate."

In Faun shape, Ember stepped beside Roland, handing him several small packets. "Dried meat and berries. High in the mountains food can be scarce. These will sustain you then."

Thea glanced from Ember to Ulfgar sprawled on the ground beside his barrel. Her heart sank. Ember wasn't going to get a chance to speak with Ulfgar at all.

Ember seemed to sense what she was feeling. Laying a hand on her arm, Ember spoke softly. "Sometimes the Deity's ways are different than ours. Trust me, your friend's journey is not over yet."

Thea gave a grateful smile. "I'll miss you, Ember."

Ember smiled. "And I will miss all of you. It has been good fighting by your side."

Thabani returned. "You have warm clothing?"

"Yes," Thea assured him. "We were sure to bring that."

Thabani nodded. "Good. I have never gone beyond the foothills myself, but from the air I have seen high passes and other dangers you will have to cross before you reach the home of the dragons. The Minathrils live in those lands. They are a proud, distant kind of people. Very disciplined and skilled, they say, but I've never heard of them coming down to fight with the Resistance. They live in the mountains, and there they stay. We don't have many dealings with them."

Thea's heart sank. They sounded so much like the Elves.

"As for the place where the dragons live, I've never heard of anyone reaching it and coming back alive. That doesn't mean it can't be done," he winked, "but I can't give you directions or offer you any advice except to be cautious, and travel with as much speed as you safely can. Mountain travel will only become more difficult as the weather grows worse."

Thea nodded and glanced at Roland. He listened to Thabani with a grim expression.

Thabani smiled. "But there is one thing I can do: Zanele has agreed to go with you and aid you in your quest."

Thea looked around in surprise. Zanele was nowhere to be seen.

"She is preparing to go as we speak."

"But she's your healer."

"Raphea has permitted her to go, and it is the least I can do. I would not have your company travel through the mountains without a healer."

Moments later, Zanele joined them. She carried a bag over her back and her satchel at her side. Cheeky rode on her shoulder, staring at everyone with big black eyes.

Thabani acknowledged her presence, then turned to Thea. "Zanele knows the forest well. She can lead you as far as the foothills, and after that you will have to find your way together. The Deity's blessing be on you all."

"Thank you, Thabani." Thea offered him a warm embrace. "The Deity's blessing be with you and the Resistance."

Ayanda came and gave Thea a farewell embrace. Inyoni grinned at her from her mother's back and waved a pudgy little hand.

Thabani stood beside Roland and spoke in a low voice. "Guard the Spark."

Roland clasped his hand. "With my life."

Calling for Sylica, Thea followed Zanele to the edge of the camp.

Sylica scampered after them, her mace and shield clattering. "We're going on an adventure again? Where are we going?"

Roland gave her an incredulous glance. "The mountains?"

Sylica beamed. "We're going to the mountains? I love seeing the mountains! They're so big and pretty. Did you hear that, Daisy? We're going to the mountains!"

Ulfgar heaved his massive bag onto his back and staggered after them, grumbling.

Zanele led the way out of the camp and west through the trees.

"Just think!" Sylica continued to chatter, "We're going to get such a good view from up there! Mountains are pointy and bald on top, just like Uncle Bob. He said he liked it that way because there was less of him to catch fire if something went boom, but my mom said he was just losing it because he was getting older. But that's funny because I'm getting older and I'm not losing anything. I still have my mace and my shield and my candy bag and Daisy and my—"

"Just shut up," Ulfgar grumbled.

They walked until staph, then set up a makeshift camp. Thea fell asleep as soon as her head touched the ground, and woke for her turn on watch feeling like she'd hardly rested at all.

Sitting with her back against a tree, she stared blearily at the forest surrounding them, shifting herself again and again in an effort to stay awake.

When staph was over, they gathered together to confer.

"Do we carry on?" Thea asked. "We've been

travelling on very little sleep and we're tired, but Thabani said to get away as fast as we could."

"Then we carry on." Zanele gave a firm nod. "Thabani only says things like that if he means it."

"But restday is for resting, unless our Generals have told us otherwise."

"And?" Zanele raised an eyebrow.

Thea sighed. "The thing is, we didn't check in this morning. At least, I know I didn't. Maybe there's clearer direction we don't know about yet."

"We should check in now," Roland agreed. "I don't like it when I miss checking in."

"Alright," Zanele agreed.

"Huh," Ulfgar muttered. "While you're all thinking, I'm going to get some more sleep."

Thea knelt and waited. The day was just as overcast and gloomy as it had been before. A fitful breeze stirred the branches overhead. Allulien was silent.

As she waited, Thea's mind drifted back to the Fauns and their fight against the enemy. Allulien must be proud of them, though how anyone could not like the Fauns, Thea didn't know. There was something so endearing about them and their selfless hearts.

And now she knew who the Generals of the Fauns and Dryads were. The Fallen General had been the guardian of the Littles, before he fell, and of course Enkeli was the General of the Elves. That only left Raphea to either be the General of the humans or the Minathrils. Now that she thought about it, what if Raphea was the General of the humans and the Minathrils were not one of the five races at all? That would explain why they lived in the mountains with the dragons and never seemed to leave.

157

After waiting for what felt like long enough, Thea got up and returned to the others.

"Any word?" Zanele asked.

Thea shook her head. "You?"

"No." Zanele glanced at Roland.

"I didn't hear anything either," Roland concluded.

"So what will we do?" Thea frowned. "We don't have direct orders."

Roland gave her a thoughtful glance. "Micai did tell Thabani we needed to get away. That sounds like direct orders to me."

"I guess. I'd just prefer to get the direct orders myself."

"We carry on," Zanele said, standing abruptly. "Tomorrow our orders may be different, but for now we are too close to the Resistance."

Ulfgar's snore rumbled the ground beneath their feet. Rousing him to resentful wakefulness, they continued on their trek.

Restday felt long. Thea walked until she stumbled from weariness, but still Zanele led them on. If she was tired, she didn't show it.

Sylica bounded along beside Zanele, with Daisy skipping at her heels. "—And then I realized that if I'm not a Little, I must be a Faun!"

Zanele shot her a surprised glance. "What?"

"A Faun! Of course, I *used* to be a Little, which made a lot of sense because I'm friendly and I'm interested in so many things and I'm short—I just grew a bit extra—and my mom and my dad are Littles of course, but the Littles in Gedwyld sort of look at me funny which I thought was kind of strange, but now it all makes sense because I'm not a Little after all. I'm a Faun!"

Zanele gave Sylica a long, slow stare. "You are not a Faun."

"Of *course* I'm a Faun! I love singing and dancing just like the Fauns, and I have an animal companion too!"

Zanele looked down at Daisy. "That is a tin can."

"Hear, hear," Ulfgar muttered.

Sylica stuck her nose in the air. "Daisy is *real*, just like I am a *real* Faun."

"Look." Zanele stopped walking and turned to Sylica. "My legs? Covered in hair. Your legs? No hair." She gestured to her head. "My hair is curly. Yours is weird. I have horns. You definitely don't."

"That's just outside stuff. That changes. *Inside* I am a Faun all the way through."

"Look." Zanele set her hands up on Sylica's shoulders and looked her squarely in the eye. "I know my people. I have healed them inside and out. You are not a Faun and you will never be a Faun. What you did on the battlefield, no Faun could ever do. I know you love to dance and sing. You bring joy wherever you go, and my people love you for that. If you joined our tribes and lived the rest of your days with us that would be a joy and a delight, but you are not a Faun."

Sylica's face scrunched up, just a little. "If I'm not a Faun, what am I?"

"Beats me." With a wry smile, Zanele turned and continued to move through the forest. "You look a lot like Thea and Roland, to be honest, but different too. I never saw anything like you before. It's not bad to try to figure it out, just don't lie to yourself while you're doing it."

Subdued, Sylica followed Zanele through the trees.

Zanele's pace was light and quick, but with her shorter stature it wasn't too hard for everyone to keep up. Her curly brown hair was tied back in a braid, as it was when they first met her.

Thea watched her with interest. It wasn't easy to get Sylica to listen to anything, but it seemed like Zanele was able to read her in a way that Thea was still learning to. Sylica had a way of changing the world to fit the way she thought, rather than the other way around.

Thea glanced around sharply. So far there hadn't been any sudden wells or other obstacles, but maybe she should walk a little more carefully for a while.

They stopped and made camp with enough time left in the day to do some hunting and foraging, saving the food packets from Ember for when they really needed them.

Leaving her bag behind in the camp, Thea took Raybow and wandered off through the trees. She tried to stay alert so she would have something to bring back to camp, but again and again she realized that she was lost in her own mind, or not really thinking at all. It might be best to just get what sleep she could, and be in better shape for tomorrow. Turning around, she retraced her path through the trees.

In the camp, the fire crackled cheerily. Ulfgar sat beside his pack, his bearded chin in his hands. As Thea approached, Zanele set an armful of mushrooms by the fire and went to sit beside Ulfgar.

She seemed to consider him for a moment, then spoke. "When I travel, I take time to check on everyone's condition, to make sure they're doing alright. I was wondering if I can help you."

"What?" Ulfgar looked at Zanele with a confused glance.

"I'm a healer. That's what I do."

"Don't need healing," Ulfgar muttered.

"Really?" Zanele leaned closer. "If you think that broken bones and torn flesh are the only kinds of wounds that need to be healed, then you are wrong."

Ulfgar frowned. "What?"

"I've seen how you treat them. They care about you, but you push them away. Even when you care about something, you act like you don't. Something is hurt deep inside you. A hurt from a long time ago."

"Hmph." Ulfgar stared at the fire. "That's just the way I am."

"No, that's called trauma. It's a wound that's in the mind and the heart."

"So? What happened happened. I can't change it and I can't change me."

"Well that's a stupid way of thinking." Zanele's eyes flashed. "It takes longer to heal than a broken leg, but that doesn't mean it can't. You don't have to live with it forever."

Ulfgar stared at her, his hands clenched tight.

Thea hardly dared to breathe.

Beyond their camp, the undergrowth rustled and Roland stepped into view. A wild turkey hung over his shoulder.

Ulfgar snorted and stared down at the fire.

Zanele gave him a keen glance. "I'll be here, if you change your mind."

Roland set the turkey by the fire and began to

prepare it for cooking. Thea waited a couple of moments, then approached the fire herself.

Sylica did not appear. Thea waited until the food was cooking over the fire, then asked the others if anyone had seen her. No one had.

Roland's hand hovered over the mushrooms he had been chopping. "How long has she been missing?"

"Since we got here. A measure at least."

Roland glanced out through the trees, concern creasing his forehead.

Zanele frowned. "She is an adult, according to circles as you count them. She should be able to take care of herself."

Thea and Roland exchanged an uneasy glance.

"I'll go look for her," Thea said.

She grabbed Raybow, just in case, and set out through the trees.

There was no knowing where Sylica had gone. Thea searched out from their camp in a long sweeping circle, but couldn't see any sign of her. Getting her bearings, Thea set out farther.

A distant voice echoed through the trees. Thea froze and listened.

"Hello!" The voice was very far away, but it sounded like Sylica.

Thea followed the voice past a swamp, up a tree-covered ridge, and into the valley beyond.

"Hello!" The call was very close now.

Thea ducked around a leaning tree and scanned the forest beyond. Sylica was nowhere to be seen.

Daisy burst out of the undergrowth, yapping and bouncing excitedly around Thea's legs.

"Daisy!" Thea crouched down and was rewarded with

a massive lick on her face. Wiping the slobber off with the back of her hand, Thea stepped back. "Where's Sylica, Daisy?"

Daisy kept yapping and running in circles.

"Hi Thea!"

The voice came from above Thea's head. She looked up.

Sylica waved cheerfully, her legs swinging off the side of a branch far above the ground.

"Sylica! What are you doing up there?"

"I'm stuck."

There were no other branches beneath Sylica's perch.

"How did you get up there?"

"I flew!"

Thea stared. "You *what*? Okay. What happened?"

"Well Zanele told me I'm not a Faun—"

Thea thought she caught a hint of a pout on Sylica's face.

"—So I was thinking about what other kinds of things I could be, and I thought that maybe I'm a Dryad! Dryads can do lots of cool things, like flying, so I tried to fly and I did! Only—" her face fell, "it didn't last very long, and then I started to fall and that was scary. Thankfully this branch got in the way, so here I am!"

Thea watched her friend for a moment. "Sylica?"

"Yes?"

"You're not a Dryad."

"Yeah ..." Sylica frowned. "I think I figured that out."

Well that was something, at least. Thea glanced back towards the distant camp. "Will you be okay up there for a while? I'll go get the others and we'll figure out a way to get you down."

"Okay!" Sylica grinned. "Daisy and I were playing

hide and seek. It was a little tricky, because there aren't many places I can hide up here, but we were still having fun!"

Leaving Sylica and Daisy behind, Thea retraced her way through the trees.

"Any luck?" Roland asked, his eyes taking in the fact that Thea had returned alone.

"Found her. She's stuck up a tree."

"Okay." Roland considered this. "It could be worse."

"I'm not sure how we're going to get her down."

Zanele hopped up. "Let's go and see."

Thea led the others to the place where Sylica waited.

Zanele stared. "You said she was stuck in a tree, but I was not expecting that." She glanced at Thea. "How exactly did she get up there?"

"She was trying to figure out if she was a Dryad."

Zanele looked at her in surprise.

"She only made it partway."

"But ... *why*?"

Thea gave a helpless shrug. "It's complicated."

Ulfgar stumped around the base of the tree. "We could cut it down. That would get her down pretty quick."

"Hey!" Sylica protested. "This is a *nice* tree! Don't cut it down!"

"I could cast shield on her," Zanele offered. "Then she could jump without getting *too* hurt." She frowned up into the tree. "But I don't want to risk her twisting her ankle or something."

Roland cut a short length off his rope. Throwing the rest over his shoulder, he strung the short length around the back of the tree and gripped the ends in his hands. Leaning back, he started climbing up the tree, inching the rope higher as he went.

Thea watched Roland as he climbed. Muscles straining, he drew closer to the branch where Sylica waited.

"Oh, hi Roland!" Sylica grinned. "That's a neat way to climb a tree! Are you going to climb down like that too? You could teach me! That would be fun!"

"Can you move?" Roland panted, bracing himself beneath the branch where Sylica sat.

Sylica scooted further down the branch.

Roland heaved himself up. Taking the rope off his shoulder, he looped it around the branch and dropped the end to the ground.

The branch swayed beneath Sylica's excited bounce. "Oh! Me! Can I go first?"

"That's the idea."

Sylica swung herself over the edge of the branch and grabbed the rope. "Wheee!" she cried, sliding down to the ground.

Letting go of the rope, she stared at her reddened hands. "Ow! The rope bit me!"

"Let's get back to camp," Zanele said, patting her on the back. "I'll wrap those up for you with some salve. They'll feel much better tomorrow."

Roland swung himself down with an ease that showed how experienced he was with ropes. Pulling the rope down after himself, he coiled it and slung it over his shoulder.

Thea realized she had been staring. Looking away, she felt her face get hot. Ayanda probably would have said something, if she was there.

Back in their campsite, Zanele bandaged Sylica's hands, then ordered her to lie down and rest. Ulfgar poked and prodded the meat that sizzled over the fire. Roland got out his knives and did some training.

Thea sat and watched. Roland worked himself hard, drilling attack after attack. She had to admit that he was very attractive. She'd never really thought about him like that before. They had always been close, but these feelings growing inside of her wanted something closer.

Roland's spirit gleamed beneath her tingling spirit sight. There was nothing else she needed to be doing right now. She let herself slip into vidlas like a warm, comforting blanket. It had been so long since she didn't care how deep she got.

The longer she looked, the more she realized she'd never really looked into Roland's spirit at all. It shimmered with vibrancy. Determination pulsed brightly, the light of the Deity glowed, warm and sure, and behind it all was a longing that ached deeply. It reached out to her, like an echo of something new rising up in her own heart. She wanted him. She wanted to be with him in a way she'd never wanted anyone else before.

Slowly she became aware of someone tapping her arm. With a wrench, Thea pulled herself out of vidlas and turned to see Zanele sitting beside her.

"You alright?" Zanele asked.

"Oh. Yes," Thea stammered, suddenly aware that her heart was racing, although she didn't know why. "I was just using my elf-sight. It makes us kind of zone out sometimes."

"Huh." Zanele seemed to consider this. "Does elf-sight have something to do with watching your attractive friend while he trains?"

"What?" Thea startled. Had it been that obvious?

What would Roland think? She glanced at him in concern, but Roland continued with his drills, unaware of the world going on around him.

"So is anyone going to eat this turkey, or is it all for me?" Ulfgar grumbled.

Chapter Ten

The next morning, they continued west towards the mountains. Thea kept a sharp eye on Sylica. She knew anything could happen, but the trouble with Sylica was that you could never anticipate what would happen next. When an old, empty berry bush was suddenly filled with fresh, ripe berries, Thea breathed a sigh of relief. That she could handle.

After eating their fill of the unexpected, out of season berries, they continued on their way.

"How far is it to the end of the forest?" Thea asked Zanele as they walked.

"It will be two or three days till we reach the foothills. It would be faster if we had an Enkeli caster in our company. When we had an Enkeli caster in the Resistance we could cross the entire forest in three days."

Thea thought about how long it had taken them to walk all the way from Gedwyld. "That would be nice. I've never met someone who served under Enkeli before. At least, not someone who was actively serving."

"In the Resistance we mostly have people under Allulien and Micai. I'm the only one who has served under Raphea, as far as I've heard."

"Why did you choose Raphea?"

Zanele shrugged. "I saw all the hurt that was happening to my people. It hurt me too. Then Raphea came and told me that's what healing is all about: taking the pain of others so they don't have to carry it alone. I have served since that day."

Thea gave Zanele a grateful smile. "Thank you for coming with us. I hope you don't mind that Thabani sent you."

"I wanted to come. I've never been outside the forest before."

Thea thought about the silver in Thabani's hair. "How old are you?"

"Fifteen circles."

Thea looked at Zanele in surprise. "You're only fifteen?"

"So?" Zanele shot her a keen glance. "I have been considered full grown by my people for many circles now."

Thea considered this. If Thabani was getting old at twenty-five, Fauns must grow up very quickly.

She glanced at Roland. He was on high alert, scanning the forest around them. He hadn't really looked her direction all day. It nagged at her mind, like something that wasn't quite right. Of course, he wanted to make sure they were safe, but once they stopped to set up camp, he still didn't pay attention to her. He was either busy hunting or training. He drilled Thea on her falcion techniques, but that wasn't the same as really spending time together.

Sylica and Zanele were always happy to talk, and even Ulfgar joined in sometimes, but more often than not, Roland would excuse himself from the conversation to go stand watch.

Thea watched him as he worked. He really was attractive, more than any other Elf she had met, and the more she thought about it, the more she hoped that he thought the same way about her.

She remembered all the times that Roland had sought her out and showed that he wanted to be with her, but she'd taken it for granted. Now that seemed to be gone, but she wanted it more than ever.

As they travelled on, the tree-covered hills and ridges became more frequent. Zanele chose her way with care, trying to avoid the steeper slopes.

One day, at the top of a particularly high ridge, Zanele stopped. "This is the end of the forest."

Trees spread out in every direction. Ulfgar shot her a skeptical glance.

Zanele gave a knowing smile. "You will see."

As they carried on, Thea began to notice a change in the forest. There were different kinds of trees, and they didn't grow together as tightly as they had before.

The hills around them grew taller. Finding a stream, they followed its course up through the foothills, which eased their passage somewhat.

Thea was amazed at the energy with which Zanele had thrown herself at getting to know her travelling companions. She had caught Zanele talking with Ulfgar on several occasions, but chose to give them a wide berth. Whatever they may have been saying, it was enough for Thea to see that as the days passed, Ulfgar's spirit seemed to soften again, a deep light gleaming through the hardened cracks.

Sylica accepted Zanele as a long-lost Faun soulmate and talked to her about everything. Zanele took this in stride, although Cheeky seemed to regard Sylica—and Daisy—with wary suspicion.

From Thea, Zanele showed a great interest in learning about the Elves, especially their medical practices, and they spent many measures talking as they walked.

Sometimes they sang. Zanele taught them a Faunic marching song, and Ulfgar regaled them with a strange ballad he'd learned in his past travels. Roland taught them one of the sea shanties he'd learned during his time on the Raven.

That didn't last long, though. Soon Roland was on high alert again, scanning the hills for any sign of danger.

Their winding path through the hills led them higher and higher, until one day they emerged from the trees to find themselves in an alpine meadow. Setting up their camp beneath the shelter of the last few trees, they set down their packs and enjoyed the beautiful vista spread out before them. They could see the mountains now, stretching up to pierce the clouds. At the far end of the meadow, rocky slopes jutted up to meet the looming mountains.

"Looks like fun," Ulfgar muttered.

"Yeah!" Sylica agreed, oblivious to Ulfgar's tone of voice.

Thea glanced at Roland, but he was already making a ring for a fire.

"Who's hunting today?" Thea asked.

"I'll go," Ulfgar offered. "Saw a promising spot just past that stream."

"Thanks, Ulf," Roland grinned. "I could use some more training time." Grabbing his knives, Roland found a clear, flat area, a distance out into the meadow.

Sylica grinned. "Daisy and I are going to go pick flowers!"

Thea glanced around. Wildflower season was clearly past, but she could see a few half-wilted blooms scattered among the grasses.

"Don't go too far," she called as Sylica skipped off across the mountainside.

Thea collected some fallen branches and started the fire. In the meadow, Roland began his familiar routine, muscles straining. Light glinted as he swung his blades.

Thea shook herself and returned to her task. The fire had burned down to a mass of smouldering twigs.

Starting again, she did her best to stay focused, and soon the campfire was crackling cheerily.

A short distance away, Zanele was sorting through the contents of her medical bag. Cheeky darted around her, then nipped inside the bag as Thea approached.

"Zanele, could I talk with you for a moment?"

"Of course." Zanele scooched over so Thea could have space to sit.

"Thanks." Thea sat down and found herself fidgeting self-consciously. She knew she wanted to talk to someone, but now she was unsure of what to say.

Zanele gave her a knowing look. "It's about Roland?"

Thea felt her face get hot. She nodded. "I keep thinking about him more and more."

"So?"

"It's like I can't help myself. I've always loved him, of course, like he was my brother and my best friend, but I don't want to just be his best friend anymore, I want ..." Her face grew hot again as she shied away from putting words to her feelings. Her voice constricted to a whisper. "Is that wrong?"

Zanele leaned back and gave Thea an amused glance. "I've spent the night with at least five different people I grew up with as brothers. Trust me, it's fine."

Thea looked at Zanele's twinkling eyes. "Really?"

Zanele shrugged. "Fauns enjoy it when the mood takes us. We can't take so long thinking about things as you do. If we did, we'd be dead before we decided anything!"

"I—I guess so." It was so hard to wrap her mind around the life expectancy of a Faun. They had so little time, but Elves had forever!

"Look." Zanele set a hand on Thea's shoulder. "Everyone can see that you and Roland like each other. There's no reason why it can't be more than that."

"But he seems so preoccupied. He used to spend time with me whenever he could, but now I hardly get a chance to talk to him."

"Of course not." Zanele gave her a wry grin. "He's just like Thabani. Whenever Thabani is travelling with people he cares about, he gets all caught up with caution and safety. Take it as a complement. Roland is taking care of you the best way he knows how."

"But he's taking care of all of us."

Zanele gave her a sidelong glance. "Sure."

Thea stared across the hillside to where Roland was repeating his drills. His red granite skin was smoother than it had been. In his body and the determination in his eyes, the last signs of childhood were fading away.

Thea became aware of Zanele's amused glance.

"Yeah. You're falling hard."

Thea scrambled to find something else to say. "You talked about Thabani, when he travels. Who does he really care about?"

"The Faunlets, of course." Zanele smiled. "He'd die for them in a heartbeat."

"Does he have children of his own?"

"Not sure." Zanele shrugged. "We don't really keep track of parentage. As soon as we're old enough, we run around with the rest of the kids like a pack of cubs. Our whole tribe is our family. The older Fauns are our mothers and fathers. The young Fauns are everyone's Faunlets. Why would we only want one or two parents to show us love and attention? That would be a very lonely life." Zanele smiled. "I've had a couple of Faunlets myself. Sometimes I forget which ones were mine, because they're all mine. That's the way it is for the Fauns."

Thea thought about her own childhood: her father busy helping his brother with the leadership of the First House, her mother hurrying from one social function to another. They never seemed to have much time for Thea, leaving her in the care of nannies, servants, and tutors.

Roland's childhood hadn't been too different. His mother was head of the merchants' guild, and his father was one of the most successful merchants in the city. Roland had practically raised himself, sneaking away from his lessons to watch the racing ships.

That's why they had found each other. They needed companionship and someone to be there for them. Now these new, overwhelming feelings made her want to risk it all, in hope of something more.

Thea sighed. "What if I do something wrong? I'd have to live with that forever."

Zanele leaned closer, looking straight in her eyes. "Or you learn and move on. That's a lesson for everyone, not just the Fauns. We just have to learn it quicker than most."

"She's right, you know."

Thea turned to see Ulfgar standing behind them.

He shuffled uncomfortably. "Sorry to listen in, but I've been learning about that too. The Deity doesn't want us to live in fear, you know. That's the Enemy's talk."

Thea looked at Ulfgar in surprise, but he seemed oblivious to her gaze.

"You never really know how long you have with someone," he muttered, "Faun or not. It'd be a shame to waste that."

Zanele gave Ulfgar a sly glance.

Ulfgar reddened and stammered, "Don't read too much into that."

Thea looked at Ulfgar. His spirit had been shifting so slowly she'd never really seen just how light it had become.

"Thank you, Ulfgar." She smiled. "I'll remember that."

Ulfgar's head scrunched down between his shoulders. He frowned. "Don't you read too much into that either."

The next day the clouds were low and heavy with the threat of rain as Sylica led the way into the mountains, skipping cheerfully with Daisy at her side. Soon she slowed to a walk, then stopped at the foot of a cliff, breathing heavily.

"Out of breath?" Ulfgar gave her a skeptical side-eye. "Thought you'd just fly up or something."

Sylica rolled her eyes. "I'm not a Dryad, remember? I

can't just fly when I want to."

"You did once," Ulfgar muttered.

Thea's stomach sank as she stared up the cliff, its upper reaches fading into grey obscurity. "There will be a way up, right?"

"There has to be." Roland's gaze turned to a small animal path skirting the foot of the cliff. "Come on, let's find it."

The path led to a scree-filled gully. Roland eyed it doubtfully, but Sylica pushed past him, eagerly scampering up the narrow incline.

With a clattering rumble, the slope gave way beneath her.

"Whoa!" Sylica fell, carried by the momentum of the rockslide beneath her feet.

"Look out!" Roland pushed Thea back as the cascade of loose stones tumbled towards them.

Magic surged and Zanele sprang across the tumbling rocks. Grabbing Sylica, she pulled her back to the shelter of the cliff.

Everyone stared as the rockslide tumbled on, slowed, and came to rest in a jumbled heap. Overhead, the rumble of falling stone echoed from the clifftops.

Sylica blinked, then her face lit up. "That was fun! Let's—"

"No!" Ulfgar glared.

Sylica deflated. "Oh. Okay."

Roland eyed the rockslide with pursed lips. "Not that way. Let's find a different one."

With a nod, Ulfgar turned and led the way along the foot of the cliff.

Workday stretched on, but no safe way presented itself. Ulfgar plodded along with his head sunk between his shoulders. Roland's worried gaze moved from the imposing wall of rock to the dark storm clouds overhead.

Thea's heart sank. If they had to, they could try to climb, but they only had one rope and no way to get Daisy up the cliff face with them. Sylica would balk at that, and anyways, they couldn't leave the dragon treasure behind.

"Wait—" Roland stopped, staring up the cliff with widening eyes. "That looks like a ledge! Hang on, I'll go look." Dropping his bedroll, Roland scrambled up the craggy rock face until he reached what looked like a smooth patch of stone, set back from the cliff face below it. Crouching half out of view, he turned to look down. "It is a ledge! It's a lot wider than it looks from down below, almost like some kind of path. I think we found our way up!"

At Thea's side, Zanele gave a sigh of relief.

Sylica clapped her hands. "I want to see!" Scrambling up the rocks, she joined Roland on the ledge, peering this way and that with interest.

Daisy whined and scratched at the rocks.

"All right," Ulfgar grumbled, lifting Daisy over his head. "Up you go then."

With a scramble of claws, Daisy propelled herself up the remaining rock face, scattering bits of stone in all directions. On the ledge at last, she sat down at Sylica's side with an expression of smug accomplishment on her strange metallic face.

"Good girl, Daisy!" Sylica beamed.

With a grunt, Ulfgar heaved himself onto the ledge.

Thea picked up Roland's bedroll and scrambled up to join them.

At the foot of the cliff, Zanele stepped back a couple of paces, then sprang up the cliffside, landing lightly beside Ulfgar with a smile.

Cheeky clung to the back of her head, pulling chunks of hair loose from Zanele's braid in a desperate attempt to hold on.

Gingerly, Zanele untangled the little squirrel's claws from her hair and lifted her back down to her shoulder, muttering something under her breath in the language of the Fauns.

"Okay." Roland eyed the ledge that stretched along the cliffside before them. It sloped gently upwards. "Step as carefully as you can. If you're having any trouble let me know."

He led the way, with Thea following close behind. They walked in single file, hugging the side of the path away from the sheer drop.

Behind Thea, Sylica's voice chattered on like a never ending avalanche. "Wow! Look at how high we're getting! We're really mountain climbing now! I wonder if this ledge keeps going up forever and ever! If it does, does that mean we're almost at the dragons now? I'd really like to see a dragon again!"

"Again?" Thea glanced back.

"Sure, I saw dragons before, haven't you?"

"No."

"Oh." Sylica considered this for a moment. "Well dragons are *really* big when they're the big ones. They came by to talk sometimes, and once they asked if I wanted to come somewhere with them but my mom and my dad said no because I wasn't grown up enough yet. Ooh! Look down there!"

The ledge wound higher and higher up the side of the

mountain. The cliff at their side dropped to a terrifying depth, but the ledge remained wide enough that they didn't have to get too close to the edge. Strands of cloud blew past, driven by the gusting wind.

Roland glanced back at Thea. "You doing alright? I've been looking for a good place to stop and rest, but we might have to push on till we get to the top."

"I'm doing alright." Thea glanced back at the others. They seemed to be keeping up without any trouble.

"I don't like how cold that wind is getting." Roland frowned. "Do you feel it?"

Thea nodded. Even though it was still workday, the sky was growing darker.

Roland's lips drew into a thin line. "We shouldn't stop here." He turned to continue up the ridge.

"Roland?"

Roland glanced back at Thea. "Yes?"

Thea's mouth went dry. She wanted to tell him that she liked it better when he was looking at her. That something hurt inside her when he turned away. But how could she say that?

There it was—that look in his eyes again. She wanted him to look at her like that forever.

Something bumped into Thea from behind.

"Hey!" Sylica called. "Why'd we stop?"

"Sorry," Thea muttered.

Roland gave her an apologetic smile. "Maybe later."

Turning, he continued along the ledge. Thea followed, listening to the clatter of Sylica and the others following behind.

Something caught her ear—a rumble like thunder in the distance.

She paused, listening.

It was louder now—a rumble of grinding rock, growing closer, echoing across the mountainside. Beneath their feet, the stone began to tremble.

Chapter Eleven

Roland froze. Thea stared past him, her heart pounding in her ears. The rocks on the path ahead of them were moving. They weren't falling, they were gathering together into a heap—growing taller—forming into a shape that looked like a troll, but much, much bigger. The creature turned and faced them with glowing eyes.

"What's that?" Thea gasped.

Roland drew his knives. "Stay back!"

"Oh look!" Sylica called. "A really big troll!"

"That is not a troll." Zanele stared out from behind Sylica with narrowing eyes. "Trolls never get that big."

The giant, stony creature stepped towards them. The rock beneath their feet trembled.

Sylica stared. "That's really big."

"Let me at 'em," Ulfgar growled. "Let me at 'em."

Roland waved him back, his eyes not leaving the giant creature's face. "Wait, Ulf. There isn't room."

Thea stared at the massive bulk of the stone monster, a feeling of horror creeping over her senses. This creature had no spirit or life inside it at all. As far as her elf-sight could see, it was no different than the stone beneath their feet, but somehow it was *alive*.

Was there a caster nearby? Thea stared across the mountainside, but the only spirits she could see were those of her companions.

"Stone golem," Ulfgar muttered. "I've heard tales ..."

Roland waved his hand with a surge of magic.

The stone golem continued its advance, every step shaking the mountainside beneath them.

"Banish didn't work," Roland hissed to Thea with widening eyes. "Why didn't it work?"

"That thing isn't dark." Thea stared as the golem stepped closer, sending shivers through the stone. "It isn't even alive."

Roland gripped his knives and leaped at the golem, blades flashing with light. There was another surge of magic, and Roland struck. His old knife skidded across the surface of rock, but the trollsbane knife cut deep.

The golem roared and swatted Roland away.

Roland slid towards the edge of the cliff, scrambling to catch himself. His legs swung out into space and he clung to the ledge, digging his elbows into the fissures in the rock.

Thea ran to him. Grabbing his arm, she pulled with all her strength.

"Out of my way!" Ulfgar shoved past and charged at the golem, swinging his great axe.

The golem stepped forward to meet him. Swinging its giant arms, the golem struck Ulfgar in the head and sent him tumbling back. Tripping over Thea, Ulfgar crashed into Sylica, landing in an uncomfortable heap.

The golem loomed over them.

Roland pulled himself back onto the ledge and darted forward, jabbing up into the golem's midriff with his trollsbane knife.

The golem's roar shook the cliff beneath their feet. It swung its arm and Roland ducked.

He wasn't fast enough.

The golem grabbed Roland's leg and lifted him

slowly into the air.

Roland swung wildly with his knife, trying to land a blow, his eyes wide with terror.

Don't hurt him! Thea threw her magic at the golem and felt it pass right though. There was no mind there to affect.

With a heave, the golem threw Roland over the side of the cliff.

Rock erupted from the ground at Thea's feet. It jutted out through the precipice, growing faster than sight into a massive ridge of rock, long and flat, with sheer cliffs dropping off each side.

It appeared in an instant, and Roland landed on its far end in a crumpled heap.

"Roland!" Thea ran to him, the strange new rock pounding beneath her feet. Crouching by his side, Thea held his hand. His knives lay beside him. Blood oozed from a gash on his head.

Footsteps hurried towards her.

"Is he okay?" Sylica demanded.

Feverishly, Thea felt Roland's chest. Was his heart even beating? "I—I don't know."

"My job." Zanele budged Thea away. "Healer coming through."

Thea watched breathlessly as Zanele knelt over Roland's motionless body.

Ulfgar grabbed Sylica, gesturing wildly at the long ridge of rock beneath their feet. "How did you do that? You just made a bloody mountain out of *nothing*! Is no one talking about this?"

Zanele glanced up at Thea. "I've seen worse." She spoke lightly, but her eyes weren't smiling.

Thea swallowed. "Is he going to be alright?"

The mountain rumbled, sending shudders through the stone beneath their feet. The golem was advancing along the narrow ridge, every step sending fragments of rock tumbling to unseen depths below.

Thea stared in alarm. With sheer cliffs all around them, there was no way to escape. "Sylica ... want to try doing that again?"

Sylica looked like she was about to cry. "I don't know how I did it! How am I supposed to do it again?"

"We can't stay here." Ulfgar looked from the golem to Roland's prostrate form. "Zanele?"

"He's stable, but we shouldn't move him. Not till I've checked his spine."

The golem continued to advance along the ridge.

Ulfgar threw a handaxe. It rebounded off the golem's shoulder and disappeared over the cliff. The golem didn't flinch.

Heart pounding, Thea nocked an arrow and shot. It glanced off the golem without leaving a mark.

Fear twisted in the pit of her stomach. If Raybow couldn't help ...

"Zanele. We need to get out of here. Now."

Zanele's eyes flashed. "Do you *want* him to die? I need time!"

"I—I've got my mace." Sylica stared at the advancing golem, her eyes wide with fear.

"Sylica—" Thea's words died in her throat. The golem was too strong. She couldn't charm it. It almost killed Roland, and it was coming. Coming closer with every step.

"I knew it," Ulfgar growled, gripping his great axe. "I knew it. Deity help me, I *tried* not to care, but I can't do it. I care, alright? I care about every stupid one of you, and now I'm going to lose you again, but I don't care. I'm going to do it, because I'm not going to watch you die."

Ulfgar straightened his helmet and tightened the straps on his pack.

"Right. Here I go. Maybe I'll see you around someday."

Lowering his head, Ulfgar charged towards the golem.

The golem swung its arm. Ulfgar jumped. Grabbing its swinging arm, Ulfgar clung to it as it swung up and over the edge of the cliff. The golem staggered, thrown off balance by the sudden weight. Its foot slipped off the edge of the cliff, and it fell.

Thea rushed to the edge of the precipice, staring as Ulfgar and the golem tumbled into the depths with a rumble and clatter of stones.

Then there was silence.

"Ulfgar!" Sylica stared. "What ..."

"Zanele, can you—" Thea turned to face the Faun, then faltered as she saw the horror in her eyes. "... shield him?"

Zanele shook her head. "It wouldn't make a difference. Not from that high."

"I don't understand." Sylica stared down the cliff with a bewildered expression. "Why did he do that?"

Daisy sat by her side and whined.

"He was saving us." Thea's voice was quiet. Something twisted in her gut until it was hard to breathe. It didn't make sense. Why did he say that he might see them someday? What did it have to do with him losing people again?

"We need to go down there." She was surprised by

the force in her own voice. "I don't know what he was doing, but—but maybe he's down there somewhere."

"And flat as a griddle." Zanele glared. "What will there be to see?"

"I need to know."

"And what about your boyfriend?"

Thea stared at Roland, surging emotions vying for her attention. "Is he going to be alright?"

"Yes." Zanele conceded. "He will have a killer headache when he wakes up."

"Then I think I need to go down. Roland will understand."

Zanele regarded her silently for a moment. "Fine. If you give me a moment, I will finish what I'm doing here. I want to come with you."

"But—"

Zanele glared. "If there is any chance Ulfgar is still alive, I want to be there."

Thea watched as Zanele carefully felt along Roland's neck and spine. Magic surged, and a shudder ran through Zanele's body. Her face contorted in pain.

Thea stared. "Are you alright?"

Zanele nodded, taking a slow, shaky breath. "It was worse than I expected. That's all."

Turning back to Roland, Zanele carefully rolled him onto his side, then bandaged his forehead.

As soon as that was done, she slung her satchel back over her shoulder. "Sylica, you and Cheeky stay here with Roland. If he wakes, make sure he doesn't move. We still have his bedroll? Good. Cover him with that so he doesn't get cold."

Turning, she trotted briskly back along the ridge. Thea hurried to catch up.

From the ledge, it was easier to really look at the new spur of rock. It rose out of the depths, solid and real, even more massive than Thea had realized. The tiny figures of Sylica and Daisy watching them go made her stomach turn.

She'd be right back. She just had to know what happened.

Thea hurried along the ledge, lower and lower, with Zanele at her heels. Soon the spur was lost in the clouds behind them.

When they reached the ground again, they hurried along the foot of the cliff until the new spur of rock loomed in front of them.

Getting her bearings, Thea made her way to the place where Ulfgar must have fallen. Would he—no, there was nothing but boulders littering the rocky ground.

She glanced around. Did she have the wrong spot?

Zanele stepped back, eyeing the spur of rock. "There aren't any ledges. There should be a body. He fell right here."

They searched between the stones, back and forth along the base of the cliff. No body. No pack. Not even any splinters of the barrel.

Zanele's eyes widened. "I don't understand. He's just *gone*."

Maybe I'll see you around someday. Why had Ulfgar said that? It was like he thought—like he *knew* he wasn't going to die. But somehow he was still losing them.

Thea turned to Zanele. "Did he tell you anything? I saw you talking with him. Did he say anything about his past at all?"

The ground rumbled beneath their feet. Slowly, the

boulders at the foot of the precipice started to move. Drawing together. Rebuilding a giant, terrifying form.

Thea stared. How was that possible?

The stone golem stood before them again—larger and even more terrifying than before.

"Get back!" Zanele hissed. "Get back!"

Panic surged through Thea's body. Turning to run, her foot struck something and she fell.

A voice shouted, loud above the rumble of grinding rock.

In an instant, everything was silent. Thea scrambled to her feet.

The stone golem stood still. Its glowing eyes faded and disappeared. Then, with a shudder, it collapsed into a heap of stones.

The stones didn't move.

Thea stared at it, then turned to Zanele. "What—"

"Quiet!" Zanele hissed. She stared around the rocky mountainside with narrowing eyes.

Something stepped out from between the rocks. It was shaped like a human or an Elf, but larger, and its features were lizard-like in appearance. It was covered in orange scales, and its head bore a large crest that stretched from its forehead to its back. A staff was in its hand and a satchel hung over its shoulder.

"Greetings, travellers." The stranger spoke in Common. "This is a fortunate meeting."

Thea stared at the strange creature standing before them.

"Who are you?" Zanele demanded.

"I am Awdub Hwasan. I was travelling through this region and I heard sounds of combat coming from these cliffs. I hope you have not been hurt."

"Not at all." Zanele eyed the stranger suspiciously. "But I'd like to know how you made that golem disappear, Awdub Hwasan."

"You can call me Hwasan." The stranger smiled. "I am a scholar. There is an old and secret language that was used to create the golems. By speaking the correct words, it is possible to unmake them."

Zanele didn't seem impressed. "If you're a scholar, what are you doing out here in the mountains?"

"Research." Hwasan smiled. "I can only spend so much time behind tables filled with scrolls before I hear the call of the wide world again. I am glad I happened upon you. Sadly it is not too uncommon to meet stone golems in the mountains. You could have been seriously hurt."

The spirit inside Hwasan was dark, but not completely. A pale glow pulsed behind the swirling darkness.

"Sorry if this is rude, Hwasan," Thea ventured, "but what are you?"

"I am a Minathril. Have you not met a Minathril before?"

"No, I haven't." She looked at the Minathril's narrow, dragon-like face. "Are you really half-dragons?"

"No." Hwasan seemed amused by the thought. "No, we are our own sort of people. We live with the Dragons, though, so I see why people might get confused."

Thea's heart leapt. "Could you lead us to where the dragons live?"

Zanele shot her a sharp glance.

Hwasan seemed to consider this. "Perhaps I could. Which Dragon are you looking for?"

Thea hesitated. "Maybe you should come and meet the rest of our party. Then we can talk about it."

Hwasan glanced around. The colour on their scales faded a little. "And where would they be?"

"You'll see," Zanele glared.

As they walked back to the ledge, Zanele kept a cautious eye on the mountainside surrounding them. "So, you're all alone, Mr. or Ms. Hwasan?"

"Mr." Hwasan supplied, "and yes, I am travelling alone. I hope that does not affect your opinion of my trustworthiness."

"No." Zanele considered this. "Just my opinion of your intelligence."

"The mountains are the home of the Minathrils. There are many dangers, but I have faced them before."

"Huh." Zanele didn't seem to be impressed.

Returning to the start of the ledge, Thea scrambled up.

Hwasan grasped his staff and climbed up after her.

Zanele followed last.

The cliffside was shrouded in mist. Thea walked as quickly as she dared, with Hwasan and Zanele following close behind. When they reached the great spur of rock, she turned to the Minathril. "Wait here. I am going to get my friends."

Hwasan stared at the narrow ridge with a strange expression. "I cannot say I remember that being there."

Thea shot Zanele a sidelong glance. "It's new."

Leaving Hwasan behind, she hurried along the narrow ridge. As Roland's motionless form came into view, worry rose to choke her again.

"Hi Thea!" Sylica called. "Did you know that clouds are cold inside? I always thought they would be light and fluffy, so it's kind of disappointing."

Thea knelt beside Roland. He opened his eyes and looked at her, a gentle smile creasing his face.

Thea grasped his hand. "Are you okay?"

"I think so." His voice was soft and distant. "Sylica said I couldn't get up."

"Zanele didn't want you moving until she had a chance to check on you again."

Roland's eyes drifted shut, then sprang open again. "The stone golem?"

"It's gone."

Roland frowned. "Sylica said Ulfgar ..."

"He pulled it down over the cliff."

Roland thought for a moment. "Is he dead?"

"He's gone."

Roland closed his eyes. Thea felt his shoulders tremble.

"He's just gone," she repeated. "There was no body. No sign of his pack. Nothing."

Roland looked at her sharply, confusion battling its way across his face. "Is my head not working right, or does that not make sense?"

"You're right. It doesn't make sense. But—" she glanced out at the fog surrounding them, "—that might have to wait till later."

Roland grasped her hand tighter. "I don't want you to leave again."

Thea stared down at Roland. Her gut twisted with how close she had come to losing him. "We're all going together. Zanele?"

Zanele approached out of the mist. "How's the patient?"

Cheeky jumped out from behind Roland and

clambered up Zanele to sit on her shoulder.

"He seems alright," Thea said. "Can he get up now?"

Zanele knelt beside Roland. After questioning and examining him, she seemed reluctantly satisfied. "You can get up, just be careful."

Gingerly, Roland lifted himself into a sitting position. His face spasmed with pain and he held his head.

Zanele pursed her lips knowingly. "Take your time."

Holding Roland's arm, Thea supported him as he got unsteadily to his feet. He reached down to grab his knives and almost collapsed.

"I'll get those." Zanele scooped up the knives and Thea put them back in their sheaths.

Roland took a few breaths and seemed a bit steadier.

"Sorry I didn't deal with the headache," Zanele grimaced, "but I wanted some magic left, just in case ..." Her eyes stared beyond the edge of the cliff, as if seeing something she never wanted to see again.

"Come on!" Sylica bounded ahead of them like a puppy that had been restrained for too long.

Zanele leaned close to Roland and spoke in a low voice. "We have company, it seems. There was a Minathril at the foot of the cliff. He has yet to give a satisfactory account of himself."

"He knows the mountains," Thea explained, "and he might be able to lead us to the dragons."

"Hello!" Sylica bounded up to the Minathril. "I'm Sylica, what's your name? I haven't met a Minathril in a really really long time! Do you like my dragon? Her name is Daisy."

Hwasan stared at Sylica, his scales blanching into a peculiar shade of grey. "Awdub Hwasan, at your service."

As Thea approached the ledge, Hwasan's eyes took in Roland leaning on her shoulder. "I see there were some injuries after all."

"That's none of your business," Zanele snapped.

Leading the way, she strode along the ledge, with Sylica and Daisy scampering after her. Hwasan followed them, and Thea and Roland came last.

As they left the ridge of rock behind, Thea glanced back down the precipice. Ulfgar was gone. She listened desperately to hear the clatter of his armour and his grumbling voice, but the wind that blew past her was empty.

Wearily, she plodded on, clinging to Roland's arm. His familiar, comforting presence eased the ache in her heart.

She never thought she'd lose Ulfgar. He was always just *there*, even though he acted like he didn't want to be. In the end he'd shown how much he cared for them, then he was gone. In a strange, horrible way, it would have been easier if there had been a body, but as it was ... would she ever know what happened to him?

She held tighter to Roland's arm. Arl was dead. Ulfgar was gone. And Roland ... Thea shivered. If it wasn't for Sylica ... Sylica and her strange, unpredictable magic.

At the top of the cliff at last, Zanele led them on, past the windswept slopes, to a patch of scraggly trees huddled in the lee of another great cliff. Once everyone had gathered around, Zanele turned to Hwasan. "Alright, Minathril. Explain yourself."

Hwasan raised his hands in a helpless gesture. "I have already said all there is to tell. I am a scholar, travelling the mountains for my research. I heard shouts and sounds of combat, and was happily able to offer some relief." His scales gleamed orange and he glanced at Sylica. "I do not wish to impose myself on you, but if you require assistance finding your way through the mountains ..."

Thea looked from Roland to Zanele. "We *are* wanting to reach the home of the dragons, and it would be helpful to have a guide."

Zanele crossed her arms. "What I want to know is how you made the golem go away."

Hwasan smiled. "I will explain it again for those who were not there. Golems are created and sustained by magic. Through study it is possible to know the secret words that are the key to their life force. Speak the proper incantation, and their life force is broken."

Thea glanced at Sylica. "Did the golem have magic on it?"

Sylica nodded. "'Do what I say' magic."

"And what do you know about magic?" Zanele eyed Hwasan suspiciously. "Are you a caster?"

"No," Hwasan sighed. "I have no skill in the art myself, but I have studied it, out of interest."

"Where are you from?" Thea asked.

"The mountains are my home. I was raised at Dark Rock, and I've wandered the mountains since then."

"So you know these lands we are passing through?"

"I do. Not as well as some other parts of the mountains, but I have been here before."

"We will not take you out of your way?"

"It would be a little out of my way," Hwasan conceded, "but that does not trouble me. I would be happy to help."

"And why would you want to help us?" Zanele's eyes

flashed. "You're a Minathril!"

The colour on Hwasan's scales faded. "Why should a Minathril not help?"

"Because you don't care about us! You hide up in your mountains and do nothing to help the world! My people have wandered the forests since Raphtova was formed and not once have I heard of any of your kind coming beyond the foothills. If the Minathrils actually did something, maybe my people wouldn't keep dying!"

Hwasan stared at Zanele, his scales fading into blue. "Your people died too?"

"Many of them have." Zanele was still shaking with rage. "And I feel it *every time*."

"My people also died." A silver sheen glimmered on the blue of his scales. "I am sorry to hear of your loss."

"Your people died?" Thea asked gently.

Hwasan looked at the ground. "My crew. Killed in a Dragon raid. I was still young at the time."

"But I thought the Minathrils lived with the dragons."

"We do, and we serve our Dragon with our life." His scales darkened into brown. "When the Dragons fight, the Minathrils pay the price."

Sylica stared at Hwasan. "You keep changing colours!"

Hwasan faded into a light tan. "Yes. All Minathrils do."

"Why?"

Hwasan hesitated. "That is just the way we were made."

"I think it's really pretty!" Sylica beamed. "I like that my skin is green, but you get to have all the colours at the same time! Well, I guess not at the *same* time, but most people only get to have one or two colours ever! My candy gets to have all the colours too. Let's see what colour comes out next!" She rummaged in her bag and pulled out a neatly wrapped candy. "Ooh! A pink one! Here you go!"

She shoved the candy into the hand of the quickly greying Minathril. He stared at it, and his scales flushed a brilliant orange. "Thank you for your generosity, but I am not hungry at the moment."

"Oh. Okay!" Sylica took the candy back and fed it to Daisy, who yapped and jumped around her excitedly.

Roland set a hand on Thea's shoulder and turned to Hwasan. "We appreciate your offer, but I hope you can understand that bringing someone along with us is a decision we shouldn't take lightly. We'll need some time to think and talk about it."

"Of course, I completely understand." Hwasan smiled. "If I can be of any service, just let me know."

As soon as Hwasan's attention was diverted elsewhere, Roland pulled Thea aside. "What did you see?"

Thea looked up into Roland's thoughtful eyes. "His spirit is mostly dark, but there is light there too."

"Do you think we can trust him?"

"He is no darker than others we have trusted before, like Arl when I first met them, or even Ulfgar. If Hwasan travels with us, maybe his spirit will start changing, just like theirs did."

Roland nodded thoughtfully. "Thabani said there were Minathrils in the mountains. The Messengers haven't been in communication with any of them yet, so I don't really know what to expect. Hwasan would be a helpful way in, though, if he's trustworthy enough."

Thea nodded. "I think it's worth it, to get to the dragons faster."

Roland considered this. "I agree."

Thea went to find Zanele. She found her building a small campfire in a sheltered spot, while keeping a not-too-subtle eye on what Hwasan was doing.

Thea crouched beside her. "I think we should give him a chance."

Zanele raised an eyebrow.

"I've told you about my spirit sight. I can see that there is darkness inside him, but there's light inside him too. Maybe we can help him while he travels with us, just like you were helping Ulfgar."

Zanele frowned.

"You heard about how his crew died. Maybe that's where the darkness comes from."

Zanele sighed. "Fine. We'll give him a chance. Just remember—that is not the same as trusting him."

Through the trees, Thea watched Hwasan approach Sylica. He gestured to Daisy. "I have never seen a creature like that before."

Sylica beamed. "Daisy is a very special kind of dragon."

"I can see that." He knelt beside Daisy and got licked in the face. "And I can see that Daisy is very friendly."

"Daisy is my best friend in the whole world!"

Hwasan smiled. "Everyone needs a best friend, I think." His scales glowed a bright yellow-orange as he watched Daisy leap about. His thick tail swept slowly from side to side, just brushing the ground.

Thea smiled. Sylica wouldn't have any problem with someone new joining their party.

As everyone was settling down for staph, Thea

approached the Minathril.

"Hwasan, we've decided that we'd like you to come with us, for a while at least. If you could show us the way, we would really appreciate it."

Hwasan's scales shone a brilliant yellow. "I am happy to help. Which Dragon are you looking for?"

Thea glanced at Roland. "We don't really know. Probably any dragon would work."

"Any *good* dragon," Roland corrected, "as long as it would be willing to speak with us."

Hwasan's scales flickered with a hint of gold. "That will be the hard part, finding a Dragon who is willing to speak with anyone. If you are not set on one certain Dragon, I can lead you to Meiling. Your chances with her are as good as any, and you will not have to walk as far."

"How far will it be?"

Hwasan gave her a sidelong glance. "That depends on how good you are at climbing."

Chapter Twelve

Thea slept, then took her turn on watch. Sitting close to the fire, she stared out over the desolate mountainside. Mist blew by in ragged threads, driven by the moaning wind. It almost sounded like voices.

Thea shivered.

Around her, the others slept.

Again and again, Thea's eyes were drawn to Roland's motionless form, trying to forget the sight of him lying bloody and unconscious at the edge of the cliff.

He was breathing peacefully now. The bandage around his head was bloodstained, but it wasn't new blood.

He was going to be okay.

Thea looked at him again, just to make sure.

As the others rose from their rest, Hwasan folded up his sleeping mat, then regarded the group with a solemn gaze. "When you are ready, I would be glad to show you the way."

Thea glanced from Roland to Zanele. "I think we will stay here today."

Hwasan's scales greyed. "You said you wanted to speak to a Dragon."

"We do, but today has been ... hard. We need to rest before we carry on."

"I see." Hwasan hesitated. "Is there any way I can be of service?"

Zanele made a face. "You don't need to be of service. We're just going to be resting, maybe looking for something to eat."

Hwasan's scales blazed orange. "I can help with foraging. I am very familiar with the plants and herbs of the mountains."

Zanele frowned, but Thea laid a hand on her shoulder. "Thank you, Hwasan. We'd appreciate that."

After Zanele and Hwasan left to go foraging, Roland got out his knives, giving them a couple of experimental swings.

Thea knew that determined gleam in his eyes. "Roland ..."

"Yes?"

Thea's mouth went dry. "I was wondering ... could we sit and talk for a while? It's been so long since we just spent time together."

A smile lit Roland's face. "Of course. I'd enjoy that too." Sheathing his knives, he joined Thea by the fire. "Training can wait till later."

She glanced at the bandage still wrapped around his head. "Doesn't it hurt?"

"It does, but I feel a lot better already."

"I'm glad." Thea couldn't keep the fervor out of her voice.

Roland's eyes grew thoughtful. "That was a close call, wasn't it?"

"If you'd died, that would have been awful!" The words tumbled out, unchecked. "I didn't—I didn't want you to die."

Roland took her hand and held it tight.

Thea took a trembling breath. "It happened so fast. Like when Arl died. There was no warning or time to say goodbye." She shivered. "At least then we knew the danger. We knew we might not make it out. This time we were just travelling. We didn't know anything was there. Then you almost died, and Ulfgar ... ."

"Disappeared." Roland frowned and rubbed his head.

"We looked everywhere." Thea gave a helpless gesture. "I don't understand what happened."

"There was no sign of him?"

"Nothing. If he'd ... if he'd died, we should have seen something. If he'd survived the fall and somehow been able to walk away, there should at least have been splinters of barrel left behind. But there was nothing."

"He's just gone."

Thea nodded. Wind hissed in the wizened branches overhead.

Roland shifted a stone with his foot. "I keep looking around and expecting to see him."

Thea looked into Roland's troubled eyes. "I know. I do too."

The fire settled in a shower of sparks.

Thea watched the small points of light fade away. "Before he fell, he said he might see us again someday. I don't know what he meant, but maybe he was right."

"I hope so." Roland stared out through the blowing tendrils of mist. "If it wasn't for him we wouldn't have made it out, would we?"

Thea shook her head. "And if it wasn't for Sylica ... if her magic hadn't done that ..."

"She made a new piece of the mountain?"

Thea nodded.

"Zanele said that, but I thought I must have heard her wrong."

"You didn't hear wrong. Sylica made a whole ridge of rock appear that wasn't there before. Just in time to catch you."

Roland slowly shook his head. "That magic of hers. Did she mean to do it?"

"No. It just happened. She doesn't know how."

"But it was just in time to save me."

Thea nodded and squeezed his hand. "I'm so glad it was."

"I am too." Roland bent closer. His arm slipped around her waist.

Looking into his eyes, Thea's heart hammered in her chest.

"Excuse me—"

Thea tore her gaze away to see Hwasan standing at the edge of the campsite, a bundle of greens and roots in his hands. He set them down. "Sorry to interrupt, but I couldn't see Sylica anywhere. Do you know where she is?"

Thea looked at Roland in consternation. Sylica was missing? Anything could have happened.

She scrambled to her feet. "Have either of you seen her since staph?"

"No." Roland grimaced. "I didn't even see which way she went."

Thea bit her lip and glanced around the mountainside. There were only two ways she could have gone, without going steeply up or down.

Roland slung his rope over his shoulder. "If you go one way, I'll search the other. Hwasan, will you join me?"

"Gladly." Hwasan bowed.

Thea hurried away. Beyond a shoulder of rock, she

found Zanele digging in the ground with a stick. Cheeky sat on her shoulder, chewing a nut.

"Zanele, have you seen Sylica?"

"Not since staph. Why?"

"None of us have seen her at all."

"Huh. She can take care of herself." Zanele pulled a root out of the hard-packed ground.

"What if she's stuck again?"

"You won't always be around to help her. She's going to have to learn to take care of herself sometime."

"But it wasn't like this before. If the dragon treasure is causing these magic flares somehow, we just have to get to the dragons."

"Don't expect the dragons to fix everything," Zanele snapped, scooping up the results of her foraging. "Now excuse me." She hurried back towards the campsite.

Thea continued along the mountainside. There were so many places to search—down narrow gorges, around shoulders of rock, in patches of scraggly trees, and through shallow caves.

Finally Thea rounded a point of rock to find a small mountain meadow, and there was Sylica, sitting next to a stream. She was scrubbing her arms furiously.

"Sylica!"

Sylica jumped and attempted to dry her arms on her glittering armour. "What? Oh, hi Thea!"

Thea sat down beside her. Sylica's emerald-like skin gleamed brighter than ever. "What are you doing?"

"I was thinking—" Sylica fidgeted self-consciously, "—that maybe my skin is only green because there's something on it, like grass stains. If I washed it off, maybe I would see lots of different colours."

Thea gave her a knowing look. "Like a Minathril?"

Sylica stared at her arms. "Ghuuuuuhhh. Hnnggaaaaa. Grrruuuungggllffff!"

Thea watched her straining muscles. "Are you trying to change the colour on your arms?"

Sylica deflated. "It's not working."

"Sylica." Thea looked straight in her eyes. "You are not a Minathril. You don't have scales and you look nothing like a lizard."

"But their colours are so pretty."

"They are, but that doesn't mean you're not pretty."

"But I don't even know what I am!"

"Maybe you're an Elf."

"Thea," Sylica sighed, "I don't look like you at *all*. You're yellow. I'm green. Your hair is all coppery. Mine is white and green."

"Roland and I are different colours too. Elves are like that."

"And I have crazy magic!"

Thea sighed. "You're right about that. I've never met anyone who can do the kinds of things you do."

Sylica put her chin in her hands. "So how do I find out what I am?"

Thea watched the cool wind blow through the long, dead grass. "Why do you have to be anything? Why can't you just be Sylica?"

Wistful sadness gleamed in her eyes. "But then it's just me."

"We're your friends, Sylica. That's not going to change no matter what you are. Different kinds of people can be friends, you know."

Sylica cocked her head. "Just like Daisy is my friend, and she's a dragon and I'm a Little—I mean, a something."

Thea smiled. "Just like that."

Beaming, Sylica leaped to her feet. "Come on, Daisy! I can still have friends, even if I'm not a Minathril! Let's go see our friends!"

They bounded off, laughing and yapping.

"Careful of the cliff!" Thea yelled after them.

Sylica avoided the cliff and scampered out of sight around the great spur of rock.

"Sylica's in a good mood," Roland grinned as Thea returned to their campsite. "What kind of problem did you get her out of this time?"

"A philosophical one." Thea joined Roland by the fire. Zanele stood over him, checking his injuries.

Thea glanced around the campsite. "Where is she now?"

"She wanted to show Hwasan the tricks Daisy can do. Ow!"

"Then hold still!" Zanele scolded. "You should feel much better tomorrow, but there will be no training for at least two days."

"But—"

"No buts," Zanele retorted firmly. "Besides, there's other things you can do, like spending time with Thea."

Roland gave Thea a sidelong glance. "We were talking about that."

"GOOD."

"What?" Roland looked up, startled.

"Just good." Zanele gave a knowing smile. "Spend all the time together you can."

Hwasan strode into view, with Sylica and Daisy trotting along at his side.

"And can you explain to me how it is that Daisy acts

this way, when she is made, like a machine, out of metal?"

"She has alive magic on her."

"Fascinating. There are not many who possess that kind of magic."

"Daisy is special!" Sylica beamed.

"Where did this Daisy come from?"

"Hello!" Roland waved for Hwasan and Sylica to join them by the fire.

Hwasan broke off the conversation and returned a smile.

Thea shot Roland a sidelong glance, but he sprang to his feet and went to join Hwasan. "If Sylica has finished with you, would you mind telling me about some of these roots and herbs you collected? I don't recognize all of them."

Hwasan's scales surged a brilliant yellow. "Of course." Joining Roland by the pile of produce, he began to describe the edible mountain plants and the best ways of preparing them.

Sylica butted in excitedly, telling them all about her favourite foods from home.

Hwasan smiled and glanced up at the sky. "Evening will be coming soon. Shall I prepare the evening feast for us?"

Zanele gave him an unimpressed glare. "I'll cook."

"Then do you mind if I provide assistance? I am familiar with these ingredients."

Zanele relented, and grudgingly tried some of the methods Hwasan suggested. Everyone agreed that the results were delicious, and Hwasan beamed with pleasure.

As the light faded from the sky, everyone spread out

their blankets and prepared for the night.

"Do you divide up watches?" Hwasan asked. "I'd gladly take one."

Zanele opened her mouth, but Roland jumped in first.

"I'll take a watch with you, Hwasan." He gave a winning smile. "I'd love a chance to talk some more."

Hwasan agreed, and Zanele settled deeper into the hollow where she sat by the fire.

Thea lay down, not too far away. Cocooned in her blanket, her eyes followed Roland and Hwasan as they settled down for their watch.

Roland's skin gleamed in the flickering light of the fire. He leaned forward, listening to Hwasan with eyes full of interest. His request to take watch with Hwasan hadn't only been to ensure safety; he was genuinely interested in learning about the Minathril as well.

Roland glanced down at Thea and saw her watching. He smiled, then turned his attention back to the conversation.

The wind blew cold from the distant cliff. Thea shivered and pulled her blanket tight.

She woke in the first light of morning, sore and cold. Struggling to her feet, Thea wrapped her blanket around her shoulders and sat by the fire to do her check in.

Allulien was silent, but that was not unexpected. She was trying to get the dragon treasure back to the dragons. If Allulien wanted her to do something different, she would have heard.

Once everyone had eaten and was ready for the day, Hwasan led them along a narrow track that ended at the foot of a cliff.

"That is very steep." Thea stared up the imposing wall of rock that seemed to stretch into the clouds.

Hwasan nodded. "You can't get far in these mountains without having to climb. This route is difficult at first, but later we will reach a gully we can follow to the top of the pass. It will protect us from the worst of the winds."

"How do you suggest tackling this?" Roland eyed the cliff with a keen gaze.

Hwasan pulled a metal spike out of his bag. "I will climb and fasten the rope to this spike, then the rest of you can climb up the rope to join me."

Sylica's eyes narrowed. "How is Daisy supposed to get up there?"

Hwasan flashed her a smile. "We can tie the rope around her middle and pull her up with us. The cliff looks sheer from this angle, but there are many ledges and places to stop and rest along the way. Look!"

Two sheep with large, curved horns leapt into view, bounding from ledge to ledge along the cliff.

"Wow," Sylica breathed. "Being a mountain sheep would be so much fun!"

When the sheep had left their sight, Hwasan turned to Sylica. "They are magnificent creatures. Now we will go scale the cliffs like they do, only perhaps without so much leaping."

Hwasan pulled his own rope out of his bag. It was thin and light, but appeared to be strong. Placing his hands on the wall of rock, he began to climb.

Thea watched as Hwasan used all four of his limbs—plus his tail—to steady himself and move upwards. It was clear that he was a confident climber.

Soon he had achieved a great height and half-disappeared onto some sort of ledge. The chime of metal rang out, and a few moments later the end of the rope tumbled down to meet them.

Thea glanced around the group that waited. With a wrench, she remembered Ulfgar wasn't there.

"I'll go next." Zanele grabbed the rope in both hands. "Hold on, Cheeky."

Nimbly, Zanele scrambled up the cliff, joining Hwasan on his perch high above the rest.

Roland eyed the rope thoughtfully. "Maybe you should go next, Sylica, and we'll send Daisy up after you."

Sylica scrambled her way up the cliff, though not nearly as gracefully as Zanele had. Halfway up she stopped and looked down. "Hi Daisy! Hi Thea! Hi Roland!" She tried to wave, then scrambled to grab the rope again.

At the foot of the cliff, Daisy began to pace.

"Come on, Sylica," Zanele's voice drifted down from above.

When Sylica reached the ledge where Zanele and Hwasan waited, Roland grabbed the end of the rope. "Here, Daisy!"

Daisy dashed back and forth along the foot of the cliff, whining nervously.

Roland tried to intercept her, but Daisy pushed past without slowing.

Roland sucked the gash on his thumb and handed the rope to Thea. "Your turn."

"Daisy!" Thea crouched down. "Daisy, come here!"

"Be good, Daisy!" Sylica's voice floated down from above.

Daisy cocked her head and paused long enough for Thea to pounce on her. Roland grabbed the rope and tied it securely around the dragon's middle.

"I'll climb beside her," Roland suggested. "We don't want to risk something going wrong halfway up."

As the people above began pulling up the rope, Roland climbed onto the wall, following alongside as Daisy rose carefully into the air. It was a slow ascent. Thea breathed a sigh of relief when Daisy and Roland were safely on the ledge.

When the end of the rope dropped again, Thea made sure Raybow was securely attached to her baldric, then began to climb. It was easier than it looked from below, especially with the help of the rope, but it still felt like a long time before her face reached the ledge and helping hands reached out to guide her up the last few steps.

"Good." Hwasan beamed. "Now we do that again." Untying the rope from the spike, he coiled it and slung it over his shoulder.

There wasn't much space on the ledge. Everyone leaned out of the way as Hwasan began to climb. The next stretch of the cliff wasn't quite so steep, Thea was glad to see, but the Minathril still climbed with care.

Sylica sighed. "Is he there yet? It's taking so long."

"He needs to be careful," Roland explained. "Without a rope to hold onto he needs to be sure he won't fall."

Sylica rested her head against the wall of the cliff with a sigh. Suddenly perking up, she glanced around, grabbed a bump in the rock, and started to climb.

"Sylica—" Thea began, then stared as the rock beneath Sylica's hands turned into the first step of a stairway, stretching straight up the steep incline.

Sylica grinned and clambered up the stairs, with

Daisy following close behind, yapping cheerfully.

Hwasan glanced down at them with a frown. "I told you to w—" His eyes widened and his scales faded into the colour of the rock beneath his hands. "What is that?"

"A stairway!" Sylica grinned and passed by the Minathril, carrying on up the mountain.

Zanele followed, her small hooves springing lightly from step to step.

Roland shot Thea an amused glance and gestured up the stairs. "After you."

They passed Hwasan who stood as if frozen, staring at the steps.

"Those were not there before," he muttered. "I know they weren't."

Thea looked at the steps beneath her hands, each stair even and perfectly formed. "They're new."

"Coming, Hwasan?" Roland grinned.

Hwasan cautiously approached the stairway and climbed up after Roland, staring at every step beneath his feet as if he couldn't believe his eyes.

The stairway reached right to the top of the cliff. Thea found Sylica and Zanele there, sitting with their feet swinging over the edge.

"Hi Thea!" Sylica grinned. "That was a lot faster, wasn't it?"

Thea had to agree. Standing behind Sylica, she watched the billowing clouds blow past, both above and below their perch at the top of the cliff.

Soon Roland and Hwasan joined them.

Hwasan stared at Sylica, unabashed. "I have never known someone who could make stairs in a moment, and without any tools."

Thea gave him a knowing glance. "That's Sylica."

"But power like that ... it—it is unheard of."

"Sure would help if she could do it on purpose," Zanele muttered under her breath.

Hwasan frowned. "But did she not—"

"Don't worry about it," Zanele snapped. "We got up the cliff. That's the important part."

"Look how high up we are," Sylica grinned. "That was a lot easier than climbing."

Hwasan bowed. "Thank you, Sylica, for your assistance."

Roland glanced around the barren slope on which they found themselves. Not far away, another cliff rose into the clouds. "Now what?"

Hwasan's scales gleamed orange as he tore his eyes away from Sylica. "That was the end of the more difficult climbing. If we follow the base of this cliff we will come to the gorge that I mentioned. From there we will reach the top of the pass."

With Hwasan leading the way, they skirted the bottom of the cliff. The ground they walked along was not steep, but they still made their way with care.

Rounding a corner, Thea saw a human-like figure partway up the cliff—spreadeagled—gingerly trying to find a foothold for one of his legs. A large, two-handed sword hung over his back.

Everyone stopped and stared.

"Excuse me!" Thea called. "Are you alright?"

"Eh?" the man called. His foot moved back and forth until it found a suitable resting place.

"Can we help you?" Thea yelled to make herself heard above the gusting wind. "We have a rope!"

"Rope? Who needs a rope?" The man's voice

sounded strangely familiar. "Back in my day they hadn't invented ropes yet."

Thea stared. "*Coham?*"

"Aye, that's me!" The elderly man glanced down and cracked a toothless grin. "Oh! I remember you! How's the adventuring life?"

He wore the same old, worn armour and trousers that Thea had seen him in before. From their current angle, they were clearly the worse for wear.

"Who is that?" Roland demanded.

"Coham. He's a blade for hire. I met him before." Thea looked back up at the spidery little figure. "What are you doing?"

"Off to get me some dragon treasure!" Coham cackled.

"*What?*" Thea yelled.

Coham inched higher up the cliff. "Gonna get some dragon treasure. Oopsie!" A rock crumbled beneath his foot and he slipped, dangling precariously by one hand.

"Coham!"

Tendons straining, Coham pulled himself back up and found his footing again. He gave a dry chuckle. "Heh heh heh. Can't go falling now, what would Beatrice say?"

Thea stared up at the wizened old man. "What *would* Beatrice say?"

"'Dumb old codger, I told yous t'stop climbin' things without doing yer stritches beforehand.' Like I need stritches," he muttered under his breath.

"Where is your granddaughter now?"

"Gettin' married." Coham found another handhold and pulled himself higher. "Found herself a nice young man, but poorer than a post. Got ta get them a nice wedding present or they'll be chewin' the soles off their old boots."

"But ... dragon treasure? Don't you know that's dangerous?"

"Gosh darnit. You think I never dealt with dragon treasure afore? Ol' Coham knows what he's doin'."

Roland glanced at Thea. "Does he know what he's doing?"

Coham reached along the edge of a ridge high above his head, his hand creeping like a spider.

"I have no idea."

"Now listen here," the old man croaked. "My bones have been creaking all day, and that wind's blowing no good news. Get yourself some shelter before that storm starts, you hear?"

Thea glanced around. The clouds were darker than they were before, and the wind was gusting stronger. "What about you? You're stuck on the side of a cliff!"

"Not for long!" Shifting his weight, Coham reached for another handhold and froze. "Huh," he muttered. "Damn arthritis."

He lowered his arm and tried again with the other one. This time it seemed to work and he lifted himself another inch.

"Coham?" Thea called. "We know another way up. If you come down we could show you!"

"Huh." He groped with his foot, finding a place to put it just above his elbow. "Off you go, I'm a little busy."

Roland looked at Thea in consternation. "We just leave him there?"

Thea shrugged helplessly. "I think he wants us to."

"The weather is closing in," Hwasan interjected. "We

should carry on before it is too late."

Following Hwasan, they hurried along the foot of the cliff. Soon a dark gap opened in the sheer walls of rock. Inside, a boulder-filled gully stretched up into shadow.

Hwasan glanced warily over his shoulder. "We seem to be making good time, but we will try to reach the top as quickly as possible."

It was dark in the gully. Tall cliffs stretched up on either side of them as they scrambled up the rocky incline. Boulders shifted and moved beneath their feet.

"Careful!" Thea called as a stone dislodged and tumbled past Roland and Zanele on its way down the steep gully.

In the distance, thunder rumbled. Wind hissed through the gap in the cliffs overhead.

"How far is it to the top of the pass?" Roland asked.

"Last time I was here it took me a measure to climb the gully."

Roland frowned and glanced up at the narrow strip of sky. The clouds were growing very dark.

With a rumble, drops of rain began to fall. Only a few made it down the narrow chasm to reach the travellers, but from the sound, Thea could tell it was raining heavily.

"Come on!" Hwasan urged them to move faster.

"Why?" Sylica protested. "We're not getting very wet down here."

Hwasan's face was grim. "Not yet."

Chapter Thirteen

Rain pattered against Thea's hood and gleamed on the stones underfoot as she followed Hwasan up the rocky incline. A bright flash of lightning lit the chasm for a brief moment, followed immediately by a roll of thunder that shook the mountain beneath them. A small trickle of water ran down the rocks beneath their feet.

"I hope that old man found shelter." Zanele stared at the narrow strip of sky where they could see rain blowing by in sheets.

Thea didn't know what to think. In some ways she questioned Coham's sanity, but there was something sharp about the old man's mind.

Roland glanced at Thea. He tried to smile, but Thea could tell he was worried.

Water splashed beneath their feet. It rushed down the gully towards them as they scrambled higher and higher.

"Hey!" Sylica tried to shake off her foot. "Where's this water coming from?"

"The rain," Hwasan replied, his scales the deep grey of the rock walls surrounding them.

"But—" Sylica protested.

Hwasan's scales flashed red. "Why do you think this gully is here? This is where the rain goes!"

Gushing down the narrow gorge, the water became a

stream. It splashed around their legs, making every step treacherous.

Thea listened to the roar of the storm overhead. If anything, the rain was louder than before. With a grinding rumble, a rock tumbled past, propelled by the force of the water.

"We need to get out of here." Roland's voice was urgent. "Now."

The water churned past them, ankle deep, dashing against the cliffsides and boulders that obstructed its way.

"Can we climb?" Roland felt along the wall, trying to find a handhold.

"Do we go back?" Zanele stared up and down the narrow gully with widening eyes.

Hwasan braced himself against the rushing torrent. "It's too strong! We'll be washed right over the next cliff!"

The walls gleamed with water running down from the cliffs above.

"It's too slick." Roland stepped back, almost staggering in the force of the current. "I can't get a good hold."

Rocks shifted underfoot, driven lower and lower by the rushing stream. The dashing spray soaked Thea to her skin as she struggled to stay on her feet.

"Thea," Sylica's eyes were wide with terror. "Thea, I'm trying to help but it's not working!"

With a cry, Hwasan staggered as if his legs had been knocked out from under him. He scrambled to get his footing again.

"Get up against the wall!" Roland yelled, gesturing everyone to one side of the gully. With a swell of magic, the rushing water surged to the other side.

Beneath Thea's feet, the water slowed to a trickle. She stared as the raging water leapt down the gully towards them, hit an invisible barrier, and swept around it to continue its tumbling cascade down the mountain.

Hwasan got unsteadily to his feet. "What happened?" It was almost impossible to see him through the gloom.

"Stay close," Roland urged everyone. "I am keeping the shield as small as I can so it will last longer."

They huddled together as the flood churned past, shivering and soaked to their skin. Daisy sat in the middle of their small huddle, water dripping off her snout.

Hwasan stared at the rushing water that surrounded their small bubble of safety. Slowly, an orange tint returned to his scales. "Perhaps I can also do something to help."

Carefully, he drew a small metal brazier out of his bag. Taking something small and black in his other hand, he struck the metal, sending a shower of sparks down onto the small nest of coals inside. Gently, he blew on them, and Thea watched as the coals began to glow. She thought she felt, for a brief moment, a small flare of magic.

A warm, gentle radiance shone out from the tiny brazier.

Thea looked at the Minathril in surprise. "Was that magic?"

Hwasan's scales faded back to deep grey. "No. Why do you ask?"

Thea paused. Why had she asked? "I just thought ... maybe ..."

"Minathrils carry these in the mountains." Hwasan nodded at the brazier in his hands. "It is not always possible to light a fire, and these provide some warmth for us when we need it."

Everyone huddled around the brazier's warm glow. Around them, the storm raged and the churning waters surged past.

Thea looked at her bedraggled friends. "Maybe Coham had the right idea after all."

"If he isn't being blown right off that cliff," Zanele retorted. "Listen to the wind howling up there!"

Thea listened to the rumble of the storm. The mountain shook beneath them. She glanced at Roland. "How long will the shield last, do you think?"

"Probably a measure. I could renew it if I needed to, but that would take most of my magic."

"I could extend it with my magic," Zanele added.

Thea looked at Hwasan. "How long does a storm last in the mountains?"

"A storm like this?" Hwasan's voice was grave. "It can last for days."

Thea stared at the mass of water that churned past them. "So we can't stay here."

Zanele's eyes widened in alarm. "There is no way we can survive that torrent. Not like this."

Something tumbled down the gully towards them. Bursting through their shield, it crashed into Hwasan. The brazier tumbled to the ground, its hot coals spilling out across the wet stones.

Thea scrambled out of the way, clinging to Roland as her foot slipped and was tugged violently by the rushing water outside the shield.

The strange bulging figure leapt to its feet. It was

short—only half Thea's size—but almost as wide as it was tall. It had a strange, insect-like face with a long proboscis and large glassy eyes.

The creature shook itself and looked around wildly.

Roland put a hand on the hilt of his knife and gestured everyone back, as much as they could move back in their small bubble of safety.

The creature grabbed its face and pulled, peeling back the facade to show a normal, human-like face. It was thin, with glittering black eyes.

"Oh!" Thea gasped. "Hello, are you alright?"

The little stranger grabbed a small white shape that hung off its bulging clothing and blew on it. A shrill whistle pierced the air.

"Goblin!" Hwasan gasped from behind Thea's ear.

Goblin? Thea stared at the strange little creature before her. It didn't look like a Little, but of course, what else could it be? Their strange outfit must be some kind of protective clothing.

"Hello!" Sylica bounded towards the Little, as much as the small, crowded space allowed her to bound.

In a flash, the Little reached behind their back and produced a sharp metal rod, which they flourished menacingly.

Something approached through the tumbling water, and three more Littles appeared, wearing the same protective clothing and face mask. They burst inside the shielded area and stared at the strangers with large, startled eyes.

The first Little hissed something, and the rest of the Littles quickly drew their own sharp metal rods from the sheaths on their backs. They pointed them at Thea and her friends, and the first Little spoke.

Thea cast comprehension magic over all of them.

"—To kill us!" the Little finished, as understanding settled in Thea's mind.

"We are not here to hurt you," Thea explained. "We are passing through and got caught in the storm."

The Little's eyes narrowed. "Magic makers. Only magic can move water like that."

"Isn't it nice to have a break from the storm?" Sylica beamed.

"We need this water." The Little's eyes flashed. "You are blocking our pipes!"

"I'm sorry," Thea said. "We didn't mean to block anything. We are just trying to shelter from the storm."

"What are you doing?" Hwasan hissed in Thea's ear. "You can't reason with goblins."

"Littles," Thea hissed back. "They aren't goblins, they're Littles."

One of the Littles pushed the end of their weapon up against Sylica's side. "You will come with us. Big Boss will deal with you."

"Hey! That hurts!" Sylica protested as the Little prodded her forward. "Thea?"

Thea glanced at Hwasan's wide eyes. "I think we should go with them. We can't stay here, and maybe they can help us."

Each Little was attached to a thin, snaking rope that stretched back up the gully. Seizing Thea's arm, one of the Littles pushed her towards the upper end of the shield where the ropes stretched out into the torrent.

"Hold on," the Little ordered in a stern voice. "If you let go, the storm will kill you for us."

The Little blew three short blasts on their whistle. Moments later, the rope began to move, drawing steadily back up the gully. Thea clung to it as she was pulled beyond the shield and into the raging water. Her feet were swept away and she fell to the ground. Clutching the rope, Thea struggled to breathe as the churning torrent crashed over her.

The tug of the rope pulled her on. With all her strength, Thea pulled her knees forward and launched herself up, gasping for air. The cascade crashed over her again.

Lungs burning, Thea clung to her lifeline. Her arms were numb from the cold. Her legs throbbed with pain from smashing from boulder to boulder. She couldn't breathe.

Darkness loomed in front of her. Suddenly, the water was gone. Thea stumbled forward and collapsed on dry ground, coughing and gasping for breath.

Footsteps thudded around her. Someone tripped over her arm, but she barely felt it. Water splattered across her as the others coughed and stumbled across the room.

Thea pushed herself up. There was Roland, collapsed on his hands and knees, a dark scab showing where the bandage had been ripped off his head. Daisy scampered out from beneath him and ran over to Sylica, who sat on the ground in a daze. Zanele stood and wiped her face with her arm. Cheeky poked her head out of her bag and made a scolding sound at the Littles.

They were definitely Littles. Thea watched as their strange, bulky clothing began to deflate. There were other Littles too, untying the ropes and helping the original four out of their protective clothing. They looked like most of the Littles Thea had met before, though perhaps a bit smaller, and their skin was pale.

Within, their spirits were dark. They shot furtive glances at Thea and her friends as they worked.

It was a bare, cave-like room. Across the mouth of the cave, Thea could see the raging flood still sweeping past. The opposite wall of the cave was filled with levers and interlocking gears. Thea glanced around sharply. Where was Hwasan?

Coughing erupted from the ground beside her elbow. Thea stared, then realized that Hwasan lay beside her, but so well camouflaged by the colour of his scales that she could hardly see him.

Sylica scrambled to her feet and started chattering cheerfully in the language of the Littles.

Hwasan's eyes widened.

Sylica gestured from friend to friend, words pouring out of her with the speed of the rain on the mountainside. Daisy bounded around her legs, equally as excited.

The Littles stared in alarm, looking at each other as if unsure of what to do.

One of them grabbed a lever on the wall and pulled. With a grinding rumble, a wall of rock slid across the mouth of the cave, swallowing everything in darkness.

"Hey!" Sylica protested. "Where'd the light go?"

Green light flared from a small lantern. Then more and more lights appeared.

In the green-lit shadows, a Little stepped forward. Thea quickly cast comprehension again.

"If you fight, we will kill you," the Little said in a firm voice.

"We're not here to fight you," Thea assured them. "We are friends."

She felt a hiss of inhaled breath beside her ear.

"We have no friends," the Little glared, "and especially not the green one who does not stop talking. Now you will give us your weapons, or we will kill you."

Thea glanced at Roland. His hand rested on the hilt of his knife in a way that said that he would not, under any circumstances, give it up.

Thea turned back to the Littles. "We do not mean you any harm. If you don't want us here, we can carry on our way. Thank you for helping us out of the ravine."

The Little scowled. "We did not help you. We captured you. Now we get your weapons."

"Oh! We were captured?" Sylica looked at the Littles in surprise. "That's fun! I've never been captured before! Did I miss something important? I might have been a bit distracted, I do get distracted sometimes. My dad says that I should really work on that, but I keep forgetting."

Roland laid a hand on Sylica's shoulder and turned to the Littles. "We can leave, or come speak to the leader you mentioned earlier, but no one is taking our weapons."

The spokesperson pointed their metal spike at Roland. "Then you will die and we will take them from you dead."

With a clatter, the metal spike landed on the ground, sliced in half by Roland's knife. The Little staggered back.

"You will not harm us." Roland's eyes flashed.

The Littles stared, agape, then with a cry they charged, metal spikes flailing.

Magic blazed into an almost-visible barrier that stretched across the middle of the cave. The charging Littles crashed into it and ricocheted backwards.

Roland's eyes blazed. "I meant what I said. You *will not* harm us."

The Littles stared at the hint of mist that hung across the room. Some glared darkly, others stared with mouths agape. One Little crept closer and tried to poke it with their finger.

"No!" The Little who had spoken jumped up and down in rage. "Kill them! They are dangerous!"

Zanele watched with her chin in her hands. "Are we allowed to attack them yet?"

"Wait." Thea stared at the Littles. Gently, she sent charm magic into their minds. "We will not harm you if you do not harm us." It was true. She just had to help them believe it. "You should take us to your leader now."

The Littles looked at each other. "Big Boss?"

"Yes, take us to Big Boss."

"I—I guess we could," one of them ventured.

Roland glanced at Thea.

Thea smiled. "Big Boss will take care of everything."

The Littles nodded uncertainly.

"We will take you." The Little who had been the spokesperson stepped forward again. "Come with us."

"Yay!" Sylica capered around the room. "Now we get to be friends again! I love making new friends, and so does Daisy, don't you Daisy? It's even more fun than eating candy and I *love* eating candy but—"

The Little turned to Sylica with a frown. "You will be quiet."

Sylica paused in the middle of her caper. "Oh."

Leading the way, several of the Littles stepped through a small door and into a narrow passageway. Thea had to crouch to fit through.

Walking in near-darkness, she felt her way along the rough, cave-like walls. She could hear the shuffle of many footsteps before and behind her. Small patches of green light glimmered between the shadows.

"Zanele?" Sylica's loud whisper echoed down the narrow passageway.

"What?"

"You're shiny."

"No, *you're* shiny," Zanele retorted. "That is literally the shiniest armour I have ever seen."

"But why do you have safe magic on you?"

"It's a shield spell. I'm not stupid."

The small, winding tunnel ended, and Thea stepped out into a larger corridor. She could stand upright now, and it was wide enough for at least two big people to walk side by side. Metal brackets on the walls held lanterns to light the way. The walls, ceiling, and floor were stone, chiselled smooth, and carved with a series of grotesque images.

"Oh!" Sylica cried as she stepped out into the corridor. "Are these your tunnels? They're so nice! You even put pictures on them! I like making pictures too, but whenever I tried drawing on the wall at home, my mom told me not to. Your moms must be really nice to let you have pictures on your walls. Oh, hello!" She turned to wave at another Little who passed by, staring at the strangers with wide eyes.

"This way." The leader of the Littles pointed, and gestured for the rest to follow.

"Where are we going?" Sylica bounced along cheerily. "Can we have a tour? One of my favourite places to see is always the kitchen, because that's where the food is, and there's always—"

The meaning of Sylica's words faded from Thea's mind as the comprehension magic ended.

The Littles led them to a door, bigger than the first, and fastened together with a large number of bolts and levers. The Little who had been leading the way turned to Sylica and spoke sharply. Sylica stopped talking.

Turning back to the door, the Little struck the knocker, which resounded like a bell. With a rumble and clatter, the bolts and bars moved back one after another, and the door swung open.

Stepping through the door, they entered an enormous cavern. Stone pillars stretched from the floor to the ceiling high above, hung all around with lanterns, which cast a plethora of strange green shadows. At the far end of the room was a large stone chair, and at its foot a huddle of Littles talked in hushed, urgent voices.

Sylica leaped forward excitedly, but the Little by their side spoke sharply, and Sylica reluctantly stopped.

The Little marched forward importantly, gesturing for Thea and the others to follow.

As they approached, the Littles by the throne turned and stared. They wore some kind of leather or untreated hide, and most of them carried spears. One particularly small, wizened Little held a long spiked mace.

Thea cast comprehension magic again.

"I bring a report." The Little that led the way stood straight and spoke in a loud voice. "The pipes were blocked by these intruders. Now we have brought them to Big Boss."

The wizened Little glared. "With their weapons? Idiots."

The Little's eyes widened slightly. "They would not harm us if we would not harm them."

The wizened Little scowled.

"They are strong magic people," the Little continued, "so we bring them to Big Boss."

"Strong magic people." The Little's eyes narrowed. "I see. Leave them here."

The escorts turned and left. The door slammed shut behind them.

The wizened Little looked at Thea with an affronted glare. "I am Big Boss. Why did you come here?"

"We were passing by and got caught in the storm," Thea explained. "We would appreciate shelter, but if we are not welcome we will continue on our way."

The Littles surrounding Big Boss shifted and held their spears tight.

Big Boss frowned. "Goblins do not shelter people. You will be sorry you ever came here."

"But you're not goblins. We all know that you're really Littles. People only call you goblins because they don't know any better."

"We are what?" Big Boss glared. "Who told you something like that?"

"Other Littles did, of course. We have lots of Little friends down in the lands beyond the mountains."

Big Boss spat. "Weak ones. We are goblins. We fight and kill and take no prisoners. We survive because we are goblins."

"We can call you goblins if you want," Thea relented, "but that doesn't mean you are evil creatures."

The Little stepped in front of her and stared up with hard, cruel eyes. The point of his mace pressed down on her chest. "Enough. No one will think we are weak. I will kill you one by one and then you can tell me if you think we are evil creatures."

Roland's eyes flashed.

"Wait," Thea whispered.

With comprehension magic, Thea gently reached into the Little's spirit, trying to understand. It was dark and hard. There was no doubt in his heart that they were, in fact, nothing but goblins. How could it be that they had so embraced the lies that had been told about them? Elora and her people had lived beneath the weight of those same lies, but they had fought against them, living in the way the Great Big Big had taught them to. These Littles had given up on being Littles altogether.

What could she do? She could charm them and probably convince Big Boss to let them go, but what difference would that make? The pain and bitterness she saw inside them made her heart ache. How could she break into their prison and show them there was another way to live?

It might be impossible, but she knew someone who could do impossible things.

"Sylica? I think our new friends would love to hear about your Uncle Bob."

Sylica's eyes lit up. "You want to know about Uncle Bob?" She squealed, and everyone stared. "You would *love* Uncle Bob! I know it! He is my best friend in all the world—except for Daisy of course—and he made so many wonderful things! There was one time he tried to make a flying machine and it had wings and everything, except that his arms got too tired and he landed in the duck pond and it took us all the way till feast time to get him out because there was this really mad goose who kept chasing us all over the place but my favourite time was when he would make his big boom lights that would shoot up in the sky and then *boom!* all the colours would be everywhere and we would be washing pink and yellow spots off the cows for days but it was totally worth it and *sometimes* he would even let me sit and watch him while he worked and he would tell me all about his plans and what he wanted to make. Did you know he gave me this bag of candy? He said it was because I always liked to share, so that's why I always share it wherever I go! I think maybe the yellow ones are the yummiest but then I eat a purple one and I remember how yummy those ones are. Do you want to see what your favourite colour is?"

Reaching into her bag, Sylica began thrusting handfuls of candy into the hands of the stunned Littles.

"And then *after* we eat candy we can have a dance! We had such a fun dance when we were staying with the Fauns. Did you know that the Fauns are my second favourite people in all the world? They love dancing and singing and they have animal friends too, just like I have Daisy. Do you have any animal friends?"

Big Boss stared. Around him, several of the guards sheepishly munched their candy.

"This is Thea," Sylica grinned, turning to the others, "and Roland, and Zanele, and—oh, where did Hwasan go? Oh well. They are my friends too! There was a really big storm on the mountain today and it almost washed us away. Did you know that? I think storms are very exciting, especially when there's all the lightning and thunder and the wind going *whoosh* and sometimes there's even hail, but there wasn't any hail today, just rain, but it was a lot of rain. Do you like it when it rains? I'm so glad we came to see you! It's so nice to make new friends!"

Big Boss opened his mouth, but no sound came out.

Sylica turned to one of the guards. "What's your name? I'm Sylica!"

The guard blanched and stared up at her. "Uh ... Akka."

"Hi, Akka! That's a nice name. I think your hair is really pretty. How do you get it to all stay on top of your head like that? I try to do that sometimes but then it all falls down right away."

"Uh ..." Akka looked around like a trapped animal. "I have a string. Like this." Akka held up a skinny arm that had a string wrapped around it.

"Oh you *tie* it up. That makes so much sense! I just kind of pushed my hair up but then it just fell down again. See?" Sylica demonstrated. Her hair fell in front of her face.

"We are not talking about hair!" Big Boss glared at Sylica.

"Why not?" Sylica gave a puzzled frown. "Hair is nice and it can look very pretty too. I like my hair because it is white and green. I like your hair because it is kind of short and sticks up all over. But if we weren't talking about hair, what were we talking about?"

Bewilderment filled Big Boss's face. He stammered. "We ... we were ... that we don't take prisoners. Yes. We don't take prisoners."

"Oh, well that's okay. I never met a prisoner before but I can always meet one another day. Say, did you make this room yourself? It's really pretty."

A gleam of pride flickered across Big Boss's face. "It took us many circles to make this room."

"And the pillars are so tall!" She waved at Akka. "Come stand beside it! Look! You're all the way up to here on it!" She glanced around the guards and gestured to the tallest one there, standing almost as tall as Zanele. "Hey! Let's see how tall you are on it!"

"No!" Big Boss glared. "We are talking about *important* things."

Sylica's eyes lit up. "Like candy! Do you need more? Here!" She pressed some into Big Boss's hand.

One of the guards gestured shyly.

Sylica beamed. "Of course! You can have more candy too!"

The guards gathered around her eagerly.

"No!" Big Boss threw his candy on the ground. "Goblins don't take prisoners! We will kill you!"

"You can't," Thea replied in an even voice. "As your own people told you, we have strong magic. We don't want to hurt you, but we will not let you hurt us."

Big Boss glared. "Goblins are strong. We are not afraid to fight."

"But you don't always have to fight. There is a big world out there, and in some places the people love and accept the Littles. They don't have to fight to be able to survive." She glanced at the guards who stood listening to Sylica's endless chatter, completely enthralled by her descriptions of the fruit and pastries she liked to buy from the market in Gedwyld. One of the guards was letting Daisy lick her face.

Big Boss gripped the handle of his mace, as if through it he could regain some sort of sanity in his world. "We never let anyone go free. Goblins must be strong!"

"Listen." Thea held out a calming hand. "Let's make a bargain. We will pay you for safe passage out of your tunnels. Then no one could say you let us go for free."

Big Boss frowned. "What kind of pay?"

Thea drew out her falcion. "This sword."

Big Boss stared at its gleaming blade. He wanted it, Thea could see it in his eyes, but he stepped back and gave her a wary look. "And is that sword better than the spike stick of the Big Boss?"

Thea swung the falcion at the ground, burying it in rock halfway up its blade.

Everyone stared.

Big Boss reached out a trembling hand. "I will take your pay."

"Good." Thea grasped the sword and pulled it back out of the rock. "I will give it to you when we are at the borders of your land."

Big Boss frowned.

"Then anyone watching can see that we gave you pay. We can give you a deposit of candy, though, as a token of our word." Thea gestured to Sylica. "Could you leave a bucket or two worth for them, Sylica?"

Beaming, Sylica swung her candy bag over her head, dumping out candy until the pile on the ground reached above her knees.

"There you go!" she beamed. "Candy for our friends!"

Big Boss tore his eyes away from the impossibly big pile. "We take you out, and you give me the sword."

"Yes." Thea glanced around her party. Roland gave her a slight nod, and Zanele watched the proceedings with amusement. She could see Hwasan more easily now, but his colour was still a deep grey.

"Come," Big Boss ordered his guards. "We will bring our not-prisoners to the gate."

The guards shuffled nervously, casting wistful glances at the heap of candy.

"Now!"

Reluctantly, the guards straightened and followed Big Boss towards the door. Thea and her friends went with them, through the door, down the long corridor, out another door, and into the narrow tunnel beyond.

Blue light glimmered down the tunnel to meet them. The drumming of rain filled the air.

As soon as Thea stepped out into the open, she was soaked to the skin.

Big Boss stood in the entrance of the tunnel. "We brought you out. Now give me the sword."

Roland set a hand on Thea's shoulder and eyed Big Boss sternly. "That sword is only one weapon of the many that we carry. No other goblins will attack us as we leave this area. Is that understood?"

Big Boss nodded, staring at the sword.

Thea removed it from her belt with its sheath and set it in the Little's trembling hands.

"This will be the sword of the Big Boss," Big Boss whispered. "No goblin ever had a sword like this."

Thea looked into his eyes. "If you ever come to Gedwyld in peace, the people will accept you there."

In his spirit there was a flicker of something that didn't seem quite as dark.

Chapter Fourteen

Sylica continued waving long after the goblin tunnel left their sight. All around them, rain pelted every surface with its relentless barrage.

Roland frowned as he peered through the gloom. "Any idea of where we are, Hwasan?"

The Minathril trudged on.

"Hwasan?"

The Minathril looked up. "How ... what ..." His grey scales dripped water onto the rocks beneath his feet.

"Do you know where we are?"

Hwasan stared around the rocky landscape. Dreary grey clouds cloaked the mountainside, obscuring any obvious landmarks. "I ... I think we must be across the pass now. I don't see any cliffs. We just ... keep going west."

Roland nodded. After consulting a compass, they set off again. Gradually the wind died down and the rain settled into a long, steady shower. The sky grew darker and darker until finally Roland made the call that they should camp for the night.

It was cold and wet. Thea huddled beneath her blanket, dimly aware of murmured conversation going on around her. She couldn't forget the feeling that landed deep in her gut when she looked in the dark spirits of the goblins. *Oh Deity*, she whispered, *help them find the light.*

She shivered as the cold seeped into her bones. The adrenaline of the day was long gone, leaving a deep, aching tiredness in its place.

"Thea?" Roland sat down beside her. "Are you doing alright?"

Thea nodded, but she couldn't stop shivering. Roland shifted her sodden blanket and spread his cloak around them both.

Thea leaned into his warmth, and Roland wrapped his arms around her.

"It was hard seeing Littles like that, wasn't it?" Roland's voice was low and gentle.

Thea nodded, tears stinging her eyes. She let herself watch Roland's spirit close beside her, so bright and alive. Maybe one day the Littles would have spirits like that too.

Roland brushed a wet tendril of hair off her face. "The Great Big Big will take care of them."

She looked up into his compassionate eyes. Yes, the Deity would take care of them, just like Arl and Ulfgar. The Littles' story wasn't over yet.

Rain continued to fall across the mountainside, blanketing all other sounds with its dull, calming murmur.

Thea felt her body relax and sink into the comfort of Roland's embrace. It felt like home.

"This is nice," she murmured as the cold and discomfort faded away.

Roland wrapped his arms tighter. "I'm glad."

In the warmth of his embrace, Thea fell asleep.

She woke with Roland's arms still around her. Zanele's hand was on her shoulder. "Sorry, Thea. It's your turn for watch now."

Thea rubbed her eyes, trying to shake the drowsiness from her head. Rain still poured down on their campsite. In the near-blackness of night, she could just make out the huddled and blanket-cocooned forms of the rest of her companions.

"Everyone else has had their watches. Yours is the last." Zanele shot Thea a grin, then huddled up against the side of a boulder, pulling her blanket over her head.

Thea shifted into a more upright position. Beside her, Roland stirred.

"It's okay," Thea whispered. "I'm just taking watch now."

Roland relaxed again. Thea shifted closer so he could lean up against her. It was nice, having Roland close. Soon his breathing was slow and peaceful again.

Thea watched as the light of day slowly crept across the mountainside. The clouds were still heavy and dark with rain.

Once everyone was awake and those who needed to check in had done so, they ate some of the food that Ember had sent and carried on walking.

It was a cold and miserable day, barraged by the relentless rain. Everything was wet, and the rocks beneath their feet were loose and slippery. As the mountain led them higher, the wind became piercingly cold. An occasional snowflake gleamed white in the deluge.

As staph approached, the weather lifted slightly. The rain slowed to a drizzle, and through the blowing cloud they caught glimpses of mountain peaks ahead of them.

Thea glanced back. Across a bare valley, she could just see the high ridge of rock that must have been the pass.

"I know this area," Hwasan said. "There is a cave not far from here that I have spent the night in before."

"Are you sure this cave is empty?" Zanele asked, one eyebrow cocked.

"It was when I was last there. Of course we will make sure it is safe."

Hwasan led the way, and soon they found the cave. It was wide and fairly shallow. After Hwasan and Roland had both explored it and declared that it was safe, everyone tramped inside. Thea set her bag against the wall and attempted to wring some of the water out of her clothes.

Cheeky clambered out of Zanele's bag, wet and bedraggled.

Sylica flopped down on the dry floor of the cave, a puddle quickly forming beneath her. She wiped her hair back from her face. "That was a lot of rain! Let's make a fire. I'm wet all over!"

Roland gave her an apologetic smile. "There's no wood, Sylica. Even if there was, it would be absolutely soaked by now."

Sylica frowned. "But I want a fire. I'll go find some wood." She sprang to her feet.

Thea glanced out the mouth of the cave. It faced east, and she could see the wide, rocky valley they had crossed. There were no trees. There weren't even any bushes.

"Here's some!" Sylica called from the back of the cave. Everyone stared as she came trotting back into view with her arms full of firewood.

Hwasan stared. "That was not there before."

Roland shook his head, a wry smile playing at the

corners of his mouth. "With Sylica, it didn't have to be."

Sylica dumped her armload of wood near the mouth of the cave and trotted cheerfully back into the shadows at the back of the cave. Hwasan followed her.

He returned moments later as Sylica skipped by with another armload of firewood.

"There is a massive pile of wood back there!" He pointed, his eyes wide with shock. "How did it get there?"

Roland shrugged. "Sylica."

"But how?"

"Your guess is as good as ours." Roland shook his head. "At least we can make a fire now."

Soon the fire was crackling, and everyone unpacked their bags, spreading their wet things around the cave to dry.

"Check up time," Zanele announced. "Roland, how are you doing?"

"I'm doing alright."

"Let me look at that head of yours." Zanele got Roland sitting down and examined the wound. "It's still healing well. Anything else hurting?"

"My bruises are aching, but that's it. Can I start training again?"

Zanele gave him a thoughtful stare. "A little bit, but don't overdo it."

Roland glanced at Thea. "You don't mind?"

"As long as you're doing what the doctor says." Thea gave him a wry smile. "I would join you, but ..."

Roland shot her a grin. "All that training, and now you don't even have your falcion anymore." He shook his head in mock disbelief.

"Maybe I'll get another one someday." Thea shook

out her blanket beside the fire. "A better one!"

Roland waved and stepped out of the cave, knives in hand.

"How are you doing, Thea?" Zanele asked, joining her by the fire.

"Better now that we can get dry. It was cold, being in the rain for so long."

Zanele nodded. "Anything hurting?"

"Everywhere?" Thea offered with a laugh. Her muscles ached from climbing the cliff, and her legs were scraped and bruised from being pulled up the gully.

Zanele sat her down and gave her some salve to rub on her bruises. Cheeky scampered around her, apparently much happier now that she was dry.

Sylica and Daisy were nowhere to be seen. Zanele sighed and turned to Hwasan. "Your turn. How are you feeling?"

"I am well," Hwasan replied. "Thank you for your consideration."

Zanele gave him an unimpressed glare. "How are you *actually* doing?"

Hwasan stared at the fire. "I am sore and tired, as I am sure we all are, but I have escaped any serious injury, for the time being. I am used to travelling in the mountains."

"You said," Zanele muttered to herself. Rooting through her bag, she pulled out a dripping wet roll of bandages. Carefully unrolling it, she hung it up to dry, draping one end over Sylica's pack and the other up over the end of her halberd.

Thea sat by the fire, enjoying its warmth.

Hwasan shifted in his place by the fire. "How did Sylica make the wood appear like that?"

Thea glanced up. Hwasan was watching her intently, his scales as grey as the rock surrounding their cave. "I don't know," she admitted. "I don't think anyone knows, even Sylica herself."

Hwasan shook his head. "I have seen extraordinary magic from her. To make rock take shape beneath her hands, make wood appear where there was no wood before, and what she did in the goblin caves ... I have never seen anything like that."

Thea looked at Hwasan's urgent face. "Like what?"

"For anyone to walk away from an encounter with goblins unharmed ... it is unheard of."

"But I told you, they aren't really goblins. They're Littles, and many of them are my friends."

Hwasan eyed her thoughtfully. "I have heard of Littles before and wondered if they were a distant relation of the goblins. Even if it is true that they are the same species, these ones were not your friends. They meant to kill us, and they were going to try."

"I know." As much as Thea didn't want to admit it, she had seen the look in the goblins' eyes.

"But Sylica changed their minds, and they didn't even realize it. How did she do that? I have never seen anything like it."

Thea stared into the dancing flames. "It's like she sees the world as a different place than it is, and when people are near her they start to see it that way too."

Hwasan shook his head. "It is a magic I have never seen before. Not in any of my studies."

"What exactly have you studied?" Zanele asked, glancing up from her work.

"Many things. I love to learn and I will study anything before me that I do not understand. Magic has been one particular area of my study."

"We were all doing magic, you know." Zanele stretched out another bandage to dry. "It wasn't just Sylica."

"I know. The kind of magic you and Thea and Roland do I have seen before. I have never heard of anything like this magic of Sylica's."

"Have you known many people who were servants of the Deity?" Thea asked.

"I have met a few. One of them was killed by goblins. It seemed to me that none of you knew how dangerous goblins can be. You didn't seem frightened at all."

"I don't get frightened." Zanele gave a smug smile. "If someone is threatening you, why give them what they're wanting? It only encourages them."

Hwasan watched the Faun at work. "So you have never been afraid?"

Zanele set down the bandage she was holding. "I have," she admitted. "When I was a Faunlet, my people were ambushed. I tried to run away, but my hoof caught and I fell. I thought the monsters were going to kill me, but our leader jumped in the way and she was killed instead." Zanele sat down by the fire. "I was frightened then. But if someone tries to make me afraid, I will not satisfy them."

Thea looked at Hwasan. "I wasn't afraid, because I knew who they could be. They could have been full of life and joy, but instead they were trapped and afraid, unable to see any way but hurting and killing."

Hwasan watched Thea in fascination. "So you tried to help them."

"They are one of the five races made by the Deity. How could we just kill them, or walk away and leave them like that? I had to show them that they don't have to be alone. At least, I had to try."

Hwasan stared down at the fire. The grey of his scales faded into blue. "Minathrils are not supposed to be alone. We live and work with our crew. They're like our tribe or our family. A Minathril is nothing without a crew."

Thea watched Hwasan intently. She had wondered about his scales and the way they changed. Could it be linked somehow with how he was feeling? "You said your crew died, didn't you?"

Hwasan nodded. "When they were killed I did not know what to do. I was alone."

His spirit was raw and open. It ached with exhaustion, fear, confusion, and a long, long road.

Thea leaned forward gently. "We can be your crew."

Hwasan stared at Thea. The edges of his scales gleamed with gold. "You would? I ... I wanted to have a crew. I do have a lot to offer. I know many things through my studies, and many secrets—"

"You don't need to offer anything," Zanele interjected. "It doesn't work like that."

Hwasan's scales faded into grey.

"We like you, Hwasan," Thea smiled, "and we're glad you're with us. There doesn't need to be any other reason than that."

Deep inside Hwasan's spirit, something shifted. The light of hope seemed stronger than it had before.

"Hi everybody!" Sylica bounded into the cave, dripping from head to toe. Daisy scampered after her, shaking the water off her scales with the chime of crashing metal.

"Daisy and I went foraging, but we didn't find

anything except for this pretty rock." Sylica produced the rock with a proud grin. "Isn't it nice? It doesn't taste good, though, so we can eat candy instead! Here's one for you and one for you ..."

Hwasan held up a protesting hand. "Thank you, but, ah, it is not good for my teeth."

"Oh. Okay!" Sylica grinned. "Daisy doesn't have teeth, so she can have as many as she wants. Can't you Daisy?"

Daisy yapped excitedly.

Roland strode into view. "It's halfway through staph! I thought I'd find you all asleep!" His eyes twinkled as he joined them by the fire.

"We're just enjoying being warm and dry." Thea slid over so he could sit beside her.

"Well we can stay here for restday too." Roland found a dry scrap of cloth to clean off his blades. "There's no point in hurrying on when we're tired and it's still raining."

"Yay!" Sylica cheered. "I like it when we have time to rest and play."

Roland put his knives away. "You said you know these lands, Hwasan. Is it much farther to the dragons?"

Hwasan thought for a moment. "I have never been to Meiling's Caverns myself, but I think it should only be another span or so of travel."

Roland nodded thoughtfully. "That would be good. We'd stand a chance of getting out of the mountains before the Great Sleep is fully upon us."

"The snow begins here long before it reaches the lower slopes."

"I know." Roland stared out at the rain. "What kind of terrain will we be facing?"

"It will be steep. Dragons live at a much higher elevation than this."

Roland frowned thoughtfully.

Zanele gave Hwasan a sidelong glance. "If you've never been to this dragon's cave before, how are you going to lead us there?"

Hwasan's scales shone orange in the gleam of the fire. "I just have to get us close enough. Her Minathrils will find us long before we reach it."

"How do you know that?"

"Every Dragon home is surrounded by Minathrils. They are always standing watch."

Zanele frowned. "Since when does a dragon need anyone to watch for them? They're a *Dragon*."

"I cannot say that I ever asked."

"For someone who asks so many questions, that really surprises me," Zanele retorted.

Sylica's snore echoed through the cave. She lay sprawled out by the fire, her head resting on Daisy's back.

"I do ask many questions," Hwasan replied, staring at Sylica as she slept, "but it seems that most of my questions remain unanswered, like where that strange metal dragon came from, and why you want to speak with the Dragons at all."

"And you think we would tell you that?" Zanele cocked an eyebrow. "We hardly know you!"

"You said you could be my crew."

"That doesn't mean we trust you." Zanele watched Hwasan keenly for a moment, then her eyes twinkled. "I don't trust half the people in my tribe to make a rational decision when it really counts, but I love them and I would die for them."

Hwasan frowned and stared into the fire, his scales a shade greyer than they had been before.

Zanele stoked Cheeky's back. "Trust has to be earned, but love and care can be given freely."

"I've never had a reason to trust or love anyone."

"Maybe that is changing now." Zanele smiled to herself and returned to organizing her medical bag.

It seemed that Hwasan had finished talking, so Thea took the chance to clean Raybow and sort through her arrows. Some of them had been damaged, and she set to work fixing them, silently thanking Elora for teaching her how.

After a rest, Roland went out hunting, but returned without any success.

Thea sat beside him as everyone gathered around the fire for the evening meal. Thankfully they still had food from Ember, though at the rate they were eating it, it wouldn't last long. The patter of rain outside the cave mingled with the crackling of the fire.

"I wouldn't be surprised if it changes to snow overnight," Roland reflected, his arms stretched out by the fire. "It's really cold out there."

Hwasan nodded. "If the water underfoot turns to ice, we may need to tread carefully tomorrow."

"I hadn't thought about ice." Roland frowned. "That would make it a lot harder to get up any cliffs. Would you recommend waiting for a warmer day?"

"There may be no more warmer days." Hwasan shrugged. "It is that time in the mountains."

"It might *snow*?" Sylica beamed. "I love snow! We can go sledding and make snow people and have all sorts of fun!"

"It won't be very fun for travelling in." Roland gave a

wry smile. "That's the problem, Sylica."

"Well it won't be fun if you don't *want* it to be fun," Sylica retorted. "I think we can have fun in the snow even if we are travelling! It turns everything into a guessing game!"

Daisy jumped around her, yapping excitedly.

"Good idea, Daisy!" Sylica beamed. "We should sing! I love singing around a campfire, and this cave sounds so echoey! See?" She started singing one of the songs Zanele had taught her. It was a lively, catchy tune. Thea found herself singing along, and soon everyone was joining in.

Roland threw more wood on the fire. "There's lots back there," he winked at Thea. "We might as well enjoy it."

The flames of the fire leapt and danced. Sylica tried to teach everyone a round, but she kept losing her place and soon there was more laughing than singing.

Thea watched Roland wipe tears of laughter from his eyes.

"I do not know many songs," Hwasan offered, "but I could tell a story."

Everyone listened as he told a tale about a strange, faraway place where sand stretched as far as the eye could see.

Then Roland told the tale of the Eagle's race against the Raven. Everyone listened breathlessly as he related the way the Raven had shortened her keel to cut across the shoals. Roland had lost that race, sailing on the Eagle, but his eyes shone as he spoke about the Raven and her crew. He mimicked Captain Svetka's brash manner of talking in such a lively way that everyone couldn't help laughing, and it was clear he thought the better ship had won.

As he finished his tale, Roland glanced out into the darkness of night. "We should sleep now." The fire had died down, and once again the cold crept closer.

Zanele nodded. "I'll take first watch."

Hwasan stood. "Could I take watch with you?"

Zanele grinned. "Be my guest."

Sylica grabbed her blanket and stretched out by the fire. Daisy flopped down beside her.

The cold night air seeped along the ground and filled the corners of the cave. Thea shivered as she fetched her cloak and blanket.

Across the cave, Roland laid out his blanket the way he did every night, with his knife close at hand.

Thea crept closer. "Roland?"

Roland glanced up.

Thea's voice caught in her throat. "Could ... could I sleep beside you again? I really liked that."

Roland smiled. "I did too. Here." He moved his blanket so there was room for her beside him.

Thea smiled shyly as she curled up next to Roland. His presence was warm and comforting. Roland shifted closer and wrapped his arm around her.

The cold night air didn't seem as cold anymore.

Thea lay and listened to the crackling of the fire. Roland's story left thoughts of Lyudmyla hovering uncomfortably in her mind. Roland was going back there, as soon as their errand to the dragons was done. Maybe she would go with him after all, just for a little while.

"Good night, Thea," Roland whispered.

Thea nestled closer. "Good night."

Chapter Fifteen

Sylica's squeal of excitement echoed through the cave, dragging Thea into the world of wakefulness. She opened her eyes in time to see Sylica scamper out of sight, followed by the scrambling clatter of Daisy trying to keep up.

Across the cave, Zanele pulled her blanket over her head.

Roland's eyes twinkled in the early morning light. "Someone is excited about the snow."

As Thea sat up, a rush of cold air tingled across her face. Beyond the mouth of the cave, the mountainside was covered in a soft, white blanket. Large flakes of slow drifted on a fitful breeze.

In the distance, Sylica began pushing and prodding a heap of snow into a vaguely person-like shape, singing at the top of her lungs.

Roland leaned out of the cave. "Sylica, you aren't wishing for snow, are you?"

Sylica looked up. "I don't have to wish for snow, it's already snowing!"

"Could you think warm thoughts for a bit?"

Sylica cocked her head. "Why?"

"We need to climb a mountain today. It would be a lot easier without the snow."

"Oh." Sylica seemed to consider this. "But snow is so pretty!"

With a helpless shrug, Roland returned to the fire.

Emerging from her cocoon of blankets, Zanele gave a wry smile. "You know she can't control her magic."

Roland's gaze turned back to the snow-covered world outside. "She can't control it all the time. That doesn't mean she never can."

Close by, Hwasan methodically folded his sleeping mat.

Thea took some time to check in, then joined the others by the fire.

Roland handed her a piece of jerky. "Anything from Allulien today?"

"No. Nothing since we left my house."

Roland pushed the last coals of the fire closer together. "I didn't hear anything either. I was hoping to get some guidance for our travel today, especially if the terrain is going to be rough."

"It's like that, sometimes." Zanele stroked Cheeky who lay curled up on her lap. "If you haven't heard anything for a while, it's worth a pause to make sure you've been listening, but otherwise you just keep going."

Thea sighed. "I know. It's just harder when there's nothing to hear."

"Sometimes hearing is harder, because then you have to do something."

Thea frowned. "Why wouldn't I want to do the Deity's will? I'd much rather have direct orders than be left to find my way on my own."

Zanele watched her with a thoughtful gaze. "Then you've never been told to do something you didn't want to do."

The mountainside was beautiful beneath its blanket of snow, but it was bitterly cold. Drifting flakes tingled on Thea's face as she stepped out from the shelter of their cave.

"Hi Thea!" Sylica scampered to join her. "Whoa!" Her feet slid in opposite directions and she tumbled to the ground.

As Thea stepped closer, her foot began to slide. Pushing a small patch of snow aside, her probing fingers met a solid sheet of ice.

Sylica struggled to her feet, grinning widely. "It's just like skating out here! Do you like my snow person?"

Thea examined the lumpy heap of snow. "It's very nice."

Roland joined them, setting his feet carefully. "You ready, Sylica? It will be slow going today, so we should start as soon as we can."

"I just need to get my bag!" Sylica scampered back to the cave, her feet sliding wildly in every direction.

Zanele eyed the snowy landscape with a disapproving gaze. "Any chance it will melt as the day goes on?"

Roland shook his head. "I doubt it. Not with how cold that wind is."

Zanele sighed. "Magic it is, then."

Thea smiled as the wave of magic washed over them. The ground was still icy underfoot, but her feet felt steadier as she shifted her weight and took a few experimental steps.

Sylica returned, followed by Hwasan. He walked confidently, the claws on his lizard-like feet digging into the ice.

He bowed. "If everyone is ready, we should proceed."

There was general assent, and they continued their trek up the mountainside.

Even with a magical blessing steadying their feet, their progress was very slow. Everyone had to walk cautiously, especially on the steeper slopes which became more and more frequent.

Hwasan led the way, venturing ahead to find the easiest path for the rest of the party. Sylica scampered after him, heedless of the ice underfoot—her perpetual motion somehow compensating for her lack of traction or coordination.

The cold seeped into Thea's bones as they waited once again for Hwasan to find a better route than the long, rocky incline that stretched before them.

"Unfortunately, this seems to be the best way forward," Hwasan reported as he returned.

Roland eyed the slope cautiously. Among the jumbled rocks, ice glimmered treacherously.

Hwasan bowed. "If you'll allow me." He held out a hand to Sylica who took it eagerly. They ventured up the icy slope together, Hwasan's claws digging into the cracks and fissures in the ice. Sylica's feet scrambled beneath her in a near-stationary sprint.

Roland had the foresight to tie his rope around Daisy's middle before she became agitated by Sylica's absence.

When Hwasan and Sylica reached the top, Zanele grabbed the end of the rope. "I'll take that. Hold on, Cheeky." Lightly, she ran up the slope, her goat-like hooves bounding from rock to rock. At the top she poised precariously on one of the larger boulders and waved to Hwasan and Sylica. "Come on, lend a hand."

Soon Daisy was pulled to the top and the rope was

lowered to help Thea and Roland in their ascent.

At the top of the slope, Thea found a secure place to stand and catch her breath. The mountain loomed large before them, stretching up into the clouds. What they had climbed was just the beginning.

Roland stared at the distant cliffs with dismay in his eyes.

Zanele grabbed the rope and threw it over her shoulder. "On we go!" she called, but her cheerfulness sounded forced. As she turned, her hooves slipped out from beneath her. The jolt sent Cheeky tumbling off her shoulder.

"Cheeky!" Sylica gasped, running to grab the little squirrel. Missing Cheeky entirely, her feet slid out from beneath her and she crashed into Zanele, landing in a jumbled heap.

Cheeky tumbled on, scrambling madly with her sharp little claws as she skidded across the rocks.

"I'll get her," Hwasan offered, hurrying after the little squirrel.

Before he could reach her, two Minathrils stepped out from behind the boulders, one on each side of him. They looked very much like Hwasan, with lizard-like features and crests. Their scales were bright orange.

Hwasan disappeared, leaving only his bag hanging in midair.

One of the Minathrils grabbed the empty air where Hwasan had been, speaking in a language Thea didn't recognize. She cast comprehension.

The Minathril's hand rested in midair, as if holding an invisible shoulder. "A strange Minathril, travelling alone. Where is your crew?"

The Minathril's hand moved, as if the invisible

shoulder had been wrenched away.

"I am not travelling alone," Hwasan's voice replied.

The Minathril's eyes flicked to Thea and her companions. "I said where is your crew, not who are these people."

"That is not your business," Hwasan replied, avoiding the Minathril's grasp again. "I am acting as guide for the people you see here. They wish to speak with Meiling."

The Minathril turned and really looked at them for the first time. "They are not creatures of the mountains. What is their business with Meiling?"

"Why don't you ask them? Their business is theirs, not mine."

The corners of the Minathril's scales were tinged with red. "Do you give your captain this kind of trouble? None of my crew would speak so." Turning away from Hwasan, the Minathril strode over to Thea and the others, eyeing them with a keen stare. Several more Minathrils emerged from the surrounding mountainside.

"What is your business with Meiling?" The leader of the Minathrils looked down at Thea and her companions with a cool, expressionless gaze.

Thea stepped forward. "We have something that belongs to the dragons and needs to be returned."

"And this something belongs to Meiling?"

Thea cringed beneath the Minathril's unblinking stare. "We don't know. That's why we want to speak with her."

"I see." The leader gestured to the other Minathrils, who circled around. "As it happens, Meiling sent us on patrol to intercept something that was approaching her territory. Whatever it was, we were to bring it to her. It seems that something is you."

Thea swallowed. "You'll show us the way?"

"We always follow the command of the Dragon. There is no question. You will go to Meiling."

"Thank you," Thea replied, though the Minathril's words sounded more like a threat.

The spirits of the Minathrils were light. Not bright like Roland's or Sylica's or Zanele's, but they did not have the presence of darkness Thea had grown accustomed to seeing in most people. It seemed as if these Minathrils followed the Deity in some way, but their manner was different than any Deity-followers she had ever met.

"I am Oreum Jeewon." The Minathril spoke in a clear, firm voice. "You are under the custody of the Oreum Crew, and I am their Captain."

"Pleased to meet you." Thea glanced around at the stoic faces of the Minathrils. "I am Thea. This is Roland, Zanele, and Sylica. Hwasan you already met."

"Yes." The Captain glanced at one of the other Minathrils. "Bring the lone one here."

Two Minathrils approached, with Hwasan between them. He was still not fully visible, but his scales were tinged with red. Cheeky scampered in front of him, past the legs of the other Minathrils, and scrambled up onto Zanele's shoulder, briefly scolding the Minathrils before ducking out of sight.

"This is Cheeky," Zanele interjected.

"And Daisy!" Sylica chimed in. "Daisy is my Dragon. Do you like her? She's just like a Dragon, but smaller."

The Captain's eyes took in Daisy for a moment, then flicked to Sylica's face. "An artificer. I see." She turned her impassive stare on Hwasan. "What is your name, lone one?"

"Awdub Hwasan."

"Awdub." The Captain's eyes narrowed. "I am not familiar with that crew."

"We come from south of here."

"What brings you north?"

"Study. Then I became a guide to these people."

"Bringing lowland people into the mountains at the cusp of the Great Sleep."

"Their business was urgent."

"I will be the judge of that."

"We can speak for ourselves," Thea interjected. "We are here because we don't want to be driven mad by dragon treasure. That's why we are bringing it back to the dragons."

The Captain looked at Thea with scales a shade greyer than they had been. "Usually lowland people come to take Dragon treasure, not return it."

"Maybe we're not like other people," Thea glared. "And leave Hwasan alone. He hasn't done anything wrong."

The Captain's scales gleamed a deeper orange. "There are very few reasons for a Minathril to not be with their crew, and most of them are not in his favour."

"So are you going to take us to see Meiling, or what?" Zanele muttered.

"People do not see Meiling. You will go to her Caverns. If she is so inclined, she will speak with you."

"So we'll go and see if Meiling would be inclined to speak with us?" Zanele's voice dripped with sarcasm.

"Yes," the Captain replied. "It is a two day's journey to the Caverns." The Captain's gaze lingered on Thea and her companions for a moment. "Actually, it may take three."

The Captain gestured to one of the other Minathrils. "This is Oreum Ssen, one of my Sergeants. He will see to your wellbeing."

The Captain turned away, giving orders to the other Minathrils in a clipped, authoritative voice.

The Sergeant took a moment to look over Thea and her companions. "You have a rope and warm clothing. That is good. If you are cold we have emergency blankets with us."

"Thank you," Thea replied. "I think we are warm enough." She glanced at the others to confirm this, but no one objected. "The most trouble we've had is trying to walk on this ice. It's very slippery for us." Like Hwasan, the Minathrils didn't seem to be having the same trouble.

The Sergeant nodded. "Even with claws it is a skill to be learned. Our young ones take a while before they can grasp it." His scales flashed yellow. "Fortunately, there are many of us, and we can provide the support you lack from your own feet." He called several of the Minathrils over and assigned two of them to walk alongside each of the strangers.

Oreum Ssen himself accompanied Thea, and they were joined by another Minathril who was a bit shorter but otherwise seemed identical to the Sergeant.

"This is Oreum Sungy. She is one of the newest members of the crew."

Thea smiled a greeting. Glancing back, she saw the others, each meeting their two Minathril companions. Hwasan was also accompanied by two Minathrils. His scales glowed a dull, pulsing red.

"Oreum Jeewon will lead the way," Ssen explained as he and Sungy took up positions on either side of Thea. "She patrolled these cliffs in the circles before she became Captain. If there is a way that will not be too difficult for you to climb, she will find it."

Thea nodded, feeling strangely small between the two Minathrils who stood a full head taller than her.

A command echoed across the mountainside, and the Minathrils began to move. After a few tentative steps, Thea felt her feet sliding again. Ssen took her arm on one side, and Sungy on the other. Supporting Thea's weight, they continued moving forward. When they reached the next rocky slope, the Minathrils walked right up it, as if its icy surface did not affect them at all. Thea tried to keep her feet beneath her, but she spent more time being dragged or carried than she did actually walking.

At the top, Thea smiled apologetically at her companions.

Ssen said something Thea couldn't understand. She cast comprehension. "Sorry, could you say that again? I don't understand your language."

Ssen's scales turned grey. "You don't speak Draconic? But how—" He paused and his scales brightened into gold. "You are a Shindah."

Thea frowned. "A what?"

"A Shindah. You follow the instruction of the Generals in service of the One."

"Yes, I am a servant of the Deity under Allulien. Roland serves beneath Micai and Zanele follows Raphea."

Ssan's scales faded to grey again. "Three Shindahs? The business that takes you to Meiling must be very

258

important. Why did you not tell us at once?"

"No one asked."

Ssen shook his head. "I must speak to Jeewon immediately." He nodded to Sungy and hurried away towards the cliff where the first few Minathrils were beginning their ascent.

Sungy seemed to look at Thea differently than she had before. "Will you continue walking?" she asked.

Thea nodded. As soon as she stepped forward, her feet slid again. Sungy half-caught her, but it took a moment before Thea stood steadily again.

"You must be careful with your feet." Sungy's scales became tan in colour. "Keep them beneath you, taking small steps. That is how we teach our young to walk on the ice."

Thea tried moving forward with small, careful steps.

"That is better. You do not need to rush."

"Thank you," Thea smiled. With her arm linked around Sungy's, she was able to move more steadily than she had before. "I heard you are new to this crew?"

Sungy nodded. "When the Great Sleep is over it will be the end of my first circle."

"How old are you? If it's okay to ask."

"Thirty-two circles."

Thea looked at Sungy in interest. She had just joined her crew, but she had already lived longer than any of the Fauns Thea had met. "How long do Minathrils usually live?"

"About a hundred circles."

"And it is around your age when you join your crew?"

"Yes. My mate also joined the Oreum. He is one of the escorts for the Faun."

Thea considered this. "So you don't always join the

same crew as your mate?"

"Sometimes we do and sometimes not. It depends on our interests and skills and where we are needed. Different crews have different purposes. Oreum is a scouting crew, and both my mate and I enjoy being out on the mountain. Others prefer to tend the gardens or learn the art of healing."

"And all of these crews serve Meiling?"

"Meiling is not the only Dragon in the Caverns. Two of her offspring live there, and they each have crews of their own."

"Which Dragon do you serve?"

"Liwei is the Dragon of the Oreum. He is our Commander."

"I thought your Captain said Meiling had commanded you."

"She did. Liwei serves Meiling and we serve Liwei. If Meiling commands us, we obey."

Ssen hurried back to join them.

"The Captain wishes to speak with the Shindahs immediately," he called as he approached.

Thea glanced back at the others who followed, spread out one cluster at a time on the rocky slope. Ssen went to speak to them, while Sungy led Thea to the foot of the cliff, where several Minathrils waited for them.

"Shindah," the Captain spoke as Thea approached. "Why did you not say that the Generals sent you to us?"

"Because they didn't." Thea watched the scales of the Minathrils fade to grey. "Our Generals have allowed us to go, but they did not send us. This errand is our own."

"I see." Jeewon stared at Thea. "We have Shindahs among our people, but neither they nor our Dragon have been told of your coming. I would have thought the arrival of three Shindahs might have been mentioned."

"We are travelling quietly."

"Hello!" Sylica cried, running up to join them. Her feet slipped and she skidded across the icy ground, landing in an undignified heap with a shriek of excitement.

Thea suppressed a smile. "Quiet, relatively speaking."

"I see." Jeewon's gaze took in Roland, Zanele, and Hwasan as they approached.

"All Shindahs are our honoured guests. You are under our protection and escort until we deliver you to Meiling."

"Thank you." Thea glanced at the stoic faces of the Minathrils. Some were grey and some were gold. Others were yellow and orange.

Jeewon gestured one of the Minathrils forward. "Oreum Tayhyang is our healer and the Shindah of our crew. He will bless our passage to make the way easier."

"Welcome, Shindahs." Tayhyang smiled. "The blessing of the Deity be on us as we climb." He gestured with his hand and Thea felt the surge of magic.

Zanele eyed the healer suspiciously, as if trying to size up how good of a healer he really was.

With a nod, Jeewon dismissed Tayhyang and turned back to Thea and her friends. "I have just returned from scouting the cliff. There is a route that should be passable, as long as the weather does not grow worse. You will each be fastened to your guides to ensure your safety. Do not be afraid to ask for help as you climb."

With her spear in her hand, Jeewon sprang lightly up the foot of the cliff, with two other Minathrils close behind.

Ssen joined Thea, a rope in his hand. Deftly, he tied it around Thea's waist and attached one end to himself and the other to Sungy.

As he worked, Thea glanced around the company of Minathrils that had gathered at the foot of the cliff. There seemed to be about fifty of them. They had all looked alike to her at first, but now Thea could see differences that distinguished one from another. The healer had a wider face. Ssen's crest had deep scallops in it. Sungy had a more pronounced forehead.

Sylica scrambled and slid across the rocks, giving out handfuls of candy, which the Minathrils solemnly accepted but did not eat. Sylica didn't seem to notice.

Ssen gestured Thea towards the cliff that towered above them. Glancing over her shoulder, she caught Roland's gaze. He gave her an encouraging smile.

With Ssen before her and Sungy behind, Thea began to climb. It was not as steep as the cliff Hwasan had led them up, but it still required great care to avoid a dangerous fall.

Along with her guides, Thea scrambled up shoulders of rock and edged along ledges no wider than her foot. Ice hung from the rocks and crunched underfoot.

The ice gave way. Thea tumbled down the slope in a shower of loose stones and fragments of ice until the rope stopped her with a jerk.

Thea clung to the rocks, her heart pounding in her ears. The rumble and crash of falling ice echoed from the depths beneath her feet. "Ssen?"

"You are safe." Ssen stood wedged between two boulders. His scales flared a brilliant orange.

Where was Sungy? The other end of the rope seemed

to be fastened on thin air.

"I am here." Sungy's voice came from just above the end of the rope. "I am sorry. That frightened me."

"It frightened me too." Thea turned her eyes back to Ssen. With one hand on the rope, he helped her back onto the ledge.

Thea leaned back against the solid face of rock. Sungy joined her, her scales a strange, almost transparent tan.

Thea stared at her. "Were you invisible?"

The tan of Sungy's scales grew stronger. "Minathrils become camouflaged when we are frightened. It is a way we can protect ourselves."

Thea nodded. Hwasan had seemed to disappear when the Oreum found them. He must have been frightened.

"Do Minathril colours mean something too?"

"They change according to how we feel," Ssen explained.

Thea looked at Ssen. His scales had turned green. "How are you feeling now?"

"I am feeling content. We stopped your fall, and we made it past many obstacles without falling."

"I see. Sungy, what about you?"

Sungy's scales became even more tan than they were before. "I am embarrassed. I should not have been so frightened when you fell, but this is my first time helping someone up a cliff like this, and I do not love heights."

"It's okay, Sungy." Thea gave her an encouraging smile. "I don't think I would ever stop being afraid of cliffs like this."

"If you do not like cliffs, you did not choose the best

way of approaching the Caverns." Sungy shook her head. "You looked so calm, I did not think you were frightened at all."

Thea glanced down at her trembling hands. "I guess we show our emotions differently than you."

"Clearly so." The tan of Sungy's scales became tinged with green. "I never met someone from the other races before."

"And I had never met a Minathril before I met Hwasan." Thea smiled. "Thank you for teaching me."

Ssen bowed. "If you are ready, we will continue now."

Thea got gingerly to her feet. "I think I'm ready."

As they continued to follow the narrow ledge, Thea glanced back down the slope at the others.

"Why does Hwasan have people helping him? He can walk on the ice as well as you."

Ssen glanced over his shoulder. "They are not there to help him, they are there to watch him."

"Why?"

"The good Dragons are not the only ones who have Minathrils. His crew is not familiar to us, so we have to be careful."

Thea frowned. "You think he comes from a bad Dragon?"

"We do not know." Ssen's scales gleamed orange. "If we did, he would be dead. As it is, we will watch him closely."

"But he's helping us."

"There can be many motivations for helping. We have seen enough of war to never let our guard down. Our Dragon depends on it."

Ssen moved on, and Thea followed.

"Do the Minathrils protect the Dragons?"

"It is the Dragon who protects us, but one Dragon cannot be everywhere at once. We are the hands and feet of the Dragon. We stand guard against the small threats. Our Dragon stands guard against the big ones."

"What kind of big threats?"

"Evil Dragons. Our Dragon is faithful to the One, but there are Dragons who prefer the lies of the Wishful One. Ever since the Wishful One fell, the Dragons have been fighting, and their Minathrils have stood with them."

"So you *are* fighting against evil."

Ssen's scales flickered grey. "Of course. Did you think otherwise?"

"You never leave the mountains. We thought you didn't care about the rest of Raphtova."

"If it wasn't for the faithful Dragons and their Minathrils, evil Dragons would roam free across Raphtova, bringing destruction and chaos."

Thea stared at the Minathrils, spread out along the long track up the cliff. Here they were, serving the Deity after all. If the five races were already accounted for, perhaps this was the purpose of the Minathrils, to be the helpers and companions of the Dragons in the fight against evil.

Hwasan's scales flickered red. Why hadn't he told them what his scale colours meant? It wouldn't have done any harm, would it?

"Careful!" a Minathril's voice rang out as Sylica slipped on a difficult stretch of cliff.

Sylica's face was drawn up in a pout. "It's too slippery!"

The ice disappeared—its absence spreading out from

Sylica in a fast-expanding circle until the entire cliff was dry and bare.

Sylica stuck her chin in the air. "That's better."

Everyone stared.

"Dragon magic!"

Thea turned to look at Ssen—where Ssen should have been. He had gone completely camouflaged, but quickly faded into grey.

Thea swallowed. "Dragon magic?"

"That toy Dragon," Ssen demanded, "can it do Dragon magic?"

"I don't know," Thea stammered. "I think it's been making Sylica do magic."

"But that's Dragon magic."

"What does that mean?" Thea protested. "What kind of magic can Dragons do?"

All along the route up the cliff, Minathrils were talking excitedly.

"Dragons don't do magic. Dragons *are* magic. They can change the world just by thinking about it."

Thea stared. That sounded like Sylica.

"You think that was Dragon magic?"

"I know it was Dragon magic. What else could make the ice disappear as if it had never been there?"

Thea tore her gaze away from Sylica and Daisy, scrambling cheerfully across the rocks. "I don't know, but that's what we are here to find out."

Without the ice underfoot, the climb became much easier. Even so, it was well into restday before they reached the top of the cliff.

Jeewon continued to lead them on, away from the cliff and further up the mountain. After another measure of walking, they reached a sheltered valley with a small stream flowing nearby.

Jeewon gave a command, and all around Thea the Minathrils began to set up camp.

Left unattended for the moment, Thea and her companions gathered together again.

"Well that was interesting." Zanele flopped down on a bare patch of ground, eyeing the Minathrils with a skeptical gaze.

"We have so many new friends now!" Sylica beamed. "Everyone loves Daisy so much! Did you see that? I knew I had the best friend in all the world!"

Finally able to stop and breathe for a moment, Thea felt the adrenaline of the day begin to fade. The bustling clamour of the Minathrils all around them seemed loud and overwhelming.

Roland put his arm around her shoulders. "You doing alright?"

Thea relaxed into the comfort of his presence. She nodded. "I'm just tired."

"That was a long day," Roland agreed, "but I'm glad we made it up that cliff alright."

Hwasan stood nearby, his scales a dull brown, watching the other Minathrils with a sullen expression. It seemed to Thea that his spirit was darker again, more like it had been when they first met him.

Ssen approached and indicated that he would like to speak. Thea cast comprehension again.

"The Captain wishes to speak with you," Ssen reported. He looked at Hwasan. "All of you."

Following Ssen through the camp, they found Jeewon sitting on a large, flat stone, talking with two other Minathrils. She stopped and turned towards Thea as she approached.

"You did not tell me that you brought Dragon magic with you. Does this have something to do with your business with Meiling?"

"Yes." Thea glanced at Sylica. "Strange things have been happening ever since Sylica found this strange ... metal Dragon. We believe that it needs to be returned to the Dragons."

The edges of Jeewon's scales were tinged with gold. "I begin to understand why you consider your errand to be urgent. Dragon magic is powerful, and I have never heard of it being possessed by any but a Dragon. Perhaps Meiling will give the answer to this enigma."

"We hope so."

Oblivious, Sylica danced around Daisy, who hopped on her hind legs and yapped excitedly.

Jeewon gestured for Ssen to approach again and turned to Thea. "You are tired from a long day. You and your companions will go and get what rest you can. We travel again tomorrow at first light."

Ssen led them to the foot of an overhanging cliff. "You can make yourselves a place to get comfortable here. Food is being prepared by the fire, which you are welcome to partake in if you do not have your own."

Ssen returned to the rest of the crew, leaving Thea and her companions alone. With the cliff at their backs, the Minathrils surrounded them on every other side. They would not be able to leave without their guides knowing or questioning why they were doing so.

Collecting some food from the Minathrils, they ate in silence, with the exception of Sylica who wandered around the camp, talking happily with anyone who would listen. The Minathrils watched Daisy intently as she scampered along at Sylica's heel.

Zanele sat on a rock and fed nuts to Cheeky. "There sure are a lot of them," she frowned, eyeing the Minathrils. "And this is only one crew."

"How many crews can a Dragon have?" Thea asked, glancing at Hwasan.

Hwasan sat removed from the others. His scales flickered red. "It depends on how old the Dragon is."

"How long do Dragons live?"

"They live forever, unless someone kills them."

Thea considered this. "So they could keep getting more and more Minathrils."

Hwasan nodded.

"How old was the Dragon your crew used to serve?"

"I do not know. I was too young to remember."

Around them, Minathrils prepared for nightfall.

"I guess you never met this crew before, since they didn't know your name."

"No. I was travelling alone, so I did my best to avoid encounters with other Minathrils. You may have seen why." His scales flared red again.

Thea gave an apologetic smile. "I think they were just trying to be careful."

"I'm sure," Hwasan muttered, and withdrew into himself again.

Zanele gestured over their sleeping area. "We didn't get to rest much today. Might as well be sure we sleep well tonight."

Thea nodded. Blessing their camp was the best way to ensure that a long day of travel didn't sabotage the next.

She yawned. Night hadn't begun yet, but weariness dragged at her limbs. "I guess we don't need to set watches tonight." She glanced at Roland to see what he would say.

He eyed the Minathril camp that surrounded them on every side. "They serve the Deity," he said in a low voice.

Thea nodded. "At least they serve a Dragon that serves the Deity, but their healer is beneath Raphea."

Roland nodded. "Then I think we are safe." He glanced at Thea. "That will be nice, for a change."

Thea's eyes followed Sylica as she continued to make friends amongst the Minathrils. Should she call her back? Anything could happen when Sylica was left to her own devices.

Nothing else had happened since the incident on the cliff, though, and the Minathrils seemed to treat her with a cautious deference.

Getting her blanket, Thea joined Roland by the foot of the cliff. They talked for a while, about the day and the climb and the Minathrils. Slowly the light faded from the sky.

Feeling Roland's arms around her, Thea closed her eyes and let the strain of the day fade away.

That was so much nicer than sleeping alone.

Chapter Sixteen

Thea woke to the murmur of the Minathril crew, feeling more rested than she had in days.

Roland lay beside her, watching her face with a sleepy, contented expression.

Warmth flooded over Thea. If she could wake up like this every morning ...

Roland smiled. "Ready to check in?"

Thea nodded, bracing herself to face the cold world outside their cocoon of blankets.

Sylica was already happily chatting with the Minathrils—if she'd ever stopped at all—though without Thea's comprehension magic, it was clear they couldn't understand a word she was saying.

After another silent check in, Thea looked up to see Ssen waiting patiently. He gestured to his ears and Thea cast comprehension.

Ssen bowed. "When you have finished, the Captain wishes to speak with you. Alone."

Thea glanced at Roland. "I can come now."

A glimmer of concern passed through Roland's eyes.

Thea laid a hand on his shoulder. "I'll be back soon."

She followed Ssen across the frost-covered mountainside to the flat rock where they found Jeewon waiting alone. Her scales gleamed gold in the early morning light.

Jeewon bowed as Thea approached, then turned to

Ssen. "Thank you, Sergeant. You may go."

With her hands behind her back, Jeewon waited until Ssen had disappeared among the other Minathrils, then turned her keen reptilian gaze on Thea. "Oreum Tayhyang, our healer, heard from Raphea this morning. Your identities as Shindahs was confirmed, as was your intent to speak with Meiling. In this you have been truthful with us." Her golden scales gleamed as her eyes seemed to read every feature on Thea's face. "We also learned that you are the Spark that was foretold. Is this so?"

Uncertainty twisted in Thea's stomach. "I have been called the Spark, but I don't know what that means."

Jeewon cocked her head. "The Dragons foretold that one day a Spark would come to bring light back to the peoples of Raphtova. I am honoured to meet the Spark in my lifetime and receive you under my protection."

"I—I don't understand," Thea stammered. "How come you and the Fauns seem to know all about this when I have no idea what's going on?"

"You met the Fauns?" Jeewon's crest moved strangely. "I am surprised to hear they are still alive."

Thea froze. "Why wouldn't they be?"

"They run around the forest with no disciple or order at all. It is a wonder they don't kill themselves with their carelessness."

Thea's face grew hot. "Thabani and the Resistance are excellent fighters. If it wasn't for them the forest would be overrun with monsters."

Jeewon examined her spear with a stoic expression. "As soon as they turn their backs they will find that the monsters are there again. If you fail to follow up on your victories properly, any advantage you have earned is lost."

"If you think they should be more disciplined, maybe you should go down there and teach them." Thea's eyes flashed. "Why do you leave them alone in their forests to 'kill themselves with carelessness'? We'll never win against the darkness if we treat each other like that."

Jeewon's scales flared red. "We follow the command of our Dragon. There are more important things to be done than running through the forests after the Fauns."

Thea stared into Jeewon's spirit. It wasn't dark, but if her eyes couldn't see it she wouldn't have believed it.

"As for your identity," Jeewon continued, "none of my crew know, besides Tayhyang and myself. It will remain so, but at my command they will redouble their security and precautions. What do your companions know?"

"Roland is my protector, appointed by Micai. Zanele is a skilled healer under Raphea. They both know about the Spark."

Jeewon nodded.

"Sylica I trust with my life, but I'm not sure how much she understands."

"Raphea told us she could be trusted." Silence hung in the air. "Awdub Hwasan?"

"We only met him a few days ago. He doesn't know anything."

Jeewon watched Thea for a moment. Her scales gleamed orange. "Regarding the lone one, we were told that he is supposed to be with the Spark, by Enkeli's intent."

Enkeli? Thea did her best to hide her surprise. She'd never even met Enkeli. What were they wanting from her?

Jeewon's eyes gleamed. "Do you know why this would be?"

"I ..." Sudden confidence surged. "I think he needs to learn about the Deity."

"Raphea said you are the only one who may be able to help him." Jeewon's gaze was piercing. "This did not ease our concern about his presence here, but it seems we do not have a choice in this matter."

Thea frowned. "If he needs help, why would you send him away?"

"Because he is dangerous. I will not tell the Spark what to do, but you must be careful."

Watching Jeewon's cold, expressionless eyes, Thea's face grew hot. "I have seen his spirit and it is dark, but I have seen darker spirits change."

Jeewon's golden scales gleamed. "You can see within a spirit?"

"I can."

Jeewon seemed to regard her in a new way.

Thea shrugged. "Some Elves can do that. It's not that special."

"Perhaps. Or it may be that there is hope for this lone one after all."

"There would be more hope for him if you weren't so harsh! He has received nothing but judgement and rejection since he met you!"

Jeewon's scales flared red. "You clearly do not understand Minathrils."

"Maybe. But I *can* see when someone's spirit is getting *darker* because of the way they are treated. And you claim to be good?"

The impassive expression on Jeewon's face did not flicker. "Our priority is the safety of our people and the success of our objective."

"Well, maybe you should care about other things." Thea glared up into the Captain's emotionless face. "Like showing mercy."

Turning, Thea stormed back to where Roland waited for her. She threw herself down on the ground, stewing in a seething mass of discontent. "They're just as bad as the Elves! Proud, stuck up, uncaring—"

Roland rested a hand on her shoulder. "Thea ..."

Tearing her gaze away from the ground, Thea looked up into Roland's patient eyes.

He offered a tentative smile. "Maybe that will start changing now."

Thea sighed. "Maybe."

Roland leaned closer. "Thea—"

"Are you ready to begin?" Ssen called, approaching from the midst of the Minathril camp. "We have another long day before us."

Thea glanced from Roland to Zanele nearby. Hwasan stood alone at a distance, and Sylica was already skipping cheerfully among the Minathrils.

Reluctantly, Thea stood. "Yes, we are ready."

They followed Ssen to where Jeewon was waiting for them.

Jeewon acknowledged their approach. "Thea, for your travelling companions today, I will continue to assign Ssen, but for the second I will offer another of my Sergeants."

"No." Thea watched a ripple of colour pass through the surrounding Minathrils. "With your permission, Captain, I would like to have Sungy with me again. She did very well yesterday."

Jeewon eyed Thea for a moment. "Very well. Sungy,

you will accompany Thea again."

Sungy stepped forward and bowed.

Thea's friends each received their two escorts, and Jeewon gave the command for the day's travel to begin.

"You are yellow," Thea whispered as Sungy strode alongside her.

Sungy nodded. "That is because I am happy to travel with you again. Thank you for asking for me."

On Thea's other side, Ssen seemed more alert and attentive than he had before. They talked a little, but when the comprehension magic faded, they walked in silence.

Over the course of the day, Jeewon and her crew led Thea and her companions up another cliff and even further up the mountainside. As restday passed, they arrived at the foot of another cliff, larger than any they had climbed so far. As Thea stared at it in dismay, Ssen gestured that he wanted to speak.

Thea cast her magic.

"We will stop here for the night. The Captain has given orders to make camp."

"Good." Thea tried to control the quiver in her voice. "I don't think I could handle that cliff just now."

Ssen's scales shifted yellow and his crest shook. "We will not be leading you up any more cliffs. The Tunnels are close."

Thea let out the breath she had been holding. "Tunnels?"

"The way into Meiling's Caverns."

Around them, Minathrils began to set up their camp. In the distance, Jeewon spoke to two of her sergeants with the same stoic expression Thea had seen on her face all day.

Ssen turned to Thea. "You upset the Captain this morning. I have not seen her like that in many circles."

"Really? It didn't seem like she was feeling anything."

"Did you see the way her crest was up and how red her scales were? She was furious!"

"I had no idea." Thea racked her mind, trying to recall anything other than Jeewon's stoic face. "I'm not used to watching for colours like that."

"You seemed completely calm."

"What? I was practically shaking, I was so mad."

Ssen's crest waved slowly, but now his scales were grey. "It seems that there is much to learn. Would you trade lessons with me? I can teach you about our emotions, and you can teach me about yours."

"I think that would help." Thea glanced around the camp. A couple of Minathrils were lighting a fire. Others were preparing food or laying out mats for sleeping. "That Minathril there. What are they feeling like?" Thea pointed to a Minathril with orange scales. "I see that colour a lot."

"We show that colour when we are determined or focused. She has a job to do and she wants to do it well. What do you look like when you are determined?"

Thea considered this for a moment. "We lower our eyebrows a little. And we stare at what we're trying to do. I think." It was harder to explain than she expected. She glanced around the camp. "How Roland looks a lot of the time, really."

"Roland is often determined?"

"These days he is. He takes our safety very seriously."

Ssen's scales faded to grey.

"What are you feeling now?"

Yellow flashed across Ssen's scales. "I was thinking about what you said. Roland seems very responsible. He would make a good Minathril."

Thea's eyes followed Roland as he crossed the camp. "Grey is thinking?"

"Thoughtful, yes, but the meaning changes along with the movement of our crest." He gestured to the long ridge of skin that stretched from his forehead to his upper back. "My crest was waving, which shows I was thoughtful. If my crest was still it would have shown confusion, and if it was back it would have shown worry."

Around Thea and Ssen, the Minathrils continued to set up their camp. Sylica was in the thick of things, chattering away, while the Minathrils around her nodded solemnly, unable to understand a word she was saying. There had been another occasion of Dragon magic during the day's travel: a fully grown apple tree—with apples—had appeared, growing out of a crack in the cliff. Sylica had enjoyed the apples immensely, though she had almost fallen down the cliff while trying to pick them.

On one side of the fire, Tayhyang sorted his medical equipment, while Zanele watched him with cautious interest. At the edge of the camp, a group of Minathrils had gathered for some kind of weapons training. Roland sat nearby, watching them with an eager gaze.

Hwasan stood alone at the foot of the cliff, his scales betraying a bitter defensiveness. No one seemed interested in speaking to him.

"You approached Meiling's territory from the east, didn't you?" Ssen asked when the lesson was over. "Did you see any sign of goblins on your way? We try to track their activities, when we can."

Thea nodded. "We met them when we were climbing the pass and got caught in a rainstorm. They took us to meet Big Boss, but we didn't learn much about what they've been doing."

Ssen's scales faded to grey, but now his crest was back. "You were able to get away?"

"I gave them my sword as payment for passing through. I never used it much, so I don't miss it."

Ssen's crest rose to show confusion. "You didn't have to fight?"

"We didn't want to fight them. They're really Littles, you know."

"Littles?"

"One of the five races. People only call them goblins because they don't know any better."

"But those creatures are fierce! I have never heard of anyone walking away from them unscathed. How did you do it?"

"I got Sylica to start talking."

Ssen stared at Sylica, who was still skipping about the camp, talking cheerfully with anyone who would pretend to listen.

"Did she use Dragon magic?"

"I don't think so. She was just being Sylica. Listen."

Thea cast comprehension across the whole camp.

The Minathrils turned to stare at Sylica as she continued talking, oblivious of the change around her.

From the snatches of sentences that drifted to Thea's ears, she caught something about boots that only worked when you screamed, something to do with Ulfgar's axe, and apple pie.

All around her, Minathrils stopped to listen. Thea

watched as amused yellow scales faded into grey confusion, but Sylica was only getting started.

"Has she stopped to breathe?" Ssen asked, his scales equally grey.

"I'm not sure if she ever does." Thea watched with an amused grin as the candy bag came out and handfuls of sweets were thrust into the hands of the bewildered Minathrils.

"I don't understand." Ssen stared, grey confusion colouring his scales. "What is she doing?"

"She is just being Sylica."

"And that is how you got away from the goblins?"

Thea nodded. "And giving them a sword."

Jeewon strode over to join them. "This was your doing, I imagine."

"Not really. I did cast comprehension, but just so they could understand what she was already saying."

Jeewon watched Sylica, her orange-grey scales tinted with red. "She has completely baffled and distracted over half of my crew. I would order you to stop her, but it is so fascinating to watch."

Thea shrugged. "This is just her natural state. Trying to get her to stop is the difficult part. Give her a moment or two and she'll probably try to start a dance. And there she goes now."

Sylica and Daisy leapt and twirled around the fire. Beneath her exuberant influence, a few of the Minathrils began to join in. One of the cooks used a set of pans to pound out a drumbeat.

Jeewon watched the growing revelry. "It is not uncommon for our crews to enjoy this kind of fun, but never when on duty. It may not be Dragon magic, but I think it is a kind of magic all the same." She gave Thea a cunning glance. "I thought you were foolish to be travelling with so small of a guard. I begin to see that you are not as unprotected as I thought."

After a while, the dance came to an end, and one by one the Minathrils returned to their work.

When the evening meal was ready, Jeewon invited Hwasan to sit next to her. Hwasan seemed to resent this, but sat where he was bid.

With comprehension magic still hanging over the camp, a couple of the Minathrils were persuaded to tell a tale, and Sylica told the story of the Littles' escape from the Deorcian. Thea could tell that both Jeewon and Ssen listened with interest. What they thought about the idea that goblins were really Littles created by the Deity, Thea wasn't sure, but if the Minathrils themselves weren't one of the five, would they even care? They didn't seem to have much concern about the fate of those who lived below them on the rest of Raphtova.

Chapter Seventeen

The next morning, Thea looked up from her check in to see Jeewon waiting for her. Bowing her head, Thea took a little longer to cast comprehension than she needed to, then got to her feet. "Do you need something, Captain?"

The Captain watched her intently, her scales gleaming with gold. Ssen hadn't explained what gold meant. Thea made a mental note to ask him later.

"You may call me Jeewon. I want to show you something."

Jeewon led Thea away from the camp. Following a well-worn path, they rounded a shoulder of rock and found themselves at the top of a tall cliff.

The clouds that had covered the mountains for the past several days were gone. All around the crag on which they stood, snow-capped mountains gleamed in the golden light of Allumen. Far below them, glittering waterfalls twinkled in the deep blue valleys. Tree-cloaked mountainsides stretched up, up, to become sheer cliffs and rocky bluffs, and above them all towered jagged white peaks that seemed to pierce the sky.

"This is the home of the Minathrils." Jeewon spoke in a low voice. Her face seemed as stoic as ever, but her scales glimmered yellow and green.

"It's beautiful," Thea replied, unable to hide the

wonder in her voice.

Jeewon pointed to the largest of the peaks. "Do you see that mountain?"

Thea nodded.

"Beneath it lies the Caverns of Meiling."

Thea stared. "I thought you said it was only a three day's journey to get there. We've already travelled two!"

"You are correct. We should be there by staph."

"But—but how is that possible?"

Jeewon's crest shook, just a little. "You are about to see *real* Dragon magic."

Leading Thea back to the camp, Jeewon called for Ssen. "Take your company ahead and report to the Dragon. Thea will travel with me today."

Ssen bowed and turned away.

Thea's heart sank as she watched him go, but it seemed that she didn't have a choice. She would be walking with the Captain.

Jeewon gave a command to her crew, and the Minathrils began to assemble.

Thea collected her bag and went to join Jeewon, standing a respectful distance from the Minathril Captain.

The atmosphere was different now. She could see it in the colours that glistened on the scales around her and the way the Minathrils stood and formed their ranks. Today was going to be different.

At another command from the Captain, the company set out.

As they rounded a spur of the mountain, the yawning mouth of a large cave appeared before them. The leading company of Minathrils marched in without a moment's pause.

Thea and Jeewon followed. Inside, the air was dry and still. It seemed warm compared to the brisk, icy wind that blew across the mountainside.

Jeewon turned to Thea with a brief, formal bow. "Welcome to the Tunnels. They will lead us to the Caverns of Meiling."

The angles carved in the walls of the tunnel carried the echoes of daylight along with them, lighting the way with a dim, luminous glow.

Thea stared at the cavernous size of the passageway—so different than the narrow tunnels of the Littles. She risked walking a little closer to Jeewon. "Was this made for Dragons to travel through?"

"No. Dragons fly, and this tunnel would be too small unless the Dragon was very young." A gleam of pride showed on her scales. "These tunnels were made to move troops, like ours. There is nowhere in our Dragon's territory that we cannot reach within two days."

"How big is your Dragon's territory?"

"What I showed you this morning was only a part of it."

After marching for about two measures, Jeewon called a halt. She turned to Thea. "There is something I wish to show you."

As Jeewon led her to the side of the tunnel, Thea noticed a smaller passage, leading away through the shadows. She followed her guide through the passage and up a long flight of stairs. At the top, another cave mouth opened onto the mountainside. Thea squinted in the intense glare of blue-white light.

"See that mountain there?" Jeewon gestured.

Thea stared as her eyes adjusted to the brightness.

"That is where the tunnel began."

Thea gasped. As far as her limited experience of travelling in the mountains could tell her, she would have guessed it was a two day's journey away, at least.

"And that is the mountain where we are going." Jeewon drew her attention to the large peak she had indicated before. It was still a great distance away, but not as far as it had been.

"How did we get so far so quickly?"

Jeewon's scales flashed yellow. "Dragon magic."

"I don't understand."

Jeewon turned her keen eyes on Thea. "Dragons simply make things happen. That is what Dragon magic is: changing the world to be the way you want it to be. Meiling wanted these tunnels to take only a few measures to travel through, so that is the way they are."

Thea stared at the distance they had travelled in only a couple of measures. "So they can do whatever they want?"

"They can, but they choose not to."

"Why?"

A ripple of colour passed over Jeewon's scales. "We do not question the Dragon." She turned her piercing eyes on Thea's face. "Remember that."

Turning, Jeewon began the long walk back down the stairs.

Thea followed. "Why do you keep saying 'the Dragon'? I'm never sure which Dragon you mean."

"Meiling is *the* Dragon. This is her territory and we are going to her Caverns. The Dragon is our Commander and highest authority. Her offspring who live in her Caverns are also beneath her command, but as they grow they are taking greater responsibility and building their own crews. Liwei is *our* Dragon. If Meiling is ever killed in war, he may become the Dragon in her place, or he may choose someday to leave the Caverns and claim his own territory. If he does so, the Oreum will go with him."

They returned to the tunnel, and the Minathrils continued their march. Periodically, Jeewon called Thea aside to show her how far they had come. It was hard to believe, but the mountain where the Dragon lived drew steadily nearer.

A large crossroads opened up on either side of the tunnel.

"We have entered the Caverns of Meiling." Jeewon's face was stoic, but her scales showed a glad determination.

The tunnel didn't appear any different than it had before, but Thea realized, with surprise, that there was no way that daylight could still be refracting along the stone walls and ceiling, but somehow they still shone with light, filling the corridor with a warm, gentle daylight.

The Minathrils marched on. Thea craned her neck to look around, but couldn't see any sign of the tunnels being inhabited.

As they entered a large, cavernous room, they found Ssen and his company waiting for them.

Jeewon turned to her crew. "Ssen and his company will escort our guests. The rest of the crew is off duty until tomorrow."

The Minathrils dispersed. No longer marching, they strolled away in small groups, talking cheerfully amongst themselves.

Ssen's company remained, standing at attention. Jeewon nodded to Thea. "The Dragon will see you immediately."

The Captain led the way through a series of corridors, each as plain and unadorned as the first tunnel had been. Voices echoed in the distance, but no other Minathrils appeared until they entered a small chamber. There, a lone Minathril stood guard. A chain of gold hung around the guard's neck and their spear was more ornate than anything Thea had seen among the Oreum.

Jeewon bowed and spoke with the guard, pointing to Thea and her companions. The guard nodded and gestured for them to pass.

A low rumble shook the ground beneath their feet. Thea glanced at Roland. His eyes were wide. Golden light refracted down the corridor to meet them, glinting off Jeewon's scales as she led the way.

An absence made Thea glance over her shoulder. Ssen and his company remained beside the guard, their ranks filling the exit like an impassive wall.

Thea hurried to keep up to Jeewon's purposeful stride. Around them, the golden light grew brighter and they stepped out into a massive cavern.

Before them lay the Dragon. It filled the cavern, its body folded upon itself into a form so dazzlingly large that Thea could not comprehend its shape. Beneath the Dragon, a bed of golden treasure stretched out in every direction.

Thea felt the sharp intakes of breath from her companions as they stepped into the cavern behind her.

Jeewon bowed and stepped aside, leaving Thea and her companions standing before the Dragon.

It stared at them with massive green eyes, its scales reflecting with glimmers of every colour imaginable. With a rumble like distant thunder, it opened its mouth.

With her heart in her throat, Thea cast—

"That will not be necessary, Small One." The cavern shook beneath their feet with the sound of the Dragon's voice. "Welcome to the Caverns of Meiling. You have travelled far to find the answers that you seek."

Thea felt Roland's presence beside her, but she couldn't tear her eyes away from the enormous, dazzling sight of the Dragon before them. Even Sylica was silent.

The Dragon's eyes gleamed. "Meiling will speak with you now."

Thea stared as the massive eyes looking down on them became a dazzling golden colour.

"Welcome, Small Ones." The Dragon spoke again, but the voice that shook the walls of the cavern sounded different than it had before. The massive, golden eyes swept across their party with a piercing gaze. Through Liwei's body, Meiling smiled. "Welcome, Thea of the Elves. I have heard your name spoken before. Welcome, Roland of the Elves, and Zanele of the Resistance. Welcome, Sylica, and welcome, Awdub Hwasan of Dark Rock."

Hwasan's scales faded to grey. "You know my crew?"

"I do," Meiling rumbled. "Julong of Dark Rock was a friend of mine, before he and his crews were killed. It was believed there were no survivors."

A surge of emotions rushed across Hwasan's scales.

"That was long ago, in circles as you count them," Meiling rumbled. "Tell me, why did you not come for our aid before now?"

Hwasan almost disappeared as his scales faded into the colour of the wall at his back. "I am just a guide," he said in an even voice. "I am not here for any reason of my own."

Meiling swept her piercing gaze across the group. "So." Her voice rumbled. "Tell me why you have come to seek the Dragons."

Thea tried to swallow, but her throat was dry. "Because we found this." She pointed at Daisy. Her voice sounded small and weak, compared with the Dragon's rich voice. "We think it's causing Dragon magic."

Meiling turned her piercing stare on the little Dragon. "A collector. It has been many circles of Raphtova since I saw one of those."

"A what?" Thea ventured.

"A collector of Dragon treasure, made to bring back pieces that have been lost or stolen." Meiling's voice rumbled. "A good idea at the time, but once they collected too much Dragon treasure, they began to generate their own magical field. We stopped using them a long time ago. Where did you find it?"

"In an old house near the sea."

Meiling nodded. "There was an artificer there who had an interest in modifying them. We sent one for his experiments."

"So you don't need Daisy anymore?" Sylica asked, her eyes wide as she stared at the Dragon.

Meiling smiled. "No, we do not."

"Oh good." Sylica ginned. "Then you won't take her away."

"I wouldn't dream of it." Meiling's rumble almost sounded like a laugh.

Thea stared in alarm. "But Meiling, it has been doing Dragon magic. Can't you make it stop?"

"The collector cannot do Dragon magic. Only a Dragon can do Dragon magic." Meiling's eyes narrowed. Raising her head, she leaned closer. Something rumbled in the back of her throat.

With a rattle of gold and jewels, Meiling lifted her arm. With a deft movement she turned Daisy over and opened the panel with a dagger-sharp claw. Scooping up a pile of treasure, she poured it into Daisy and shut the panel. Daisy jumped to her feet and shook herself.

Thea stared. The cavity inside Daisy was already full, but at least twice as much treasure had just been added without overflowing it.

"That will be enough," the Dragon rumbled. "The magical field will be large enough to contain the outbursts. Make sure it never leaves the Green One's side."

"I—I don't understand," Thea stammered.

"If a Dragon does not have enough treasure to maintain their magical field, it spills out into the world, causing uncontrolled surges of magic like you have seen."

"But Daisy isn't even a real Dragon!"

"I was speaking of Sylica."

Thea stared.

Sylica's hands flew to her mouth. She squealed. "Am I a *Dragon*?"

"No." Meiling rumbled. "There is not a drop of Dragon blood in you, but you do have Dragon magic."

Thea's mouth hung open. "How is that possible?"

"I do not know. I must take council with the Tilaryn and see what I can learn. I will speak to you again in two spans' time."

Thea looked at Roland in alarm. Did they have to wait in the mountains for that long?

"Your time here is not for nothing," Meiling rumbled. "As we speak, a storm is rolling across the mountains that will make travel impossible for many days. And do not think that your errand is the only reason that brought you so far to the Caverns of Meiling. The Deity has other purposes for the Spark."

Thea's stomach felt hollow. Out of the corner of her eye, she saw Hwasan's scales gleam gold.

Sylica raised her hand. "Can we go exploring now?"

"Soon, Little One. Jeewon will ensure that you are all comfortable and cared for during your stay. She will tell you where you may go, and where you may not. Then you will be free to explore."

Thea felt Meiling's gaze pierce her mind. "Go. Be the Spark among my people."

An unseen presence disappeared and the Dragon's eyes became green once again. Liwei smiled, showing hundreds of teeth. His massive presence was intimidating enough.

"Jeewon," Liwei rumbled, "the Oreum will stay within the Caverns until the storm passes. When you go, tell Arrum that I will speak with her."

Jeewon bowed and turned to leave.

Glancing down, Thea saw mushrooms growing out of the cracks and crevices along the edge of the room, glowing with a pale, iridescent light. The vast expanse of treasure contained countless pieces of golden metalwork, scattered with silver and heaps of precious stones. Among the shimmering expanse, she thought she caught a glimpse or two of pale white bone.

She looked up at Liwei. "Excuse me, there is an old man we met as we were travelling, and he was coming this way. I think he was looking for Dragon treasure."

Liwei gave an amused rumble. "Coham is known to us. I wondered when we would see him again."

The Dragons knew Coham? Thea tried to wrap her mind around the thought. "If he takes Dragon treasure, won't he go mad?"

"He would, if he took it," Liwei rumbled. "If it is given to him that is a completely different matter. When a Dragon gives a piece of their treasure away, it loses its Dragon's touch and becomes safe for those who are not Dragons."

"But if someone just takes it?"

"The treasure continues to make its magical field. Without its Dragon nearby, it affects the minds of those who possess it."

"That's why Dragon treasure is so dangerous?"

"Yes." Liwei rumbled. "But if someone takes Dragon gold without asking, perhaps they deserve it."

Jeewon led the way out of the Dragon's cavern. Once they were back in the adjoining chamber, she gestured that she wished to speak.

"You will be billeted in the Oreum quarters," Jeewon explained, once Thea had cast comprehension. "I will show you the way there now." Turning, she led Thea and the others past Ssen and his company and out through the maze of corridors.

Thea walked beside her. "I knew Dragons were large," she ventured. "I didn't realize they were *that* large."

Jeewon gave her a sidelong glance, but her scales

and crest showed her amusement. "You thought Liwei was large?"

Thea stared. "They get bigger than that?"

"Meiling has lived for more than a thousand circles, and Dragons never stop growing."

"But ... but she must be ..."

"Larger than you can comprehend."

"How can something that big even exist?"

"Dragons are magic. If they want to exist, they do. Very few guests see Meiling in the flesh. She prefers to speak through Liwei."

The tunnels they now passed were clearly inhabited. Through open doorways, Thea caught glimpses of Minathrils at work and play. Other rooms appeared to be sleeping quarters.

Jeewon gestured to one of these. "This is my room. If you have need of anything, you can find me there when I am off duty."

Passing several more doors, Jeewon gestured to another room. "This will be your room while you are staying with us." Opening the door, she stepped inside.

It was a small room, with a bunk along each side. Against the far wall were four small chests, with four hooks hanging above them.

"I will give you time to settle yourselves. When you are ready, meet me at my room and I will show you around the Oreum quarters." With a bow, Jeewon turned and left.

Thea put her pack in one of the chests and hung her oilskin on the hook above it. Sylica flopped down on one of the lower bunks, and Daisy scrambled up beside her. Hwasan set his satchel on the bunk above Sylica.

"How about you and Roland take the other bottom

bunk, and I'll sleep up top," Zanele suggested.

It suddenly struck Thea that there were only four beds in the room, but five of them. Of course, she wanted to sleep beside Roland, but somehow it felt different having other people assume that she would.

Roland gave her a wry smile. The beds were not wide, being clearly made for a single person. Of course, they'd slept close together before, but that was to stay warm. Inside the tunnels of the Minathrils, everything seemed to be maintained at a comfortable temperature, but they would have to sleep close just the same.

Thea didn't mind at all.

After a short rest, they went to find Jeewon. She showed them the mess hall where they were to eat their meals, and the large room where those who were off duty spent much of their time. There were a couple of private meeting rooms, and a large assembly hall that completed the quarters of the Oreum crew. The large, immaculately clean bath rooms were shared between the crews.

Wherever they went, Minathrils turned and stared.

"Do you not have guests very often?" Thea ventured, as Jeewon led them back to the Oreum quarters.

"It is not uncommon for a crew from another mountain to come on an errand from their Dragon. To have guests who are not Minathrils is almost unheard of."

"It is a long way to come," Thea admitted, thinking of the journey all the way from Gedwyld on the coast. If they hadn't found the dragon treasure and had to do something about it, she never would have come so far.

Jeewon nodded. "Today you will stay in the Oreum quarters. Tomorrow the rest of the crews will know about your presence, and we can show you more of the Caverns. As it is, I am sure you are tired from your journey."

When the time came for the evening meal, Thea and Roland joined the Oreum crew in the mess hall. Sylica was already there, mingling cheerfully amongst the Minathrils. Daisy trotted eagerly by her side.

Jeewon gestured for Thea and Roland to join her table. With a smile, Thea sat in the indicated seat and cast comprehension over the table's occupants.

A flash of red caught her eye. Hwasan sat alone at a table in the corner of the room. His scales and his spirit both showed his bitterness and discomfort. Thea glanced at Roland, but he was already deep in conversation with Ssen.

Across the hall, Zanele entered, eyeing the throng of Minathrils with an expression of barely-concealed contempt. Skirting the edge of the room, she sat beside Hwasan.

Hwasan's scales betrayed his surprise at this intrusion, but Zanele didn't seem to notice.

After the evening meal, Thea and Roland excused themselves and retired to their room. Zanele was already there, but she didn't seem to feel like talking.

Tired from the day and their long trek up the mountains, Thea climbed into bed and nestled close to Roland.

She was only dimly aware of the slam of the door and Sylica's cheerful voice talking to no one in particular as she flopped onto her bed, followed by the clatter and scrape of Daisy scrambling up after her.

Chapter Eighteen

Thea woke in darkness, with Roland's arms around her. His deep, even breathing filled the silence with its gentle rhythm.

Was it morning yet? It was impossible to tell, but she felt surprisingly awake.

"Daisy," Sylica's whisper seemed loud in the silence, "when do you think they have breakfast?"

"They're military," Hwasan murmured from his bunk. "They will have a signal to let everyone know."

The walls began glowing with radiant light. They grew brighter and brighter as Sylica sat up, beaming with pleasure.

"It's morning! Come on, Daisy, let's go see everybody!" She scrambled out of bed. "Good morning, Thea! Good morning, Roland! Good morning, Zanele! Good morning, Hwasan! See you later!" With a wave, she skipped out the door.

Sounds drifted in from the corridor outside, filling the room with the murmur of Minathrils preparing for the day.

Hwasan climbed down from his bunk and followed Sylica.

Roland stretched.

"They certainly make sure you're awake on time," Zanele muttered, flopping down to the floor. She scratched by the root of one of her horns, her head cocked at a contemplative angle. "I wonder if they have a quiet place for Shindahs to check in. I haven't even seen a window in this place."

Thea swung her feet over the edge of the bed. "I can ask Jeewon."

"Don't worry. I'll find somewhere." Springing up, Zanele trotted out of the room.

Roland watched her go. "Tell you what, Thea, I'll go find a place for my check in, and you can use this room."

After Roland had gone, Thea stood in silence for a while, running her hand along the walls. They were plain, grey rock, but somehow they lit up the room as brightly as if there had been a window.

Settling herself in a corner, Thea knelt to check in. With a rush, the warm glory of Allulien's presence flooded her senses, filling the tiny room as if it would burst. Her heart leapt as she stared up into her General's face.

Allulien's gaze bore an expression of deep joy that was almost overwhelming, as if they could see into the core of her being and had no doubt of what they would find there.

It had been so long since Allulien had come.

"You have orders for me?" Thea whispered.

"I do." Allulien's eyes twinkled with light. "It is something you were already going to do, but I want you to know that it is also the will of the Deity. Be the Spark."

The Spark? Fear rose in Thea's heart. "How do I do that?"

"The Spark is who you are, Thea. As long as you are being yourself, you will be the Spark."

"But I'm just me. I'm not anyone special."

Allulien's face was stern. "Who else among the servants of the Deity have had all four Generals walk with them and teach them? Ever since you were young, our eyes have been on you, and all that you have learned and experienced has led you here. Among the Minathrils, be who you are. They have more need of the Spark than they realize."

Thea bowed her head. If Allulien said she was the Spark, it must be true, however untrue it felt.

"For the rest of your time here, you will receive the gift of language, allowing you to understand and speak the language of the Minathrils, without the need to cast your magic throughout the day."

"Really?" Thea swallowed. "I didn't—I mean, that would be nice, but what about the others? They don't know the language either."

"Sylica will be given a translator, and Zanele will find one for herself. I foresee Roland spending much of his time on the training grounds, and the language barrier will not be an issue for him there. Military language is all basically the same."

"Hey!" Micai's voice echoed in the distance. "I heard that!"

"You know it's true, Micai," Allulien retorted. "Don't complain."

"Hello, Micai!" Thea called. "I miss you!"

"See you 'round, Thea!" Micai's voice echoed back.

"Now be quiet and let me finish!" Allulien called, and winked at Thea. "Your companions will be cared for, but I do not want language to hinder the Spark's effectiveness. Two spans may seem long, but they will pass soon enough. Once you depart, the gift of language will be gone and you will have to learn the language of the Minathrils the slow way, like everyone else."

Thea nodded. "Thank you Allulien. I will obey."

Allulien smiled and placed a hand on Thea's head. The warm tingle of magic swept over her, filling her with an assurance and confidence she hadn't felt before.

Allulien's form faded away, leaving only an imprint on Thea's spirit sight, like footprints in the sand.

Thea stared at the place where Allulien had been. "Wait—you said all four Generals have taught me? I've never even met Enkeli before!"

A faint echo of a smile formed in Thea's mind, and the impression of three words: "Have you not?"

A bell rang in the distance. After a long breath to steady herself, Thea stood and set out for the mess hall.

When breakfast was finished, Thea and her companions gathered together in the midst of the dispersing Minathrils.

"Did you know that every Minathril I have talked to so far doesn't know what a pie is?" Sylica informed Thea in wide-eyed dismay. "How can anybody not know what a pie is! Pies are delicious! If I had a pie bag as well as a candy bag, I could—"

"Hello." A Minathril with a narrow snout approached and bowed to Sylica.

"Hi!" Sylica grinned. "I'm Sylica, what's your name?"

The Minathril bowed again, speaking Common in a strong Draconic accent. "I am Kureum Noonie. I would be honoured to accompany you as a translator during your time in the Caverns."

Sylica stared in surprise. "For me?"

"Yes. You are the Green One with Dragon magic. You

have much to say, but my people cannot understand your language. I am old, but when I was young I travelled and learned some Common. I would be honoured to translate for you."

"That would be great!" Sylica grinned. "We'll have so much fun and go exploring all over and we can talk to everybody! Come on, let's go!"

Daisy jumped and yapped excitedly.

"Oh right—this is Daisy, my best friend in all the world. You can translate for her too!"

"It would be an honour." The Minathril bowed. "Would you and Daisy be interested in having a tour of the Caverns?"

"Oh yes, we'd love that!" Sylica scampered off towards the far door. "Let's go! Oh wait—we're going that way? Okay! Let's go!"

Thea smiled as Sylica skipped away, with Daisy at her heels and Kureum Noonie hurrying to follow.

Ssen stepped through the door, moving aside just in time to avoid a collision. Thea waved a greeting.

"Good morning." Ssen's scales shone yellow as he approached. "I trust your night was good?"

Thea cast comprehension for the sake of Roland and Zanele. "Yes, thank you."

Ssen bowed and turned to Roland. "From what I have seen, you are a military person. I will be training with my crew this workday. Would you like to join us?"

A smile lit Roland's face. "I would really enjoy that. Is that alright with you, Thea?"

Thea nodded. "Go join them. You've missed your training for a few days now."

Roland gave her a grateful smile and followed Ssen out of the room.

Ashes

A few steps away, Tayhyang was having a private conversation with Jeewon. Approaching Zanele, he bowed. "I have seen that you are a Shindah beneath Raphea. We have extensive medical rooms here in the Caverns. Would you like to see them?"

Zanele eyed him cautiously. "I would like to see them."

Tayhyang bowed. "I can show you the way now, if you care to accompany me."

Zanele considered this for a moment. "Alright." She grabbed Hwasan by the arm and dragged him along.

"What—" Hwasan stammered, his scales a grey transparency.

"I need someone to translate for me," Zanele retorted. "Thea won't be around to do her magic all the time."

Dragging Hwasan after her, Zanele accompanied Tayhyang through the door and out of sight.

Jeewon stepped beside Thea. "And I will be your guide for this day."

Thea looked up at the Captain in surprise. "Isn't your crew training today?"

"That is Ssen's responsibility." She gave Thea a keen glance. "My task is to show the Spark our life in the Caverns. And it is an honour."

Thea followed Jeewon out of the mess hall and down one of the many tunnels.

"You have already seen the crews' quarters. That is where we eat and sleep when we are not on duty. Today I will show you where our food comes from."

They walked on, through long corridors with their strange, angled walls, refracting light that seemed to come from within the walls themselves.

"As you have seen, there is not much food to be found in the upper reaches of the mountains, especially during the cold seasons. Instead, we grow our own."

They stepped through a door into a large, brightly lit cavern. At their feet, pools spread out in every direction, filled with plants of all descriptions. Water trickled from one pool to another, filling the warm, humid air with its delicate song.

The walls of the cavern were carved into shelves. On them, Thea recognized lettuces, beets, and several kinds of herbs. Vines growing tomatoes, cucumbers, and squashes hung from trellises overhead. In a nearby pool, waterlilies and tall grasses swayed in a gentle breeze that seemed to come from nowhere.

Amongst all the beauty, Minathrils were hard at work, tending to the plants, repairing trellises, and harvesting the produce. Thea followed Jeewon between the pools.

"We grow everything we need," Jeewon explained, her scales gleaming with pride. "It does not matter to us when the storms come or if the snow lasts longer than it should. We are well fed."

Thea stared at the abundance surrounding her. "You don't eat anything from the outside world at all?"

"There are a few healing herbs that do not adapt well to our gardens that we must forage on the mountainside. Sometimes our Dragon brings back a kill for us, or we go hunting when the weather is good. Then we work hard to dry and preserve the meat. It is useful for long scouting expeditions."

Light glistened off a small cascade as it trickled from one pool to another.

"Where does the water come from?"

Jeewon nodded. "Come and see."

Leaving the garden cavern, they entered another large room, where water flowed through several channels carved in the rock.

"Our spring of water comes up through the rock not far from here. Some of the water flows to the gardens and the kitchens. The rest goes here." Opening a door, Jeewon led Thea into a new room where they were enveloped in a cloud of steam. "This is where we heat the water. The hot water flows to the bath rooms and the medical rooms."

The hot, humid air filled Thea's lungs. "How do you heat it? Is there a fire?"

"All of the heat and light in the Caverns comes from the Dragon. It is the Dragon's magic that allows us to live like this—with all we need and more." Jeewon gestured. "Come see the medical rooms. We are not far from them now."

Stepping through another door, Thea found herself in a room filled by a large pool. Steaming water flowed into it from every side. A Minathril stood waist-deep in the water, filling an ornate bowl from one of the steaming cascades.

"This is the bath where the healers perform their cleansing," Jeewon explained. "They are careful that no dirt contaminates their important work."

Beyond the bath room, they stepped into a clean ward lined with beds. Only two of the beds were occupied, while several Minathrils bustled around them, attending to their patients' needs.

"Is Zanele here?" Thea asked one of the Minathrils.

"She is in surgery room B." The Minathril bowed. "Would you like me to take you there?"

"Yes, please."

Thea and Jeewon followed the Minathril down a long, brightly lit passageway, lined with doors.

"The medical laundry room is through there," Jeewon explained as they went. "That corridor leads to the kitchens so food can be brought for the injured."

Their guide stepped through an open door into a large, bright room. Several Minathrils stood around a single bed in the center of the room. It took a second glance to spot Zanele's short figure among them, with Cheeky perched on her shoulder.

"—And we place our tools here, so they remain sanitary," Tayhyang explained. Hwasan relayed this information to Zanele.

"So this whole room is *only* for surgeries?" Zanele asked. Hwasan passed on the question, and Tayhyang affirmed that it was so.

"Do you not have surgery rooms for your people?" he asked.

Zanele shook her head when Hwasan relayed the question. "I just do them on the battlefield."

"What?" Tayhyang stared when he was told Zanele's answer. "How do you keep your tools clean?"

Zanele shrugged. "It's war. You do the best you can."

"She says it is war. She does the best that she can," Hwasan translated.

"Like I had a choice," Zanele muttered.

"She has no choice," Hwasan repeated.

The Minathrils shook their heads in disbelief.

Without drawing attention to herself, Thea nodded her thanks to her escort, and followed Jeewon back down the corridor.

"Your people seem to know a lot about healing,"

Thea said as they left the medical rooms behind.

Jeewon's scales showed her pleasure. "Raphea has taught us well."

"You have many Shindahs who serve beneath Raphea, don't you?"

"Yes, but that is as it should be. Raphea is the instructor of our people."

"Wait—" Thea turned to stare at Jeewon. "Raphea is the General of the Minathrils?"

"Yes. Did you not know that?"

"No, I didn't." Thea's mind raced. "But then ... that means you are one of the five races made by the Deity."

"Of course." Surprise showed on Jeewon's scales. "Did you think we were not?"

"No," Thea admitted. "To be honest, I didn't. There are already five races on Raphtova, and since you live in the mountains with the Dragons I thought that would explain it."

"Explain what?"

"Why you're here, shut away from the rest of the world."

"We are here to serve our Dragon. I already explained that."

"But if you are one of the five races, you are supposed to be a part of the life of Raphtova, like the Dryads and the Fauns and the Littles. That is what the Deity wants, for the five races to live together and care for each other, not be hidden away in the mountains with the Dragons."

Jeewon's crest rose into a defensive stance. "Our life is in the mountains. We follow the commands of our Dragon, and through the Dragon, we serve the Deity."

"But your Dragon is not the Deity!"

Jeewon's scales flared red. "You accuse us of worshipping the Dragon?"

"No, I'm not." Thea's heart beat loud in her chest. "And I'm not saying you can't serve your Dragon, but it is wrong to shut yourselves away from the rest of the world like this. Trust me, I know. My people shut themselves away from the world and their spirits all died inside of them!"

Jeewon stared at Thea, a tumult of emotions rippling across her scales.

Thea stared back, willing her to understand. When the silence stretched on, she took a long, trembling breath. "The Deity's call is stronger than the Dragon's command. Maybe it's time to figure out who you really serve."

Jeewon's gaze was cool and distant. "You give me much to think about. I will show you back to the Oreum quarters and continue my duties for the day."

After Jeewon had gone, Thea made her way to the room where off-duty Minathrils often spent their time.

There she found two Minathrils having a wrestling match, while several others watched and cheered. At a large tapestry loom, a broad-shouldered Minathril was absorbed in their work. Others dozed in comfortable-looking chairs.

Sylica and her translator were there, sitting around a large table with several other Minathrils. They seemed to be playing some kind of dice game.

"Oh, I understand!" Sylica clapped her hands. "It's kind of like a game I played with some Fauns once, only in that game you had to put money in the middle and I didn't have any money so I put in candy instead, and—"

Kureum Noonie gestured desperately. "She says that she understands, and that—"

"—they thought that wasn't fair because I had as much candy as I wanted and they didn't have as much money as they wanted, but they did like my candy, so—"

Minathril laughter swept around the table.

"Slow down!" A Minathril with a long crest waved a hand. "Poor Noonie is going to explode!"

Sylica realized something was wrong and paused in her tale long enough for Noonie to catch up.

"Good. Good." One of the Minathrils laughed. "We're glad you understand the game."

Noonie translated for Sylica, who beamed with pleasure.

One of the Minathrils dozing in a chair opened one eye. "You missed the rules about trading."

"Come on, Uhnhey!" the Minathrils at the table protested. "She is just learning!"

"What's going on?" Sylica wanted to know.

"Uhnhey is our champion at the game," Noonie explained. "She is complaining that we taught you the simple way."

"She is the champion?" Sylica grinned across the room at Uhnhey. "Can I play with her?"

Noonie seemed startled and translated for the Minathrils at the table.

"Uhnhey!" a Minathril at the table called. "Bring your lazy tail over here. The Green One challenges you to a duel!"

The Minathrils pounded the table, their crests waving excitedly. "Duel! Duel!"

Slowly, Uhnhey got up from her seat, to cheers around the room. Sitting across from Sylica, she leaned forward. "I accept your challenge."

Noonie briefly explained to Sylica the rules that the others had originally simplified. Another of the Minathrils handed Uhnhey and Sylica their handful of tokens.

"Trade." Uhnhey swapped some of her tokens for others laid out on the table.

"Uh ..." Sylica stared at her tokens. "I'm happy with what I have."

"And you must call your hand."

"Come on, Uhnhey!" the rest of the Minathrils protested. "This is her first game!"

"It is not a duel unless you call your hand."

Noonie turned to Sylica. "In the tradition of the duel, you must say what hand you want to throw. You only get the points if the tokens land as you called."

"Oh, okay." Sylica nodded. "Which call is worth the most points?"

"The Dragon. If you throw a Dragon, you win the game," Noonie explained. "But that is a very difficult hand to throw. A River or a Spire would be more likely."

"I'll call a Dragon then." Sylica nodded decisively.

When Noonie translated her call, the Minathrils around the table erupted in excitement.

"You can't do that, it's your first game!" a Minathril cried.

Another pounded the table. "Courage like a Minathril! Well done, Green One."

The rest of the Minathrils crowded around the table. Thea crept closer, peering through the surging throng.

"Ready?" a Minathril called.

Uhnhey nodded. "I also call Dragon."

The Minathril stretched a hand over the table.

"Three, two, one, throw!"

Uhnhey threw her tokens down.

With a grin, Sylica threw her tokens down too.

The Minathrils exploded in excitement. "She threw a Dragon! She threw a Dragon!" They slapped Sylica on the back and pounded the table, shouting and cheering.

"I told you," one of the Minathrils shook a finger at Uhnhey. "The Green One has Dragon magic. Beaten in a newcomer's first game!"

Uhnhey gestured helplessly. "Congratulations to a worthy opponent."

"Uhnhey says congratulations," Noonie explained. "But tell me, did you really throw a Dragon or was that Dragon magic?"

"I didn't use magic," Sylica beamed. "I just wanted to win, so I did."

Noonie shook her head, amusement gleaming on her scales. "That is exactly what Dragon magic is."

"I've never trained with anyone like them." Roland's eyes shone as he put his knives away that evening. "Any one of them alone would be a dangerous opponent, but the way they work together is astounding. They can bring their shields together and advance through anything as if they were a moving fortress. And their discipline! I've seen Khariton try to whip the new recruits into shape, but if Ssen says a single word his crew jumps as if their lives depend on it!"

"You were practically beaming when you came back to the mess hall." Thea leaned back, unable to help a smile at Roland's enthusiasm. "I can tell that you and Ssen get along really well."

"Absolutely!" Roland climbed into bed beside her.

"He said I could join them again tomorrow."

"You'll enjoy that."

Roland nodded. "The more I learn, the more I can share with the others back home. I can't wait to hear what Khariton thinks of it all." He lay back and closed his eyes.

Thea shifted uncomfortably. Would she really go back to Lyudmyla with Roland? Their forced stay with the Minathrils delayed her need to make a decision, for now.

Roland seemed to be enjoying his time anyways, and of course Sylica was too. At the evening meal, the news of her victory had spread like wildfire around the mess hall, and all the Minathrils made a fuss over her.

Zanele seemed to regard the Minathrils with an indifferent sort of disdain, avoiding them whenever possible, although it did seem that she enjoyed her time in the medical rooms, in a way. Once Hwasan was released from translating for Zanele, he sat alone in the corner of the mess hall and refused to speak to anyone. His scales betrayed his discomfort and frustration, but Thea thought she caught glints of gold as his eyes followed Sylica wherever she went.

Their presence was certainly making ripples amongst the crew of Minathrils. Thea couldn't help but notice that Jeewon hadn't come to the meal at all.

Chapter Nineteen

Life with the Minathrils fell into a kind of rhythm. Sylica roamed the Caverns with Noonie, bringing excitement and chaos wherever she went. One day a crew's worth of apple pies appeared out of nowhere. Another day the Minathrils were astonished by a magical display of fireworks in the middle of the mess hall. As everyone ducked for cover, Sylica proudly explained which fireworks were like the ones her Uncle Bob had made and which ones were inventions of her own.

Zanele spent much of her time in the medical rooms. The healers there accepted her as an honoured Shindah, which she seemed to resent somewhat. Still, she appeared to enjoy learning from the Minathril healers, and taught them about what the Minathrils began to call "battlefield medicine".

At Zanele's insistence, Hwasan continued to translate for her. When he wasn't accompanying Zanele in the medical rooms, he could be found watching Sylica and the excitement that followed wherever she went. He was not treated poorly by the Minathrils of the Cavern, but it was clear that he wasn't fully accepted by them either.

Roland spent every day with Ssen and the Oreum crew as they trained, returning every evening with more stories of the prowess of the Minathrils.

Thea found herself once again in Jeewon's care. Every day the Captain showed her more of their life in the Caverns, one day climbing up to the lookouts high on the mountain, another day venturing deep beneath the Caverns to the mines, where Minathrils unearthed precious metals and gemstones for their Dragon's treasure.

One day they joined Roland and Ssen at the training grounds, watching the way the Minathrils brought their shields together in a circle, edging their way across the vast space in a maneuver designed to rescue the injured from a battlefield. At a command from Ssen, the wall of shields bristled with spears, ready to threaten any who would attempt to bar their way.

The next day, Jeewon showed Thea the family quarters, where Minathrils of a mating age lived and raised their young.

"We will not venture far," Jeewon cautioned as they watched a cluster of Minathril children at play in a large common room. "The presence of strangers can harm the growth and health of our young, if special precautions are not taken."

Thea stared at the tiny Minathrils tumbling across the floor. Every delicate scale twinkled in the light.

A new shade of determination gleamed on Jeewon's scales. "The task of raising children requires complete effort and dedication from both mates. During this time, all their needs are cared for by the crews."

Minathrils bustled by, many of whom were clearly male or female—a distinction that had been missing from any of the Minathrils Thea had met so far. "All they do is raise their children?"

"Without that devoted care, their children will die. It

is intensive, but the time for mating only lasts ten circles of our lifespan, then any desire or ability to reproduce disappears. Once our children are grown, we can dedicate the rest of our life to the service of our crew and our Dragon."

As they left the family quarters, Jeewon seemed lost in thought.

"I was speaking with Meiling," she said after a long silence. "Julong, the Dragon of the Awdub crew, was killed 32 circles ago. Hwasan would have been very young at the time."

"He told us he was very young," Thea replied. "Does it matter?"

Frustration flared on Jeewon's scales. "Did you learn nothing from what you saw today? Our young cannot live alone. Even after they have passed the most vulnerable stage, they still require dedicated care for eight circles or more. Hwasan could not have survived on his own, but there were no other survivors."

"He said he's always been alone."

Jeewon gave Thea a sharp glance. "Someone must have cared for him. The question is who, and why he is not telling us."

"Why should he tell us? We aren't entitled to know everything about his life!"

Silence fell across the corridor. Jeewon seemed to study Thea's face for a moment before turning and continuing down the corridor.

Thea followed.

When Jeewon spoke again, determination glinted on her scales. "Ssen told me he was teaching you our colours and what they mean. I will teach you more. Then you can watch Hwasan and see for yourself." She gave Thea a keen glance. "His scales do not always match the words that he says. Be careful, Thea."

Loud voices clamoured, cutting through the noise of the busy mess hall. At the table where Thea and Roland sat, conversations halted. Minathrils in every direction craned their necks to see what was going on.

Thea's heart sank. A large crowd had gathered around the corner of the room where Hwasan and Zanele usually sat. At Roland's side, Ssen's scales faded into grey.

Zanele appeared, elbowing her way through the growing crowd of Minathrils. Her gaze locked onto Thea's. "Cast comprehension! Now!"

Thea's mouth went dry. "How ... how big do you—"

"Just do it!"

Thea cast comprehension over the whole room. "What's going on?"

Zanele's eyes flashed. "I'm going to give some Minathrils a piece of my mind!" Turning on her heels, she stormed away, pushing her way into the crowd.

Thea hurried to follow.

"Leave him alone!" Zanele's voice rose above the clamour. "Listen to me! Those were *my* words. I said it! He was only translating! How dare you treat him like that for something I said!"

Thea pushed her way through the growing crowd. Zanele stood in front of Hwasan, glaring up at the Minathrils that pressed in around them.

"Lone ones are not welcome here," a Minathril replied, scales flickering red with anger.

"*You're* not welcome here!" Zanele snapped. "Go away! Now!"

"What's going on?" Thea demanded, hurrying to Zanele's side.

Zanele was shaking. "I told them. I told them they are not true followers of Raphea. Raphea teaches us to bear the pain of *all* of Raphtova, but they only care about their own people!"

Roland and Ssen pushed their way through the milling crowd.

"You told them that?" Thea looked in the Faun's rage-filled eyes.

"Yes, I told them to their face!"

"And ... Hwasan had to translate that?"

"Of course he did," Zanele snapped. "How else were they going to know what I was saying?"

"But ... Zanele, they already don't like him ..."

"And that's wrong! Why should they treat him like an outcast just because he came from somewhere else? He hasn't done them harm. And I was right, you know. That is what Raphea teaches."

"I know." Thea held the Faun's shaking hands. "I know you're right."

"And now they're mad at Hwasan." Zanele's eyes filled with pain. "They should be mad at me, not him!"

Footsteps approached. Silence fell as Jeewon stared down at them, her scales a brilliant red. Her crest stood on end, quivering violently.

"End your magic." Jeewon's voice was firm and cold. "I must speak with my crew."

Thea ended the effects of her spell and nodded to the Captain.

Jeewon turned on her heel and marched to the other side of the room. Her clear, hard voice cut through the air—words Thea could still understand because of the gift of language from Allulien.

"I gave you orders on how to treat the lone one." Every word cut like a knife. "I said you will not trust him, but you will treat him with kindness and respect and honour, and this is how you act? I will not have insubordination in my crew, in front of the honoured guests of the Dragon!"

The Minathrils in the hall had become almost completely transparent. Thea turned her mind back to her friends around her. Sylica was there, staring at everyone with large, confused eyes. Hwasan sat, unmoving, as if he could not believe what he was seeing and hearing. Roland glanced at Ssen, his mouth set in a thin, hard line. Beside Thea, Zanele was still shaking in fury.

Ssen stepped forward and bowed to Zanele. "I see you are angry."

"No, really," Zanele glared.

"I am learning." Ssen bowed again, a hint of pride gleaming on his scales. "My understanding is not good, but Roland teaches me."

He was speaking in Common. Roland gave him an encouraging smile.

Across the hall, the Captain's tongue-lashing continued.

Zanele regarded Ssen with a solemn expression. "Thank you. It seems like most Minathrils aren't interested in learning anything."

"Minathrils are deep like ... mountain. Maybe we need ..." Ssen frowned and continued in Draconic, "an earthquake to shake them."

"An earthquake to shake them," Hwasan repeated in Common.

"Earthquake." Ssen nodded. "Or a Faun-quake."

A reluctant smile spread across Zanele's face. "Ssen, you're alright."

They fell silent as Jeewon approached once again. Ignoring the rest of them, she stopped directly in front of Hwasan.

"Forgive the behaviour of my crew. They will not do so again." Turning, Jeewon walked away, slamming the door behind her.

Silence filled the room.

Hwasan stared at the ground, his scales the pale grey of the stone at his back.

"Hwasan," Thea sat down beside him. "I'm so sorry."

Hwasan shrugged, his scales showing his embarrassment. The darkness in his spirit made Thea's heart ache.

She took a careful breath. "I hope you don't listen to those people who are being cruel. We are glad you're with us, and we won't send you away."

"The choice may not be yours," Hwasan muttered.

"Listen." Thea leaned closer. "The Deity made the five races of Raphtova to live and work together. That is what you are doing. You are here with us, helping us and being our friend, and that is what the Deity wants. The people here don't understand that, but we do. And we get to show them that."

Hwasan looked down. "I had not thought about that." His voice seemed pensive, but something about the colour of his scales and the quiver of his crest showed that he was feeling very uncomfortable.

Around them, the room continued in silence.

Thea glanced up at Roland. "Maybe it would be best if we go to our room for the night."

Hwasan nodded. "I agree."

"Daisy and I are coming too!" Sylica grinned.

Zanele shot a disapproving glare at the silent Minathrils and turned towards the door.

As Hwasan got up to follow, Ssen set a hand on his shoulder. "You have a very good crew."

Thea watched a hint of pride gleam on Hwasan's scales as he bowed. "Thank you."

The next morning, the Minathrils seemed more subdued as they ate in the mess hall. Thea saw several of the offenders on their hands and knees, scrubbing the floor.

Without discussing it beforehand, Thea, Roland, and Sylica joined Zanele and Hwasan at their regular table. It was the first time since coming to the Caverns that they had all eaten together.

As they finished their meal, Jeewon strode up to their table. Bowing in greeting, she turned to Hwasan.

"Awdub Hwasan, I admire your courage. I have heard a full report of the events of yesterday. Regardless of what I may think of what was said, it took a very courageous person to stand in the middle and be the spokesperson. I honour you, and will see no repercussions come to you because of that event." Turning, she nodded to Thea. "I have business to attend to today. You must find something else to do with your time."

Turning sharply, the Captain strode away.

Hwasan slowly let out his breath.

Thea glanced at Zanele. "What are you going to do today?"

"I'm going back to the medical rooms, of course."

Zanele's eyes flashed. "You think I'll let them scare me away?" She stood up and stretched. "You ready, Hwasan?"

Hwasan's scales faded into grey transparency.

Ssen approached their table with a friendly wave. Thea cast comprehension so everyone could share their greetings.

Ssen turned to Roland. "I'm giving the crew a day off, so there's no reason to go to the training grounds today. You'll join us again tomorrow?"

"Of course."

Ssen's scales glowed yellow. "I would like to join Zanele and Hwasan in whatever they plan to do today, if they will have me." He looked from Hwasan to Zanele.

Zanele pursed her lips. "Oh, alright. I'll tolerate that." A smile glinted in her eyes. "To the medical rooms?"

Ssen bowed.

Thea watched a gleam of light shine in Hwasan's spirit as Ssen fell in step alongside him. Together they walked out the door.

A few moments later, Sungy approached. "Excuse me, Thea. If you aren't busy today, could I have the honour of introducing you to my family?"

"Of course! I'd love to meet your family." Thea smiled as pleasure surged across Sungy's scales. "Can Roland come too?"

"Of course." Sungy bowed. "He would be most welcome."

Roland smiled as he and Thea followed Sungy out of the mess hall. "This is nice. It's a long time since we've had a day together."

"It is nice." Thea squeezed Roland's hand, then cast

comprehension so Sungy could join the conversation.

As they walked through the family quarters, Roland looked around with interest. "So this is where the families live. I wondered why there weren't any children around."

Sungy nodded. "The crew quarters are not designed for young ones and families. Here they are much better cared for."

Leaving the large, common area filled with the noise of chatter and children playing, Sungy led them down a long corridor.

"My younger brother Kachy and his mate have said I can bring you to meet them and their young. This is their room here." Giving a brief knock on a door, she opened it and stepped inside.

Following, Thea and Roland found themselves in a large, pleasant room. Comfortable-looking seats surrounded a thick, brightly coloured rug, littered with toys. On the far side of the room, a large granite-topped table held an assortment of dishes and half-eaten snacks.

"Sungy!" A Minathril who was clearly male ran forward and embraced her. "Cheehey! Sungy and the guests are here!"

A female Minathril stepped out from a side room that appeared to be a sleeping quarters. In her arms, a young Minathril blinked sleepily. Another child peered out from behind her legs. "It is good to see you, Sungy!" Cheehey's scales gleamed yellow. "And welcome to your friends!"

"This is Thea and Roland," Sungy gestured. "They are honoured guests of the Dragon."

"We are very pleased to meet you." Cheehey and

Kachy bowed. The child behind Cheehey waved shyly.

"Hello," Roland crouched down to the child's level. "What's your name?"

"Dacdak," the child said in a quiet voice. His scales faded to make him almost invisible.

"It's nice to meet you, Dacdak," Roland smiled.

"And dat's my sister, Beayul," Dacdak added, pointing to the smaller child in Cheehey's arms.

"It is very nice to meet you too, Beayul."

The small child blinked and nuzzled her face into her mother's arm.

"Come in," Kachy urged them. "Just be careful where you step."

Cheehey lifted a plate off one of the chairs and gestured for them to come sit down.

Roland picked up a ball off the floor. "Is this yours?" he asked Dacdak.

Dacdak nodded.

"Can you catch?"

Dacdak held out his hands, his scales turning a brilliant yellow as he caught the gently thrown ball.

"Where are you visiting from?" Cheehey asked.

"My home is east of here, on the shore of the sea," Thea explained, sitting in a chair large enough to make her feel a little small.

"I do not think my people have ever been so far." Cheehey watched her with interest. "What is it like?"

"It's a beautiful old stone building, high on the cliffs above the sea. It's not far from Gedwyld, a city of humans and Littles. Have you ever met humans or Littles before?"

"No. We have never been beyond the walls of the family quarters. First we were children, then we came of age and found a mate, and now we are raising our young. When they have grown there will be time to see what there is in the world. Perhaps we will meet humans and Littles then."

Kachy nodded. "You can see our life here. We are warm and comfortable and well cared for. This lets Cheehey and I devote all of our energy to raising our young."

Thea looked at the child in Cheehey's arms. She was so small, her scales so delicate and tiny. Her narrow crest wobbled from side to side as she squirmed in her mother's arms.

"Would you like to hold her?" Cheehey asked.

Thea nodded, gingerly accepting the small child being placed in her arms. Beayul was heavier than she expected. She wiggled and babbled, tapping Thea's amber diamond skin.

"That looks funny to you, doesn't it?" Thea smiled, moving her arm so it reflected the light.

With a shriek of laughter, Dacdak tumbled across the room, colliding with Thea's legs. It was like being struck by a tumbling rock, but with a thousand sharp little blades. Thea gasped and almost dropped the child in her arms.

"I'm a stone golem, coming to get you!" Roland rumbled in a low voice, thumping across the floor on his hands and knees.

Giggling, Dacdak scrambled to get away.

"I remember this time of life very well." Sungy's scales shone a golden yellow. "My mate and I raised two daughters. Our eldest is becoming interested in finding a mate of her own."

"Where are your daughters now?"

"They serve in the childbearing rooms. It is a busy day for them there, so they could not be spared to come meet you. Perhaps another day they can."

"I would love to meet them."

In Thea's arms, Beayul lay peacefully, watching the gleam of the light on Thea's skin.

Behind her, Roland tumbled across the floor. Dacdak was in hot pursuit, waving an oversized broom.

"I getcha, golem!" Dacdak cried, smacking Roland over the head.

"Ow!" Roland winced, then groaned dramatically. "Ohhh you got me!" He closed his eyes and lay very still.

Yelling in triumph, Dacdak jumped on Roland's stomach.

Roland burst out laughing and lifted Dacdak into the air. Dacdak giggled, his arms, legs, and tail waving.

Warmth flooded Thea's heart. Roland would be such a good father one day.

Roland looked up at Thea and saw her gaze. Setting Dacdak back on his feet, he came and leaned on the back of her chair. "She's a cute one, isn't she." He smiled down at Beayul's peaceful figure.

"Would you like to hold her?" Thea asked, glancing at Cheehey to see her approving nod. Standing, she lifted the child into Roland's arms.

His gaze met hers. The love and desire in his eyes were clearer than they had ever been before.

Thea's heart leapt to respond. She wanted to marry him. Even if it meant going to Lyudmyla. She wanted to be with Roland, to have children with him, and to spend the rest of her unending life with him.

She wanted it more than anything in the world.

In his arms, Beayul began to fuss.

"She must be hungry again." Kachy reached out for his daughter. "I'll go feed her."

As Beayul was carried away, Roland stayed close to Thea, his arm around her waist. The thrill of his presence tingled through every fibre of her being. She wanted him, and the passion in his gaze told her—he wanted her too.

"Attack!" Dacdak yelled, taking Roland out at the knees.

Laughing, Roland tumbled to the ground. Dacdak clambered triumphantly on top of him.

Across the room, Sungy gave a knowing smile.

"Dacdak is quite the little warrior," Roland grinned, struggling back into a sitting position beneath the little Minathril's onslaught.

"I know." Cheehey's scales gleamed with pleasure. "Perhaps he will join the Oreum one day, and go scouting with Sungy."

"Are you a part of the Oreum too?" Roland asked.

"No. We do not join a crew until we have finished mating."

"Really?" Roland staggered as Dacdak tugged on his arm. "Why's that?"

"Come eat, Dacdak!" Kachy called.

The little Minathril scampered away, and Roland got back to his feet, returning to Thea's side.

"We do not wish to divide our loyalty," Cheehey explained. "When a Minathril's time for mating is done they can discern which crew they are best suited for, and perhaps receive the calling to become a Shindah."

Thea looked up in surprise. "Anyone is welcome to serve the Deity. Why can't you be a Shindah when you're raising a family?"

"Why would we? The time for mating and raising our young is not the time for such an important commitment. Our work as a Shindah would be compromised, and our young would suffer."

It *was* an important commitment. Thea shifted uncomfortably. How could anyone hope to give a husband and children the love and care they would need while still being fully dedicated to the service of the Deity? On the other hand, Ayanda of the Resistance served under Allulien and carried her child with her into the middle of battle. Who was right?

"Will you eat the evening meal with us?" Kachy asked, returning from feeding the children. "We would love to hear more of your journey through the mountains. From what Sungy has said, it sounds like there is a tale to tell."

Roland shot Thea a grin. "Of course. As long as Thea doesn't mind, we'd love to stay and eat with you."

Chapter Twenty

"What's wrong, Thea?" Roland asked as they got ready for bed that night. He spoke in Elvish, which allowed them to have some privacy in their shared room, but even so he spoke in a low voice. "Halfway through our visit with Kachy and Cheehey it was like you weren't there anymore."

Thea felt her face get hot. Had it been that obvious? She'd tried to engage in the rest of the conversation, but she hadn't done very well.

Roland sat down beside her. "Do you want to talk about it? You were acting like I wasn't even there, but for a moment I thought something very different was going on."

Thea shifted uncomfortably. "I was thinking about what Cheehey said, that Minathrils can't be a Shindah while they are raising a family. It made me wonder if ... if maybe I shouldn't hope to have a family someday. If you wanted to have a family, I mean—" she stared at her hands, not daring to look up. "I love you, Roland, but I don't know if I can love you like this and really serve the Deity too."

Thea's heart pounded in her ears. What would Roland think?

Gently, Roland took her hands in his. "Thea."

Thea looked up into his tender, compassionate eyes. His gaze seemed to reach deep inside her, filling her with steady reassurance.

"I can see this is worrying you." Roland's smile was gentle. "You'll ask Allulien about it tomorrow?"

Thea nodded and squeezed his hand. "Thanks." Leaning her head against Roland's, she gave a long, trembling sigh. His presence was so comforting.

"Thea," Sylica's sleepy voice called from her bunk across the room. "Are you kissing Roland?"

"*Finally!*" Zanele commented from above. "It took them long enough."

Thea stared at Roland in consternation. He gave her an embarrassed smile. "Maybe we'll try to find somewhere alone next time."

The next morning, Thea woke before anyone else in the room. Quietly, she got out of bed and slipped out the door, feeling her way through the darkness. The long corridor outside was empty and quiet, the walls glowing with only the faintest light.

After wandering the empty rooms for a while, Thea settled herself in a corner of the large common room. Kneeling, she waited in silence.

"Something is troubling you?" Allulien's voice was quiet, but somehow it still filled the room.

Allulien's warm glow flooded over Thea as she looked up into the face of her General. "I love Roland."

"You say that as if you are confessing something wrong," Allulien reflected. "Why?"

"I am sworn in the serve the Deity. Can I love someone like this at the same time?"

Allulien's face was both stern and kind. "The traditions of the Minathrils are not without reason. The time in which they can bear children is very short, and their children die if they do not receive proper care. This is the way Minathrils were made. Fauns are different. Their children can go with them into any part of life and grow just as healthy and strong."

Thea hardly dared to whisper. "And Elves?"

"Elves live forever, and remain fertile throughout their lifespan. If they had to wait until their time for childbearing was past, there would be no Elves in the Deity's service at all." Allulien's eyes glittered. "It can be difficult to remain faithful to the Deity's call while providing the presence and care that a family requires, but it is not impossible, nor is it wrong to desire it. You and Roland are both loyal to the Deity and are well suited for each other. You do not need to be afraid of loving him." Allulien's face grew serious. "Remember, though, that your first commitment and loyalty is to the Deity, not to a mate or to children. Even good things can become a false deity if they are worshipped, and you have seen what becomes of the spirits of those who do so."

Thea nodded. She had seen too many dark and dead spirits, and she'd sworn that hers would never be like that.

A smile returned to Allulien's face. "But in its proper place, love honours the Deity more than anything else."

Assurance flooded Thea's heart. It wasn't wrong to love Roland, and it was not forbidden. She bowed her head. "Thank you, Allulien."

Allulien disappeared, but the walls around Thea continued to glow with a light of their own. In the distance, the breakfast bell rang.

Stepping into the corridor, she saw Roland and her other companions on their way to the mess hall.

Hurrying to join them, Thea slipped her hand in Roland's and fell in step beside him.

"How was your check in?" Roland asked in a low voice.

Thea's heart beat faster. "Allulien said it's okay." Keenly aware of the eyes of the others on her, she gave Roland a quick kiss on the cheek. "I love you."

Together, they stepped into the morning chaos of the mess hall.

All through breakfast, she felt Roland's presence beside her, though they didn't talk to each other at all. Sylica had a way of dominating the conversation, and Thea was glad to hear from Zanele that there hadn't been any further incidents with Hwasan and the rest of the Minathrils.

As everyone began to go their separate ways for the day, Roland gave Thea an apologetic smile. "I promised Ssen I'd help run training today. You don't mind, do you?"

Thea squeezed his hand. "Of course not. I'm glad you can help Ssen." Across the room, she caught Jeewon's gaze. "I wouldn't mind talking with the Captain again."

That day passed, and the next, falling back into a familiar rhythm. Roland trained with the Minathrils, but Thea was surprised to find that Ssen spent most of his days with Zanele and Hwasan. Zanele seemed to tolerate this, maybe even enjoy it, but it was in Hwasan that Thea saw the biggest change. The bitter anger that so often showed on his scales was slowly replaced by contentment, sometimes even happiness, and every day the light inside his spirit grew.

Thea didn't see Jeewon much. She was busy with her

duties as a Captain, only taking a few moments each day to make sure her guests were comfortable. Instead, Thea spent more time with Sungy, or joined Sylica in her daily adventures.

There, Thea witnessed the most astonishing change of all—that Sylica was actually learning to talk a little slower. It had certainly been her translator's doing in some way, but perhaps it was the realization that her words would be translated, and more people would understand them, if she spoke fewer words at a time.

A change had also seemed to come over the Minathrils of the Caverns. They were quieter than they were before, no longer including their guests in spontaneous games or storytelling. Sometimes conversations would die down when Thea stepped into the room, but her ability to decipher the Minathrils' scales was never quite good enough to be able to tell what was going on.

One day at breakfast, Jeewon approached Thea. "Today you will have a private audience with Meiling. She wishes to speak with you as soon as you have finished your meal."

Thea tried to hide her surprise. Had it already been two spans since she spoke with Meiling?

"I'll walk you there," Roland offered.

Thea shot him a grin as Jeewon bowed and turned away. They hadn't been able to have much time together—not just the two of them. Even in their room, there were always other people around.

As Thea and Roland left the mess hall, they fell in step beside each other.

"Ssen says the storm on the mountains is passing," Roland told her as they walked. "He thinks we should be clear to leave tomorrow."

Of course—the storm. She'd forgotten that was one of the things keeping them at the Caverns all this time. Living in the world of the Minathrils, it was surprisingly easy to forget about the world outside.

They walked in silence, past the sleeping rooms and through the corridors that had once seemed so maze-like. Now they were quite familiar.

Before they stepped into the antechamber, Roland stopped. "Thea, I have something I want to tell you, before it's time for us to go." He looked down into her eyes and took her hands in his. "I love you, Thea. I see the person you've grown up to be and I think you're beautiful, inside and out. You're the only person I could want to spend my life with."

With a pounding heart, Thea stared up into Roland's earnest gaze. A small, mischievous smile pulled at the corners of her mouth. "I know. You told me in other ways."

Roland gave a wry smile. "I guess it was obvious, but it's still important for you to hear it. I don't know what you're planning to do now, but I have to go back to Lyudmyla, and I wanted to say it now in case I can't see you for a while."

Thea felt her face get hot. "I … I want to go back to Lyudmyla with you, Roland. Just for a while, of course. If I make things right with Uncle Mykyta then I can come back and see you whenever I want, and you can come see me too."

Joy filled Roland's face. "I'm glad, Thea. I was really hoping you'd come."

Lifting up her face to his, Thea kissed him, then stared into his glimmering emerald eyes. "I'm not ready to say goodbye yet."

"Me neither." Roland stood with his arms around her, watching her with an expression so glad it took her breath away.

Finally he gave a wry smile. "I guess you have a Dragon to talk to."

Thea nodded. "I'll see you after, though."

Roland smiled. "I'll be here."

As Thea walked into the antechamber, the Minathril on guard stepped aside. "Meiling is expecting you."

"Thank you." Walking softly, Thea passed through the corridor and stepped out into Liwei's cavern. The massive Dragon watched her with Meiling's golden eyes.

"Welcome, Thea," the Dragon rumbled.

Thea stepped carefully between the iridescent mushrooms and stood at the edge of the great heap of treasure on which the Dragon lay. "You wanted to speak with me?"

Meiling rumbled. "You came here out of concern for your friend. I have learned all that I can, but it seems that there are mysteries even the Tilaryn do not understand. What I can tell you is that Sylica is magic, in the way that a Dragon is magic. We do not *do* magic or *possess* magic. It is who we are. Sylica, however, is not a Dragon. In her blood I smell the Elves, but Elves alone cannot explain her existence as she is. Perhaps something happened early in her life, but I cannot guess what that would have been. However it may be that she is magic, she is. Is there anything else you wish to know?"

Thea took a moment to absorb what the Dragon had told her. "If Sylica is magic, why can't she control it?"

"That was because her hoard was too small. When a Dragon does not have enough treasure to contain their magic, it spills over into the world in unpredictable ways, threatening to tear a hole in the fabric of reality. That is why every Dragon must have their hoard, and why our Minathrils labour to increase it."

"Sylica has a hoard?"

"When she accepted the collector dragon as her own, the treasure inside of it became her hoard and started refracting her magic, but it was not enough to contain it. That is why you saw unpredictable surges of magic once the collector was found. It amplified her magic, without containing it. When you arrived here, I added more treasure to her hoard, which is why the surges have stopped."

An image of pies and fireworks rose in Thea's mind. "But I'm sure I've seen her do magic since then."

"Having a sufficient hoard does not mean she cannot do magic. It means the magic is now under her control. As long as she sleeps by her hoard, there should be no further issues."

No further issues was not a phrase Thea was used to associating with Sylica. "And she needs to add treasure to her horde?"

"No. The amount of magic a Dragon contains is dependent on their mass. We continue growing, and our hoard must grow too. Sylica will not grow anymore, so her treasure will be sufficient."

"But Sylica is a very ... generous person. What if she gives the treasure away?" Thea's eyes widened. "Will it make people go mad?"

"As long as she gives it away, it will cause no harm. It would be a problem if her hoard becomes too small, but since it is stored in a collector, I am sure more treasure will replace anything that is given away. The collectors were made to collect treasure, after all." The Dragon shifted in a clatter of tumbling gold. "I spoke with Sylica earlier this morning. As Dragons do for their young, I taught her how to be careful with her magic. She is small enough that a burst of magic from her will not be too harmful, but over time even she could put too much strain on the fabric of reality, given the right circumstances."

Thea felt a pang of misgiving. "You told her, but did she listen?"

The rumble of Meiling's voice almost sounded like laughter. "It was no more difficult than teaching a young Dragon. Trust me. She understood." The rumble died away. "You do not need to worry about your friend. Though her fate is a mystery, I can tell you this: she will find her purpose and her people."

Thea considered this. "She won't cause too much harm with her magic?"

"I do not think so. Reality has had to bend around her actions many times already, but fortunately, reality is stubborn. When given enough time, it can adapt to most unexpected changes."

"All the Dragons have to be careful about this?"

"Yes, and the larger we are, the more careful we have to be. Even the evil Dragons are cautious about the impact their magic has on Raphtova. They still want a world to live in."

"And you control your magic by having enough treasure?"

"Yes, and by rarely leaving it. As long as I rest here on my treasure, my need to eat is sated. My hoard reflects the shedding magic back to me and sustains me. When I fly, I must eat, and what would a creature my size eat to sustain them? That is why, when I can, I send my children or my Minathrils. I only leave my cavern to complete the task given to the Dragons by the One on the Throne that you call the Deity."

"What is the task of the Dragons?" Thea's voice quivered beneath the vast expanse of the Dragon's presence.

"Our task is to do battle with the Dragons and Tilaryn who have set themselves against the One on the Throne, to stop them from holding dominion over the people of Raphtova."

"You can fight Tilaryn?" Thea stared at the massive, golden eyes that looked down at her.

"Dragons are magic, and magic can interact with the spiritual. Tilaryn are as tangible to us as the treasure we lie on. When we wish, we can step into the Throne Room of the Deity."

The Throne Room? Thea felt in her spirit a distant echo of the wonder and terror of the moment she had stood before the One on the Throne.

"It was there that I learned of you," Meiling rumbled. "The name of the Spark is spoken in the presence of the One."

Thea shivered. In her mind she could see Allulien and Micai as they stood before the throne, their glory and power revealed in a way Thea had never seen before or since. She could still hear her own voice, accepting a position in the war against the Fallen One. Apparently that position was the Spark.

Thea swallowed. "Everyone keeps telling me I'm the Spark, but no one tells me why. Apparently it's just who

I am, but I don't understand what it means!"

Meiling rumbled and the golden eyes moved closer. "Tell me, Little One, what does a spark do?"

Thea's mouth felt dry. "A spark starts a fire."

The Dragon settled back into the bed of gold. "And wherever you go, the light of the Deity begins to spread. It is a light that has long been absent from much of Raphtova. We Dragons knew that it would return someday, and for it to return there would have to be a Spark to begin the fire. That is why we foretold that the Spark would come, to bring the light of the Deity to the five races again."

"Wait!" The words burst out of Thea. "I thought I had the five races figured out, but I was wrong. The Minathrils are one of the five, because they were taught by Raphea. The Elves, the Dryads, the Fauns, and the Littles all have their General, but what about the humans? Are they not one of the five, or were there six and the Halls of Knowledge are wrong?"

Meiling smiled, a large, tooth-filled smile. "You are correct. Humans are not one of the five."

"But—but I thought they must be!"

"Humans are like the Dragons. We are not one of the five, because we were not made for Raphtova. Humans are the Deity's response to the rebellion of the Fallen One. They are the glue to hold the people of Raphtova together, when the Fallen One would drive them apart."

Thea frowned. Images of angry, fearful faces rose in her mind. "How are they doing that?"

Meiling's voice rumbled. "They have the choice to follow the will of the Deity or not, as we all do, but it might not be as infrequent as you think. The tale has been relayed to me of the Littles' acceptance by the humans in Gedwyld, and I wonder if a human had any part to play in your own story of returning to the other races of Raphtova?"

Thea's heart leapt. Of course—it was Davis's coming to Lyudmyla where it all began. He had shown her what a spirit could look like when it was fully given to the service of the Deity, and after that she could never have been happy to stay in Lyudmyla. She smiled. "You're right. I would not be here if it hadn't been for a human."

"And it was that human that lit the spark in you. Given enough time, the spark will spread, and the peoples of Raphtova will be ready to fight together once again in the war against the Fallen One."

Responsibility fell over Thea like a weight. "And that's all my job?"

"All it needs is someone to begin it, and it has already begun. You may not be aware of the chaos your presence has caused here in the Caverns, but many of my Shindahs no longer have access to their magic because of the events that have transpired since you came here, and others have left the Caverns under new orders from Raphea. Apparently there are reparations to be paid for their neglect of the peoples of Raphtova." The Dragon's eyes glittered. "I did not expect this when I accepted the Spark into my Caverns, but perhaps I should have."

"You yourself said that the five races are supposed to come together. Why didn't you do anything about it?"

The Dragon settled deeper into the bed of treasure. "The choices of the Minathrils are not my responsibility."

"What?" Thea glared at the glittering figure towering before her. "You're their *Dragon*! They do whatever you say!"

Meiling's golden eyes flashed. "I do not pretend to hold sway over all the actions of those who have placed themselves beneath me, nor do I try to do so. If they have fallen short in their commitment to the ways of the Deity, the blame rests on their own heads, not mine."

"You think the Minathrils decide anything for themselves?" Thea glared. "Everything they do is to serve the Dragon. If they have forgotten to care about the rest of the world, maybe that is because you never told them to!"

Silence hung in the air. Slowly, Meiling stirred and a low rumble filled the cavern. A slow dread crept over Thea as she considered who it was she had just challenged. But it was true. Would the Minathrils ever return to the other four races if their Dragon didn't tell them to?

"I will consider your words," Meiling said at last. "And now your time in the Caverns is drawing to an end. Tomorrow morning you will depart." The tension in the air seemed to ease away. "Jeewon will direct you towards a more northerly course, easier to traverse than the way by which you came."

Thea nodded. "Thank you."

"I have a favour to ask of you as you go," Meiling continued. "There has been a magical disturbance, a span's journey north of here. Would you be willing to investigate its cause for me? It is beyond the borders of my territory, so I am reluctant to send a crew out that far."

Thea stared at Meiling, waiting for her to see the irony in what she had just asked.

Meiling rumbled. "Especially while there is so much

turmoil here in the Caverns." Her piercing, golden gaze met Thea's with a burning intensity.

Thea lowered her eyes. This seemed to be the line that should not be crossed. "Yes, we can do that."

"Good. You can tell what you find to your General, and I will inquire after you when I am next in the Throne Room. You may go."

Meiling closed her eyes. Thea waited to see if Liwei would say anything, but the Dragon lay motionless, breathing peacefully.

As Thea hesitated, a massive green eye opened slightly, regarded her for a moment, then closed again. It seemed that her audience was over. Thea turned and left the cavern.

"What did Meiling say?" Roland asked as he and Thea began the walk back to the Oreum quarters.

"She said that Sylica is going to be okay, as long as she has Daisy with her."

Roland considered this. "She won't have strange magic anymore?"

"She'll still have magic, but she should be able to control it."

"That doesn't sound a lot better to me," Roland frowned. "What's to stop her from still making a well to see what it's like to fall down one?"

"Nothing, I guess. The only one who can stop her is herself."

Concern etched itself on Roland's forehead. "And we're supposed to let her wander the world like that?"

"Meiling seemed to think she would be okay." Even as she spoke, Thea's heart sank. What sorts of things could happen to someone with the magical potential of a small Dragon and the self-control of a puppy? She grimaced. "At least she'll be travelling with us for a few more days. After that, I don't know what she wants to do."

Roland sighed. "I guess a lot can happen in a few days."

"Meiling says we need to leave tomorrow. She wants us to look for something for her, about a span's travel north of here. Some kind of magical disturbance. After that we can carry on to Lyudmyla."

Thea could feel Roland's glad smile.

"Alright. Did she say anything about what we're looking for?"

"No. I don't think Meiling knows what it is, just that it's something magical."

Roland frowned. "No advice on how to find it, or how to know if we found the right thing?"

"Um ..." Thea floundered. "Sylica can see magic. Maybe she'll be able to find it."

"I guess," Roland conceded.

"Meiling did end the conversation quite abruptly. I think I made her angry."

Roland's eyes widened. "How did you make her angry?"

"By being the Spark, I think. Things won't be the same here after we leave. I guess that's part of what it means to be the Spark."

"Like when you left home." Roland gave a wry smile. "You should have seen it."

Something twisted in Thea's gut. "I can't believe I'm going back."

Roland took her hand. "I'm glad you are."

Looking up into his eyes, Thea's heart beat faster. It

was worth it, to be with Roland.

As they approached the mess hall, Roland slowed his pace. "I promised Ssen I'd help with training today. I'd really like to, if it's going to be our last day here."

"I understand," Thea smiled. "We have the whole journey to spend time together."

Roland nodded and squeezed her hand before heading off towards the training grounds.

At the next mealtime, Thea found Sylica and told her it was their last day with the Minathrils.

"What?" Sylica gasped, her eyes wide. "Come on, Daisy, we have so many people to say goodbye to!" She scampered off as quickly as she could, with Daisy in hot pursuit.

When Sylica was gone from sight, Thea went to join Zanele and Hwasan at their table. She had hoped to speak to Hwasan alone, but Zanele always seemed to be around him.

"What's up?" Zanele asked, as Thea pulled up a chair.

"We got the news that the storm is dying down. We can leave tomorrow morning."

Zanele nodded. "I'm glad to hear it. What's the plan then?"

"We'll take the northern route out of the mountains. Apparently it's easier than the eastern route, and we're going to check something out for Meiling on the way. Roland and I are going to Lyudmyla, but we can all travel together for a while before you head back to the forest."

"Sounds like a plan," Zanele agreed, and busied herself with finishing the contents of her plate.

"Hwasan," Thea slid her chair closer to the Minathril,

"could I speak with you for a moment?"

Hwasan's scales showed a slight nervousness, but he nodded.

"I just wanted to say that you're welcome to come with us, to Lyudmyla, or the forest, or wherever you want to go. You're a part of our crew, and we'd like to have you with us." Thea paused, considering the best way to share the thought that had been growing in her mind. "But I've also seen you spending time with Ssen. It seems like you really get along. If you'd rather stay here with your people, I would completely understand. We'd miss you, but I think you would be happy here."

Confusion and disgust rippled across Hwasan's scales. "Why would I stay with the Minathrils? They've never accepted me before."

"Ssen has accepted you, and I think the others would learn to as well. When you spend time with him I can see a light and peace in your spirit that I hadn't seen there before. I think this is what you want, deep down inside."

"In my spirit?" Hwasan's eyes seemed mildly curious, but concern spread across his scales. On the other side of the table, Zanele ate her meal with delicate precision.

Thea gave an apologetic smile. "Yes, I can see the spirit inside of people. It's a gift that some Elves have. Others can see lightwaves or the connections between people or other things. We call it elf-sight."

Hwasan frowned thoughtfully. "Can Roland see the spirit inside of people?"

"No. He can see through physical things, like your actual heart pumping blood."

"And can Sylica see the spirit inside of people?"

Thea hesitated. "I'm not completely sure what Sylica can do, but I don't think she can. She can see magic, though."

"I see." Hwasan stared at Thea, a rush of colours sweeping across his scales.

Thea watched him in concern. "Are you alright?"

"Yes." Hwasan looked down at the table. "I am just thinking about what you said." His manner seemed unconcerned, but his scales showed fear.

"If you need to talk about anything, I would be glad to listen," Thea offered.

"No, thank you. I just need time to think."

"Okay." Thea stood up. "You can let me know later if you'd like to come with us or not. It's completely up to you."

As Thea turned to go, she felt the weight of Hwasan's stare.

"Hey." Zanele's hissing voice caught Thea's ear as she walked away. Stopping, she looked back.

Zanele was not talking to her. She was leaning over the table, staring intently at Hwasan. He gave her his attention, resentment flickering across his scales.

Catching the urgency in Zanele's voice, Thea stopped to listen.

"Listen to me," Zanele continued, her eyes not leaving Hwasan's. "I know who you are. You're a spy, sent to find the Spark. I know."

Fear and anger flashed across Hwasan's scales.

"I've seen the way you watch Sylica and stalk her movements." Zanele leaned closer. "You thought she was the Spark because of her magic and how powerful she is. As long as you were barking up the wrong tree, I let it go. It gave you more time to come to your senses.

But now you've figured out who the Spark really is, haven't you? I can tell. So figure out whose side you're on."

Hwasan stared at Zanele. "You were pretending to be my friend. Why?"

"I wasn't pretending." Zanele glared. "We like you, Hwasan, and you're a part of our crew. That is what mercy looks like—accepting people who aren't perfect—and that is something you don't get from your master, is it? Now it's your choice: accept us, or abandon us. Until you make your decision, I will be watching you."

With a wrench, Thea forced herself to turn and walk away. She was shaking. She had to find somewhere to be alone.

Leaving the mess hall, Thea stumbled back to their room and shut the door.

Hwasan was a spy. How was that possible? Of course, she knew there was something strange going on inside of him, that he was somehow connected to something dark or dangerous, but a spy? A spy sent especially to find *her*? She had never considered that the Enemy might be interested in finding or harming her. Now the behaviour of Roland and others who had taken her into their protection started to make more sense. There was real danger, but she hadn't seen it before.

What should she do? She had seen the light growing inside of Hwasan. Perhaps he would change his allegiance and choose to serve the Deity instead. Jeewon had said the Generals wanted Hwasan to be with her. It must be in the hope that he could be saved.

Thea's heart welled up with the unbelievable mercy

of the Deity, to welcome an agent of the Enemy into their midst, in the hope that he might be changed.

He could be changed, and he would, but she couldn't let Hwasan and Zanele know what she had heard. That would ruin everything. She would just have to be on her guard, and keep showing mercy.

Roland. Thea's heart fell and a knot grew in her stomach. She couldn't tell Roland. He was so concerned about her safety. If he knew Hwasan was a spy sent to find her, he would never let him stay. But if Roland sent Hwasan away, that would be the end of the story. There would be no more hope for redemption.

Thea's heart pounded as she paced the room. Zanele knew, and she would be watching. That had to be good enough. Roland could never know.

Chapter Twenty-One

The rest of the day passed in a blur, although outwardly it was no different than a usual day. The Minathrils hardly seemed to acknowledge that their guests would be leaving. With all the turmoil they had caused, Thea wondered if their departure would be a relief.

Wherever she went, it seemed like Hwasan was always there, watching her. And if Hwasan was there, Zanele was never far away.

When they all retired to their room for the night, Thea was doubly aware of Hwasan's gaze. Sylica and Roland were the only ones who seemed unaffected by the change in atmosphere.

"Thea, look at the knife Ssen and his company gave me!" Roland beamed as he held it out for her to see. "It makes a perfect set with my trollsbane knife. See the dragon carved on the handle?"

Trying to ignore Hwasan's looming presence, Thea gave the new knife the attention it deserved.

"Ssen said I can come back any time. Maybe I'll have a message to deliver here someday." Putting his knives away, Roland climbed into bed beside Thea. "How was your day?"

Thea's heart sank. "It was fine. Not very eventful."

"What did you do?"

Thea shrugged. "Just wandered around and talked with people." Her heart pounded. She had never tried to hide something from Roland before. It was hard to look in his eyes.

"Is something wrong?"

Thea forced herself to look at him. "I think I'm a bit nervous about travelling again."

Roland nodded. "Ssen said travel can be rough after a storm, but we'll take our time. There are lots of caves to shelter in along the way, so our nights should be comfortable enough."

Thea gave him a wan smile. "That's good."

Lying in Roland's arms, Thea stared up at Hwasan's bunk, just visible in the shadows. Even though she could feel Roland's peaceful breathing close beside her, he felt further away than he ever had before.

When morning came, Thea stayed behind to do her check in. Closing the door after everyone else was gone, she knelt by the far wall and waited.

Thea.

Thea glanced around the small room. Allulien wasn't there. She bowed her head again.

Thea. Allulien's voice entered her mind again. *As you travel north, there is one danger you must be aware of.*

In Thea's mind, the image of a cave appeared: a large, domed room with moisture glinting on the walls.

Our scouts have discovered a cave in the northern reaches of the mountains, overlooking the Deorcian. Inside this cave there is a stone, enchanted with dark magic. We suspect that it is connected with the increase of monsters in the Deorcian, but we have not found a way of neutralizing it without retaliation from the Fallen One.

As Thea's internal vision adjusted to the gloom of the

cave, she saw a stone pedestal in its exact center. On the pedestal rested a shadowy orb.

If you enter this cave, you must not touch the stone. If someone tries to touch it, you will do whatever must be done to stop them. Do you understand?"

Thea nodded as Allulien's words sank deep into her spirit.

You will stop them. At all costs.

"Yes, Allulien." Thea blinked, and the vision faded from her mind.

Slowly she stood, and found that her hands were shaking. She had never heard Allulien speak in that tone of voice before.

In the distance, the bell rang.

Fervently whispering a prayer that they would not happen upon that cave, Thea opened the door.

Hwasan stood in front of her.

Thea startled, then tried to steady herself, her heart pounding.

Hwasan's scales turned transparent-grey. "Forgive me for surprising you." He bowed. "I wanted to say that I will continue travelling with you. I thank you again for your warm welcome."

"Of course." Thea forced herself to smile. "We are glad to have you with us."

Hwasan smiled and bowed again. His crest was back. Was he worried?

"Shall we walk to the mess hall together?" Hwasan offered.

Thea nodded, and walked beside him in silence. Meiling had spoken about some kind of magical disturbance to the north. That wouldn't be the cave Allulien had warned her about, would it?

After the meal was finished, Thea and her companions prepared to depart, packing their bags with the travelling food the cooks provided for them.

Although most of the Minathrils had gone to their day's tasks, a few lingered in the mess hall, gathering around Thea and her companions to say goodbye. Instinctively, Thea cast comprehension so everyone could freely speak.

Ssen shook Roland's hand, then bowed to Thea. "It has been an honour to spend time with you both."

"And it has been an honour to get to know you, Ssen." Thea bowed in return. "Hopefully we can see you again someday."

Ssen's scales gleamed gold. "That will be a day of joy for me." Bowing again, he strode across the room to speak with Zanele and Hwasan.

Thea turned to Sungy, who was also present. "Thank you for welcoming us and introducing us to your family."

Sungy's scales shone yellow. "It was a pleasure. I am glad you could stay with us for this time."

Nearby, Sylica was giving a tearful goodbye to Noonie.

"We'll miss you so much!" Sylica threw her arms around her translator's neck. "Won't we, Daisy?" At her side, Daisy cocked her head and whined.

Removing herself from Sylica's tight embrace, Noonie bowed. "I must thank you, Sylica. You have improved my Common very much."

Thea joined Jeewon by the door. "Thank you for your hospitality."

Jeewon's scales churned with glints of red and grey.

"I will lead you to the end of the tunnels and show you your way. You can thank me then."

When everyone was ready, Jeewon led them out of the mess hall and through the vast network of corridors. Soon they passed fewer and fewer side passages, and the corridor became a long, straight tunnel, like the one they had entered the Caverns through so long before.

"Is this the same tunnel?" Thea asked.

"You entered through the eastern tunnel. This one leads north."

Silence fell once again, broken only by their footsteps and the clatter of Sylica and Daisy running on ahead.

After several measures of walking, a gust of cold wind blew down the tunnel to meet them. Thea glanced at Jeewon, but the Captain said nothing.

Soon real daylight shone ahead, and they found themselves in the entrance of the tunnel, staring out at a snow-covered world.

Jeewon pointed north. "Follow that valley between the two peaks. Beyond it, the Great North River will guide you. When you reach the slopes above the treeline, you can turn east or west, whichever way your road is leading you."

Thea turned to the Captain. "Thank you for your help, and for teaching me about your people."

Jeewon bowed, her scales a dull grey orange.

Thea glanced at Roland, less than eager to venture beyond the shelter of the tunnel entrance.

He gave her a wry smile. "Let's go. Goodbye, Captain."

Roland stepped out into the snow, and Thea followed.

Sylica scampered past. "There's so much snow! Can

we make *tunnels*?"

Zanele made a face. "Haven't you had enough tunnels for a while?"

"Come on, Sylica," Roland gestured her on. "You'll have time to play when we camp for the night."

Slowly, they trudged down the slope, away from the tunnel entrance.

Jeewon's voice rang above the hissing wind, her arm raised in farewell.

Thea had not understood what Jeewon said. The gift of language was gone.

She waved, and watched as Jeewon turned and strode away into the shadows.

The wind hissed, blowing wisps of stinging snow off the overhanging rocks. The cold bit deeply through Thea's warm clothing. The Great Sleep had come to the mountains. The sooner they got down to the lowlands again, the better.

"I could play in the snow and walk at the same time if I wanted to," Sylica reflected, tramping cheerfully along behind Thea. "I have lots of magic juice, you know. I could do lots of fun things in the snow with magic!" She hesitated. "But Meiling said the world doesn't want too much magic juice spilling all over the place. It gets things too sticky."

"Magic juice?" Thea eyed her skeptically.

Sylica grinned. "I'm full of magic juice, like a berry is full of berry juice. That's what Meiling told me."

"Did she use those exact words?" Thea gave a wry smile.

"Yup! She was super nice, and soooo big! Lots bigger than Liwei."

"Wait." Thea stopped. "You actually saw Meiling?

You didn't just talk with her through Liwei?"

"Of course I saw her. Meiling said I could, because I'm basically a Dragon except not a Dragon at all. We had a really good talk, but my brain hurt a bit afterwards. I think she made me do too much thinking."

Zanele made a face. "It couldn't have done too much harm." Adjusting her pace, she fell in step beside Hwasan. "Do you know this northern route at all?"

"What? No." Hwasan eyed the slopes surrounding them, his crest flat against his back. "I think the Captain's advice was good. East of here we'd have to deal with the cliffs again."

Zanele gave him a keen glance. "Good. We'll carry on, then."

As they entered the valley, the snow grew deeper. Soon they were trudging through drifts reaching above Thea's knees. Daisy hopped in Sylica's wake, disappearing after every bound in a poof of snow.

As they walked, Thea scanned the mountainside nervously. If they passed near the cave, would they have any warning?

A shadow caught her eye and she stopped. Hwasan bumped into her.

"Sorry," Thea muttered. Where had she seen the shadow? There. It was the darkness beneath an overhang. Nothing spiritually dark about it at all.

"No, *I* am sorry." Hwasan bowed, his scales flaring a tan colour. "I should have been more careful."

"It's alright." Thea moved over so Hwasan could walk beside her. "I hope your time with the Minathrils didn't end up being too hard after all."

Hwasan seemed to consider this, his scales becoming greyish-green. "You're right, it was not as difficult as I expected it to be. I learned much about the field of medical practices," he shot Zanele a glance as amusement flashed over his scales, "and I learned that there are people in the world who are willing to stand by me. I never had that before." A hint of gold flickered at the edges of his scales.

Thea smiled, forcing herself to stop her anxious scanning of the mountainside. The cave wouldn't be this close, would it?

"Look!" Roland called, from where he was breaking a trail up ahead. "There's a cave here. Do we want to stop and rest? I'd say we're well into staph now."

"No!" Thea's voice burst out, more urgent than she intended it to. "I mean—" she stammered, "I don't think it's quite so cold out, now that it's staph. Shouldn't we keep walking for a while?"

Roland gave her a curious glance. "I guess so. Should we travel a long day today?"

Thea nodded. "I think so. We don't want another storm to come before we get out of the mountains."

"Alright. We'll keep going, then." Roland watched her thoughtfully for a moment, then continued the trek down the valley. Thea took a shaky breath and followed.

Tramping through the snow, the cold sunk deeper and deeper into Thea's bones. She was tired, but stopping to rest meant finding a cave, and who knew what they would find there?

Finally restday was passing, and at Roland's insistence they began to look for a place to shelter for the night.

"Here's a cave!" Zanele called, from where she was searching further down the rugged slope.

Thea cringed. "Careful!" Scrambling through the

snow, she hurried to get there before the others did.

Pushing past Zanele, Thea crouched down and stared into the shadowy gloom of the cave. It was small, and nothing like the cave Allulien had shown her. She took a shaky breath. "It seems safe enough."

Roland followed her inside and checked around the nooks and crannies, trailing snow with every step. The cave was too low to stand in and just large enough to fit all five of them inside, but it was dry and the floor was smooth. "This will be alright," Roland nodded.

Zanele and Hwasan crawled inside.

"Sylica!" Zanele called over her shoulder. "Aren't you coming?"

"Daisy and I are going to play in the snow!" Sylica's voice echoed from outside. "Roland said that I could!"

Beside Thea, Hwasan pulled his brazier out of his bag. Lighting it, he set it in the center of their small shelter. Everyone huddled around its warmth.

Finally Sylica joined them. Panting heavily, she scooched close to the brazier. "That was fun," she grinned with sparkling eyes. "Daisy and I had a snowball fight. Daisy can't make snowballs, but I couldn't hit her, so in the end we were even." Melting snow puddled around her feet and gleamed on Daisy's metallic scales.

"Are you hungry?" Thea asked, taking some food from the Minathrils out of her bag.

"Oh yes! I could make a—" Sylica's face fell. "Oh right, I'm not supposed to do that. I'll eat some of that food then." She munched on a piece of dried meat with a surprisingly thoughtful expression.

Cheeky sat on Zanele's shoulder, nibbling a bit of something Zanele had offered her.

The food from the Minathrils was simple, but good. Thea ate in silence, watching Hwasan from the corner of her eye. Both light and dark still showed in his spirit. She wanted to say something to him, but she couldn't think of what to say. If there was just something that would tip the scales, that would convince him to turn to the Deity ...

She was too tired to think, but her mind wouldn't stop churning everything over and over again.

Knowing how hard it would be to fall asleep, Thea offered to take the first watch. Around her, everyone else shuffled to pull out their blankets and get comfortable on the bare cave floor. Thea sat by the brazier and stared out the small cave mouth to the shadowy snow beyond.

Hwasan was watching her. Thea pretended not to notice.

After a long silence, Roland stirred and sat up.

"Can't you sleep?" Thea asked.

Roland shifted closer. In a low voice, he spoke in Elvish. "Can you tell me what's going on? I'm not used to seeing you nervous like this."

Thea glanced around their small cave. Hwasan lay peacefully. His eyes were closed. "It's something Allulien said. There's a cave somewhere along our route that has something dangerous in it. That's why I've been so nervous about caves."

Roland watched her closely. "This cave—you'll know if we find it?"

Thea nodded. "Allulien showed me what it looks like."

"Okay." Roland's eyes were thoughtful. "I'll check any caves with you before deciding if they're safe to stay in. Is there anything else I need to know about?"

"No." Thea's heart sank. Roland was watching her, waiting for what else she would say. "I'm nervous about going back to Lyudmyla," she offered. It was true, after all.

Roland took her hand. "I'll be there with you."

Thea forced a smile. She wanted to feel close to Roland again. She could just tell him, but then he'd make Hwasan leave.

"Thea?" Roland's gaze was gentle, begging to be let in.

Thea's heart beat faster. "I—"

Beside her, Hwasan shifted and rolled over.

Thea squeezed Roland's hand. "I love you, Roland." She took a trembling breath. "It will be okay."

Days passed as they continued to make their way north. The snow and bitter cold made their progress slow, but with magic to ease their travel and take the worst bite off the cold, they were able to make their way further and further down the mountain slopes.

With each day that passed, Thea's anxiety lessened. Hwasan wasn't acting any differently than he was before, and none of the caves they found matched the image shown by Allulien.

On the fourth night, their cave overlooked rolling, wooded foothills, where snow had not yet fallen.

"By staph tomorrow we should drop below the snow line," Roland shared as they ate their evening meal.

"Finally!" Zanele stretched her hooves out towards the glowing brazier. "I've seen enough snow to last a lifetime."

"Thanks for doing so much with your magic, Zanele,"

Roland grinned. "It really helped us make good time."

"That's what healers are for," Zanele shrugged, scratching Cheeky behind the ear. Cheeky leaned farther and farther until she fell over, then scrambled sheepishly onto Zanele's shoulder where her glaring eyes dared anyone to comment.

Roland's gaze scanned the hills stretched out below them. "Once we drop below the snow line we'll need to turn east or west. I don't know how far south the Deorcian stretches, but I want to avoid the forest down there, just in case." He glanced at Thea. "Thea and I are going to Lyudmyla. The rest of you would be welcome to join us, of course, but you might have other places you want to go."

Silence drifted through the cave on the cold evening air.

"I have nowhere to go," Hwasan replied, his scales a cautious grey. "If you will have me, I will come."

"Of course you can come," Thea assured him. "We'd be glad to have you." She watched the light swell in Hwasan's spirit as yellow glowed across his scales.

Zanele traced her finger along the rocky floor of the cave. "I don't know what I should do. My leader sent me to help you, and I'm not sure if that duty is done. If it is, I will go home. My tribe needs me."

"You were sent to help us through the mountains," Thea replied. "You don't need to go further with us if you don't want to."

Zanele glanced at Hwasan. Thea could see why she was hesitating. She had warned Hwasan that she would watch him until he made his final decision. But surely he was close now. The light in his spirit was so much brighter than the darkness.

"I think we will be alright," Thea assured her. She couldn't explain why, here in front of everybody, but maybe Zanele would understand.

Zanele shrugged. "Perhaps. I will ask Raphea in the morning." She stared out the cave mouth, towards the forest far below. "I miss my people. Everything is so much simpler there, compared to the Minathrils' rigid, complicated ways. No offence." She glanced at Hwasan.

"No offence taken." Hwasan bowed.

Zanele's eyes twinkled. "Still, they're not all bad. I'm glad I got to meet them. There's a few things I learned that will come in handy on the battlefield, even if I can't have an entire room devoted only to surgeries."

Thea watched Allumen's light fade from the sky. "Every race really does have something to offer, when we're able to work together. Maybe we taught the Minathrils something too."

Zanele grinned. "I think we did."

Sylica dozed by the brazier, her head resting on Daisy's back. She hadn't done any magic on their whole way down from the Caverns so far. Thea was surprised by her self-control. That wasn't something she was used to seeing in her.

"What will you do, Sylica?" Thea asked.

"Hmm?" Sylica opened her eyes. "What?"

"Roland and Hwasan and I are going to Lyudmyla. Zanele might come with us, or she might go back to the forest. What are you going to do?"

"Oh. I like the Fauns. I think I'll go see them some more." Snuggling closer to Daisy, Sylica closed her eyes again.

Silence fell over the cave. Outside, occasional flakes of snow drifted by on the fitful breeze.

"Tomorrow is going to be day five," Roland said, "so we have to keep our eyes open for that magical disturbance Meiling asked us to watch for."

"A magical disturbance?" Zanele frowned.

Hwasan straightened.

"Yes, she wanted us to find out what is causing it, since we were going this way anyways," Thea explained.

"What do you think it is?" Zanele asked.

"I have no idea." Thea shrugged. "I guess we'll know it when we see it."

"Do you know where this disturbance is?" Hwasan asked. A hint of orange gleamed at the edges of his scales.

"Just that it was about a five day's journey from the Caverns, but that doesn't tell us much."

Hwasan nodded. "We will see what we can do."

"And if we don't find anything?" Zanele frowned.

"Meiling just asked us to look. If we don't find anything I think that is fine," Thea assured her. "She can send a crew out if she really needs to know."

The orange on Hwasan's scales grew stronger.

Chapter Twenty-Two

Thea stared out the mouth of the cave at the morning's new dusting of snow. Zanele sat nearby, tying her hair back in its customary braid.

"Any word from Raphea?"

Zanele shook her head. "Nothing today."

"What will you do, then?"

Zanele shrugged. "Not sure. I don't have to decide just yet, so something might come up."

Thea nodded. A chilly morning breeze gusted across the mountainside, reaching into their small cave with its icy fingers. She shivered and pulled her cloak tighter. "If there's something strange going on nearby, that could be why you didn't hear anything. Sometimes the Generals can't risk showing themselves, if that means drawing the Enemy's attention."

Zanele stretched, a small smile playing at the corners of her mouth. "Oh, I'm not worried. The Generals have their ways of showing us what to do. I'm sure I'll know when the time comes."

Thea smiled. "Whether you come with us or go home, I'm glad you've been with us, Zanele. I think you were the Spark to the Minathrils just as much as I was."

Zanele gave a wry smile. "I think it's catching." Her sharp gaze scanned the empty cave around them. Sylica was often out and about as soon as it was light, and Roland had made a habit of doing his check in away

360

from the group in a private place.

Thea looked down at Zanele's bright, eager face. "The Fauns have been faithful to the Deity in a way that none of the other races have. I admire them so much for that."

Zanele's eyes twinkled. "The Deity made us stubborn. If we don't want to give up, we don't. That can be a blessing and a curse, you know," she winked, "but it's done the Resistance well. We'll be true till we die."

Thea nodded. There was no doubt about that. "I think we could all do with being a little more like the Fauns."

Zanele's smile became almost impish. "I wouldn't say no to that."

Roland strode into the cave, bringing another gust of cold, damp air with him. "Finished checking in?"

Thea nodded. "Anything we should know about?"

"No. Nothing since we left the Caverns. We just need to get back to the Raven as soon as we can."

"Where's Hwasan?" Zanele asked.

Roland glanced outside. "I haven't seen him. Maybe he's with Sylica?"

Collecting their bags, they stepped out of the cave. In the distance, Sylica and Daisy slid down a large, snowy rock.

"Sylica!" Thea waved, waiting as Sylica and Daisy scampered back up the slope towards them. "We're getting ready to go. Have you seen Hwasan?"

"Nope. He left the cave during the last part of my watch. Isn't he back yet?"

A look of concern crossed Zanele's face.

Roland frowned. "That's strange. He doesn't usually wander off."

"Hwasan!" Thea called. Her voice echoed off the distant crags.

Scattering around the area, Thea and the others searched for Hwasan, but he didn't seem to be anywhere nearby. They found his footprints, though, and Roland set out to follow them.

A short while later, he returned with Hwasan following close behind.

"Found him!" Roland grinned. "He heard us calling, so he was on his way back."

"And where were you off to?" Zanele gave the Minathril a suspicious side-eye.

"I could not sleep, so I thought I would wander a while and went farther than I realized." Hwasan's scales flickered a dull grey-orange. "I lost my way, but your voices brought me in the right direction again."

"You didn't try retracing your footprints?" Zanele raised an eyebrow.

Hwasan looked down as if he was embarrassed. "I did not think of that." A hint of red flickered on his scales, and Thea saw a shadow grow in his spirit.

"That's alright," Thea assured him. "I'm glad you weren't lost for long."

The shadow in Hwasan's spirit seemed to fade. Thea let herself breathe again.

"Does everyone have their packs?" Roland asked. "We might as well get started."

As they walked, Thea kept her eyes open for anything unusual, but the snow-covered, rocky land around her appeared unchanged.

After several measures of walking, they found themselves at the top of a high bluff. Below them, forested hills stretched as far as they could see.

Thea glanced back. Behind them, rocky slopes stretched up into white obscurity. "We've reached the end of the mountains." She glanced at Zanele, but the Faun did not comment.

"It's almost staph." Roland fingered the handle of a knife thoughtfully. "Do we want to find somewhere to rest for a bit, while Zanele decides what she wants to do?"

"There's a magic rope coming up from that big rock there." Sylica pointed. "Maybe that would be a good place."

"A what?" Thea demanded.

Hwasan's scales went almost transparent.

"A magic rope," Sylica grinned. "It comes up out of the rocks and then goes over the mountains."

Thea glanced at Roland. "Maybe that's the magical thing Meiling was talking about."

Roland looked with interest in the direction Sylica had pointed. "Let's go have a look."

"Come on," Sylica gestured. "It's over here!"

Thea and the others followed Sylica as she tramped cheerfully up and around the boulders.

"There!" She gestured triumphantly.

Thea stared around the barren, rocky hillside. A scrubby bush waved slightly in the wind.

"It comes out of the ground here," Sylica explained, "goes up in the air, and off that way!" She pointed south.

Roland squinted at the vacant air in front of them. "What would anyone want a magic rope for?"

"It's talking magic, so I guess you can talk from one end of the rope to the other end. I wonder where it goes!" Sylica poked at the ground beneath their feet, but the rock seemed solid.

Thea glanced around the group. Hwasan was gone.

Wait. His bag was there, hanging just behind Roland's elbow. Something must have frightened him, but his scales quickly flared orange again.

"Alright." Roland nodded. "Let's have a look around. There might be a cave below us somewhere."

"I do not think that is necessary," Hwasan interjected. "You found what Meiling wanted you to see, did you not?"

"Maybe," Roland shrugged. "But since we're here we might as well find out all that we can. The whole point of us looking was so Meiling wouldn't have to send a crew out."

Zanele gave Hwasan a shrewd look. "You wouldn't happen to know anything about this kind of magic, would you, Hwasan?"

"I—I cannot see any magic here at all," Hwasan stammered, the colour rapidly fading from his scales. "The only reason we're looking is because Sylica says she sees something. For all I can see, it is the same as any other rock on the mountain."

Thea nodded. It did look like any other rock on the mountain, but Sylica could see magic, so something must be there.

"Come on!" Sylica skipped off down the mountainside. "Let's try downhill first!"

Thea hurried to follow. Who knew what would happen if Sylica found a strange magical place without anyone else there to supervise?

The rocks underfoot were slippery and treacherous, but Thea managed to catch up to Sylica at the foot of the slope. Where two boulders met, a large, shadowy crack could be seen.

"Do you think that's the entrance to a cave?" Sylica asked, panting.

Thea tried to stare through the darkness. "It might be."

Roland's hands rested on his knives as he stepped beside her. "Do you want me to scout?"

"Perhaps I should enter first," Hwasan replied, his scales glinting orange once again. "I have studied magic for many circles. If there is something magical inside, I can make sure it is not dangerous."

Zanele frowned.

"I think," Thea said slowly, "I should go first." She glanced at Roland. If there was any chance this was the cave Allulien had warned her about, she needed to know before anyone else stepped inside it.

"What if there is some danger you cannot see?" Hwasan protested, his orange becoming even more vibrant. "I wish to be of service."

"Thank you, Hwasan," Roland replied, taking in Thea's glance, "but Thea can see things that are unseen. I agree that she should go first."

"Then allow me at least to follow her," Hwasan insisted.

"Alright," Roland conceded.

Thea stared at the tumult of light and dark in Hwasan's spirit. What was going on? If this was just some sort of magical phenomenon, as Meiling had implied, perhaps there was a simple explanation, but if not ...

Thea's heart beat faster. She needed to know if this was the place Allulien had spoken of. If it was, maybe that would be the key to what the darkness was doing in

Hwasan's spirit.

Turning, Thea stepped through the crack. Almost immediately, it widened out into a smooth-floored passage, with two walls of rock sloping to meet overhead.

Orange light glowed behind her. Thea glanced over her shoulder to see Hwasan holding out his brazier.

"It is also useful as a light source." He smiled as he stepped beside her. Gold shimmered across the orange of his scales. "Allow me."

Holding the light aloft, Hwasan strode beside Thea, further down the stony passageway. After several paces, he slowed. "I will ask you again: allow me to go ahead and see what may be found here. I will make sure it is safe and return at once."

Thea looked at the strange blend of colours evident on his scales. Something was going on, and Zanele had said he was a spy. She wanted to believe that he meant well, but orders were orders. "I have to go first, Hwasan. My General told me to."

Anger flickered at the edges of Hwasan's scales. "You don't trust me?"

"I do trust you, Hwasan, but I have orders to be careful of one particular cave. I need to know if this is that cave, before anyone else enters it." Without waiting to hear his protest, Thea continued down the passageway.

With the glow of the brazier behind her, Thea's hurrying figure cast a large, dark shadow before her. She just needed to know, then she could make everything right with Hwasan.

The sound of her footsteps echoed through the darkness around her. Thea stopped and stared through the shadows. The passageway had ended, opening out into a large, domed cave. In the center, a stone pedestal rose out of her shadow, holding a dark, orb-like stone. It looked just like the one in her vision. It was the cave.

Thea's heart sank. Now what?

"Careful," Thea said as Hwasan stepped beside her. "Make sure you stay back from the center of the room."

More footsteps sounded behind her.

"I wanted to come too!" Sylica's cheerful voice rang through the silence, along with the clatter of Daisy's eager trot.

Beyond her, Thea saw the green glow of Roland's lantern. Orange brazier-light shone from the ground by her side.

"Okay everyone, listen to me." Thea took a careful breath. "We all have to stay away from the center of the room. We'll find out what we can for Meiling, but then we need to leave."

Roland stepped beside Thea, scanning the cave with a keen gaze.

Thea glanced at Sylica. "Can you tell us about the magic you see?"

"It's talking magic, like I said. The rope ends at that stone thing, so I guess it's for talking."

Thea frowned. For talking to what? And who would use this place, on the edge of the cliffs between the mountains and the Deorcian?

She felt Zanele's hiss of breath. Hwasan had circled partway around the perimeter of the cave and was cautiously approaching the stone.

"Hwasan?" Thea called. "Stay with us, please. That stone could be dangerous."

Hwasan's scales flashed red, then glowed orange

again. "I know about magic. I will find out what it does."

"We are staying away from it," Thea repeated. "You can learn what you can from the sides of the room."

"Meiling wanted us to learn about this stone," Hwasan insisted. "I cannot study it properly from so far away." He continued moving closer to the pedestal in the center of the room.

"Sylica says it is talking magic, so we already have a pretty good idea of what it's for," Thea replied. "Please stop, Hwasan."

Hwasan stopped, but he did not step back.

"Come over here." Thea gestured for Hwasan to join her by the passage entrance. "It's safer, and we can talk about what we've seen."

"Why?" Hwasan's scales flared red. "Why should I do what you say?"

"Because she's the Spark." Zanele's eyes flashed. "What she says is important."

"She isn't *my* Spark." Brown tinted Hwasan's scales.

"I thought you said we were your crew," Zanele countered.

Hwasan hesitated. A gleam of light within his spirit threw into relief how dark it had suddenly become. Thea hardly dared to breathe.

Hwasan's scales gleamed orange. "We will talk about that later," he conceded. "First I need to learn about this stone."

"Hwasan!" Thea cried as he took another step towards the center of the room. "Please listen. We're saying this because we care about you."

"What's he doing?" Sylica asked. "Does he want to talk to someone?"

Fear rose in Thea's spirit. "No one is to touch that

stone. Do you understand?"

Hwasan's crest waved, a slight hint of yellow gleamed. "I understand." He stepped forward again.

"Listen!" Thea hurried towards him. "You have to trust me. You can't touch that stone."

"Why not?" Hwasan demanded.

"Because Allulien said so!"

"And why should I care about that?"

"Because Allulien's words come from the Deity!"

"I never needed the Deity before," Hwasan's scales flashed red. "That is not changing now."

Roland put a hand on his knife.

"No!" Thea gestured Roland away. "Listen, Hwasan. The Deity cares about you. Whatever you have done before, the Deity wants to show you mercy. *Please listen to me!*"

Hwasan continued striding forward. Darkness was closing in on his spirit again. What was happening? Why wasn't he listening to her? Just a couple more steps—

Don't touch it. Thea threw her magic at Hwasan. She didn't want to charm him, but what choice did she have?

The wave of magic hit a counterspell and disappeared. Thea stared. Who would counterspell her? Roland or Zanele wouldn't. Was it possible that Hwasan—

Thea cast charm again. *Don't touch it.*

With a surge of magic, her spell disappeared.

Zanele darted forward. A knife gleamed in Roland's hand.

"Stop!"

Hwasan touched the stone.

A wave of magic exploded across the room. It filled Thea's body and mind with a feeling like lead. She couldn't move. She couldn't think.

Around her, everyone froze—

Not everyone. Zanele darted forward with lightning speed. Shouting, she waved her arm.

Magic swelled and exploded around Thea into a golden dome, completely surrounding her. The magic freezing Thea's muscles melted away and her mind was free. Staggering, Thea touched the golden dome. It was solid, obscuring her view of anything that happened outside. Its golden surface swirled and glittered beneath her hand. It was magic, but she could see it, and she couldn't get out.

Thea thought she felt a swell of magic. What was happening out there? She hammered against the golden walls.

Wait—comprehension would show her what was going on. As Thea cast her magic, the golden wall before her became transparent, showing Hwasan standing before the magical stone. Zanele swung her halberd with a surge of magic. Hwasan countered her.

"Let them go!" Zanele yelled.

Roland and Sylica stood frozen in place, just like Thea had been, with Daisy standing motionless between them.

Hwasan struck out with his staff, but Zanele dodged aside.

"Release the Spark." The Minathril's eyes flashed, his scales red with anger.

"What, so you can charm her again?" Zanele glared up at him, crouched in a fighter's stance. "She is safe where she is."

Hwasan gestured and there was another surge of magic, which Zanele countered.

"My shield stays," Zanele growled.

Thea stared, her face pressed to her invisible wall. Hwasan was a caster? How could that be? There had been so much light in him. How could he serve the Enemy like that?

"So, what did you tell him?" Zanele swung her halberd at Hwasan's legs and he jumped back. "That you found the Spark?"

"That is none of your business," Hwasan growled. Moving his staff with snakelike precision, he struck Zanele on the face and she staggered back.

Hwasan stood tall, his tail lashing. "Go now and I'll let you live."

Zanele spat blood and looked up with a reckless smile. "Have you learned nothing about Fauns?" Jumping up, she caught him in the stomach with the butt of her halberd. Before he could react, she struck again, forcing him backwards.

Step by step, she drove him back, away from the stone. "You will *not* hurt them," she spoke through gritted teeth. "And you will not say *anything* about them to your master."

Hwasan stumbled, transparency flickering on his scales. With a swell of magic, he cast again, and Zanele counterspelled.

"Don't even try." Zanele's eyes flashed as she struck again.

Hwasan parried her blow, his scales blazing red. "You won't be able to counterspell every time." He swung his staff for a blow of his own. "Magic runs out eventually."

Zanele caught it with the shaft of her halberd. "As does yours, I imagine."

Hwasan glanced at the stone. A hint of gold rippled across his scales.

Zanele had seen his glance. As Hwasan turned to reach for the stone, she swung with her halberd.

Shifting out of his feint, Hwasan struck her unprotected side. Zanele tumbled to the ground.

As she fell, a small figure launched itself out of the shadows and landed on Hwasan's head. He waved his arms wildly, trying to fend off Cheeky's assault.

On the ground, Zanele seemed dazed.

"Get up!" Thea yelled, her face pressed to her immovable window. "Get up!"

Collecting herself, Zanele staggered to her feet as Hwasan ripped Cheeky off his face and flung her across the room.

Zanele crouched to spring, and Hwasan kicked her in the face. Zanele crumpled to the ground.

"No!" Thea pounded on the shield. "Don't hurt her!"

Wait, if the shield was magic—she threw the rest of her magic into a counterspell. The shield shimmered, but held firm.

Hwasan pulled something that looked like a short, thick piece of wood from his belt. With a surge of magic it sprouted a blade: long, thin, and wickedly sharp. He stabbed it into Zanele's chest.

Thea screamed and pounded on the shield. It would not move.

"Do something!" she yelled at Roland's motionless figure. "Don't just stand there!"

He stood, immobile, as if he had been frozen. Sylica was just as motionless.

Tears streamed down Thea's face as she hammered on the walls of her prison. Outside, Hwasan kicked Zanele's body aside and turned to face the others.

A glimmer of gold shimmered over his scales as he stared at Roland, the dark dagger still grasped firmly in his hand.

"No!" Thea screamed. "Don't touch him!"

Hwasan flicked his dagger and the blade disappeared. Setting one hand on the stone, he smiled. "Tell me, Roland, where does the Spark live?"

Roland opened his mouth. "She lives in a manor house on the coast. A measure's walk north of Gedwyld." The words came slowly, like they were being dragged out of him.

"Thank you."

There was nothing but darkness in Hwasan's spirit now. All Thea could see through her failing sight drove her despair deeper. Zanele was dead. How could Hwasan do that? She had been so kind to him!

"Zanele was part of the Resistance." Hwasan's words broke through Thea's consciousness. "Tell me about them."

A horrible understanding filled her mind. Roland knew all about the Resistance. Hwasan must have seen that, or why would he be questioning him? Now the Enemy would know about them. Thabani said their only safety was that the Enemy didn't know. Now they were in danger, and she couldn't do anything to stop it.

She hammered on the shield, she screamed and cried, but Hwasan did not even glance in her direction.

Everything before her became tinged with gold. What was happening? Thea stared in alarm. Her comprehension spell was ending. Before her eyes, her window into the world disappeared.

Thea collapsed against the wall of her prison, sobs racking her body. There was nothing she could do. She was trapped. Her magic was gone. She was alone.

Not alone. Thea felt a presence in her mind. It was filled with holy anger. Thea fell to her face.

Thea. Allulien's voice filled her mind. *You did not obey.*

Guilt tore through her heart, flooding over her grief and terror.

"I tried!" Thea gasped. "He didn't listen to me!"

Your orders were not to reason with him. Allulien's voice was more stern than anything she had heard before. *Your orders were to prevent it at all costs.*

"But I tried everything—"

You did not. You should have killed him, rather than let him speak to the Enemy.

"What? I couldn't kill him! What about mercy? I was trying to save him!"

Sometimes mercy looks like judgment. What about mercy for the countless people his betrayal has put at risk? Hwasan received his mercy—it led him to your party, in the hope that he might find redemption. Mercy was there for him to choose, right until he made his final choice. Allulien's words sank into her consciousness like a death knell. *Your disobedience has brought danger to everyone you love. As we speak, the Enemy is learning all that he wishes to know.*

"What can I do?" Thea stared at the floor with burning eyes. "I'm trapped!"

You are saved. Zanele followed her orders to her dying breath. Now you follow yours. Go save the Resistance.

"But how—"

No magic lasts forever. When the shield falls, be ready. You will only have one chance.

Allulien's presence left her mind. Thea sagged on her hands and knees, fear and horror filling her mind. She had to obey. She had to stop Hwasan, no matter how much it hurt.

Willing her feet to hold her, she forced herself to stand. How long would it be until the shield ended? Was there any way to know?

With shaking hands, she unclipped Raybow from her baldric and put an arrow to the string. Heart pounding, she sighted toward the place where she remembered Hwasan to be. The golden shield glimmered across her vision.

Her arms started to shake.

With uncanny silence, the shield disappeared.

There was Hwasan, standing in front of Roland, his hand on the stone.

Thea released her arrow.

Hwasan's scales faded in surprise and he opened his mouth. The arrow struck him in the chest.

For a moment everything was unchanged, then Hwasan crumpled to the ground.

Roland staggered. A shriek burst out of Sylica, as if her voice was finally released.

Thea ran to them, throwing her arms around Roland as he sank to his knees. Sylica ran across the cave to Zanele's side, with Daisy clattering after her.

Roland was shaking. "I couldn't stop him!" he cried, his head in his hands. "I couldn't stop him! My body wouldn't move. My mind couldn't cast magic. She's dead and I had to watch—"

"Roland!" Thea clung to him, her hands shaking almost as much as his.

"I tried—I tried, but there was nothing I could do." He stared, as if part of him was still trapped in horror. "I couldn't save her, I couldn't do anything!" He slammed his fist on the ground, his shoulders heaving.

"She's dead." Sylica voice was small, but it seemed to echo around the cave. Zanele's lifeless form was in her arms. "I—I hoped that maybe—maybe she was faking, or something. But—" Sylica's lip trembled and she looked down. "I don't think my magic can fix this."

"Oh Sylica." Thea reached out a hand. "I'm so sorry."

Carrying Zanele's slender form, Sylica walked over to them and set her gently on the ground.

"*I'm* sorry." Roland's voice was hoarse. "I should have seen it coming, but I didn't. I was too late."

"It wasn't your fault, Roland. It was *my* fault." Thea's heart ached as she stared at Zanele's bloodied form.

"You don't understand." Roland's voice was low and urgent. "I told him ... I told him everything! About Thabani and the Resistance. Svetka, the Raven, your uncle, everything. I couldn't stop myself! The Enemy knows now, and it's all my fault!"

"It was not your fault!" Thea held his shoulders and stared into his panic-stricken eyes. "You were charmed! None of us realized he had magic like that, or we would have been more careful."

Roland nodded. His hands seemed a bit steadier.

"He's gone now. He can't hurt us anymore."

"You killed him." Roland looked at Thea with a mixture of awe and horror.

"I had to." Thea felt sick. She couldn't bring herself to look at Hwasan's motionless form. "I should have done it before. This is all my fault. I'm so sorry."

"No. No it's not." Roland struggled to his feet and walked over to where Hwasan lay, the end of Raybow's arrow protruding from his chest. Blood soaked the ground beneath him. Roland shook his head. "Why did he touch it? You told him it was dangerous, but he did it anyways."

"I know." Thea sighed. "I think he knew what it was all along. He wanted to talk to the Enemy, because he was a spy."

"What?" Roland stared at Thea.

"He was a spy," Thea repeated. "Sent to find the Spark. I overheard Zanele challenging him on it one day. He didn't deny it."

"How long have you known?"

"The day before we left the Caverns."

"And you didn't tell me?" Baffled rage filled Roland's face. "Why didn't you tell me!"

"I couldn't! You would have sent him away!"

"With good reason!" Roland's voice rose to a yell. "Because he was going to do that!" He gestured at Zanele's body, lying on the ground.

"Not necessarily! The whole point of him being with us was that he might have changed! We had to give him that chance!"

"So he could kill us and threaten everything we've worked for?"

"No! We were supposed to give him a chance until he made his final decision. That was when I was supposed to shoot. If I had just done that, none of this would have happened!"

"And if you had just told me what was going on, maybe I would have been prepared for this!"

"And I wasn't going to let another Elf ruin the work of the Deity!"

Roland stared at her, his body as tense as a bowstring.

Thea's hands started to shake as she realized what she had said. "I—I don't …"

Roland stepped back. His eyes scanned the cave as his hands checked that his knives were still in place. He took a slow breath. "I have to go. Svetka and the Raven are in danger." His dark, hurt-filled eyes rested on Thea's. "Are you coming with me or not?"

"I can't." Thea's heart sank. "The Resistance is in danger because of me. I have to go help them."

"You promised you would come with me."

"I know. I'm sorry."

"But—"

"My place is with the people of Raphtova, not the Elves." The words leapt out of her, stronger than she intended.

Roland's eyes flashed with anger. "Why do you hate the Elves so much? They are your own people!"

"They are not my people!" Thea glared at him, her heart pounding. "They have abandoned Raphtova. They don't even worship the Deity! Instead they worship Enkeli and their own precious temple and don't care about the Deity's ways at all!"

Roland's stare turned cold. "And you say I am just one of them."

"No," Thea protested. "You're different. You serve the Deity. You're the only Elf I could ever actually trust."

"But you still didn't trust me."

"No." Thea's heart sank. "No, I guess I couldn't trust

you."

"Because I'm an Elf." Baffled hurt filled Roland's eyes. "You show mercy to everyone else. Why not the Elves?"

"Because they know better." In her mind she saw again the ponderous traditions of the Keepers of Knowledge, poring over their gilded scrolls and tomes that mattered more to them than the living people, fighting and dying across the sea. "They have all the knowledge they need and they have rejected it. If you want to save the Elves, go try to save them. As far as I'm concerned, they deserve their judgement."

Silence fell across the cave.

Roland stared at her, pain and anger dark in his eyes. Turning, he strode away.

Thea's gut twisted as she watched him go. She wanted to call out, but she couldn't. There was nothing she could say.

Roland didn't look back. His footsteps faded into silence.

A horrible feeling of loss overwhelmed her senses. He was gone, and he was never coming back. The horror of the day returned with the ache of isolation and despair. Bowing her head, Thea cried.

Chapter Twenty-Three

Thea's heart and body ached. The stony floor beneath her was cold and hard. She shivered, isolation and grief throbbing deep in her spirit. Roland was gone. Zanele was dead. Hwasan was dead. And she had failed to follow her orders.

A small shuffling sound echoed from across the cavern. Thea looked up to see Sylica standing in the distant shadows, something small held in her cupped hands.

"He killed Cheeky." Sylica spoke in a trembling voice. "Why would he do that?"

Shakily, Thea got to her feet and walked to Sylica's side. The lifeless form of the little squirrel was curled gently in her hands. Tears glistened on Sylica's cheeks.

Thea put her arms around her friend. "I'm so sorry, Sylica."

By their feet, Daisy stared up with mournful eyes.

Around them, silence filled the desolate cave. They were alone, far from help or any other friendly presence. The bodies of their two dead companions lay on the ground, not far away.

"Sylica," Thea's voice shook. "I don't know what to do. We can't just leave them."

Sylica looked down at Cheeky, still cupped in her hands. "After the fight in the forest, the Fauns burned their people who died. Should we do that?"

Despair surged through Thea like a sob. "I wish we could, but that would take so long. We'd have to go all the way down to the forest, and—"

"Thea. I have Dragon magic." Sylica looked at her with large, gentle eyes. "Technically I can do anything—as long as it doesn't break the world too much." She offered a sheepish smile. "I think a pile of wood wouldn't be too much."

Thea smiled gratefully at her friend. "We'll do that. We'll give Zanele the farewell her people would have given her."

Letting Sylica carry Zanele and Cheeky out of the cave, Thea forced herself to walk back to the place where Hwasan lay. His scales were a strange, lifeless colour. She touched them gently.

"I'm sorry, Hwasan," she whispered. "I tried." Tears stung her eyes.

Carefully, she reached beneath him and tried to lift his body. It was heavy. She struggled for a while, then realized she couldn't do it alone.

Hwasan's brazier flickered by the wall, with Roland's lantern nearby. Collecting them, Thea carried them outside to the place where Sylica had placed Zanele's body.

There was no sign of Roland.

Thea and Sylica returned to the cave and together carried Hwasan out. His cold, hard scales made it hard to lift his lifeless body. To Thea, that burden seemed the heaviest thing in the world.

Outside at last, they lay Hwasan down beside Zanele. Thea shivered. The mountain wind chilled her to the bone as she stared out across the wooded hills that stretched below them.

Sylica found a flat piece of ground not far from where their dead companions lay. At her feet, a pile of wood began to appear. Thea watched in fascination as piece after piece materialized out of nothing.

"Do you think that's enough?" Sylica asked after a while. "I don't want to break the world too much, so I'm just bringing some wood from the forest down there."

Thea contemplated the pyre heaped before them. "I think it will be enough."

Gently, they carried Zanele, Cheeky, and Hwasan onto the pile of wood. Thea placed Zanele's halberd in her hand, but her bag she set aside. Hwasan's staff was also placed on the pyre.

With cautious interest, she opened Hwasan's bag. There wasn't much in it. A simple sleeping mat, his rope, and a bit of dried food. She set it aside. Maybe Hwasan wouldn't want them to have it, but maybe he would. There had been light in his spirit.

That was what hurt most. There had been light, then it was gone.

When everything was ready, Thea tipped the coals from Hwasan's brazier onto the wood. Slowly, the pyre began to burn.

Thea and Sylica sat together and watched in silence, with Daisy sitting beside them.

"I don't know the words to the song the Fauns sang," Thea said after a while. "It's a shame. It was such a beautiful song."

"You could make up a new one," Sylica offered.

"No." Thea watched the fletching of Raybow's arrow flicker in the fiery breeze. She didn't feel like singing.

Above them, smoke rose into the sky.

It almost seemed to Thea that the pyre held more

than the bodies of her fallen friends. It also held her belief that she understood the world, or what her place was in it. Soon nothing was visible but the dancing flames.

After a long time, the fire began to die down.

Sylica looked at Thea. "Do you think we can go now?"

Thea sighed. "Yes. I guess we should."

"That's good." Sylica cocked her head. "We probably don't want that Dragon to find us."

Thea stared at Sylica. "What Dragon?"

"There's a Dragon coming, and it doesn't feel like a nice Dragon."

Thea jumped to her feet and stared around the mountainside. "Where? How do you know?"

"That's another Dragon magic thing Meiling told me about. I can feel where there's other Dragon magic, if it's strong enough."

"Where's it coming from?"

"Over there." Sylica pointed south above the mountains.

Hurrying to grab the bags, Thea and Sylica left the pyre behind and returned to the edge of the bluff.

"We'll go east." Thea gestured.

As Sylica scampered on ahead, with Daisy clattering at her heel, Thea glanced back over her shoulder. The coals of the fire glowed hot, and the smoke was all but gone. Beyond, she could just see the lowlands to the west. Roland had gone that way, down to the western sea to sail north to Lyudmyla.

She was not going there. She would never go there.

Hurrying, she caught up to Sylica. At their side, the cliff dropped steeply to the forest far below.

"There has to be a way down eventually," Thea

panted as they hurried on. "Once we're in the forest we can hide."

"Do you think—" Sylica began.

With a rush of wind, a shadow fell across the mountainside. A Dragon wheeled above them and plummeted to the ground, landing on the cliffside with a powerful flap of its wings. Though smaller than Liwei, it still towered above them, barring their way with a sweep of its massive tail. Its blazing red eyes pinned them down, reading every twitch of every muscle.

Thea froze. There was no way to outrun something like that.

The Dragon roared, fire erupting from its mouth in a wave of searing heat and stench.

"No!" Sylica leapt to meet it and the flames sprayed aside, as if they had struck an invisible wall.

The Dragon snarled. "What? Where is the Dragon?" It swivelled its great head.

"There isn't any Dragon." Sylica stared up at the beast towering over them. "Just Daisy, but everyone says she doesn't count."

"There was Dragon magic," the Dragon snarled. "I felt it."

"Oh." Sylica grinned. "That was me."

The Dragon's eyes narrowed. "You? Impossible. I was sent for the Spark, not a strange mongrel pup."

"Well this strange mongrel pup says you can't have her!" Sylica waved her mace defiantly. "Want to try?"

"Sylica—" Thea gasped, fumbling to draw Raybow with shaking hands. "You can't—"

The Dragon's head darted forward, snapping with razor-sharp teeth.

Sylica darted aside, faster than sight, and smashed

her mace on the Dragon's jaw.

The Dragon snarled. Rearing onto its hind legs, its wings beat the air as fire spewed from its mouth, forming a seething ball of flame that grew larger and larger, as if fuelled by the mighty wingbeats. Heat crackled through the air.

Sylica raised her shield with a shout.

The flame disappeared, as if it had never formed.

The Dragon hissed. At Thea's feet, the ground rumbled and split apart, a cascade of stones tumbling down into the suddenly gaping chasm beneath them.

Thea scrambled frantically away.

"No!" Sylica yelled, her feet standing firmly on empty air.

Thea stared. Sylica shouldn't be standing there. She should have fallen with the crumbling rock, but instead she stood as firmly as she had on solid ground.

Because she had decided the solid ground was still there.

She was fighting Dragon magic with Dragon magic ... and she was *winning*.

"Charge!" Sylica ran at the Dragon, mace flailing.

"Sylica—" Thea's voice disappeared in the Dragon's roar. Drawing Raybow, she shot. The arrow was engulfed in flames.

Sylica screamed. Her gleaming armour was blackened, the hair around her face singed and curled.

"Sylica!" Thea gasped. She shot again, but the arrow glanced harmlessly off the Dragon's scales.

Daisy charged at the Dragon's heel. She bit, hung on, then tumbled to land in a heap.

"Thea, help! My magic juice is gone!" Sylica cowered behind her shield as Dragon fire blazed around her again.

Thea ran, drawing another arrow from her quiver.

The Dragon was faster, slashing at Sylica with its giant claws. She tried to dodge out of the way, but the blow caught her off balance and she staggered. Her shield was wrenched from her hand, landing on the ground with a clatter.

Rearing back, the Dragon opened its mouth.

With a flash, a small, dark figure appeared in the air above the Dragon. It fell, yelling loudly, and landed with a clatter on the Dragon's back.

Thea stared. It looked like a human, but short, with a wild mess of a beard. A gleaming axe was in his hand and a tattered-looking barrel teetered precariously on top of his oversized pack.

Thea gasped. "*Ulfgar?*"

Magic surged, and a golden wall of magic appeared inside the Dragon's mouth. The Dragon convulsed, thrashing its head wildly.

Ulfgar clung to the Dragon's neck as it shook violently beneath him. The Dragon clawed at its mouth, but the magical shield did not move.

Ulfgar swung his axe. It flashed with light and struck the Dragon on the back of the neck. The Dragon convulsed.

Clinging to a long, pointed horn with one hand, Ulfgar swung his axe again. It sank deep into the Dragon's neck.

With a shudder, the Dragon collapsed, throwing Ulfgar to the ground with the crash of splintering wood.

Thea ran towards Ulfgar as he staggered to his feet and swung his axe at the Dragon again.

The Dragon convulsed as the blow struck, and did

not move again.

"And stay dead," Ulfgar muttered.

"Ulfgar!" Thea cried. Grabbing him by his shoulders, she stared at his face. His matted beard stuck out in every direction and his pack was drenched with wine, but his face appeared unharmed and he looked at her with a surprised smile.

"Thea! I didn't think I'd see you so soon." He stared around the mountainside. "When is this? Oh, hello Sylica!"

Sylica half ran and half staggered to join them, with Daisy scampering after her. For once, she seemed completely speechless.

"What happened?" Thea stared at Ulfgar, so real and tangible in front of her. "You disappeared almost five spans ago!"

"Five spans?" Ulfgar stared at her in surprise.

"We're just leaving the mountains now."

"But I've never been back so soon." Wonder and delight grew in his face. "Micai said it would be alright, and ... and I think it just might be!" He grinned and sheathed his axe. "Come on, I've got a job to do." Picking up Sylica's shield, he tossed it to her, then turned and strode west, back the way they had come.

"Where are you going?" Thea called, hurrying after him. She hardly dared to let him out of her sight for a moment, for fear he would vanish as suddenly as he had appeared.

Sylica scampered at her side, trying to wipe the soot from her face with her even dirtier sleeve.

Ulfgar retraced their steps back to the cave and strode inside.

Thea stopped. She did not want to see inside that

cave again. Close at hand, the final coals of the funeral pyre were still glowing among the ashes.

"What's he doing?" Sylica asked.

A magical shock wave swept over Thea, sending her blood tingling.

"Oh." Sylica stared up at the sky with a curious frown. "The magic rope is gone now."

Soon Ulfgar stepped out of the cave and joined them on the mountainside. "Micai thought we might as well deal with that, since the Enemy knows we're here anyways."

"What—" Thea struggled to find words. Micai said what? How did Ulfgar know? And what was he doing there at all?

Ulfgar flourished his axe. "Trollsbane. Also effective against magical rocks, apparently." He grinned.

Ulfgar's spirit shone brighter than Thea had ever seen it before. She recognized it now—the intensity of light that showed its bearer to be in the service of the Deity. "How—" she stammered.

"Actually, we should go," Sylica interjected.

"But—"

"Thea, we need to go NOW!"

With a rumble like thunder, a shadow appeared in the sky. Thea looked up to see an enormous dragon—larger than a mountain—begin to eclipse the sky.

"Yeah," Ulfgar grunted. "I don't have enough smite for something that big."

Thea stared at the Dragon, terror freezing her mind. It was bigger than big. More enormous than anything she could have dreamed in her most terrifying nightmare.

It was coming for them.

With a roar, a second dragon erupted from the sky. It was just as large as the first, and dove at its adversary with lethal speed, its golden eyes flashing in the light.

Thea recognized those eyes.

Meiling lashed her long, serpentine body at her opponent's and they crashed into the mountainside, sending shock waves through the stones beneath Thea's feet. The mountain began to crumble and collapse, caving in on itself with a rumble like thunder. Above it, the massive Dragons rose again into the air, entangled with convulsing fury.

"Run!" Ulfgar yelled.

Thea ran. Beneath her, the stone turned to mud. Sinking up to her knees, Thea struggled to move.

Ulfgar grabbed her arm and pulled her out. "Keep going!" He pushed her in front of him. "Don't stop!"

The roar of the Dragons tore through the sky, casting dark shadows over the mountainside.

Thea, Sylica, and Ulfgar ran. A heap of rocks by their feet sprouted wings and flew away, squawking wildly.

"What?" Thea stammered.

"It's Dragon magic!" Sylica yelled. "There's too much in one place!"

Out of the ground in front of them, a tree sprouted and grew into an ancient oak, rotting and falling to the ground before their eyes. Ulfgar leaped over its decaying trunk.

Thea scrambled after him. The mountainside beneath them convulsed as if it was trying to breathe.

Overhead, the battle of the Dragons continued, falling gradually further and further into the distance.

Breathless and stumbling, they scrambled down a

gully to the forest below. Beneath Thea's feet, the ground shook less. The tremors became fewer, and further away. Terror and panic slowly gave way to exhaustion. Thea stumbled, then sank to the ground.

Ulfgar sat beside her, a worried frown creasing his forehead.

Thea buried her face in her hands. "I ... I need to rest."

Nearby, Sylica flopped to the ground, panting heavily.

As Thea's heartbeat began to settle, Ulfgar cleared his throat. "So what happened? You both look like the cat just dragged you in."

"We got to meet the Minathrils!" Sylica piped up. "They took us to their caverns and there were Littles before that too but they called themselves goblins, and then after we left the Minathrils we were walking in the snow every day and we found that cave and Hwasan wanted to use the magic stone and he charmed us and killed Zanele and then Thea killed him and then we had to go and then the Dragons came!" She stopped, her face a strange mixture of excitement and horror. Daisy set her head on Sylica's lap and whined. Sylica sighed and hung her head. "I don't think I'm the best person to say what happened."

Thea felt Ulfgar's glance. Grief ached in her chest and filled her mind. "I failed. That's what happened."

Ulfgar watched her in silence.

"I had orders." Thea spoke slowly, then faster as the words spilled out of her. "I had to stop Hwasan from contacting the Enemy, but instead I let him do it. He killed Zanele, and he told the Enemy all about the Resistance. Then I had to kill him." Her throat tightened as another wave of grief threatened to overwhelm her. "I couldn't save him, and I tried until it was too late. I didn't tell Roland what was going on, then he was charmed and forced to tell Hwasan everything. I couldn't stop it, and now it's too late. The Resistance is in danger. Zanele and Hwasan are dead. Roland is gone, and he is never coming back." Her head sank into her hands. "I failed, and I feel like I don't know anything anymore. I don't know who I am or what to do, just that it's all my fault."

Silence hung across the clearing. A distant rumble echoed from the mountains.

"Here. I think you could use some of this." Ulfgar held out a tankard filled with beer. Thea stared at it. She knew that tankard.

"From a friend." Ulfgar smiled and pressed it into her hand.

Thea took the tankard and drank. The familiar taste brought back memories of walking with Micai and their long conversations together. Micai had taught her about mercy. She hadn't realized mercy could hurt so much.

Ulfgar looked up into her eyes. "You're still the Spark. That hasn't changed."

Thea stared. "After what I just did?"

"You think you can't receive mercy?" A wry smile played at the corners of his mouth. "Anyone can receive mercy, even an Elf."

Thea's heart ached. "How do you know?"

"You still have orders, don't you?"

Thea nodded. It was true. She still had orders, and she would obey until her dying breath.

At her side, Ulfgar watched her with a thoughtful expression. There was a peace in his eyes that she hadn't seen in them before.

"Can ..." Thea hesitated. "Can you tell us what happened to you? You fell off the cliff and then you disappeared."

Ulfgar's gaze fell to the moss beneath their feet. "I went somewhere else." He thought for a moment, then continued. "I don't know why, but when something happens that should kill me, I don't die. Instead I end up somewhere else." He sighed. "At first it wasn't bad, but it happened again and again. Every time I had to build a life all over again, with nothing but what was on my back." He gestured at his oversized pack. "I found ways to work around that. What I couldn't change was losing the people I cared about, every single time. It made me want to end it all, but I couldn't."

He took the tankard back from Thea and looked at it thoughtfully. "But now I have a purpose in it all. Micai told me that wherever I go, there will be a reason, and I have a promise that ... someday there will be a home. That I can return to again, after I've been gone." He looked up and smiled. "I'm glad that today I got to be here, with both of you."

"I'm glad of that too." Thea smiled, the pain inside of her easing, just a little.

"I'm glad too!" Sylica cried, clapping her hands. Daisy hopped up, looking around for the source of her excitement.

Ulfgar nodded. "Thank you. It's good to have friends again." He stretched and got to his feet. "And now?"

Thea took a slow breath. "Now we go save the Resistance."

Ulfgar nodded. "Any particular plan? Or ..."

Thea stood. "We're going to take them home. There's

safety magic on my house, remember? If we bring them there we'll be safe, and we can figure out what to do next."

Ulfgar grinned. "Sounds like a plan."

"Come on!" Sylica skipped off through the trees, Daisy yapping at her heels. "Let's go save the Fauns!"

Thea glanced at Ulfgar at her side. He was there, and the light of the Deity shone in his spirit that had once been so dark. Somehow, the world didn't seem quite as hopeless as it had a short while ago.

Ulfgar grinned. "Go get them, Sparky."

Epilogue

The old building was not empty. Since the Elf and her friends had left, it seemed like there was always someone coming or going from its ancient, rusted gates. There were the Little people, building and making repairs. A couple of humans stopped by on their way to the city and stayed for a day or two before continuing on their way. Other visitors from Gedwyld came and went.

There were two Littles who seemed to return almost every span. They swept the floors and tended to the gardens, treating the old building with a love and care it had only experienced from the Elf and her friends. Then one day they left, and they didn't come back again.

The building waited. Something deep in its stones seemed to say that the Elf would be back.

The days grew colder. Storms rolled in off the sea, blowing wildly through the trailing vines that clung to its ancient walls. Still it waited.

There was a change. The building felt it—creeping through the ground like a frost. Danger. Somewhere, far away, evil was stretching out its hand again. The building shuddered, deep in its stones.

People began to return. First one, then another. They came to the building as if they had been drawn, knowing somehow that it was a safe place, and they were afraid.

Rumours drifted through the air, rumours of monsters lurking in the woods, drawing closer, monsters more dangerous than any they had seen before.

The two Littles returned—but now they were three. The building felt the pulse of new life as they stepped through its ancient gates. The people who had taken refuge within its walls reached out to them, seemed to see them as their leaders.

"What is happening?" they asked. "Are we safe?"

The two Littles did not have any answers.

"Thea will come," one of them replied. "She will tell us what is happening."

They waited, with the door closed against the cold wind off the sea, while outside the storm clouds drew closer.

The old building waited, too.

TOVA

a tabletop roleplaying game
designed by Jesse and Leane Winger

◇ Create characters in any of the ~~five~~ six races of Raphtova

◇ Serve under a General and wield magic

◇ Explore Arvera and beyond

◇ Lead your friends on an epic quest against evil

◇ Encounter the heroes of Raphtova

◇ Expansion races and more coming soon

◇ Free digital download

WWW.RAPHTOVA.COM

Digital Downloads - Raphtova Wiki - Updates and News

Ashes

Leane Winger

Ashes

Leane Winger

If there had been a door, it would have been slammed.

"Are you serious?" Micai yelled, storming up to Allulien. "You just let him walk away like that?"

Allulien did not flinch. "It was not my place to intervene. They were both following their orders."

"Do you realize how much therapy they're going to need?" Micai shook their head. "Or how much I'm going to need?"

"We all know you already needed therapy, Micai." Raphea gave Micai a wan smile. "Do you think any of us wanted to watch that?"

"But things are now in motion that cannot be undone." Allulien's glance was stern. "War is returning to Raphtova, whether we are ready or not. Micai?"

Micai nodded. "We will do what we can. Judgement has been declared, and it will come. We do not have much time."

The three Generals turned to look at the fourth. Enkeli looked down at the table full of maps and charts they had been scouring. Shuffling awkwardly, Enkeli stood. "There is a plan. It's almost ready."

Allulien raised an eyebrow. "How soon?"

"You'll see." Enkeli smiled and glanced down at the map of Raphtova, stretched out before them. "My turn."

Ashes

Leane Winger

Ashes

Leane Winger is a multidisciplinary creator and recovering perfectionist who always dreamed about going on an epic quest—as long as there would be plenty of snacks. Author of the mountaineering adventure novel, The Door, Leane is thrilled to be diving into the world of fantasy with The Reawakening Trilogy, the first of many stories to be set in Raphtova—a world co-created with her sword-wielding husband Jesse. Together they live in Mackenzie, BC with their growing crew of littles who keep pestering their mom for "the next chapter of the story".

Learn more about Leane's books and other projects at:

www.leanewinger.com